PHOENICIA'S WORLDS

BEN JEAPES

For Richard Baxter, 1964-2012.
Far too soon.

SOLARIS

PHOENICIA'S WORLDS

BEN JEAPES

ACKNOWLEDGEMENTS

I owe a great deal to the members of two writers' groups for feedback, advice and occasional scorn and abuse during the writing of *Phoenicia's Worlds*.

From 3SF: Chris Amies, Tina Anghelatos, Liz Holliday, Andy Lane, Janet Mattes, Gus Smith.

From Cantonese Sussex Writers' Group: Cherith Baldry, Deirdre Counihan, Liz Counihan, Christopher Evans, Leigh Kennedy, Christopher Priest, David Rain, Liz Williams.

And also many thanks to Jamie Barras, Paul Beardsley, Tim Bellerby and David Fickling, all of whom helped nudge or keep a randomly careering story onto a straight line that actually made sense.

CONTENTS

PART 1

LA NUEVA TEMPORADA

CHAPTER 1

THE MOTHBALLED SPACESHIP

Two days before everything changed, the Mateo brothers went to claim their starship.

"It's getting in touch," said Felipe at last from the pilot's seat. It had taken two hours for the capsule to reach *Phoenicia's* orbit above La Nueva Temporada. Two hours for Alex to put up with his older brother's chatter and silently work his nerves up to fever pitch. "Wants to know if it should put the heating on."

Alex was surprised to feel a stab of jealousy – *Phoenicia* spoke to Felipe first! But then, he thought, his older brother and the starship would be together for many years while he stayed safely at home. They should probably get acquainted.

"It had better," he agreed.

The ship had spent fifty-seven years powered down in space. Yes, it would need to put the heating on.

Phoenicia loomed large on the radar but the view ahead was full of the gas giant El Grande. Clouds of glowing stripes and continent-sized hurricanes, so vast they seemed frozen. The starship was just a speck against the gas giant if you knew where to look without the help of headspace. Alex twisted round in his seat, body straining against the straps, to peer back through the stern viewport. La Nueva Temporada had emerged from the shadow of the giant. The orbiting sunlets were pinpricks of light above the clouds, and with the unaided eye he could see both poles with their massive icecaps and make out the coastline of his homeworld's single continent. Rio Lento, their family home, would be well into night time and their father would probably be asleep. For all that they were making history, Alex wished he was there too. Feli wasn't the one who would have to face Papá when he learnt of this.

He turned to face forwards again and tried to work out if the glimmer that was *Phoenicia* had got any bigger in the last thirty seconds.

ANOTHER HOUR AND it was much more than a glimmer. The struts and framework of the starship filled the viewports. The capsule's blackbox took them in for the final approach. Felipe released the controls and shot his younger brother a sideways glance.

"Relax," he said with a grin.

Alex grunted. Relax? Easy for Felipe to say. Felipe wasn't the one who would have to face Papá…

The capsule passed over the ice shield's loose meshwork of struts at the ship's bow. Two kilometres of ship stretched ahead of them. *Phoenicia* was a fishbone of styrosteel with long, thin ribs. On the journey from Earth, the ribs had been laden with the modules and cargo containers and machinery that held the makings of a new colony, as well as the colonists themselves, ten thousand of them, preserved in longsleep. Now the bones were picked clean.

Halfway down, separating the forward and aft spines, was the ring of the Command & Habitation module. The ship had thoughtfully spun it up for them over the last hour. *Phoenicia* reported that it had purged the preserving inert gases and replaced them with an atmosphere the brothers could breathe.

The capsule was heading for the docking port just aft of Command & Habitation and the hull ahead of them was a wall of dull, grey-white styrosteel. A spotlight picked out the circular recess of the port and both brothers smiled at what they saw.

"Oh, ha, ha," Felipe said.

Long ago, some joker had stencilled a greeting on the airlock's outer hatch: WELCOME. PLEASE WIPE YOUR FEET.

Felipe felt around inside a locker and produced a pair of face masks.

"Better put this on." He handed one over. "The air will feel mighty raw until it's warmed up."

"Really? I had no idea," Alex muttered as he put it on. The autostraps released them from their seats, and they both pushed themselves up at the same time. Alex bounced away when they bumped into each other in mid-air and swore when a sharp edge dug into the small of his back. His face blazed red. He knew how to handle himself in microgravity – as a point of pride he wasn't wearing an exo, which could have guided his movements for him – but Felipe actually worked in space. Alex had taken a conceptual before they set out but his body and reflexes simply lacked the ingrained physical skill of his more experienced brother.

Meanwhile Felipe was already halfway through the hatch. Alex got a fine view of his brother's receding backside and Felipe was the first to see the inside of *Phoenicia*.

"Bring the crystals," Felipe called back at him. Alex pulled a small, slim box from a locker above the pilot's seat and made his own way headfirst down the narrow docking tunnel. He pushed himself through the membrane and into *Phoenicia*.

He could feel the cold through his shipsuit. The ship's air flowed like ice down his throat, even with the mask on, and his sinuses ached. Felipe was waiting for him and his crinkled eyes above the mask showed he was smiling.

"Welcome on board!"

The inner hatch opened onto a dimly lit passageway. For a moment the brothers were silent, savouring the sheer experience of Being On *Phoenicia*. It was like opening up some ancient tomb, except that the inhabitant was embedded in the very structure, alive and well.

A drone was waiting for them – a sphere the size of a human torso, studded with probes and manipulators, a mindless extension of the ship's will. *Phoenicia* spoke in headspace. The ship's voice was androgynous, using only stock phrases with the minimum of courtesy.

Welcome. Please follow the drone.

An elevator took them outwards towards the rim of the module and Alex felt the gentle tug on his body pulling him towards what was now the floor. By the time the elevator came to a halt his feet were firmly planted on the flat surface. Carefully balanced magnetic repulsion let the drone continue to hover.

They stepped out into *Phoenicia's* main concourse, an empty space where several of the ship's passages met. The scene was lit dimly with emergency lights that the ship had put on for their benefit. Marks and scars in the padded plastic walls showed where equipment and gear had been stripped away before the mothballing. The dim lights threw the corners into shadow and turned the corridors leading out into tunnels that curved away into darkness. The drone led them across the concourse without giving them the luxury to pause and look around, into a passage on the far side that led ultimately to the bridge.

Not even this place had completely survived the locust-swarm that stripped the ship. What had been the hustling, bustling control centre of the *Phoenicia* mission now held couches for a couple of command positions, some slightly old-fashioned looking instrumentation, and that was it. The pilot's couch faced a blank, curved wall. The drone retreated into a recess in the ceiling and Alex ran a hand over the wall's smooth surface. Nothing happened. He sent a command word at it.

Display.

Still nothing, except the distinct feeling in headspace that the ship gave a polite cough, waiting for a certain formality to be completed.

"Box?" Felipe said. Alex opened the box for him; Felipe extracted a crystal and held it up for all to see.

"*Phoenicia*, my name is Felipe Mateo. I officially represent the consortium that claims ownership of you and intends to commission you for a fresh mission."

He inserted the crystal into a hole in the wall. Alex found himself staring at it as if the ship's blackbox consciousness was located there and sheer concentration could speed up the processing time.

Thank you. And your companion?

Alex took out the box's other crystal.

"Uh, yeah. I'm Alex... Alejandro Mateo and I, uh, endorse what he said."

He inserted his crystal next to Felipe's.

They had spoken to the ship before. Anyone could. It maintained a presence in the Lawcore on La Nueva Temporada and anyone could get in touch, chat, ask questions... but it reserved its true allegiance for its owners, which under the ship's charter meant any group of people prepared to stump up a very large sum of money, incorporate a company and claim ownership. The charter also said that the claim had to be made in person by at least two representatives of the consortium, at the same time. The crystals were the assurance of the Lawcore to *Phoenicia* that the brothers had deposited the required sums of money, pulled together the pledges that bound the consortium, and created the company.

And then, in headspace, there was the unmistakeable brush of the ship's mind.

Thank you. I accept your command.

"Thank you!" Felipe rolled his eyes and lowered his voice for Alex's sake. "Did you know there was a time when computers just did what they were programmed to do?"

There was a time when a log canoe was the most sophisticated form of transport invented. What point are you making?

Alex quickly had to suck in his cheeks and stare at the floor. It was the first time the ship had shown a hint of character and Felipe wasn't fond of being the butt of a joke.

"Systems status," said Felipe after a moment. "Display all."

In headspace, data began to run down the walls. The wall opposite, the wall next to them, the wall by the door; lines and lines of text and images, scrolling from the ceiling to the floor like softly falling snow.

"Thruster tanks down to seventy-eight per cent," Felipe murmured. His head was on one side as he studied the data flow. "Hull integrity... some micrometeoroid scoring... it'll need fixing..."

Alex ran his hand again over the bulkhead in front of the couch, and this time there was no difficulty. The datastream gave way to a real-time headspace view from the ship's forward cameras. *Phoenicia* faced away from La Nueva Temporada and looked out into deep space. It was a bottomless pit of rich velvet black, studded with a million diamond stars.

Felipe put an arm round his shoulders.

"Where do you want to go, little brother?" he asked, and it was only half a joke. It was an intoxicating thought. They had their ship. They could go *anywhere*.

PUERTO ALTO SAT dead ahead of the capsule. The captured asteroid was 35,000 kilometres above La Nueva Temporada, lit from below by the glow of the planet. In the shadows, spots of light speckled the dark rock where viewports and airlocks capped tunnels that had been drilled into the natural surface. Elsewhere the workings of the port burst out into view – cabins and gantries, eruptions of steel and plastic, and the ring of the carousel that intermittently reared up from the rock and plunged back in. It looked like a space station buried inside the asteroid was clawing its way back out. When Alex looked down he could see the thin thread of the elevator cable, a gleaming filament stretched taut between the asteroid and La Nueva Temporada's cloud layer below. A small pearl far below was an elevator car clinging to one of its faces. As he watched, another car slid smoothly out of the base of Puerto Alto and down towards the planet, dwindling within minutes to a dot.

Felipe was in the pilot's seat again and hadn't stopped talking since they undocked.

"We may have to replace the shield struts," he was saying now. "They took a lot of battering on the voyage out. Can't risk a failure..."

"Uh-huh," Alex said noncommittally. Whenever Felipe started talking like this it was more a series of statements than a conversation, and the function of whoever Felipe was talking to was to go "uh-huh".

A liner was just coming in to dock at Puerto Alto, fresh from its passage through the wormhole from Earth. The hull was painted with clan colours, meaning it was a Terran ship rather than Nuevan, meaning it would be carrying passengers as well as freight, meaning Puerto Alto would shortly be packed with another crowd of frightened newbies unused to microgravity. Alex groaned silently. He would be sharing the elevator with them all the way down to the ground.

While the liner headed for the docking towers, the station ordered their capsule to hold its position until the way in was clear. Felipe shot him a sidewards glance as they waited.

"Kind of blew your last day of holiday, didn't I?"

"Uh-huh... what?" Alex was taken aback at his brother actually showing awareness of his feelings. Felipe looked abashed.

"I'm sorry. Maybe I just like having you around."

Alex wasn't sure how to answer that.

"And that's why I'd really, really like you to come, Alex."

Alex groaned silently. Just when you thought a subject was buried, up it popped again.

"And I really, really don't want to," he said.

"But..." Felipe thumped the console in abrupt frustration. "What can keep you here? Hey? I just don't get it!"

"No, you don't."

"Is it..." Felipe cast his hands helplessly in the air. Then he looked suspiciously at Alex. "Is it a girl?"

Alex rolled his eyes. "Yes, Feli, it's a girl." He looked away and added in a mutter: "I managed to find one you hadn't got to first."

"Hey!" Felipe actually jabbed him in the arm. "I thought we agreed not to talk about..."

Alex just looked at him.

17

"It's just…"

Alex kept looking and Felipe swore.

"Okay, so it's not a girl. But I still don't get it."

Alex looked away.

No, Felipe didn't get it. His brother's brain just wasn't wired for the fact that some people didn't loathe La Nueva Temporada, and so Alex had given up trying to explain. Felipe couldn't wait to set off into the dark; Alex had no intention of ever leaving home.

But Felipe's mind had snapped back to the subject of the ship.

"Tomorrow I'll take some tios out to give her a proper investigation," he decided. "Eventually we'll have to take a tug and bring her closer in…"

"You're going public?" Alex asked, with a sudden, nervous hope. He had hated the secrecy, the tiptoeing around any subject that might lead to what they were doing, the not-quite lies when anyone (like their father) came too close. He would love for it to be over.

Felipe flashed his usual, confident grin, the dig about girls now completely forgotten. "That's why I said eventually. No, for now, we'll keep it a secret."

A message popped into headspace. It was labelled LINDA HAHN PORT ADMINISTRATOR and it invited them both to lunch.

THE THREE OF them sat in the canteen next to a wide glass wall that overlooked the docks. The heart of Puerto Alto thrummed with activity: elevators taking goods and passengers to and from the ships in their docking cradles above; cranes moving about above and below with purpose and precision.

"So, how did it go?" asked the Port Administrator.

"She's ours, Mama." Felipe was as happy as a small boy. "Still haven't persuaded Alex to come with me, though."

Alex managed a weak smile. "Someone's got to run Papá's errands."

Felipe grunted with a sudden impatience. "All you ever do is run Papá's errands!"

"I'd rather run Papá's errands than clear up your messes!"

There was a frosty silence for a moment and their mother scowled over at both of them. She spoke as if to a pair of small children.

"Apologise to each other and give each other a big hug."

They both groaned, but the deliberate childishness cleared the air. "Oh, please!" Felipe muttered. But he cleared his throat. "I'm sorry. You do much more than run errands."

"I know," Alex said, still a trifle cold. And then he couldn't resist: "and you don't make that many messes."

Felipe's eyes narrowed and burned.

"There, that's better, isn't it?" Linda asked.

"I don't know why you're so happy," Alex pointed out, still a little hurt by the unexpected barb from his brother. "You're the one with a son going into longsleep for seventy years."

Maybe her smile was a little sad, but it was also sweet and just for him.

"I know, but I get to keep you and you were always my favourite."

And even though he knew it wasn't true, he had to laugh. After that he withdrew from the conversation as it turned technical. He watched the goings on down in the docks with idle interest.

A goods elevator was coming down, laden with containers from the recent wormhole arrival. He already knew what was in those crates, even without checking the manifest in headspace. Heavy-duty machinery, or the parts thereof, for major landscaping work. Frozen embryos of flora and fauna, genetically modified from native Earth stock for a cold climate. Mulch and chemicals to be ploughed into the soil so that it could grow plants humans could eat. All part of La Nueva Temporada's great Thaw, to push back the glaciers and claim the land beneath them for human habitation. And it was all coming in from Earth.

He automatically glanced over at the return elevator that was making the up journey. It should have been equally loaded with goods for the ship's homeward voyage, and it was only a quarter packed. And how was it economical to run a freighter full in one direction and almost empty in the other? He knew the answer with a sense of dull resentment. It was by charging so much for the cargo that it paid for the flight in both directions. La Nueva Temporada was at the mercy of the Terran price setters. It was no way to run a world, and yet, something about this place still drew people here.

A group was heading for the Customs port down below – the tail end of the crowd of passengers disgorged by the ship. Alex casually queried them in headspace. They were all families, a sub-clan from Earth, men and women and children of all ages, and even the children looked thoughtful and subdued, though that could have just been the concentration required to let their exos guide their movements in microgravity. Having your movements guided by a strap-on plastic skeleton with a mind of its own did take getting used to.

They were first generation settlers. They believed the promises – that they could work hard now to carve out a place for themselves in a thawed-out La Nueva Temporada that would be like the Earth of old.

And Alex believed it too, or at least, he told himself that he did. And that was why he was staying.

CHAPTER 2
REVISED CIRCUMSTANCES

THE DAY BEFORE everything changed, Alex arrived back home at Rio Lento.

"Ladies and gentlemen, welcome to this scheduled elevator service from Puerto Alto to Puerto Bajo, Altiplano City. We will begin our descent in twenty minutes and the journey will take approximately twenty three hours and ten minutes. Please note that your seat restraints are for your own comfort and safety while the car is in a microgravity environment, and cannot be manually released by passengers whilst the seatbelt sign is on. If you experience any discomfort or need to leave your seat for any reason while the restraints are activated, please signal cabin staff..."

As he had feared, the elevator was packed with the new arrivals, being guided by their exos to their seats as the safety statements cycled through their routine. Alex's seat stood out like a missing tooth in the full row facing the panoramic window. His heart sank still further when he saw he was sitting next to an immigrant family with far too many children. Not yet integrated into Nuevan headspace, they only had the minimum amount of tags.

As he took his seat he peered down through the glass. La Nueva Temporada was a fragile gemstone overlaid by a thin oil film of clouds and vapour. It made him proud to be Nuevan.

> "Approximately half an hour after our descent begins, passengers will be able to release their restraints and explore the facilities available on this service. These include the bar and restaurant on deck two, the entertainment centre on deck three, and the panoramic observation gallery that may be accessed from all decks. From here, depending on cloud cover, you may catch splendid views of La Nueva Temporada including the Sierra Grande and its subsidiary ranges, the Altiplano plateau directly beneath us, and the western coast of the Océano Grande ..."

"Are you a hee-ho?"

It took Alex a moment to realise that he was being addressed by the child next to him. The girl regarded him with such owlish solemnity that he had to fight back a smile.

"I'm half a hijo," he said, and wondered if his father would psychically pick up the treacherous sentiment even over the 35,000 kilometre gap between them. Tomás Mateo had been the first child born on La Nueva Temporada to Los Hijos de Castilla, the Sons of Castille, the Terran micro-clan dedicated to reviving the mores and culture of old Spain that had dominated the *Phoenicia* mission and everything that followed. As far as he was concerned his sons were 100% hijo themselves, and the fact that his first wife and their mother distinctly wasn't was only a trivial detail.

The girl scowled thoughtfully and Alex wondered not for the first time what it must be like on Earth for people to be so desperate to want to come to La Nueva Temporada, of all places. The original settlers on *Phoenicia* had been the ones with no choice. Everyone else came with their eyes wide open.

"We're Euros," she said.

Ah, that explained it.

"Most of us are too," Alex assured her. "Descended from Euros, I mean. But we're all Nuevans now."

"My dad says the hee-hos are in charge of everything and you all speak a funny language and we have to do what you say."

She scowled at him as if it was all his fault. The girl was so obviously against the idea that Alex could have hugged her. The father was shooting horrified, embarrassed glances at him over the kid's head, obviously wishing his child would shut up and stop jeopardising whatever chances they had in their new home.

"We only speak it among ourselves," Alex said with a very straight face, "and everyone gets a chance to be in charge."

The father summoned his courage.

"Darling, stop bothering the man…"

"Do we have to do what you say?" the kid asked stubbornly.

He wondered if the kid had already learnt the other word that mattered on Nueva, the flipside to 'hijo' – 'segunda', meaning 'second', which applied generically to everyone who had come to Nueva after *Phoenicia*. If her family settled in the wrong area, she might learn that segunda essentially meant second-class, not quite as good as the rest. Or, she could learn it meant a perfectly normal person, a citizen just as good in the eyes of the law as everyone else and with just as much stake in the planet. He hoped it would be the latter.

"No," Alex assured her, "you don't. The Lawcore says everyone is equal." It was as good a description of Nuevan democracy as he was honestly prepared to give. "Excuse me." He gave the father a reassuring smile and, with his bit done for social harmony and progress on La Nueva Temporada, dipped into his savings and upgraded to a seat on the first class deck above.

"Cabin staff will now demonstrate the emergency procedures to be undertaken in the unlikely event of a loss of cabin pressure and exposure to total vacuum. Thank you for your attention."

* * *

THE ELEVATOR DEPOSITED its passengers on schedule in Puerto Bajo, the planetside terminus at the highest point of the Altiplano plateau. Then a quick ride into Altiplano City, their capsule a small bubble of warmth and light trickling down the roof of the world while freezing winds scoured the rocky field on either side.

La Nueva Temporada had been settled for fifty-seven years. Fifty-eight years ago not one human had set foot on this planet and glaciers lapped at the foot of the Altiplano itself. The original settlers who slept for forty years on the slow journey here from Earth, towing the wormhole terminus with them, had awoken to find a planet that was almost exactly what the astronomers had told them to expect: Earthlike in size, gravity and atmosphere; and (the detail that the astronomers hadn't picked up on) stuck in the grip of an Earthlike ice age such as humanity's original home hadn't seen since prehistory.

But they had stayed, and now there was a glacier-free strip all along the equator, thirty kilometres at its narrowest, and on the Altiplano plateau the Nuevans had carved themselves a capital city as a statement of faith. One day, they were saying, people will *want* to stay up here.

Forty minutes later Alex was comfortably ensconced in the warm carriage of the ringrail. It curved in a loop down a spiralling tunnel and then out onto the icy equatorial tundra at the foot of the Altiplano. A line of hoops stretched dead ahead, shrinking into the distance, and the ringrail picked up power until it was a supersonic needle threading its way through them towards the south east.

The ringrail soon passed through the Sierra Grande, its shockwave knocking avalanches down from the mountains on either side. After the mountain range it crossed more plainland and then, imperceptibly, began to climb again into higher ground. The Barreras were not as sheer or as high as the Sierra Grande, but there were more of them – some sixty kilometres of steep slopes and deep valleys before the land suddenly gave out and tumbled into the sea.

Finally the ringrail was cruising slowly along the side of a valley where rocky slopes were dark with fimbulweed. They were fifty metres above the shattered and dirty face of the glacier, the original slow river that gave Rio Lento its name. Then the ringrail turned a corner and there was the town, clinging to the slope of the valley, with the dull steel grey of the sea beyond it.

The buildings were mostly prefabricated foamcast – low, two-storey, with steeply pointed eaves to shed the snow that lay in untidy heaps on the ground. There was none of Altiplano City's aspiring to art and culture here. This was a town built so that people could survive the high latitudes. Groundcars with ballooning tyres bounced along roads of compacted gravel.

It was home. The doors hissed open, Alex's coat warmed up and he stepped out with a bounce in his step.

Technically he still had half a day of leave. Maybe he would head down to the harbour, say hello to his friends at Reef Control, help out with a couple of experiments on cell cultures. But the bounce faltered when he saw the tall and very broad figure standing next to a groundcar. Then he decided he had nothing to be ashamed of and he put the spring back as he walked up to the man.

"Hola, Ilo," he said. "What's up?"

Ilo Bast had cropped, bristly hair and cheekbones so pronounced his eyes seemed to swell up from some allergy.

"Hola, Señor Alex. I've been sent by your father to fetch you."

Alex swallowed. *He can't know, he can't know...*

"Actually I was going to go down to the harbour. There's stuff I..."

Ilo smiled, but it didn't quite reach his eyes. Ilo had no specific job title in his work for Alex's father; perhaps *facilitator* described it best. If Executor Tomás Mateo wanted something done, he sent Ilo to do it.

"The Señor told me to make sure you got home, Señor Alex," he said. "Or to be more precise, he said, 'Ilo, I want my idiot son up here thirty seconds after the ringrail gets in.' And that makes us five minutes late already, so would you mind?"

Oh God, Alex thought as he slowly climbed into the car. No matter how slowly he moved, it all seemed to happen too fast. Oh God, Papá knows, and I don't have Feli with me...

THE MATEO VILLA was built into a hollow at the highest point of a promontory above the valley, looking down on the town and the glacier below it. Foamcast cabins were arranged in a square around a courtyard, many of them cut back into the rock to expand into further rooms, with other extensions made of native stone or brick.

A slim, dark haired woman was waiting in the tiled hallway. Her face was pinched with anxiety and she shuffled nervously from side to side with imminent catastrophe woven into the air around her. It was the first time Alex had seen someone actually wringing their hands. They positively writhed, clasped together protectively over the bump of an advanced pregnancy.

"Hola, Maria," Alex grunted as he pushed the door open. When he remarried, Tomás Mateo had at least had the decency to pick a wife who was just old enough that she could have been the biological mother of his sons. Still, with one thing and another Alex was never quite sure where to look when his stepmother was around, and he certainly never called her 'Mama'. He had pretty good reason to believe Felipe never had either.

"He's in his study, Alejandro," she said anxiously. "He's very..."

"Yeah, yeah," Alex grunted. "I'll get it over with." He shuffled through to meet his destiny.

Tomás Mateo, Executor for Rio Lento, was in his seat by the great window that overlooked the sweep of the glacier. He glanced up when Alex entered, dark brown eyes blazing under bushy black eyebrows, but did no more than that. Alex knew better than to interrupt. His Papá was getting the latest download from the Discourse – a daily ritual vital to the duties of any of the planet's Executors. His head was full of the composite frame of mind of one-thirtieth of La Nueva Temporada's population and his thoughts were elsewhere.

For a moment, Alex debated simply turning round and walking away. If his father had to choose between breaking contact with the Discourse and being angry at him then the Discourse would probably win. But the older man could spare him enough attention to wave a hand at the chair opposite, and (as much as Alex loved his brother) walking away was Felipe's answer, not his, so he dropped himself into the chair and got glared at. He practised returning the stare unblinkingly, trying not to show the nerves he was feeling.

Finally his father sighed, stretched, and reached for a glass of water from the table beside him.

"So," he said, as if they were already halfway through a briefly interrupted conversation and tempers had already been rising steadily for about five minutes. "My sons are the new owners of *Phoenicia*."

"Can't think of anyone better," Alex agreed. He got the full blaze of those dark eyes.

"Debateable. It's just that I seem to recall some small proviso in the charter that requires a deposit of one hundred thousand nuevos. And since I know that you don't even have one thousand between you..." His voice went very quiet, deceptively pleading. "Where did it come from, Alejandro?"

"Fe–" Alex decided he wasn't going to shift all the blame onto his absent brother, though Felipe was the one who had driven the whole thing. "We formed a consortium. With..." He steeled himself to utter the unpleasant truth. "Some backers from Earth. And Mars."

Tomás didn't blink.

"And your own share? Your friendly backers surely didn't put up all the cash?"

This was it. At the back of his mind, a drum rolled.

"We mortgaged off our rights in the East Range," Alex said. "We keep title but the bank–"

"Are you insane?" his father bellowed.

"It's under a kilometre of ice!" Alex protested. "No one can use it and we pay off the mortgage just as it becomes usable. Did you have other plans for it?"

He knew there were no other plans for it, simply because of the kilometre of ice. One day the East Range would be prime agricultural land but not today.

He also knew that wasn't the point. The idea met with resistance because it was *Mateo* land. Unfortunately for Tomás, it was not *his* Mateo land. His sons had each been given half as a Confirmation present.

"So, you have a starship," Tomás said, the sneer a bare fraction of a tone away from his voice. "Your very own toy."

I will not rise to this, Alex told himself. *I will not rise to this.*

"Our very own," he agreed.

"And you're going to get her out of mothballs and go prospecting for a new world."

"Feli is, with Mama's help. I'm staying."

"Hmm." His father seemed torn between approval that at least one of his sons showed some sense, and disappointment that it was this one: the spare, not the heir; the one who went by the non-hijo-sounding name. Alex wondered with a sudden bitterness just how upset his father would be if *he* was the one going on a seventy year voyage.

Either way, it seemed to have headed off whatever it was his father was about to say. The older man shifted in his seat slightly.

"I take it that the balance of what you got from the mortgage will set up the new company, purchase equipment, advertise for more idiots to join you..."

"Correct."

"And people will just come flocking to this venture led by a pair of fool boys ..."

"Papá, please," Alex said wearily. "You know how it's done. It'll take years. And we've found a lot of useful hints and tips in the histories of the first expedition. What to do, what not to do."

"The original mission was sponsored by a government!"

"Yes, and it went broke!"

And there lay the nub of the matter. It had been the last of Earth's dictatorships that had built *Phoenicia,* and it had fallen, bankrupt, in the four decades it took the ship to arrive at its destination. Earth today would find it hard to build another ship like it and La Nueva Temporada certainly couldn't. Therefore, the ship was unique. Anyone who wanted to travel to another system needed *Phoenicia.*

"But now we *have* the ship," he added, "so that's the most expensive item paid for. Spending duties for new equipment will be spread around the consortium, a blackbox will deal with the admin... Papá, it will work!"

Suddenly his father was on his feet and pacing.

"But why didn't you *tell* me?"

"Because you'd have stopped us!"

"Too damn right I'd have stopped you! You're both insane, and once I've dealt with you, I'll be on to Puerto Alto and letting Felipe know exactly where he stands too."

Alex couldn't help a half smile. His father still couldn't get used to the idea that Felipe was no longer at his beck and call.

The pacing continued. "It's not too late. There has to be a cooling off period. We can get onto the bank..."

"Papá, we're not going to cool off, and you can't make us..."

"I can get you declared legally irresponsible..."

If Felipe had been sitting where Alex was, the next line would have been, "Try it." But Alex always wanted to placate instead. Their expedition wouldn't leave La Nueva Temporada for years. He would really rather have his father as an ally in that time, and after, when he stayed behind.

"Papá, I don't understand why you're so against this," he said slowly. "The estate is still our property. Once the loan is paid off, we get all the rent anyway. It's going to be a great venture and it can be a *Mateo* adventure..."

"Right." His father snapped the one word as he flung himself down into the chair once more. He rested his chin in one hand

29

and glared at his son. "Talk me through this. *Phoenicia* leaves Nueva with your brother's worthless presence on board in...?"

"Well, there's..." Alex was about to detail all the preparations still to be made, but a look at his father's face made him get quickly to the bottom line. "Five years?"

"Five years, for the sake of argument. He travels for...?"

"Seventy years to the most likely prospect, which is..."

"Seventy years," Tomás said. "I'll be 126. I can probably make that. And he finds, presumably, an Earth-type?"

"Well, probably, I can show you the astronomical..."

"And then what?"

"I'm sorry?"

"And then what? I'm assuming he opens up a wormhole from Mundo de los Idiotas back here to Nueva? So his new colony can be supplied?"

"Nueva will have changed in seventy years," said Alex. "We'll be able to support a colony."

The Executor was up again. "But you cretin, you know how we are for materials! We're always going to be an agricultural exporter. We'll sell food, not raw materials. We'd be no more than a transit stop..."

He trailed off, looking at Alex suspiciously.

"But you know that, don't you?" he said.

"Materials would be imported direct from Earth," Alex confirmed. "There'd be no need for Nueva even to be a transit stop. The goods could just come straight through without unloading."

"But..." His father looked almost aghast. "Alex, we need that money! We need to be a financial centre. If no one comes through us then..."

"You'd have all our agricultural exports," Alex said hopefully.

"But that would be all. Once the colony started growing its own stuff we'd be the centre of... nothing. We'd have no influence. We'd be a bunch of farmers and that would be it." He sank back into his chair, still staring at his son. "Does Nueva really mean that little to you?"

Alex sighed, rolled his eyes. "Not to me, Papá. This is home." He tried to smile, something to soften his words, but he couldn't, and as he spoke he had the feeling of driving in nails. "But to Feli... yes, Nueva really does mean that little. He'd tell you himself if he was here. I'm sorry! But it does."

His father was silent for a long time. Sometimes he would half open his mouth, then close it again and shake his head minutely.

But then he sat up straight, and Alex had the feeling of shutters coming down over the holes he had blown in his father's shell; of new supports swinging in to replace the ones he had knocked away.

"I think we've said all that can be said by civilised men," he murmured. "Go away, Alex."

Dusk had come down and the town's streets below were empty. No one lingered outside this far to the south, and it was that dead time between the end of the day shift and the start of what passed for Rio Lento's nightlife.

Alex leaned on the balustrade with a glass in his hand and looked down into the valley. The terrace was enclosed by a glass shield that made it warm and comfortable, but one look into the chill dark could make a man shiver. He tried to imagine the streets painted in streaks of glowing light, like the cities of Earth at night, with snatches of music and wafts of food and parks reaching up the hillside towards him.

He tilted his face back to the sky as he waited for the drink or three inside him to do their work. It was vintage whisky, all the way from Earth, a sixteenth birthday present from his godparents which he had nurtured for the last three years. He had taken a couple of sips every few months to acclimatise himself into liking it.

Streams of data pulsed across the sky in headspace and floating tags identified their start and end points. Other tags would snap into existence if you looked at any of the orbiting points of light for more than a second or two. Alex sometimes found it odd that there were people, native Nuevans like him, who couldn't look up at their world's sky and immediately name and identify every visible point of light unaided. How hard could it be? To prove his point to himself he cut headspace and looked up with only his own naked eyes.

A quarter of the sky was dominated by the faint glow of El Grande, which never moved. Storm patterns larger than his entire world were motionless, intricate swirls beneath the translucent glaze of its hydrogen clouds.

If you looked very closely you could see two faint stars, one just dropping below the horizon and one just coming above it: Sols 3 and 1, two of La Nueva Temporada's three sunlets. Sol 2 would be the other side of the world right now. Regardless of the red twilight hue that came when El Grande was more prominent in the sky than the sun, they were currently set to heat-only, to fool the body clocks of the humans living below that it was actually night. On a world that kept one face always towards its parent body, but whose inhabitants were cued by evolution to expect a twenty-four hour day with regular periods of dark and light, it was the best anyone was going to get.

Alex had often tried to imagine what it was like to live on a world that spun so that its sun seemed to move in a regular pattern across its sky, day in, day out.

Puerto Alto was a fixed star in the north west, forever poised above the Altiplano. You could never see the cable by looking directly at it, but if you looked away then your peripheral vision became aware of the thin hairline of light. It was like the tiniest crack in space, barely healed over.

Another star moved now in the corner of Alex's eye, dimmer than Puerto Alto, rising sedately above the horizon. A corner of his mouth crooked when he saw it. It was *Phoenicia*, the cause of all his woes. He watched the rising star close in on yet another point of light in Nuevan orbit – Sulong Station, the wormhole terminus, named after Alex's very own Uncle Nathan and Aunt Marietta Sulong, who as well as being the whisky's donors had been the engineers who opened up the link with

Earth. This one was further out and orbited much more slowly, though from down here it looked like the two stars were going to collide. He raised the glass in salute.

"Thanks, Uncle Nathan."

Lost in his reverie, he hadn't noticed that *Phoenicia* had moved well beyond the wormhole and was already about to disappear below the far horizon. Uncle Nathan's whisky had had its anaesthetic effect. It would be all right. Their father would come round. This would be a Mateo adventure, and a glorious one too.

But he would miss Felipe, God, he would miss Felipe. Seventy years!

Alex sighed and turned to go back inside, just as a flash of white light swept across the patio.

"*Aargh!*"

He looked up again, cautiously, eyes half closed, just in time to see the burning light dwindle into nothing. And while he strained his streaming eyes up at where it had been, suddenly a wash of shimmering light flung itself across the sky like a worldwide aurora. For just a moment the mountains around Rio Lento and the town down in the valley were picked out in shades of shifting green and blue, and then they were swallowed up again in the dark and their bright neon outlines slowly began to dissolve into his retinas.

"What... the..."

He was standing with his mouth hanging open, still staring upwards. Whatever it was it had been spectacular, something he had never seen before. Unfortunately he was scientist enough to know the implications. Bright, burning lights in the sky; an aurora this far from the pole... La Nueva Temporada had just been bathed in a very, very strong burst of radiation.

Instinctively he tried headspace. The meteorological service. Orbital control. Anyone! But now there was nothing, not even static. Headspace was dead.

Following straight on from the shocked exhilaration of the event, a strong sense of foreboding was settling down on him.

Just to be sure, Alex looked up into the sky again, straight where the source of the burning light had been. He knew it well enough that he didn't need to ask headspace which quadrant he was looking at. His eyes had adjusted back to the dark and he could pick out the stars again; he was looking directly at the wormhole. Except that he could no longer see a star there.

Alex turned and fled into the house.

CHAPTER THREE

IN THE EVENT

"GO EASY ON your brother." Linda Hahn made her way with her eldest son down one of the transparent tubes that criss-crossed the passenger lobby of Puerto Alto. The lobby was a vast, crystal-clear dome set into the surface of Puerto Alto, polarised so that when you glanced upwards you looked out into a firmament of stars. The tubes led to the departure gates and were there to stop those passengers unaccustomed to microgravity from flying off.

Felipe grunted. "I just can't understand that boy."

"And?" Linda glanced up. The dome gave a grand view of the docking towers spaced around it, and ahead of her Linda could see a liner in Earth clan colours perched at the end of its docking tower. There was a vacant tower next to it and a Nuevan freighter was coming in. It will fire its thrusters, she thought, any moment... *now*.

"He could be such an asset on the mission!"

"And?"

Sure enough, the freighter started to turn with puffs of white vapour from its flanks. Another thirty seconds and they would puff again to cancel the movement, then it would move in for final docking.

Felipe burst out in frustration. "I just don't see why he won't come with us!"

"And?" she said again.

He glared sideways at her. "Got anything else to say, apart from 'and'?"

She rested her fingers lightly on his chest and he stopped, looking down at her resentfully. Bigger than her, stronger, the spitting image of his father, and she could make him stop just like that. She was so glad her two children were both boys.

"Maybe it doesn't matter that you don't understand him," she said. "Maybe it doesn't matter how useful he could be on the mission. Maybe he has his own plans for his life. Maybe he wants to stay on Nueva for reasons you will never get and that you never need to. Just respect his judgement, the way he respects yours."

"'Course he respects mine." Felipe tried to look sullen but she could see the faintest hint of a smile. "I'm right."

Linda opened her mouth to give a suitably sarcastic reply, and it turned into a gasp as something fizzed inside her head and a sharp pain lanced through her skull. She clutched at her temples, as did Felipe and every other man, woman and child in the docks area, all at the same time. Then the lights went out. For a moment the lobby was dimly lit by starlight only, and everything was grey and ghostly, until the red emergencies lit up around the edge of the open space.

"Hey, what..." Felipe's surprise was probably mirrored on her own face. "What's happening?"

The usual background murmur in the lobby was growing into a rumble, a shout. Linda shot off a query into headspace and just got static. Headspace was down. So was power for the lighting, and (now she came to think about it) the background whisper of the air con that you never even noticed was missing, and...

It was a heart-freezing moment of realisation. Linda looked up again. The freighter hadn't fired its thrusters for the second time. It was coming straight at the dome.

Others followed her horrified gaze, and screamed. Suddenly the tube was packed full of thrashing bodies, trying to get away.

The panicked shrieks doubled as the ship drew closer to the dome's fragile cover.

Felipe grabbed hold of a pair of handles set into the side of the tube, either side of an emergency access panel, and used them to brace his body as he kicked the panel away. Linda put a restraining hand on his arm.

"Wait," she said, though her voice trembled with the effort of staying still while a five thousand ton spaceship fell towards her. Felipe shot her a look of horrified amazement, but he stayed, and looked up, just as the ship hit with a crunch and a scrape. It grazed the transparent ceiling and bounced off again.

Silence replaced the screaming, and then a slow laugh spread around the room, growing from incredulous to embarrassed and finally almost hysterical. Linda found herself joining in, though it was what she had expected. Her heart was pounding, her whole system charged with adrenaline... but she had known that the dome was surrounded by docking towers and it had been built with the possibility of a collision in mind, even as the most extreme and unlikely emergency. She knew that. She had supervised it. But self-preservation is a powerful force.

But the freighter, spinning away from the dome, struck the liner. Both ships crumpled silently, with no atmosphere to carry the heartrending screech of torn metal and lives. Internal air and bodies erupted out into space with a silent grace, and Linda realised that the tower was only reinforced for collisions from above, not sideways shoves. Slowly, with a grand inevitability, its roots tore loose from the rock and a fountain of vapour jetted up from where it had been planted in the surface of Puerto Alto. Linda felt her ears pop as pressure inside the station began to drop. Elsewhere, automatic bulkheads should be closing. *Should* be...

The screams had started again, ten times worse than before. The air gushing out of the severed tower turned it into a slow, erratic and deadly missile. It spun lazily down to the asteroid and ploughed into several unreinforced modules, shattering them and tearing them apart. It continued its way into the heart of the docks and the two entangled ships now fell together towards the dome.

Felipe wasn't going to wait a second time. He dived out of the tube into the great open space of the lobby, with Linda close behind.

The space spun dizzyingly around them. Well accustomed to freefall, Linda instinctively moved her arms and legs about to shift her centre of gravity and stabilise the spin. The side of the chamber loomed and then they thumped into it. It was padded, precisely for the sake of passengers who lost their footing. She grabbed at a strap before they could bounce off again, and her body turned around and she grunted as her shoulder was twisted at an angle. But then she and Felipe were both steady, just in time to look up and see the combined weight of the two entangled ships, twice as much as the builders had planned for, thump against the dome. The screaming reached an all-round crescendo.

The *snap*, the *crack* was more felt than heard, but the dome began to star at the point of impact.

In Linda's imagination a dozen alarms were klaxoning. The port should have been echoing with their warning. In reality all the systems were down and there was just an eerie silence, broken only by the screams and shouts behind her. Felipe moved with a space worker's grace: grab this, spin around that, kick from the other. Linda followed after him and even at this time she let herself feel so incredibly proud of her son. Give him an emergency and he was immediately grown up, competent, unthinkingly taking command. Just like his father. Felipe pulled them to a halt at the main exit from the lobby. The luckier passengers and dock workers, those who also knew how to get about in microgravity, were streaming past them. "We have to get this closed." His hands grasped a spoked wheel that stuck proud of the wall. All the port's automated systems seemed to be out; anything that had to be done, had to be done manually, and that included shutting the emergency pressure bulkheads.

She arrested her motion with a mid-air twist and a soft landing on the wall beside Felipe. She glanced back at the lobby.

"There's hundreds of people..." she began.

"And we've got to..." Felipe said, almost at the same time.

The dome shattered with a roar that sounded like the sky exploding, spewing air and people out into vacuum. A hurricane tore up from the innards of Puerto Alto and boiled along the passageway. Linda was only saved because the blast jammed her body between the wheel and the wall.

Felipe still held onto the wheel, but his body was stretched out back in the direction they had come. His arms trembled as he tried to pull himself back against the force of the wind. They looked helplessly at each other and he tried to speak, but the howl was too loud.

The flange of the bulkhead already jutted out from the side of the tunnel, a metal ridge between her and the devastation. Linda wriggled round, carefully keeping one arm wrapped around the wheel. Then she grabbed Felipe's wrist with the other hand and tried to pull him up. She lacked the strength, and she knew she should be doing something much more important – turning the wheel to close the bulkhead. Which she couldn't do while he hung onto it.

Felipe must have realised it at the same time as she did. He shouted something again that Linda still couldn't hear, and then closed his eyes and let go and was sucked back out into the lobby.

Linda didn't even watch him go. She was already applying all her strength to the wheel. It gave so suddenly that she slipped and almost was sucked back into the lobby herself, but she kept her grip and set her feet on the metal surface again. She cried out as the wheel began to move once more, and the bulkhead slid out of the wall. A moment later and it had sealed the tunnel.

The hurricane died at once. Linda let herself sag in microgravity, along with the many other people who had been sucked towards the lobby and were only just daring to let go of the supports that had held them.

Only then did she look back at the blank bulkhead, knowing there was only unbreathable, suffocating vacuum behind it, and Felipe was behind it, which meant Felipe was dead. And only then did she scream. Closed her eyes and screamed, howled out her grief.

But then her duty took over. She was Port Administrator; she had to get this place back on its feet again, and fast. She ignored the cries for help, the frightened yells, the sobbing, and set off down the debris-choked passage.

ALEX AND HIS father staggered up the steps from the cellar with a large, heavy box between them. It was the last of several items they had already hauled up from below.

"I bet you never thought you'd need this again," Alex said. His father just grunted.

Maria appeared at the top of the stairs, face twisted in discomfort as she held her swollen abdomen in both hands.

"Tomás? What's happening?"

"The wormhole's exploded." They dropped the box onto the tiles of the hall.

"What? Can that happen?" She began to come down, one stair at a time, carefully supporting her increased weight with each step before taking the next.

Alex looked up at her.

"No," he said.

Tomás grabbed a lead from the box and plugged it into a power outlet in the wall. The box began to whine, the noise fading as it grew higher, and red LEDs flickered their status.

"We're getting back in touch with the world," he said. "Wormhole, whatever, something has taken headspace down and apparently fried the sat network." He was bent over a console in the box, face taut with concentration as his hands moved over the controls. "Damn, I'd forgotten how fiddly this is when you have to do it by eye."

Alex was connecting the fibre and other control cables to a satellite dish that sat on a tripod.

"Papá has access to more robust systems than the ordinary link," he told her without looking up. "They're land-based and shielded. They might be salvageable. But we need a high-level blackbox that hasn't been wiped."

"Where did all this come from?" Maria asked, blinking at the gear. Alex grinned.

"Papá was Rio Lento's comms specialist, once upon a time, remember?

The box began to hum.

"We're on," his father said. "Get the doors open. No, querida..." he added sharply. Maria had made a move towards the doors herself. "Not you. It's freezing."

"I won't go outside," she said tightly, and she determinedly began to pull one of the doors open, pregnancy not withstanding. Alex ran to help her with the other, and then he and his father manhandled the satellite dish to stand outside the entrance. Alex crouched and squinted up over the rim, angling the dish with his hands towards the star of Puerto Alto.

"First job is to get hold of the Discourse," his father said. "Panic will be growing. They have to know that things are under control."

"Are they?" Maria asked. He scowled.

"They have to believe it," he said, "or have a reason to kid themselves they believe it." He held up his hand with his finger and thumb barely apart. "We're *this* close to losing everything. So let's get it right. We get in, we invoke the emergency protocols–"

"Try that," Alex said. His father plugged a fibre into a linkset, tucked the linkset behind his ear and concentrated. After a moment he swore.

"It got Puerto Alto too. Nothing up there ... What are you doing?"

Alex was squatting down by the rim of the dish again, repositioning it to another point in the sky, waiting for its target to emerge above the horizon.

"Alejandro?" he said, more loudly.

"There are other blackboxes in the sky, querido," Maria pointed out, and Tomás fell into the profound silence of someone feeling a penny drop. After a moment, he silently handed the linkset down to his son. Alex fastened it on behind his ear and a very limited headspace opened inside his mind. It was the purely local network of the comms equipment, but it was better than nothing.

"Trying now," he said, and projected up into the cold night, feeling for what he hoped was there. Suddenly he felt something brush against his headspace – something coming from the other direction. He had made contact with *Phoenicia*.

Identify?

"Alejandro Mateo," Alex sent back. "I need your help. I want..."

I have assessed the situation. Stand by.

And Alex gasped as a sensation of a mighty void flowed over him. It was like stumbling forward and finding yourself going over the edge of a chasm, but a moment later he had caught himself and he knew where he was. *Phoenicia* had given him access to its full processing power. It was inside his headspace, and it was all his.

"Papá," he said out loud, "let me know how to get to the Discourse..."

HEROES EMERGED THAT night, in the strangest of ways and unlikeliest of places. People like Linda Hahn, who spent the next thirty-six hours co-ordinating the damage control and rescue teams on Puerto Alto.

Later, the enquiry would state at greater length what Alex had already guessed. It had less to say on the how and the why but there was no doubting the what.

The wormhole had ceased to exist and the latent energy contained within it had burst out of the terminus. The effect had been like a nuclear explosion, a single massive blast of radiation and an electromagnetic pulse, that fanned out in the shape of a cone from where the terminus had been. *Phoenicia* had been the other side of the world, sheltered by billions of tons of rock.

The people of La Nueva Temporada were protected from the radiation by the shielding of the atmosphere and the planet's magnetic field, and an electromagnetic pulse wasn't going to hurt them. But every spacecraft and satellite within the cone got the full hit, and even down on the planet the pulse covered most of the continent and wreaked the havoc that Alex had already experienced.

The elevator cars that were en route to and from the surface were designed for systems failure and they simply clung to their tracks, awaiting a reboot.

Any unshielded electromagnetic equipment on the planet simply failed to work. Blackboxes were wiped and their control of the planet's systems evaporated. Over ninety per cent of headspace nodes failed. Cars crashed. Patients died on operating tables. The fields that supported the ringrails as they hurtled at supersonic speed between the hoops vanished. No one travelling on a ringrail that night survived.

Two more of that night's heroes were Alex and Tomás Mateo. Their contact with *Phoenicia*, through a primitive comms link and a tight beam that was interrupted every time the ship went below the horizon again, let them use the processing power of the ship's blackbox to bring the confused, damaged systems of Rio Lento back online.

With that power base they could roam further, through fibre optic links, into the Discourse. Blackboxes were reinitialised and they could pour messages of reassurance into the reactivated headspace. They knitted together a network so that the emergency services could communicate once again. It was slow and it was primitive and the planet-wide bandwidth was a fraction of what it had been, but it worked. Slowly, La Nueva Temporada could begin to piece itself together again.

As a side effect, by the time dawn reached Rio Lento, Tomás Mateo effectively ran the planetary government. He ruled a wounded planet that was cut off from Earth and a bare step away from a new dark age.

CHAPTER FOUR

EMERGENCY PROTOCOLS

ALEX HAD BEEN summoned to his father's office and then just made to sit in one corner. It was an unwanted intrusion into the misery that had engulfed him ever since the news of Felipe's death had come down from Puerto Alto.

His father, apparently untouched by the news, paced the room and spoke to disembodied voices. Alex glared up at him through red, moist eyes. How could the man be so *unaffected*?

"Linda," Tomás said to the air, "tell the others what you've told me. Report from orbit?"

"*Sulong Station was slagged by the blast. The wormhole has vanished.*"

The voice of Alex's mother was just as abrupt and business-like as his father's. He instinctively reached out to see her, to witness the bereavement that was surely stamped on her face, but of course headspace was closed to him. Yesterday a call like this would have dotted everyone around the room, able to see and hear each other and interact as if they were all physically present. Now it was just voices, routed through shielded optical cables, and that was the least of the changes forced on La Nueva Temporada.

"*Sol 3 failed completely and has re-entered the atmosphere.*"

"I presume no one was hurt or I'd have heard…"

"*It hit the middle of the Océano Grande. No one hurt. Sol 1 is struggling – currently at about twenty-five per cent capacity,*" *my people should be able to get it up to at least seventy-five but that takes time. Only Sol 2 is working properly."*

Like Tomás, Alex had already heard this. He had spent much of the previous night envisioning what it meant. Only one and a half of the three artificial suns working, the wormhole closed so no new supplies could be brought in...

La Nueva Temporada was in deep trouble. The Thaw programme would have to be scaled down. Populations would shift as winter returned. More and more people – sixty million of them, all told – would be moving onto land less and less able to support them. Every minitok on the planet would have to join forces with every windmill and every hydro plant and every geothermal sink, and that should keep people warm enough to live... while the spare parts lasted. And no amount of raw energy could feed people. Headspace contained the full sum of recorded human knowledge, but that was no good to anyone without the ability to transform that knowledge into food and goods.

There were no two ways about it. La Nueva Temporada needed the wormhole back, and Alex could only think of one way that was going to happen.

"The wormhole has closed before," his father said. The man continued to pace around the room and Alex jerked his head up in surprise. Tomás gazed coolly down at him in passing with a 'didn't know that, did you?' sort of look. "We've always reopened it and no one even noticed."

"Señor, the terminus was always intact in those cases." That was a new voice, a man's. Alex guessed it would be an expert from the university, probably from the Sulong Institute. *"The link breaks naturally from time to time but we had plenty of reserve particles to open it up again."*

"Remind me."

There was the frustrated pause of an expert assembling his knowledge into non-technical phrases that could be understood by the less well educated.

"Before Phoenicia *left Earth,"* the voice said with forced patience, *"sets of particles were entangled at the quantum level.*

That makes them able to interact instantaneously, regardless of the distance between them. The ship brought one half of each set of those particles with it, and the interaction over the twenty light year gap enabled us to open a wormhole back to Earth. Whenever the wormhole closed again, we could simply reopen it with a fresh pair of particles. And we brought several million, enough to last for millions of years."

"And why can't we do that now?"

"*This wasn't a routine failure. The nature of this event has broken the link between all the particles. Our reserve collection is useless.*"

"So the only thing for it is to send *Phoenicia* back to Earth with a new collection of particles."

"*Or for them to send a ship to us, except that at as of yesterday Earth didn't have any more ships like* Phoenicia."

No one had any ships like *Phoenicia*, Alex thought with savage pride, except for La Nueva Temporada. To be precise, except for the consortium, which was to say him and Felipe...

Who was dead. Well, except for him and the consortium's backers...

Who were all on Earth, the other side of the twenty light year gap between worlds. It suddenly struck Alex that he was now the sole owner of *Phoenicia*. Up until then, it hadn't been important.

"*That is,*" said another man's voice, "*if we want a new wormhole.*"

The voice was familiar: Alex frowned, trying to place it. The disadvantage of the voice-only call was not seeing any faces or tags; the advantage was that only he could see his father contain a sigh of frustrated patience.

"Share your thoughts, Luis?"

Oh, him, Alex thought dully. Luis Alcantara – another of the planet's Executors, Maria's father and, technically, his step-grandfather. Alcantara continued with the kind of slow, careful emphasis that suggested he had worked this out long ago and now just needed to explain it to people of feebler minds.

"*It's a forty year trip to Earth…*"

Forty-three, Alex thought, *and less for the people on board due to time dilation.* There was a strange comfort in pedantry.

"*… and that's a long time to exist on emergency protocols. Phoenicia's main drive has power enough to keep us warm for generations. Obviously, we can open a wormhole eventually but we can send a robot probe to do that in the meantime.*"

Both Alex and his father rolled their eyes. Yes, the power output of *Phoenicia's* Matter Annihilation drive was more than enough to serve the planet's energy needs – while the parts lasted. They wouldn't last because the drive couldn't run non-stop for forty years. It was designed to blaze away for a decade at the most before shutting down and letting the ship cruise the rest of the way. And yes, it took *Phoenicia* forty years to get to Earth, but that was the fastest possible time. A smaller ship, without the drive, would take centuries. No, *Phoenicia* had to go to Earth, and that was all.

"Thank you for your thoughts, Luis. Professor, can we create new entangled particles?"

"*You can do it in any classroom, Señor. Give me five minutes and it's done.*"

"And reopening the wormhole?"

"*The procedure is well documented. At a pinch, anyone could train themselves up with a couple of conceptuals. Using an expert would minimise the risk, of course.*"

Tomás was already nodding, a look of grim satisfaction on his face. Suddenly Alex had a feeling that nothing in the previous conversation had been news to him. His father had already drawn the conclusions he wanted, and now he had them supported.

"Thank you, all of you. Emergency protocols continue to apply and I'll be in touch with my decision. End call."

"*Tomás.*" That was Señor Alcantara again, and even in the depths of misery Alex had to bite back a smile at the sudden spike of annoyance on his father's face. *End call* was an instruction you gave headspace and even Tomás had forgotten.

"*The emergency protocols were drawn up fifty years ago when we were nudging Puerto Alto into place, just in case we nudged too far. They weren't invented to make you planetary dictator.*"

"Thank you, Luis, and I have no intention of being one. But this is an emergency and it needs protocols." Tomás crossed to his desk and jabbed a button, hard. "End call," he said distinctly, and this time the voices fell silent.

Father and son looked at each other. There wasn't the slightest triumph or satisfaction anywhere on Tomás's features and suddenly Alex knew that, of course, his father felt the loss of Felipe just as badly as he did. But Felipe was one dead Nuevan out of sixty million live ones and while Tomás Mateo might mourn him, Executor Mateo couldn't allow himself that luxury right now.

And if both his parents could do that, Alex vowed, then so would he. For La Nueva Temporada.

"You want the ship, you can have it," he said, looking his father in the eyes. "I'll give all the assistance I can."

A fleeting tenderness showed behind his father's stony exterior.

"Of course you will. Come with me, will you? I can take five minutes and there's something we both need to do…"

ALEX REALISED WHERE they were going when they were halfway up the stairs, but it was too late to back out by then. Tomás ushered him in to Maria's room with a gentle hand in the small of his back. The room was quiet, lit only by the glacier-tinted reflection of the sun through the window. Maria was asleep in bed. It was a place Alex had no interest whatsoever in being at the best of times and the item currently asleep in the nurse's arms just doubled his lack of interest.

His father quietly lifted the baby away from her and turned towards Alex.

"Alejandro, this is Joaquin." He gently prodded the child's nose. "Quinito, this is your very big brother Alejandro and he's going to look after you and be your best friend until you're old enough to choose friends for yourself."

Alex gazed down at the tiny bundle that had so inconveniently decided to arrive, on top of everything else, just as they were finally getting the planet under control again. *This* was meant to replace Felipe? The baby was wrapped tight like a cloth skittle. Only his face showed. It was smaller than Alex's hand and stamped with a furious scowl that exactly matched Alex's own feelings.

His father cleared his throat.

"I've not behaved well," he said abruptly. Alex looked up in surprise. His father looked down at his feet, around the room, then steeled himself to look Alex in the eye. "I've not been a great father."

Alex didn't know what to say. He opened his mouth because he should probably say something. His father shook his head.

"I've not been a great father," he repeated, distinctly. "I never gave you due recognition when in fact we were eye to eye on almost everything. The way you managed to steer a middle ground between Feli and me – well, you're one of life's peacemakers and diplomats and that's a huge strength that I never properly appreciated."

Alex protested automatically. "I didn't–"

His father fixed him with a piercing look that said he knew his sons down to the core. "And now we've both lost him anyway."

Alex bit his lip. Oh God, was his father going to get weepy? Oh, please no...

But the man simply patted him on the arm.

"There's a huge amount of work ahead of us, and I have to say that right now I can't think of a better tio to have by my side. You're a good son, you were a good brother to Feli... and I know you'll be a good one to Quinito too, because I'm going to be way too busy to be a decent father. And I'm going to give him to you now."

"But I don't..." Alex protested again, but his arms reached out for the child as if there was a switch hidden in his chest – a baby-taking mechanism that was activated when his father pressed the bundle at him. The body was surprisingly light and the head that rested in the crook of his elbow was surprisingly heavy. The smell of new, clean baby filled his nostrils.

"Hola, Quinito," he murmured with resignation. "Yes, I suppose. What he said." He cocked an eyebrow up at his father. "By your side, eh?"

"Figuratively speaking." There was the tiniest suspicion of a twinkle in Tomás's eye. "And you already know your first job."

Decision of the Planetary Executive convened under the emergency protocols.

1. Spaceworthiness of starship *Phoenicia* to be established without delay. Port Administrator of Puerto Alto to supervise a party of engineers to advise on condition of ship.

2. Sulong Institute, Altiplano University to take all necessary technical steps to facilitate the opening of a new wormhole between the systems of La Nueva Temporada and Earth, including preparation of requisite amount of entangled particles, advice on construction of new terminus equipment and provision of specialist training to oversee wormhole opening.

3. Port Administrator of Puerto Alto to assemble a skeleton crew of trained spacers that will take *Phoenicia* to Earth.

4. *Phoenicia* to be compulsorily purchased from present owners by government of La Nueva Temporada. Present owners to be compensated at cost.

"AIRLOCK SIGHTED. WE'RE *transmitting the code.*"

Port Control at Puerto Alto was unusually empty. With no soft bodies around to absorb the sound, the voice had a harsh echo. Usually the room was much busier as the teams who worked for Alex's mother co-ordinated the bustle of orbital activity – the ships coming in from the wormhole and going out, and maintenance of the satellites and the Sols, and the very lives of the crews of men and women who were out in space around La Nueva Temporada at any one time.

But today there was no one out in space except the retrieval team about to set foot on *Phoenicia*.

Alex lurked at the back of Port Control. His mother and a small group of technicians were at the main console, standing behind one of the traffic controllers and watching the display as the man talked the team in. Part of the display was a long-range telescope view. *Phoenicia* was a slightly blurred skeleton with nothing to suggest the scale or the length of the kilometre-long ship.

It was a strange kind of masochism that had brought him here. Yes, he had said he would help any way he could, but as he wasn't an engineer and wouldn't be needed on board, his father had made it quite clear that he could best serve the cause by staying in Rio Lento out of the way. But Alex was glad he had had come up to Puerto Alto. He and his mother could mourn Felipe together, in between all the vital tasks she had to perform, and Felipe for a while would burn bright in both their hearts again.

This was one of the more vital tasks and Alex had wanted to be in on it. Felipe's vision of founding a new colony wasn't going to happen. It was the final slap in the face for the dream and the least he could do was say goodbye.

The voice came through again.

"*Commencing docking... Airlock is fifty metres away... forty... thirty... thirty... uh, still thirty, hang on...*"

Alex's mother frowned. "Team, why are you holding station?"

"*We're not! Uh... It's moving! Phoenicia is moving away from us! It fired its thrusters. Um, it's stopped now...*"

"Close in, team. Resume approach."

"*Complying... oh Christ, now it's spinning!*"

Alex glanced at the telescope image. At this distance the rate of rotation looked very slow, but *Phoenicia* was indeed turning purposefully about its long axis. Not fast, but fast enough to move the airlock out of range of the pod.

His father's voice broke into the proceedings, dry and commanding.

"Linda, tell Alejandro to stop arsing around and let the team on board!"

His mother glanced suspiciously at Alex. He managed a weak smile and a shrug.

"I didn't do a thing," he said truthfully.

"No telemetry to or from *Phoenicia*," the controller confirmed. "It's doing all this on its own initiative."

"Tomás, you run your planet and let me run my station. Puerto Alto out." And she turned on Alex. "Just what the hell is happening?"

"Get me a linkset," he said. "I'll ask…"

A linkset was duly produced and for the first time in days he had headspace again, however limited. It was just him and the big, anxious presence that was *Phoenicia*.

There you are. Why are these people trying to board me?

"They're an engineering team come to check you over."

Understood. However, I have been monitoring their communications and I detected an untoward possessiveness in their attitude.

"Um…" Alex bit his lip, and gestured to his mother to listen in. She nodded and the sound of the ship's half of the conversation filled Port Control. "Under the emergency protocols you do belong to the government."

I am older than the emergency protocols. I belong to you.

"Well, your owner says to let the engineers on board."

Very well. However, be warned that at the slightest sign of their attempting to take control–

"They won't. They just need to prep you for the voyage."

Very well, the ship said again. Then: *when will you be coming on board?*

"I won't be. I'm relinquishing control."

I decide when control is relinquished! I was chartered by your consortium for a specific purpose and I intend to see it through.

Alex looked anxiously around at the other humans who were listening to this. A range of pennies seemed to be dropping. People were turning away from him, bowing heads together, discussing urgently.

"But... the mission has changed! We're not going anymore. You need to return to Earth."

The mission was to undertake one interstellar voyage and open a wormhole at the end of it. My programming says that changing the destination to Earth is an acceptable alternative to the original plan. Changing my ownership is not. I am not leaving this solar system without a duly constituted owner on board. That is a fundamental of my charter.

"Alejandro?" Tomás Mateo was on again. "*Tell it that I'm now legally the senior owner!*"

As indeed he was. Felipe had died with no will and no official next of kin. That meant everything went to their father.

The ship answered before Alex could say anything.

Ownership transfers to surviving members of the consortium before next of kin, Señor Mateo. If Alejandro were to die with no spouse or offspring then what you say is true. Under the circumstances, the ship's honesty was unintentionally brutal. *As I assume this is not an attractive option, however, he must therefore come with me on the mission.*

The background noise was getting louder. Overheard snatches of conversation included discussing the possibility of reprogramming the ship; of installing a slave blackbox that could overrule the ship's own consciousness; of altering the ship's perception so that it thought it was getting its own way when in fact...

But Alex knew that none of those schemes would work. The ship's consciousness was distributed throughout its frame and was more advanced than anything La Nueva Temporada could throw against it.

He looked aghast at his mother. She had got there a moment ahead of him and she already looked stunned, pale with a second bereavement.

"Oh, Christ, I've got to go to Earth!"

PART 2
THE ISOLATION YEARS

CHAPTER 5

QUINITO

Quin is 4

I WAS BORN into a broken world and my father was putting it right. That's the first thing I remember learning.

There were other lessons, some of which had to be unlearned, some of which were never officially taught in the first place.

I was taught that there were two kinds of people on Nueva, them and us. *We* had names like my own, Joaquin Luis Salvador Mateo y Alcantara. *They* had shorter names, with fewer syllables and vowels. To make it easier for them, we would keep our names short and standardised like theirs, so to everyone outside the family I was Joaquin Mateo. *We* would privately laugh at *their* lack of sophistication and unfortunate tendency, say, to call me 'Jo-aykwin' rather than the more proper 'Hwa-keen'.

We were hijos, because we were the first to arrive on this planet. We had discovered and settled the frozen ball that became La Nueva Temporada; we had named the planet and most of the places on it. If we called *them* anything it was just 'segunda', another word taken from the old Castilian language and culture that our grandparents had decided to revive, despite the fact that we all spoke perfectly good Angla.

We got here first and so we ran the world. This made sense, when I was a boy. It took me far too many years to work out that there was a bigger picture. We may have been here first but right from the start we had been a minority. We weren't even the largest of Nueva's ethnic groups.

Of course, my perceptions were distorted from the beginning, because the day I was born my father Tomás Mateo became ruler of the world.

I was born in Rio Lento at the family home, the villa, set on a peak above the town and the glacier. I came out a month too soon, on the same day as the Event which shaped the world I grew up in. When I was little I had friends in town, boys and girls my own age at the town crèche, where we spent our days while our mothers and fathers worked hard to make food and keep us warm. Some of them were segunda but adults seemed to tolerate mixing between children. As I got older we drifted apart, and by the time of my first Communion party I understood without being told that I was only expected to invite the right kind of guest.

Under my father's regime everyone worked, even my mother, a woman whom I was to discover had been trained in no useful skills whatsoever. I remember her tears during one of her increasingly rare lucid moments, in later years – tears as she studied her fading features in a reflection, and hugged me tight, and whispered, "This wasn't what they told me, Quinito. This wasn't what it was meant to be."

But I'm getting ahead. I lived where I was born, in the villa, and it was dominated by two unseen presences. My father, the Planetary Director, and my hero brother.

That's the *other* hero brother. It took four years to learn I had two of them.

I FOUND THE picture one day when a razorstorm billowed up the valley and ice crystals crackled against the windows.

It was the limbo hour between the crèche sending the kids home and the end of the adult working day, so I was on my own. I had heard the storm alarms go off and I ran to the terrace to watch. On a clear day, the freezing air was sealed outside and the room was full of beautiful, mellow light. Years later the memory can still make me feel warm. But on a day like this it was dull and grey and the walls seemed to be closing in.

I knelt on a chair and pressed my face against the glass shield. In the fields on the slopes, either side of the glacier, I could see people hurrying to pull the protective domes over the crops. And here it came! Billowing over the far ridge, tumbling down into the settlement like a living thing, an animated cloud, dark and glittering. It struck the buildings, swamped the fields, hit the other side of the valley and kept going. Up, up, up...

The storm hit the glass with a *thud*, and millions of ice crystals scraped and shattered just centimetres from my face. I watched it without blinking, staring entranced into the heart of the creature that wanted so badly to consume me.

But there was only so long that even a class three razorstorm could hold my interest. Eventually I wandered off, and that was when I found the picture.

It was in one of the many boxes stacked at the back of the storeroom. Exactly what I was doing among the boxes at the back of the storeroom, I could never remember. Doubtless I had my reasons, but once I saw the picture, I had other concerns on my mind.

I held up the transparent plaque and tilted it to get the image from all directions. I recognised the scene immediately because there was a close-up of it in the main living room. It was my Mama and Papá, standing poised before the camera, arms linked on their wedding day. She was dressed in white and her smile was warmer and happier than I had ever seen in my life. He was dignified and noble in a dark suit, looking down his nose at the camera.

That was the living room picture. This showed the wider scene and there were other people standing on either side. I recognised my grandfather – Mama's own Papá – on the right. Next to him was my big brother Felipe. Felipe's picture was everywhere and I was very proud of the hero brother I had never met.

And... someone else, the other side of the happy couple, standing between Papá and Father Adolfo.

I studied the tio carefully. There was a smile on his face but the camera had caught him just as he was blinking, so he seemed to be sleeping on his feet and enjoying it. He looked like Felipe – slimmer, maybe a little taller, same dark hair – but he wasn't Felipe, because Felipe was over there, glancing off camera and looking sulky.

I took the picture to Mama.

THE TOP FLOOR of the villa was the preserve of the Mateos and I had the run of it during the day. The ground floor was where my father worked and there were always people coming and going, holding hushed, rapid conversations in corners or striding purposefully from room to room and talking as they went.

I could see my mother down in the hall. She had come in when the alarms went off, along with a lot of other field workers. They were clustered at the foot of the stairs, still dressed for outside, chatting amongst themselves or glancing out of the windows to check the storm's progress. They looked out of place in their work togs, and even then it struck me as odd that my mother looked a stranger in her own home.

For a long time, I had simply assumed she was in charge of the field hands, because my father was in charge of Nueva and how else would it be? It had come as quite a surprise to learn that she was just another one of the workers. There was a manager who could tell her what to do. When I had asked why, she had just shrugged and said "Because Mr Bast knows more than I do." *Mr* Bast. Not even a hijo!

I still didn't have much notion, then, of the colossal pressure that came with marriage to my father. He ran the planet, so his wife had to be seen to be doing something useful and inspiring, and what was more inspiring than putting your back to the land? So out she went each day, meek and uncomplaining, to work that would slowly destroy her.

She smiled when she saw me. She always did, though sometimes there was just a small delay between her gaze falling on me and the smile appearing.

"Hello, mi amor. Are you safe and warm?"

I handed her the plaque without ceremony.

"Who's this?" I asked, pointing at the stranger.

Her eyes went wide. "Wherever did you..." She shook her head as if to chase off unwelcome thoughts. "Come upstairs, querido."

In the living room on the first floor, she told me. "That's your..." I remember she pulled a face, as if taking some effort to find the right way to phrase a very simple answer. "That's your big brother."

I was annoyed. She hadn't understood the question. "No, not Feli." I jabbed a finger at the stranger. "*Him.*"

"That's who I meant, mi amor. He's your... *other* big brother. He's called Alejandro and you only met him when you were very, very little."

Another brother? It was like discovering I had a third hand no one had ever told me about. I looked at the stranger in a whole new light.

"Is he alive?" I asked.

I remember her pause; even then I thought it must be significant.

"We all hope he's alive, mi amor. He had to leave Nueva soon after you were born."

Leave Nueva? I thought. But no one left Nueva.

"Where did he go to?" I asked.

"He went on a very important mission for Papá. He went to a world called Earth. He'll get there when you're forty-three." She smiled. "But he'll still be nineteen, so then you'll be his big brother!"

I wasn't interested in any number bigger than five. She might as well have said "he'll be a thousand." What was much more important was:

"Have I got any more brothers?" It seemed a reasonable question, given that I had just found out about this one. Someone else from that mythical time when everyone could be as warm as they liked, and as full of food as they wanted, and could link to headspace anywhere and anytime, just by thinking about it.

Suddenly she looked sad. It only lasted a second and I wasn't sure I had spotted it before she was smiling cheerfully down at me again.

"No, querido. You see, no one's allowed to have more than one baby now. Papá would love for you to have a little brother or sister, but sometimes grown-ups have to make sacrifices."

"What's sacrifices?"

"Sacrifices," she muttered under her breath, and I was surprised, because the tone was suddenly harsh and not at all like the way she usually spoke to me. But then the smile was back, though slightly dimmed by a sadness that lurked behind it.

"Sacrifices are when... well, you want to make nice things happen for everyone, but you can't. So you have to be a little bit unhappy, so that more people can be happy in other ways."

Two neurons collided inside my head and sparked off an insight.

"Like Feli," I said, and got another hug.

"That's right, querido! Felipe made a *big* sacrifice. He had to let himself die so that his mama could save a lot of other lives."

I studied my mother carefully. That sadness was still there and it disturbed me slightly. I wanted to probe it more. It was like picking at a scab – painful, but I needed to know.

"Does Papá love Alejandro?" I asked.

"Of course he does, querido! Only... well, Papá was unhappy Alejandro had to go and... and that's why Papá doesn't talk much about him."

But my question had only been the vanguard for the real issue at hand.

"Who does Papá love more?" I asked.

She looked at me, then wrapped her arms around me and squeezed. It wasn't really a hug this time.

"Papá loves us all the same," she said.

But that didn't make sense, I thought. What about sacrifices? You *can't* all be the same – she had just said. My mother really ought to get her story straight.

CHAPTER SIX

THE ENEMY WITHIN

Quin is 10

YOU CAN LEARN and learn and learn and still get it completely wrong. You can be biting your tongue to keep quiet for years on end, and no one ever notices until the one time you let the cat out of the bag.

Such innocent words. "We don't normally eat this much..."

And immediately I knew it was the wrong thing to say. I flushed when everyone around the grand dining table looked at me. Grandfather, his bushy grey moustache bristling with a hidden smile. My father, with that fixed, dark look which I never knew meant if I was in trouble or not. And my mother...

Visits from Grandfather were a mixed blessing. On the plus side: Grandfather (and sometimes other Alcantaras too – aunts and uncles and cousins), presents, my mother happier than usual. But on the minus side there was always that elusive something I could never quite put my finger on. It was like tiptoeing over bad ice on the glacier. One wrong step and down into the icy depths you went.

My mother was looking like she had just felt the ice shift beneath her.

"Well... we don't," I added, in a small voice.

Grandfather's smile came out into the open from behind his moustache. He lifted his glass and raised it to me.

"Well, it's a special occasion, Quinito!" he said. "We've got to celebrate your birthday!"

It was indeed my birthday – my tenth – but I knew full well I wasn't the reason for the three course spread. We had had soup to start, a casserole with real meat and vegetables, and a delicious fruit salad, all washed down (for the grown-ups) by my father's precious supply of red wine. All home grown, of course. No black market provisions in *our* house.

No, Grandfather was the reason. We always ate more when someone from the Alcantara household came to visit, only once or twice a year, usually for my birthday or my mother's. Travelling, like everything else on Nueva, was rationed. I couldn't remember the time I put two and two together, but I do remember my mother's reaction when she learned that I had worked it out. I had – correctly – deduced that someone was coming to stay, because all the meals for three days beforehand had been smaller than usual, which must mean we were saving up for a big splash. Mama had listened with a nervous smile to this theory, and simply said I wasn't to mention the fact in Grandfather's presence. Grandfather was very modest and wouldn't want to think anyone was making a fuss over him.

Making a fuss, my nads. We were showing Grandfather that the Mateos could eat well.

Who was it said that every society is only three meals away from revolution? It's an old saying but its wisdom has lasted, because it's true. I firmly believe one of the few factors to prevent an uprising against my father's rule was that there really was no more food than we were already eating – at all, anywhere – and all the demagoguery in the world couldn't turn thin air into a nice juicy slab of myco.

It also helped that he didn't rule from the seat of government in Alti. In the name of resource conservation, he governed via headspace from Rio Lento, and encouraged the other Executors to do the same in their own provinces. Any angry mob would have two thousand kilometres of tundra and mountains to cross.

* * *

BUT MY FATHER'S Directorship was not without its critics; and one of them, I was to learn, was his former ally Executor Luis Alcantara – his boyhood buddy, his colleague in political arms, and (despite being almost the same age) his father-in-law. Once my father had got over the minor brainflip of marrying a segunda and having not one but two half-blood sons, he did it properly and married his friend's daughter. She had been raised in the lap of Nuevan luxury, a new world princess, and the marriage was to be a liaison between two great dynasties. The children of that union – hi! – would be kings and queens of La Nueva Temporada.

Then everything changed, including the relationship between the two men. It's hard to stay on good terms in a partnership when, frankly, you think the other man is doing it wrong, and he is untouchable in his wrongness.

And this particular birthday meal was when little Quinito learnt of these divisions. It was comparable to that day when I learned I had another brother. Life would go on as normal, but from now on I would always have this added dimension to my view of the world.

MEANWHILE, BACK AT the meal where I had just let the good Mateo name down, my father's face was completely neutral.

"Everyone eats enough," he said gruffly. "That's something we can all be proud of." And he also raised his glass to me.

"Not what they're saying in Orellana," Grandfather murmured as he took a sip.

Crack. I heard the ice go.

My father's eyes and voice went hard. "If they could follow some simple rules then there'd be enough for everyone."

My mother closed her eyes.

"It's getting colder, Tomás..."

My father snorted. "Luis, I can't control the weather!"

"Oh, is just controlling the planet getting too much?"

"*Please!*" my mother blurted. And when everyone looked at her, more quietly: "Please. It's Quinito's birthday."

Quinito had rather been hoping the conversation would go on. Apparently there were hungry people on Nueva; how could that be happening? Everyone knew – my mother reminded me almost every day – that my father was holding the world together, making sure no one went hungry, conserving Nueva's precious few resources until Alejandro opened the wormhole up again, around thirty years from now. The very hint of a crack in the grand scheme was fascinating. My father and my mother wouldn't lie to me, but nor would Grandfather. So, the truth must be something that encompassed both versions. I wanted to know more.

But instead, both men looked penitent, my father kissed my mother's hand, Grandfather ruffled my hair, and the conversation reverted to nothing at all.

As soon as it was decent I asked, "May I leave the table?" Permission was granted and I bolted out of the room.

There was a second door into the dining room, leading from what had been the servants' quarters in the days I had never known when the Mateos had apparently had servants. My father wouldn't allow such frivolities now; everyone's work was expected to contribute to keeping Nueva alive, not to personal luxury. But the door was still there.

The servants' quarters had been pressed into service as government offices, where I wasn't strictly meant to go. But there was only a skeleton weekend staff in that day and they barely looked up as I scurried through from the hallway. Those that did got a shy grin and an apologetic shrug from me to show I was just passing through and it was easier to let me be. So they did, and a minute later I had finished up with my ear pressed against the second door.

As I had guessed she would, my mother had also withdrawn and the two men were alone together, continuing to put a small dent in the wine reserves. Their voices were slightly muffled by the door but they were clearly raised. God, this was fascinating.

What I gathered was: Orellana county hadn't upgraded to the colder weather strains of myco spores. To my father, this was just evidence of inefficiency. To my grandfather, the fault lay in the inertia of the centralised distribution ministry.

"They *tried* to upgrade, Tomás! They'd petitioned, they'd almost been begging..."

My father's voice was calm, flat. "There's a planet-scale famine coming if we don't..."

"For God's *sake*, Tomás, we know that...!"

To my surprise, I was with Grandfather on this. I knew nothing about myco distribution or Orellana. I did know that my father's way of bringing any conversation to a dead halt was to cite the emergency, as if planet-wide starvation was the only alternative to any course of action he didn't approve of. It was quite heartening to know he spoke to grown-ups in the same way.

"We, Luis? You keep saying *we*. Who is *we*?" My father's voice was so quiet I could barely hear him, and when I had, I could barely believe it. I knew that tone. It was the same tone that asked if I had tidied my room, when both parties knew full well I hadn't, and the consequences for telling a fib would be too terrible to imagine. He was using that tone on Grandfather?

If Grandfather recognised the danger, he gave no sign.

"You know who we are, Tomás."

And they went on talking, using terms I didn't understand like "malcontents" and "unite the factions" and "no-confidence vote".

"What is it you want, Luis?" I heard my father ask. Grandfather answered promptly.

"Announce that the emergency is over. The emergency protocols no longer apply and that means we no longer have need for a Planetary Director. Government returns to the ordinary Executive, including you, and you remain one of its most senior and respected members. And together we all get on with managing Nueva, making sure no one goes hungry again. Or, you're unseated against your will, kicking and screaming all the way."

"Is that a threat, Luis?"

"It's a statement."

"But Luis, the protocols do still apply, because the emergency is still very much on." My father's voice grew harsher. "We don't even know my son will succeed. A hundred things could go wrong between here and there. *Phoenicia* could be space debris even as we speak."

"What a shame you bulldozed through the motion that we send it away when the drive could be feeding power to every–"

My father just talked over him.

"I'm planning for every contingency and Nueva needs me. I have given everything to making this work and I will not let a bunch of doomsayers prevent it. I will not *permit* it."

A pause...

"Is that a threat, Tomás?"

"No, Luis, it's a statement."

"Then everyone knows where everyone stands," Grandfather said quietly.

"Apparently they do."

"In that case..." The sound of a chair scraping on the floor. "With your permission, I'll seek out my daughter to talk to her, and my grandson to play with."

"That's an excellent idea," my father agreed. "Let's all stick to our strengths, eh?"

I hurried off so that Grandfather could find me.

IT WAS A good afternoon, and I retired to bed nicely tired. I got a hug and a kiss and an instruction to sleep well.

I didn't. My father and Grandfather had come out of the dining room smiling and chatting like best friends, casual and relaxed in each other's presence, but I had had a glimpse into the truth. There was a divide between them. My father was Planetary Director and the one man who was holding Nueva together – that was a fundamental fact, no contest – and Grandfather, of all people, seemed opposed to him.

I fell asleep to strange dreams of crumbling buildings and glaciers creeping down from the poles and feasting on the remains of what had been human civilization. And even in my sleep there was the unwelcome but simple conviction that one of those two men – but I didn't know which – was the enemy.

CHAPTER SEVEN

COME, HUNT A MUSGOVORE

Quin is 15

SPAIN. AN AREA of old Earth, the ancestral land of the Mateos, and known for being *warm*. None of us had ever set foot there, of course, but I had at least gathered that much about the land of my forefathers. I am genetically a warm-climate man. You could almost get high on historical conceptuals that made you feel you were there, lounging among the sun-baked olive groves while the air shimmered about you.

Trudging down a rocky gully on a planet doomed to an incipient ice age, straining my eyes into the chill, damp mist around me and clutching the unaccustomed weight of a gun in my hands... well, just say I was struck by the contrast.

It's easy to feel sorry for yourself when you're fifteen. Permanently undervalued, never appreciated, old enough to want lots of sex, too young to have any of it. The drive and energy to take on the whole world, and the emotional maturity to handle maybe a small pebble.

If, on top of this steady background condition, you are also cold and tired and hungry, and you know it's all entirely your own fault and your very own personal screw-up, it doesn't improve the mood.

But at fifteen, blaming yourself is out of the question, so I blamed my father and most of all I blamed those hill farmers. They had started this.

I had been down in Rio Lento, running some errand for my father, and round the corner came these men and women, wearing furs that shimmered a bleached blonde.

They were wearing musgovore fur. You saw the little flat creatures from time to time around the outskirts of Rio Lento – small furry rugs, quietly flowing over the ground on their own business, or more usually wrapping themselves around a rock to lick up its mossy covering. They were harmless, they bred very slowly and they didn't eat our crops, so they presented no problem. You couldn't eat what little meat they had on them, so they weren't hunted. Only now, apparently, they were.

I remember wrinkling my nose. The furs were unkempt and smelly; I would much rather be wearing my own thigh-hugging synthetic coat. It had a waterproof shell covering several thin, air-breathing layers of artificial insulating fabric. But then a chill blast of wind had cut down the valley and I had shivered. The farmers had not.

A little elementary research back home had done the rest. Musgovore fur was an excellent natural insulator, waterproof yet light and downy...

"No," SAID MY father.

I blinked, the figures still clutched in my eager, outstretched hand. I kept my smile on.

"Why not?" I asked as politely as I could.

My father pushed himself back from his desk and stretched, hands behind his head.

"It's been done," he said.

"What, farming musgovores?" I knew it hadn't.

"People have looked into it. The figures didn't work out."

"But..." I knew that my figures decidedly did work out, and very nicely too. I proffered them again, still with a smile which was beginning to feel foolish. I glanced over at my mother, who was sitting in a chair by the window and gazing down at the valley. "Mama, you can..." I began, hoping to get some back-up.

But she turned her head slowly to look vaguely at me, eyes not quite focused, and I saw that today was one of Those Days. She had started early.

She smiled, because she usually did when she saw me, and she murmured "That's nice, querido..." but then her attention was caught by a cloud through the window and she went back to studying it.

I could remember the days before her condition sank its claws into her, when she actually moved about, talked, smiled, hugged me. But I had other things to worry about now, so I turned back to my father. He looked at me with thin patience.

"Musgovores are picky eaters," he said. "They won't go back to the same rock within two days of eating. It has to be a *new* rock. So, just a few of them will cover an enormous area. And they're not quick breeders either. It's, what, one, two pups every couple of years? Breeding them would be time and resource intensive. Nice try, good initiative, won't work." He looked back down at his work.

"Then redivert..." I began.

It was the wrong words, as – I cursed myself bitterly, hours later – I of all people should have known. The one thing you did not do with the Planetary Director was suggest an alteration to the Plan. Resources were not diverted, and that was it. Civil servants backed up by years of research and the brightest blackboxes didn't try it. One adolescent boy who had grown up in the same house really should have known better.

I remember my father's fist smashing down on the desk.

"I said, no! We don't have time for dreams, Quin. If you want a fur coat then go out and shoot one, but don't bother me with this again."

DREAMS WAS THE word that did it.

Because – and it hadn't even occurred to my father to check – my figures went way beyond a nice theoretical scenario where musgovore food miraculously appeared from nowhere and everything worked out just fine. Sure, I knew they were picky eaters. They ate the mineral oxides that accumulated in a particular kind of moss on a particular kind of rock. That was why they had to move on after eating. They had to wait until more of the moss had oxidised, then come back.

If we took just three myco farms out of production, adapted the machinery to cultivate and churn out pre-oxidised moss to send every musgovore on La Nueva Temporada into furry ruggy heaven, we could do it. It would take time, four or five years... and yes, some food resources would need to be diverted. But get twenty-five per cent of Nueva into musgovore fur and the savings on artificial fabrics could be ploughed back into myco. Everyone would be warm, happy and – best of all – slightly better fed.

The least I could do was have faith in my own figures, I reasoned. The hill farmers in their fur coats would never be seen outside Rio Lento but a fur coat worn around the house, right under the nose of the Planetary Director (and any important visitors he might have) – well, that was different. Who knew what seeds might be planted?

Two small obstacles stood in my way. The first – my utter lack of hunting experience – was easily taken care of with a conceptual. With the newfound skill at taking life burning in my forebrain, I tackled the second – my lack of a gun.

"YOU EVER WANT *something, Spawn, you come to Ilo.*"

I couldn't remember the first time Ilo Bast said that to me but it had been repeated many, many times, always when no one else was looking or nearby. A wink, perhaps a nudge, would accompany the low murmur.

Ilo was a big tio with greying, short hair that looked as stiff and unpliable as his face stubble. High cheekbones pushed his eyes into two dark, accusing slits. Ilo was our foreman, supervisor, major domo and general fixit.

I first really tested this invitation when I decided it was time to learn what getting drunk was like. He hadn't been put out, just amused when this smooth-faced pipsqueak with the unbroken voice turned up at his hab to demand some of his rumoured stash. But he had risen to the occasion, and never failed to remind me of it ever after.

Lately, I had been seriously considering asking him to get me a woman so I could learn what that was like too. It wasn't just Father Adolfo's gleeful descriptions of the fate of fornicators that held me back. I reckoned that if Ilo's women were as cheap as his hooch then I could do a lot better with a little patience and my own good looks. Plus he would forever be reminding me of that favour too, and that would just be humiliating.

I had no illusions. He wasn't generous because he was a friend or because he fancied little boys. No, I was his employer's only heir and he had an eye on the succession.

He was in his Constabulary uniform, unbuttoned, when I came knocking. Putting him into part-time law enforcement had been the most legal solution to his occasional habit of breaking heads – only the slackers, he had assured me; only the ones needing a little motivation. It was also why I knew he would have a gun.

He filled the door when he opened it. He wasn't flabby, he just took up a lot of space, and he occupied that space with a resolve that suggested no one should dispute his right to do so.

"Hey, Spawn," he said with a sly grin. "Come to shop yourself for underage drinking?" He shook inside as if this was hilarious.

"I need a gun," I said. "A stunner will do." Even he probably wouldn't let me loose with a lethal weapon.

For once, he looked vaguely surprised. "You in trouble, Spawn? I can handle it for you if you point me at 'em. Unless it's the Señor, 'cos then you're on your own."

"I want to shoot a musgovore," I said honestly, and he shook mirthfully again.

"Everyone should have a hobby." He stood aside to let me in. "Let's see what we can do."

Five minutes later I had my stunner – and though he got it from his desk, I couldn't help noticing it wasn't regular issue, lacking the Constabulary crest stamped on the butt – and, for good measure, a satcomm and a bonus tracker on my wrist.

"You never know when folk will wander off," he said vaguely when he saw me looking at it, and I wondered what folk he had had to track. "You got a conceptual inside you? Good. You'll find big ones over the top, down the far end. There's satellites going over every few minutes so we won't lose you. Happy hunting, Spawn."

"OVER THE TOP, down the far end" meant "go over the ridge that divides the Rio Lento valley from the one beyond, then head inland." I knew the route and I set off with a confident stride. The way was plain from my bedroom window and I saw it every day – skirt the edge of the glacier, go up the valley side to the crest and the terraces that had once been planned to be vineyards, and over.

I was fifteen, healthy, fit and armed. The most dangerous things in the hills were wolves imported from Earth, and they were gengineered not to attack humans. What could go wrong?

Well, for a start, who'd have thought something you could see so clearly would take so long? It took me an hour to reach the terraces, lungs heaving in the cold air and legs aching. The gun was surprisingly heavy and it didn't have a sling or a holster. I had to put it into my backpack, next to the satcomm, so now it hung between my shoulders like a heavy stone. I paused on the rocky peak and gazed down into the next valley. It was narrower and steeper than the one I had come from. A smaller glacier made its leisurely way down the valley floor, fed by the same motherlode of ice deep in the Barreras as the Rio Lento. The valley was a conduit for cold, icy winds gusting down from the high ground. The earth was dry and barren with only the churned earth of cavador burrows and a few shoots of rogue fimbulweed for colour.

I ran my gaze up and down it. Well, I hadn't been expecting it to be heaving with musgovores, but even so...

Perhaps the conceptuals were wearing off; perhaps it's just amazing how cold, hunger and general discomfort can turn even a determined adolescent from his course. But suddenly the whole musgovore farming dream evaporated into Nueva's cold air and I didn't miss it one bit. A slow smile of self-disbelief spread over my face and I let out a reluctant chuckle.

"You're an idiot," I told myself. "Muy estúpido." I looked back at Rio Lento, framed by the fur of my hood. The lights were just coming on. It also looked cold and uninviting, but it was paradise compared to this slice of native Nueva. That was where I belonged. There had to be easier ways of getting on with my father.

I turned away and had taken one step when the tracker beeped. It was set to musgovore pheromones and it was picking something up.

Give up? Never! I moved the tracker about slowly, letting it define the trail. It said a musgovore had passed this way within the last hour. I heaved the gun out of my backpack and gave a last, wistful look at Rio Lento. Then I turned back to the valley.

The musgovore must have come up to the crest, also had a look at the town, and turned away again. It had headed down into the valley at a leisurely, meandering angle of descent. I followed slowly after it, constantly checking the gun's power levels, just in case. I turned the tracker's sensitivity up by ten per cent to make sure. I followed it down to the glacier and discovered it had headed straight over the ice. But I had a sensor to detect the hidden crevices, and for good measure I put the tracker up another ten per cent.

When I reached the other side I found that the musgovore had been here within the last twenty minutes. The tracker gave a seventy-five per cent probability that it was within two hundred metres.

I clipped the tracker to the gun and waved it slowly in front of me, clutched in both hands, until it had the most likely trail. I set off after my prey.

On the far side of the glacier a layer of boulders and rubble from a massive landslide, centuries old, stretched almost to the top of the valley slope. Most of the boulders were bigger than me and I was just about fully grown. It would be quite a labyrinth to pick through.

I glanced back the way I had come and saw just a blank grey wall. Mist had come flowing down the slope behind me and I hadn't even realised. Making my way home would take me into a void where I could only see for a few feet; less, once the sun was down. But I had the tracker to guide me, and I *wasn't* going back now.

The trail led into a natural rocky gully through the rubble and I moved in slowly. It wasn't fear that made me move with caution – musgovores aren't known for rapid movements much, or attacking humans at all – but somehow it just seemed the right thing to do. I was forming a psychic link with my distant ancestors, stalking game across the plains of old Earth armed with no more than a spear or a bow and arrow. My heart pounded, my blood and adrenaline pumped, and I was a little surprised to feel intensely horny, though that could have just been my age.

The unaccustomed weight of the gun made my arms ache and the mist threw a slick and damp surface over everything. My Nuevan weather instinct told me it was only a fraction of a degree from turning to ice. Then I peered round a corner, and saw it.

It was a furry quilt humped over a boulder, looking like the shimmering silver hide of a small animal had been spread out flat to dry. It pulsated slowly as it guzzled on its oxides. I could walk right up to it and it wouldn't even notice. Ilo had told me to set the stunner to max, then aim at the midpoint of its four eyes. The charge would fry its tiny little brain and that would be it.

A sliver of rock turned under my foot and I stumbled. My foot slid into a gap between two rocks and held firm while the rest of me carried on down. For just a moment a single point of my tibia was the fulcrum for my entire body weight, and then the bone cracked with a loud snap. I shrieked as I slammed into the ground.

It's one of those moments when the universe changes. Your first thought is relief that you're still alive. A split second later the pain hits, and oh my God you just want to *die*. I was lying on my front with my foot still caught and held straight up. I screamed, and whenever I moved the pain struck, and I screamed again, while my mouth filled with foul tasting grit.

Maybe the musgovore had had its fill or maybe it didn't like high pitched noises. It sidled around on its rock to scowl at me, then slowly slid down to the ground and flowed away.

"You bastard!" I howled at it. "It's your fault, you... you..." I scrabbled for the gun. It lay a couple of feet from me, and a world of agony lay between me and it. "I'll get you and *oh my fuck this HURTS!*"

That final scream left me breathless. I had to gulp in cold air through clenched teeth until I felt strong enough to act.

I had the satcomm. It was in my backpack. All I had to do was...

I moaned. To take my pack off, I had to free my shoulders from the straps, and unbuckle it at the waist. I could already see how that might go, but I had to try. I cautiously pushed myself up...

...and screamed, and slammed back into the dirt again. I tried once more, but it was no use. It just hurt too much. I could *feel* the weight of the sodding thing, pressing between my shoulders, but I couldn't get at it.

I began to sob, one self-pitying tear after another. I was cold *and* damp *and* hungry *and* in pain and I had absolutely no chance of getting back home by myself. I had a subzero Nuevan night ahead of me. I forced myself to reckon on my chances.

I could still be rescued but other things had to happen first. First I would have to be missed. I couldn't rely on either of my parents to do that in a hurry. Then Ilo would have to hear of it. He would immediately know my rough whereabouts. Then they would have to send an aircar for me.

Precious resources would be consumed, unplanned for. Oh dear God, I was in trouble. Maybe I should just lie here and die.

"Quite a scream you got there. Think I saw a stunned bat falling out of the sky."

I scowled at the retreating musgovore. No way was I going to let my hallucinations make fun of me.

"Oh, fuck off."

"Well, if you insist..."

But I'd realised, of course, even before I heard the booted feet scuff on the gravel as the man turned away.

"No! Please! I'm sorry!" I screeched.

"Hey, only kidding."

The man crouched down by my foot. By twisting my head round I could just squint at him. He was a segunda in his forties, lean and grizzled and insultingly wearing a coat of musgovore fur.

"I can get you out of this, kid, but it's going to hurt," he said.

He could, and it did.

I RECOVERED CONSCIOUSNESS slung over his shoulders. White hot pain stabbed into my leg with every step he took. I remember thinking bitterly that he could at least have splinted the break first. Turned out he had; it didn't seem to make much difference.

He carried me further up the valley until I could see the lights of a foamcast hab, close against the headwall of a cirque where it would be sheltered and out of the wind. The light created a small luminous apron and strange, shapeless masses of machinery lurked in the gloom just beyond the glow. The hab was shabby and visibly patched up.

"Open up!" the man shouted. "Got my hands full."

The door was opened by a woman and the bright light made me sneeze as he carried me in. More pain. But then he lay me down on a couch in the warm and clamped a blocker to the back of my neck, and the pain vanished. I felt exhausted and wrecked, but there was just a vacuum where my broken leg had been and I never wanted it back.

When I opened my eyes after the long, blissful sigh, I could take the room in. The woman, a teenage girl and a younger boy were all looking at me with undisguised curiosity. I tried not to be equally curious in return. The girl's birth, like mine, must have just pre-dated my father's one-child rule, but the boy's certainly hadn't.

"Look what I found, everyone." Their father passed the girl a first aid kit from behind the door and held his hand out to me. "Krauss," he said. It took me a moment to realise he was introducing himself.

"Joaquin," I said. Mr Krauss grinned as he knelt down beside me.

"Had to be a hijo. Guessed it the moment you showed." He pulled my boots off with two sharp tugs, and I felt the bones grate painlessly as he did it.

"I showed?" I asked.

"We got sensors," said the little boy harshly. If he had been well fed then he would have been podgy – round face on round body. His glare was cold and hostile. "We can tell when anything gets on our land. Dad could have shot you."

"Don't be stupid." The girl gave the boy a friendly, gentle cuff on the top of the head, and then she reached for my belt buckle and opened my slacks. "Lift your butt up."

I just stared up at her. I had often fantasised about all the things the first girl to loosen my belt might say, but that wasn't one of them. "Today?" she added.

Still I couldn't move, so she sighed and yanked my slacks down for me. Her father pulled them off, and all I could think of was how skinny and hairy and generally unattractive my bare legs must seem. The area around the broken bone was mottled and purple and I looked away. I was dimly aware that a strange combination of every fantasy and nightmare I had ever had was happening all at once.

Mr Krauss took a healing mould from the kit and wrapped it around my leg. I felt it writhing, tightening up and binding the broken ends of my bones together.

"Davy's right," he said conversationally, while he watched the mould squirm. I could only watch with half an eye. It's one thing to know it's making you better but it's quite another to know that tendrils of fungus have penetrated your skin and are doing things inside you that you can't even feel. "Technically you were poaching. I'd have been within my rights."

I flushed. "Oh. I'm, um, sorry. Sir."

"Oh, he never would." The woman bustled forward. "We were about to eat. Let us get you something."

I found myself decently covered up with a blanket and propped up with cushions. Then the girl was pressing a bowl of hot soup into my hands, straight off the stove. She managed a half smile at me before looking away quickly and joining her family at the table.

"Thanks," I said, while strange feelings coursed inside. I would like to see that smile again. But then I looked down at the soup. It was dark brown and translucent, with an oily steam that went straight to the hunger centres of my brain. I had picked up my spoon before I realised.

"Don't let's stand on ceremony," said the woman.

It took me about five spoonfuls to finish the bowl off – there wasn't much in there. I thought I should compliment the hostess, in all sincerity.

"That was delicious," I said. "Is there more?"

The boy opened his mouth as if to speak, and suddenly jolted in his seat as if someone had kicked him under the table.

"Course there is," said Mr Krauss. "Give our guest a second helping, Isabel."

The girl slowly pushed her chair back and took my bowl over to the counter. She handed it back with a lot less grace than before, and certainly no smile. I couldn't help but notice that no one else had seconds. I went back to eating, more slowly, paying more attention to what was going on around me.

I saw that the light flickered, ever so slightly. I knew it meant a less than reliable power supply. The hab would be powered by a minitok, but even they ran down eventually. The furniture was serviceable, but worn and scuffed. Much the same could be said of their clothes.

"So, what do you farm, Mr Krauss?" I said to make conversation.

"You're eating it," Krauss said. I looked more closely at the bowl. Beneath the strong roast tang of the spices, I finally recognised the flavour.

"I thought all the myco production had moved to the equator," I said without thinking.

"Don't believe everything you hear," said Mrs Krauss, though she looked at her husband as she said it. There was an exasperated fondness in her words and her glance.

"Government says it will relocate us," Krauss admitted. "But we came here all the way from the European Dustbowl to farm our very own bit of Nueva, not some parcelled off corner of a collective."

"You'll have..." I said, and bit my tongue to stop himself. I was used to stubborn pride – I saw enough of it at home. But it was one thing to argue it out with the Planetary Director; it was quite another to do it to these kind segundas who had taken me in and mended my leg and served me some of their hard-earned food.

Because, I knew about myco farming. All the cold weather strains were now in full production, but they were only available on the official collective farms at the equator. If the Krausses were still farming myco then they were farming the old strains, and that meant there would be less and less of it each year as the weather grew colder and colder.

And now I knew why the hostility from the boy. They could barely have enough to go round themselves; even one guest would put a dent into their daily ration. My presence meant less for everyone else today. My foolish request for a second helping meant even smaller helpings tomorrow. But none of them was going to say so. None of them was going to admit to being hungry.

Mr Krauss seemed to guess what I had been going to say. "We'll have to move eventually," he agreed. "One day the glacier'll force us off this land. But until then ..."

"I understand, Señor," I said quietly. And the strange thing was, I did. I thought it was foolish pig-headed pride, but I understood.

I had heard rumours of stayers-on like the Krausses. They weren't alone. There were isolated outposts of tios like them throughout the Barreras, and probably more, elsewhere throughout the continent. No doubt my father's plans accommodated them. There would be enough for them all if they moved to the collectives and did as they were told.

But some people didn't want to do as they were told. There would be growing numbers of discontents; dispossessed men and women – and their children too – who had been lured to Nueva as settlers by promises that now could never be kept. Were they part of the plan? Were they in the Discourse?

I sneaked a glance at the boy. His eyes as he stared back at me were coal black with resentment and hostility. Maybe Mr and Mrs Krauss were in the Discourse and their views had been accounted for. But what would happen when little Davy Krauss – when all the little Krausses – hit the Discourse themselves? Which would be long before *Phoenicia* arrived back at Earth.

Mrs Krauss was saying something about calling my parents to say I was safe – they would be worried. And I heard myself agree, but my thoughts were far away.

CHAPTER EIGHT

BIRTHDAY SURPRISE

Quin is 17

THERE WAS A howling wild animal inside me. I slammed my foot against the door of Ilo Bast's hab and it shuddered in time with the throbbing in my ears.

"Ilo, you fucker!" I kicked the door again and pounded on it with my hands. "You shit! Open up!"

There was no answer in the split second of grace I was prepared to give him, so I stepped back and looked about for a stone while snow whipped around me in the dark. I kicked the drifts on the ground apart until I found one. I would chuck it through one of the brightly lit windows. I would climb in. I would...

"Hi, Spawn." The door had opened and Ilo was scratching himself thoughtfully. "What's up?"

I flung the stone at his head from a distance of about three metres. Being me, I missed. I pushed past him into the warm fug of the hab.

"Where is it?" I demanded. I stopped inside and looked around.

"Where's what... hey!"

I strode to a cupboard and flung it open. Cups, plates, bottles. I couldn't see what I was after so I began to pull things out.

"Is it in here?" I yanked a drawer out from the wall and turned it upside down. Cutlery clattered on the floor. I turned away and bumped into Ilo's rock-like chest. He looked a lot less friendly than usual and a small, distant part of my mind was aware of how big he was.

"You been drinking, Spawn?" he said coldly. "I hope so 'cos you're going to need a good excuse."

I pushed him back with both hands. He didn't move. "Where is it?"

"What's 'it'?"

I hit him. The skin split on my knuckles but it felt good. My brain made a note of the pain and tucked it away for future reference. He shook his head and rubbed his jaw.

"The stuff! Where's the stuff!"

"What st–"

I hit him again.

"The stuff!" I began to sob with rage. My voice was shaking, so I covered up by hitting him once more. "The stuff you give her!"

He put a hand on my shoulder and held me away at arm's length.

"You know, that's getting kind of annoying..."

"Show me!" I screamed at him. My arms were still flailing. "Show me where it is!"

"Look, Spawn, if this doesn't stop then I'm going to have to hit you back, right? I'll count to five. One, two..."

He made it to five and I didn't stop, so he sighed and clouted me casually on the side of my head.

My world exploded. I wasn't aware of the next few seconds, except that time passed and pain roared within my skull and I must have fallen against something, because there was a cut on the other side of my face. I lay on the floor and tried to pick myself up. All I could do was twitch feebly while the stars faded from my vision. I moaned pathetically because somehow I knew the dark blurry mass standing over me was Ilo Bast, and I was afraid he was going to pick me up and hurt me again.

In fact, he just dumped me into a chair. He crouched in front of me and held me up, patting my face ungently until I could focus on him.

"If you're not happy with the arrangement, take it up with your Papá," he said coldly. He stood up and I slumped, so he crouched down again to prop me up. He also tucked a small package into my pocket which on later examination turned out to contain a couple of pornographic conceptuals. "Oh, and happy birthday," he added.

NOT LONG BEFORE that, I had been celebrating seventeen years of life.

Life was still liveable on Nueva – you just had to take a bit more care with it. Resources were rationed but people could still have fun, celebrate, enjoy themselves. People could still have birthdays.

I had got a job as soon as I turned sixteen, three months after the broken leg incident. My limp had cleared up, I had reached Nuevan adulthood and my father couldn't ground me anymore (though he could, and did, continue to charge me by instalment for the cost of the aircar sent to retrieve me). He had made it clear I was expected to contribute to my upkeep somehow and so the job suited us both just fine. I had been looking at a low rung job at the Town Hall – an administrative position, of course. I had always known that my brain was my best asset and the perceived romance of hard toil in the fields that deluded me as a child had long since evaporated. I had seen my mother's looks fade and her shape change – though by now she had given up even pretending to work herself – and I had no desire to be working under Ilo Bast.

I made my feelings known on the subject, and I could see my father approved. The Director was happy to hint very heavily that there was an opening for his son and heir right at home, at the villa, working directly for him, if I wanted.

So, Town Hall it was.

A year later, I had a structure and purpose to my life. For the first time since my crèche years, I was mixing with segundas as equals. Quite unusually for me, I was making friends. So when my seventeenth birthday came round, I felt I had something to celebrate.

It would be a small, select party, because I loathe crowds and because I couldn't afford bigger. My father made his disapproval obvious, but I waved my carefully hoarded ration tickets under his nose and he had to give in, with bad grace.

"Just make sure it's all legal," he said, yielding to the inevitable the same way another father might advise his teenage son to "just take precautions".

I shared a department at work with three segundas. Nic was short, ginger and the one I got on with best. Robert with the long, lugubrious face was our manager and several years older, but I felt sorry for him so I invited him too. And... oh, let's name names. Paula. If making her blush is the worst I've done to her then she's got off lightly.

They arrived together, sharing a cab to carry them up the track from the town. Robert instantly earned my contempt as an artless oaf by looking about him when he came in, nodding his head slowly with a thoughtful grimace, and asking how much it all cost. Nic gave me a bottle of plonk and Paula slipped a small box of sweetened myco into my hands, followed by a kiss on the cheek as she wished me a happy birthday. At that point it could not have been happier.

Then it was outside to the terrace to eat, drink, talk, play silly games, listen to music and generally help Quin feel like someone who belonged to the human race.

We were doing fine until my mother came in.

"Mama!" I protested.

"Just need to..." she murmured vaguely, and slipped into a corner to sit down and gaze out of the window. She showed no sign of moving.

Everyone in Rio Lento had probably heard of the mad señora up at the villa. Maybe they'd heard of her condition – a congenital tendency towards depression mixed with a misfiring gene that stopped certain neural conditions forming, all quite treatable with a good, positive attitude and the right kind of resources that no one was able to give her. But not that many had seen her, certainly not from my generation, and I can't blame my friends for having no idea at all of how to deal with her.

"Thank you very much for having us here, Señora Mateo," Paula said after a while, sounding a little unsure. Robert and Nic immediately added their own gabbled votes of thanks. My mother ignored them all and just sat, a conversational vacuum that sucked all normal talk out of the room. We looked at each other for a moment.

"So, uh, yeah, I told him it had to be ready by tomorrow..." Astonishingly, boring, socially inept Robert managed to kick-start the conversation again with the work-related anecdote he had been telling when she came in, and we all gratefully paid a lot more attention than before.

Then my mother started to sing. We tried to ignore it. You try.

"Mama..." I said, as patiently as I could, though my heart was sinking. Of course, I was well used to her little moments and I thought I'd got the hang of managing them, but even the best plans can slip up, as I have had cause once or twice since to remember.

It was dark outside and the window showed a perfectly reflected twin of the room. She was leaning forward and looking at her reflection in the glass, and her head rocked slowly from side to side as she crooned.

Nic tapped me on the knee.

"I don't think she's well," he whispered. I could have thumped him, until I saw the genuine concern in his eyes. Paula and Robert were looking at me with appeal, so I did what by now I knew I should never do when my mother was like this. I got up and went over to her.

I put a hand awkwardly on her shoulder. "Mama, we'd really..."

She began to cry. Oh God, she began to cry. Silent, shaking sobs. Then abruptly she pulled me into a crushing embrace, her arms wrapped tight round my waist and her head pushed into my side.

"This wasn't what they told me, Quinito." She whispered, but it was a loud whisper and everyone could hear it. "This wasn't what it was meant to be."

Of course, by now I was well aware of the dynastic ambitions of the Mateos and the Alcantaras, but I still really didn't know what to say. But then Paula came to the rescue.

"Señora?" She knelt down beside me and gently pried my mother's arms away from me. "Can we help you? Can we take you somewhere?"

My mother looked at her kind face and began to sob more loudly.

"Quinito doesn't want me at his party," she wailed.

"I'll show you where her room is," I muttered, and together we helped her to her feet while Nic and Robert fluttered about like worried flies.

"Thank you." The sobs stopped suddenly and my mother could stand erect. "I can manage it." Her voice shook. "I'm sorry I embarrassed you, mi amor." She took a couple of steps. "Hang on…"

She groped about in a pocket, and suddenly there was a small bottle of something clear in her hand and she was raising it to her mouth.

"Mama, *no!*" I snatched it away before she could take a swig. "What the hell are you doing?"

Her features were transformed in an instant into icy hatred. "Give me that!" she demanded.

I was studying the bottle, trying to see what it was. No label. The contents were clear but there was a viscosity that told me it wasn't water. If it had been booze, even I would have noticed years ago, from the smell. No, the thing that had enslaved her and rotted her mind was polite, socially acceptable, easily hidden.

"Give it to me, you little bastard!" she screamed. I was too shocked to register when she suddenly snatched it back and drained half the contents in one swallow. Then she staggered out of the room.

"Oh God, Quin, I'm sorry," Paula said eventually.

I couldn't speak. I'd had seventeen years of a mother going slowly to pieces. I couldn't remember not knowing she had problems, but I had taken all that knowledge, every scrap of evidence, and buried it behind a wall seventeen years high.

In all that time I had never seen her actually taking a drink stronger than the occasional social glass of wine. Yet when she produced that bottle, somehow I had known it was bad. And she had screamed at me, called me a bastard, and the wall had come crashing down. The full mass of evidence stared me in the face and I had no idea what to do about it.

"What was it?" I murmured vaguely. It really wasn't a relevant question but it was all I could fix my mind on. "What was that stuff?"

"I, um..."

"Well..."

Both Paula and Nic didn't know what to say either.

"You could ask Ilo Bast," Robert said. All eyes turned to him and he flushed. "Uh, sorry. I thought everyone knew."

MY HEAD WAS still ringing from Ilo's blow and my face was swelling up when I stormed into my father's study. Unusually, he was on his own.

"I want Ilo fired!" I said.

My father didn't look up from what he was working on. "Yes, he told me you were on your way up."

Of course he had. It explained the absence of everyone else. My father had thoughtfully dispersed the usual hovering crowd of civil servants to save the embarrassment of what was coming.

"Did he tell you why?" I said, a little more calm and a lot more suspicious. The significance of Ilo's words was trying to sink in, but it was bouncing off the usual shell of denial.

He looked up, pushed himself back from the table.

"You were born just after the Event," he said abruptly. I was baffled.

"And?" I said. I knew this much. The stress of the wormhole collapse, and everything that came with it, had brought on my birth. Big deal.

"It... affected her. I should have been there for her. I couldn't be. I had to deal with the disaster and then with *Phoenicia*, and then with..." He waved a hand to signify, *everything*. "All the Alcantaras were stuck in Alti. Feli was dead. Alejandro was busy with the ship."

It was one of the very rare occasions he even mentioned the name of my other brother. At the time I just didn't notice.

"All she had to get her through the emergency was you," he said, and shrugged. "And Ilo's happyjuice."

I couldn't believe my ears.

"But... but once the emergency was over...?" I said pathetically.

He gave me his patented look of contempt for when someone had just said something brainless.

"Emergency's still on, Quin."

It made me angry enough to focus.

"Yeah, but there was time to help her! Treat her! *Something*, before she got... hooked!"

"You think we didn't try? Of course we did. But she started going back to Ilo the moment you were on solids."

"So..." It still wasn't quite making sense and I snatched at anything that would help me understand. "So why didn't you fire him then?"

"Because I told him to carry on."

"You *what?*" I screamed.

"It's best." He was looking back at his work, a sure sign he considered the interview over. "There'll be no more children – it would be hypocritical if the Director's own wife couldn't stick to the one-child rule. She's never going to be the mother and the fine lady she deserves to be. This is all she has."

All she has?

"But..." I was through the anger, and back out to pathetic. I couldn't quite say the words, though they howled within my heart. *But she has me!*

"Does... Grandfather know?" I said instead.

He threw his tablet down in frustration.

"Of course he does! He's been trying to lure her away to live in Alti for years."

"Why does she stay?" I whispered, horrified I might actually get an answer. I had to ask the question; I just wasn't sure I could cope with whatever the response might be.

"Because you're here, because I'm here, because she loves us both."

I just stood and looked at him for a long time, while he bent his head back to his work. I knew I wanted to say something. Anything. But all the thoughts, all the comebacks, all the screaming imprecations I had in mind were jumbled into a solid lump that wouldn't come out of my mouth.

Eventually he looked up again.

"Are you still here?"

"You..." I managed that much that was coherent. I kept talking to see where it led me. "You *disgust* me!"

"You're no trophy. Now, unless you have a brilliant solution to the problem that algae production at Stoneberg seafarm is way below quota, could you please be somewhere else?"

You MIGHT REMEMBER I had guests still on the premises. I didn't, and I have no memory of them leaving. I do remember sitting by my mother's bed, watching her sleep.

It was the way he had said *because you're here...* It wasn't even a condemnation, just a bald fact. Was my sheer presence responsible for my mother's state?

Well, so was his, apparently. And he wasn't going to move away. Which left...

Look, I was seventeen, I was confused and upset, I can be forgiven some shaky logic. And remember, we Mateos know how to make sacrifices.

If I was somewhere else, I reasoned, then perhaps she would follow. And I couldn't stand the thought of staying a moment longer in the same house as a man who could so cold-bloodedly let this happen. I had to go, and there was only one place apart from Rio Lento that had people to take me in.

The ringrail for the Altiplano left the following day, and I was on it.

CHAPTER NINE

THE DISPOSSESSED

Quin is 21

IT WOULD BE nice to think I spent my years in Alti working closely with my grandfather, plotting and scheming at the heart of Nuevan politics.

Well, we both plotted and schemed, but on different things. Grandfather and his cronies had set their sights high, focusing on nothing less than the downfall of the Planetary Director. My own more modest concern was how to pry my mother away from Rio Lento. Astonishingly (to me), she continued to choose my father's company over mine. After I left, she singularly hadn't been on the next ringrail out after me. Whether it was because she was old-fashioned enough to value her marriage vows or she just stayed because it kept her close to her supplier – well, the fact was, she stayed.

We kept in touch after a fashion. I wasn't brave enough to call home very often – I never knew what I might get at the other end. Writing was easier. We could both take our time over what we said and how we said it, and her replies were generally lucid. And sometimes she would call me, audio and even visual, when she was having one of her good times, and then you couldn't tell there was anything wrong with her at all.

I moved into a shared apartment with a group of strangers. It was a shock to the system but sole occupancy for single tios was a rare thing on Nueva in those days.

Father Adolfo kindly sent me details of a good church near where I lived. I let the message gradually get buried by other things until I honestly couldn't remember what it said. Weekends, I lay in. Evenings I would venture out with my roommates. Getting on with large numbers of people, I found, is really quite easy. If they're friendly, you're friendly back at them. If they're dolts, you are non-committally doltish in return, and forget them the moment they move away.

Family ties got me a much better job than I was entitled to. My grandfather was then Minister of Supply and I got a place in a subgroup of his department, the Bureau of Displacement. Back at Rio Lento I had worked in the Town Hall because I wanted to work indoors in the warm and I wasn't willing to accept any favours from my father. Nepotism from my grandfather, on the other hand, caused me no problems at all. So I toiled away and earned a decent salary, and gradually, bit by bit, I shed Rio Lento.

Cosmopolitan Alti probably couldn't hold a candle to the ancient metropolises of old Earth, but by Nuevan standards it had fun and bright lights and a much more relaxed attitude to the black market than we poor bumpkins ever did. It was the place for young, single professionals to do what they always have done – get drunk, get high, get laid, regularly and often, with abandon and impunity. I suspect all those things even happened to other people from time to time even in Rio Lento, but not to the Director's son, no, no, no. But now I was just Quin Mateo with the world at my fingertips.

From time to time, tiresome reality would intrude, and if I wanted to maintain my lifestyle I had to do what it wanted. That meant regular visits to APRA – the Accommodation Pending Resettlement Area, the archipelago of displacement camps on the plain about ten kilometres west of Alti.

APRA was where you went to have your dreams scraped off.

Once upon a time, you or your parents or your grandparents had settled an area of the planet full of hope and visions for the future. Then you were forced off again by the return of winter. If – like most segundas – you lacked the contacts in the right places to get you swiftly resettled somewhere nice then a grateful government promised to resettle you on an equatorial collective farm. But first you went to an APRA camp while they waited for a place to come up for you and your family. You might be there days, or weeks, or months; and by the time you moved on, you had all that silly independent thinking knocked out of you and a much more realistic view of the future.

It wasn't a cheerful place, unless you were cheered by the notable absence of hijos. It was a flat plain broken by foamcast huts that the biting wind barely registered as it passed on through. It was big sky country at the heart of the continent, with El Grande hanging above it poised to fall down and crush us all. Even though you only saw the tiny ball of our little sun as it squeezed itself through the gap between gas giant and horizon, and even when the Event-damaged Sol 1 was the brightest thing in the sky, there was still something about the light here that was just *too* bright, bleaching the colour out of everything.

The dark lump of the Altiplano plateau loomed on the horizon and the silver needle of the elevator cable rose straight up into the sky above it. From time to time I would look at it thoughtfully and think about what lay beyond our small little world. But nothing could be done about that for another twenty years, and I generally tried not to daydream.

At first I just had responsibility for the distribution of resources. My nominal boss was an idiot who thought the job could be done while sitting comfortably in his warm office in Alti, delegating the brainwork and assuming people would just follow orders. If he hadn't been a hijo he would have been sacked years ago, but eventually even my grandfather had to admit the job could be done better. He gave it to me. My new responsibility was overall charge of APRA, and also the Resettlement Area Patrol, who policed the camps and the collective farms.

The Resets, note: not the Constabulary.

"They won't be there for more than a few months," my father reckoned, speaking of the evacs. You needed to be a properly settled community to get Constabulary. So instead of professionals the displaced population got the lowest common denominator of law enforcement. The advertisements for the Resets had said 'smart uniform, regular work, pension' and they attracted precisely the kind of tios whose priorities fell in that order.

In just a few short years the population of the camps had burgeoned. Which meant more supplies, and hence more opportunities for goods disappearing into the pockets of those smart Reset uniforms.

On one particular day I was trudging through APRA 4 in a foul temper. The morality of the black market is a fluid commodity. I was willing to pay a little extra in the city for those small items that made life more bearable, but taking from people who had nothing else but memories was another matter. I had supervised the offloading of several crates of provisions from a rigi and I knew, I just *knew* that some of them would be missing by the time they were opened in the warehouse. I couldn't be everywhere at once. It was the insistence my lords and masters had on stockpiling that was the problem. If the stuff could be brought in and handed straight out again, the possibilities for random disappearance would be far fewer. But no, they had to have reserves; stuff had to sit around doing nothing, there in case of emergencies. And that was when the sticky fingers came out.

"Excuse me, Señor..." A gentle, apologetic tug on my sleeve, but it was enough to make me swing angrily round at the speaker. "We're new here and we wondered..."

The man trailed off; I assumed it was because he recognised me. I certainly recognised him. My memory for names and faces was always good. And because I assumed that, I waited for him to finish speaking. Eventually I realised he hadn't recognised me at all and it was my glare that had put him off.

"I'm, um, sorry, Señor," he said, "you're obviously busy…"

And he turned to shuffle away. I looked beyond him and yes, there were the mother and the son. She hadn't changed much; he had, but was recognisably the same boy. The roundness had turned to square – broad shoulders, firm chin, looked well able to take care of himself.

How long was it since Mr Krauss had slung me over his shoulder and carried me back to his hab? A quick mental count – I had been fifteen – six years. Long enough for a young boy to get much bigger.

I could already see the contempt squaring up in the boy's gaze, aimed not at me but at his father, brushed off like dirt by a young hijo overlord. It hurt to see a man who had been so self-sufficient and secure out in the wilderness, now brought so low here at APRA – low in the eyes of the world and low in the eyes of his ungrateful snot of a son.

"I'm sorry, I was dreaming," I said loudly. Mr Krauss turned back to me with wary hope. "How can I help you, Señor?"

"Oh…" He paused for just a moment, then almost leapt forward with a tablet outstretched to show me, in case I changed my mind. "We just came in. It says here that Martha and I should report to block 17 and Davy has to go to Block 87, and that's the other side of the camp, and we did ask for a place where we could all be together…"

"How old's your son?" I asked, taking the tablet, but I could guess the answer already and the tablet was backing me up. Tobias Krauss, 47; Martha Krauss, 48; David Krauss, 16. Evac code nine – meaning, they were voluntary exiles, not yet forced off untenable land. Rio Lento was still habitable but their little farmstead in the next valley presumably had got too much for them.

"He's sixteen…"

"Then he'll get a bed in a single person's dormitory," I said, as apologetic as I could. "That's automatic."

"Oh, but he's never lived alone…" Martha Krauss squeezed her son's arm and looked at him sorrowfully.

I shot a glance at her little boy, fifteen centimetres taller than her and looking quite capable of being on his own. Or was he? Perhaps he was like his father, totally capable in the wild but thrown to the wolves in a place like this. He met my gaze with a neutral stare. It was impossible to guess what he wanted for himself.

I didn't owe David Krauss a thing, but the Krauss family per se still had a special place in my heart. I looked down at the tablet and used my supervisor's privileges to change some things.

"I can get him moved to Block 19," I said. "It's still a singles dorm but it's just round the corner from where you'll be..."

It seemed to be the best of all worlds because it made them all smile, and I ended up escorting them as far as the corner of the street where they would all be living.

"This will mean so much to the missus," Mr Krauss told me in a confidential whisper. "First our girl gets married, then it looked like we have to lose the boy too... it was really worrying her."

The boy was patiently putting up with his mother's clutches for a few minutes longer and was now trying very hard not to grin. Life minus family seemed to hold no terrors for him.

"This is very good of you, Señor," Mr Krauss said when we reached the corner, and even though he knew I had just read his name off the tablet, he held his hand out. "Tobias Krauss."

I couldn't really put it off. "Quin Mateo," I said, and I took my leave before the recognition could settle in. They went on to their new lives, I went back to my old one and my existing problems.

Five minutes later, I was wondering how I could be so blind. Ten minutes later I was outside a door in Block 19. A stranger opened it. Inside, David Krauss was slowly unpacking his meagre goods onto a bed. He shared the room with three other single men. He looked suspiciously up at me when I came in.

"Want to earn fifty nuevos, tio?" I asked.

He looked mighty sceptical when I got him alone and told him what I wanted.

"Why me?" he said, reasonably enough. He didn't know me from Adam.

"You're new in the camp. They won't think you know their game. They'll ignore you."

"You could have chosen any newcomer," he pointed out.

"Yes, I could," I agreed. "I chose you. If you want some other newcomer to get the fifty then..."

"Hey, I didn't say no." He continued to study me, as if I had hidden a cunning twist on my face for him to discover if he looked hard enough. "Seems to me you're just using segundas to do your dirty work."

"That's exactly what I'm doing," I agreed, already liking him less and less. "I've never done a hard day's work in my life. In fact, just walking up the stairs made my feet blister because I usually get a segunda to carry me."

He held out his hand. "Half now," he said. I checked my wallet.

"Too bad, I've only got tens."

"Better pay me sixty, then, and give me thirty now."

"Done," I said, and his face lit up with triumph. I handed him the notes. "Three tens – sixty per cent of fifty nuevos."

THE CALL CAME later that evening when I was back in my room in Alti and halfway through dinner. In my position I could wangle a video channel too, and David's face on the display was grim.

"No luck?" I said.

"Oh, I got him." He glared at me. "He's one of your lot."

"And?"

He was silent for a moment, but then seemed to decide it was still worth a try.

"It's the short Reset with the badge number D188," he said, without a lot of hope. "He's in charge, anyway. They opened a couple of the boxes – didn't see where the stuff went to."

"D188," I said. I cross checked and got the tio's name. Sure enough, the name looked hijo. Well, even we had the ones who fell through the cracks. Dusky trash. Someone had had to clean the toilets on *Phoenicia*.

So, there was one man whose day tomorrow would be spoiled by news of his imminent promotion to a collective somewhere.

"Thanks. Good work. I'll come by tomorrow with the last twenty." I reached out to clear the display.

"No problem," he said with a sly smirk. "I made a hundred out of it. Beats farming."

Oh God, he was going to play games, was he?

"Fifty," I corrected him. "That's what we agreed."

"Yeah, and when I told him you'd paid me, he gave me another fifty to look the other way." His smirk got bigger and to my irritation it was infectious. I could feel it spreading to my own face. My earlier dislike may have been overzealous.

"And then you told me anyway?" I said.

He shrugged. "Sure. I figured it's more important to keep in with you, in the long run. Señor Mateo."

And from the way he said my name, I had a feeling he had worked out exactly who I was.

"Got any more jobs going?" he added, as if he could read my mind, where the grand plan was already forming.

"Maybe. Good night, Davy."

His smug look vanished and he opened his mouth to say "It's David." I took pleasure in cutting him off.

DAVID MANAGED TO snitch a couple more Resets for me, at fifty nuevos a head. The next time he called me after that, one eye was swollen so tight he couldn't see through it and he was mumbling because of the massive bruise on his jaw.

"Jesus! What happened?" I said.

He smiled a very carefully triumphant smile. "They figured out what I was doing."

"They could have killed you!" I said, aghast.

The grin got wider and only then dissolved into a wince of pain. "Nah. You should see what we did to them."

David, it turned out, had recruited some of his dorm mates, then set himself up as bait in a carefully planned trap. The Resets pounced on him, the others pounced on them. From the proud way he described this self-sacrificial sting, I could tell he was loving every moment of it.

"You're mad," I told him.

"Yeah. Look, do you want the badge numbers or not?"

The exact same badge numbers appeared as signatories on the charge sheet that crossed my desk the next day. The Resets had arrested David's Block 19 Irregulars and charged them with assault. It just needed my rubber-stamp approval and the whole lot of them would be put away for six months.

I turned up at the Reset compound later the same day. Two lines of cells stretched away behind the front desk. My name was enough to get the undivided attention and an ingratiating smile from the junior ranker on the front desk. The smile vanished when I said I wanted the prisoners out of their cells, now. He began to dither about needing authority so I coldly asked him his name. He quickly started jabbing buttons on his desk to make cell doors open behind him, but I couldn't help noticing that he also punched a large, red button which I suspected was an urgent call for backup.

The Reset sought refuge in officiousness. "Come on, you lot! Out here! Don't keep the Señor waiting!"

David's eyes went wide when he saw me, but then he murmured something to his neighbour with a wide grin and marched confidently out. One by one the others sidled suspiciously after David and they all lined up in the front room.

I walked up and down the line, taking them in and not meeting David's eye. They all looked as bruised and battered as him.

"Well," I said coldly. "A fine sight you all are. I hope you've learnt your lesson." I watched the Reset swelling out of the corner of my eye. Normality had returned to his world. The hijo master was a little odd but fundamentally sound. I turned abruptly to him. "Okay, release them."

It was fun to see the smirk vanish.

"Señor?"

"I think you heard," I said. "None of the charges against them have any substance. Release them."

His mouth moved as if to generate the courage needed to face up to me. He was spared by the arrival of his superior.

"What the hell are you doing?" This was an older and uglier man, not so easily daunted, even by the Mateo name. "What is this?" he said when I had presented my demands again. "Why are you taking the side of these scum?"

I gave him the version of events that I had heard from the scum's mouth. He drew himself up haughtily.

"Look, Mateo, perhaps you don't quite get the picture. My men are in a highly charged and demanding situation and the antisocial elements that you are defending are only making it worse." He jabbed an angry finger at the prisoners. "They've taken to spying on my people and..."

"*Spying?*" I said, drawing the word out. "Then should I assume that there's something to spy on?"

To his credit, he didn't try to bribe me. He had some intelligence.

"Look," he said, "I don't know what game you're playing, but here's the deal. You stop interfering, you send these people to the cells where they belong, and you back off. Or, I withdraw my people altogether. I'm head of the union here. I can order a complete walkout. You see if APRA can run without them."

If anyone ever threatens you with their resignation, my father had once told me, *accept it on the spot.* The old bastard wasn't wrong about everything.

"Done," I said.

I HAD ALREADY drawn the plans up; it just took a day to get them into operation. APRA would be run by citizens' committees and policed by a volunteer guard force of evacs. I already had the core of these in David's group of friends. A self-balancing, self-checking system.

David wanted uniforms for the volunteers; I resisted. They got a badge and a stunner, and that was it. I didn't want a whole new army, a new set of Resets. I wanted a force that was visibly of, by and for the people.

Still, I couldn't resist making the trip to APRA to hand out the first batch of badges myself. As I handed David's over, his proud smile covered his face and he winked when he caught my eye. I couldn't help smiling back.

"Speech!" some idiot called when I had finished. We were in the Block 19 refectory and quite a crowd had managed to squeeze in. They all took up the refrain. "Speech! Speech!"

I hadn't planned one; I had to say the first thing that came to mind. "I think we've pressed the reset button," I said feebly, and the crowd roared.

"Your own little empire, eh, Quin?" my grandfather murmured thoughtfully when he finally got round to reading my reports. I had been quickly summoned to appear before him.

"I'm just making things work," I said piously. "And I'm only replacing the Resets who were already under me, so technically it's the same empire with a different management."

And it was working. It wasn't perfect, of course – there were still disappearances of goods, still the occasional discrepancies in manifests. Technically (a fact I kept out of the reports), APRA had become more lawless. The Volunteers were meant to report malfeasance to me, but in fact, they tended to dispense their own arbitrary justice. Sometimes they exceeded their duties; sometimes complaints were made, even charges pressed against them, which I had to quietly lose. But – the main thing – distribution was up and losses due to petty theft were way down.

He ran his eyes over the report again.

"They're very... *young*," he commented.

"Starting age for the Volunteers is sixteen and up," I said. Lawless APRA might be, but even there they had to pay lip service to what Nuevan law said about adulthood. And it was true that the initial intake were all David's friends, but I had every hope of it spreading to people who really were adults by age and experience, rather than just technically.

"Hmm. It's the 'and up' that seems to be missing. Quin, these are kids!"

"They're legally adults," I insisted.

"If you say so." He scratched his nose. "Just be careful with them. Children don't have the... the maturity, the experience, to know when to lay off. To be blunt, they can be self-righteous little brutes."

"They may be inexperienced," I agreed, "but they can recognise a thieving bastard stealing out of their mouths, whatever age."

"Hmm." He looked at me long and hard, but then tossed the report aside. "As you say. Still, it's clever how you make everyone be grateful for the privilege of doing your job for you. It must be in the blood."

CHAPTER TEN

VOLUNTEERS WELCOME

Quin is 23

MY TWENTY-THIRD birthday present was my promotion to Resettlement Co-ordinator. There were mutterings in dark corners about too much, too young, and I was well aware of claws being sharpened while people awaited my inevitable fall. I resolved to disappoint them. The Empire of Quin was no longer just the APRA camps and their idiosyncratic volunteer constabulary. It stretched from coast to coast across the continent – APRA, plus anywhere colonised by resettled Nuevans displaced from the north or the south, plus the Resets, who clung onto existence in any new community, until that community was big enough to elect its own officials.

Mine, all mine.

Personally, socially, professionally, I was making progress on all fronts. People paid attention when I ventured an opinion. I had friends and allies.

I also had enemies, whom I thought I could ignore, until a visit to Cabrera.

Cabrera is a post-Event manufacturing plant on the west coast of the Nariz Doblado. It's a giant foamcast box perched atop massive granite cliffs where equatorial winds howl in from the sea. No one had settled there pre-Event, as the salty blasts make the land unworkable and sources of fresh water are few and far between. But there's wind and waves a-plenty for its turbines, and the best quality sand for its nanolathes.

In the best tradition of putting all his eggs in one basket, it's where my father had decided to locate most of Nueva's micro-manufacturing capability.

This was just a routine auditing visit. The final task of the day was to take some figures off some machines and make sure they tallied with the official reports. The helpful management presented me with nicely tabulated columns of figures out of a blackbox, so I smiled, and got treated to lunch, and then without telling anyone I decided to go to the source. It meant going down into the deepest basement and finding some meters that recorded their output on purely mechanical displays. Not that I'm saying the management would try and fob me off with fake figures... Actually, that's exactly what I'm saying. It made sense to check, anyway.

It was a dim corridor with lights every few metres, and someone was coming down it – a powerful-looking tio, for some reason dressed for outdoors. He seemed to be heading straight at me, so I just moved to one side. And then he was joined by another, out of a side passage. Together they effectively blocked the way.

I kept the annoyance off my face, privately thinking that at least someone could show a little social grace. I stood to one side, pressed against the side of the passage, and that was when I saw two more of them approaching from behind, solid and well built.

There was a purpose to their stride that I didn't like, but you can't just assume every hard-looking tio you meet is out to hurt you. I reckoned the best thing to do was to start walking again and not make eye contact, which I did, and I was doing fine until a couple of them reached inside their coats and pulled out stunners.

I put my head down and tried to charge between the two in front of me, but then a stunner buzzed and my leg went completely dead and I nose-dived into the concrete floor. I felt the skin scrape off my face. I managed some incoherent roar as they picked me up and turned me over, sheer anger fighting its way through my fear, and then they went to work.

The first kick was right in the balls, which did me a favour because it made me scream and curl up tight while more kicks and blows rained down on top of me. I still had no idea who these people were or what I had done to them. The rational, politician part of me was trying to negotiate – I think, or maybe the words were just inside my head and all that came out through the pain were my cries and yells. Another part of me seemed to think it was worth covering all bases and was busy negotiating with someone I might be meeting shortly. *Dear Lord, I can't remember my last confession and I'm not sure I believe in you anyway and I have impure thoughts and I do impure things and I haven't been to church in years but I'm not a bad man so please help me...*

"Hey!"

I heard the shout dimly, and for one glorious moment I dared to think I was being rescued. But through one swollen eye I saw a distant figure, further down the corridor, a safe distance from my attackers.

"Beat it," said one of the thugs, and the distant phantom turned and fled. Then they went back to work.

There are scientific ways of torturing a man, so that the pain lasts, and awareness of it lasts too. Part of it becomes not just the pain but the fear of pain.

These ones weren't scientists and their idea of hurting people was a non-stop beating up. And yes, it was bloody painful, but after a while it settled into a routine, and the ever-optimistic back of my mind was saying that if I could just hang in there, I'd get through it.

Until it stopped, and I lay there, still in my curled-up ball, sobbing quietly. Then strong hands seized my arms. I heard the sounds of bolts being thrown back and I was blasted by a freezing cold wind. I tasted salt on the air and the sound of crashing waves merged with the roaring in my ears.

I hadn't realised the corridor was against the outer wall. They dragged me through an external door and dumped me on a metal platform that stuck out from the side of the building. Through the grating I could see the waves foaming pure white on the rocks beneath. I squinted up through tears and blood, and *that* was when I finally felt mortal terror. One of the men had his stunner out again and was slowly, thoughtfully, turning it up to max. Then, just as slowly, he put the muzzle against my head.

I knew a few things about stunners. I knew a full charge that close would fry my brains, like I had once intended to do to a harmless musgovore. The best that could happen was I'd be left a paralysed, drooling idiot.

I had no strength to fight or run or even weep. All I had was words.

"Can't," I whispered, through teeth that were already chattering in the cold.

"I do believe Señor Mateo is telling us something," the tio said, which at least told me this wasn't a random beating up, though what I had done to deserve this, I still had no idea. He pulled the gun a few centimetres back. "Got something to say, you hijo fuck?"

I swallowed. "Can't get away," I whispered again. I didn't sound like someone pleading for his life, but in the absence of thunderbolts from God in response to my prayer, that's what I was doing. "They'll find you."

He grinned. "No, Señor, *we'll* find *you*. We'll be out doing our routine maintenance and we'll see this figure floating in the surf down below." He jerked his head at the edge of the platform. "Oh what a shame, the Co-ordinator took a wrong turn and he slipped and fell and the rocks pounded him to pieces. I don't think anyone's going to check for–"

I stopped listening and just shut my eyes as the muzzle touched my forehead.

And then there was much shouting and movement all around me, and the hands holding me let go so I could curl up again and hear the sound of fists and punches and kicks and *none of them were on me*, which was a good thing, though by now my shivers were more like spasms and I knew I badly needed to be warm soon.

Someone was shaking me, gently, one hand on my shoulder.

"Señor Mateo? You all right?"

I opened my eyes again, slowly, and I found myself looking into the anxious face of David Krauss, peering out from the depths of a fur-lined hood. I wanted to kiss him.

"Sorry we're late..." he was saying as I straightened up. He helped me to my feet and someone hung a coat round my shoulders. I pulled it tight about me, still trembling with shock and cold.

My former attackers were kneeling, hands on their heads, covered by their own stunners which were held on them by a group of young men and one young woman. My rescuers were all David's sort of age and all complete strangers.

"Who..." I said vaguely, gesturing at them. I meant, who were my attackers, who were my rescuers, who was everyone?

"Resets," he said contemptuously. "They got transferred here when you closed them down at APRA, and all they do is bitch about the kickbacks they don't get any more thanks to you. Um..." He swallowed. "We really had no idea they were going to try this, not until Per saw them beating you up..." He nodded at one of the others who I assumed was Per, the one who had been told to beat it. I was very glad he had beaten it so fast.

I gently pried away his supporting hands so I could stand on my own two feet. Then I hobbled over to the creature who had been about to fry my brain. He was being held at gunpoint by the only girl among my rescuers.

"A *Reset?*" I said. "And you were going to *murder* me, because... just because..."

I couldn't finish the sentence because he wasn't worth the amount of coherent thought I had to give it. And something else was dawning on me. I looked at the stunner, and at the girl, and only then saw that she was wearing a Volunteer badge, and so was David, and so were the rest of them. Volunteers – the citizen's constabulary I had set up for APRA. Only, the nearest APRA camp was a thousand kilometres away.

"And what are you doing here?" I demanded. She looked puzzled – hadn't I just been told? – and she shot a look at David.

"Not what he means, hon," David said, interpreting her look correctly. "Fact is... well, the Volunteers were a pretty cool outfit and when I finally got transferred here... well, I set up some new ones." He glanced at the girl and his battle hardened features faded into a grin of astonishing soppiness. "Maddy was the first," he added.

Maddy smiled back, proud and shy, and that answered any questions I might have had about those two. I still had questions about the Volunteers, though.

"I mean, we did right, didn't we?" he finished hopefully.

"You did damn right," I agreed. "So, uh, what do you do here?"

I had completely lost touch with David after he left APRA. Maybe that had been a mistake. I should pay more attention to my protégés.

"Oh, you know, the usual. We keep an eye on the hijos, no offence, make sure none of the bosses are on the take, report them if they are." He pulled a face. "Lawcore says we're not official, so we don't get guns."

He rubbed his fist thoughtfully as he said it. I knew there were other ways the Volunteers could take punitive action against offenders. Funny how none of this got into the charge sheets filed by the Resets; funny how none of it therefore reached my ears.

"So... do we hand them over to the Constabulary?" Maddy asked. Cabrera's official law enforcement was an avuncular, fat, middle aged tio from the nearest town, fifty kilometres away. On average he managed a monthly visit.

And what would be the point of calling him in? These guys could probably draw a dozen alibis out of thin air to put them somewhere else entirely. They would outweigh any testimony my rescuers could bring.

"You escort the Señor to a first aid station," David said firmly. He looked me in the eyes. "Right, Señor?"

I looked at him back and tried not to let my thoughts show. A civilised man does not just abandon people to vigilante justice. But what was the worst that could happen?

Well, the worst was that David would zap them all and throw them off the balcony. But I didn't see that happening yet. Whatever arc David's life was taking, he wasn't yet at the point where he would be doing cold blooded murder.

So, God help me, I just said "right", and let Maddy take me back into the blessed shelter of Cabrera.

SOON AFTER THAT, I got the message that a body had been found. An engineer, an ex-Reset – just the one, but I recognised the face – had been discovered frozen to death on an external maintenance balcony. Autopsy suggested he may have been in some kind of fight – but then, this particular individual was always getting into some kind of fight, and there was alcohol in his system. It was the cold that did him in. A routine investigation was launched, and shelved; foul play was not suspected.

So David hadn't, technically, committed cold blooded murder. He had just let Nueva take its best shot.

I looked at the report for a long time. I could turn David in for this. He and his posse could go to jail. And what of me, the one who could have stopped them but who deliberately just left them to their own devices? Well, I would probably get a ticking off.

I was used to bending the law – turning a blind eye when I had to, not taking action when perhaps I should. And always the result had been that corrupt, dishonest men and women had been taken out of the system much more quickly than if the Lawcore had had to deal with them. How was this different?

Eventually I filed the report in my system and the memories at the back of my mind, both with the express intention of forgetting them.

CHAPTER ELEVEN

ENFORCEMENT

Quin is 23

IT FELT FAINTLY surreal to be flying in an unscheduled rigi towards Rio Lento, sharing the cabin with some muscular backup, with the intent in mind to arrest my father.

It had to work. The Lawcore had firmly defined treason laws but no Nuevan had ever tested them. It was interesting to think that we might be the first and interesting to think what might happen if we got it wrong. The prospect of thirty parole-free years in jail concentrates the mind.

You will hear many variations on the fall of my father. There's no harm in setting the record straight here.

After six years in Alti, I was doing pretty well and considerably better than my grandfather's party in the Executive. They still wanted to topple my father and their problems were the same as they had always been – he was just too popular, and he controlled Nueva's limited supply of bandwidth and headspace. There were slip-ups, there were people who fell between the cracks, but the overall mood of the Discourse was happy with the status quo and that kept the Planetary Director safely in power.

But you can have too much of a good thing, and the feeling was that by now (twenty-three years after the Event!), with things settled, he really ought to relinquish his control.

And the Executive actually summoned the balls to tell him so. It took years – literally – of lobbying by my grandfather and his friends, but they finally sent a message to my father requesting and requiring that he appear before them to answer some questions. It was the first time in two decades the Executive had shown any hint of cojones at all and I think they were carried away with excitement at their daring. It was inconceivable that anything could go wrong.

When I heard this, the sudden sense of hope that hit me like a body blow had nothing to do with my father's fate. It just struck me that if he could be winkled out of Rio Lento then so could my mother. We were still keeping in touch but I hadn't seen her face to face in the flesh since leaving home. Unlike the Executive, though, I kept one foot in reality and could very easily see how their plans might not work out. I sat back to see what would happen.

Soon after that, I had my run-in at Cabrera and discovered the existence of the unofficial Volunteers. When I got back to Alti I started work on what to do with this unexpected new asset. I soon discovered that David wasn't the first to franchise the operation. Volunteer chapters were springing up the length and breadth of the equator. If they could be organised properly then I could have an army of them. So, what to do with it?

Meanwhile my father replied to the Executive. As I had expected, he told them exactly where, when and how to jump, and what to do when they got there. He added that he was quite capable of answering questions remotely; even post-Event Nueva had enough bandwidth going for a simple conversation.

They turned to the Lawcore but it couldn't be drawn on the matter. Not answering a summons from the Executive was the highest form of contempt... unless you were in the unprecedented position of being Planetary Director, and he had indicated he was perfectly willing to communicate from a distance. The rights of each side cancelled out the other. What it basically said was, if you can get him, you can charge him.

The Executive had no one who could get him. I did.

* * *

"UH... IS THIS legal?"

Not the best question to ask, and not the best time to ask it – in a rigi with thirty Volunteers, closing in on our destination. The jeers and groans that went up from the other twenty-nine showed what they thought of it.

I was pleased with the volunteer Volunteers that David had picked. They were mostly but not all male; big, strong and muscular, but a gleam in their eye that suggested intelligence too. There wasn't a lot of chat in the cabin but there was a lot of thinking going on; they knew they were doing something big. Yet, if you met someone's eye, you got a frank stare and a nod in return. They knew they were up to the task.

"You got briefed," David snapped. "The Señor has been through it."

We had both taken strategy conceptuals. I wondered if he had taken one on sergeanting too.

"It's legal," I said quietly, looking not at the speaker but out of the cabin window, where each snowy peak of the Barreras that whipped by to the hum of the rigi's jets was marking one step closer to Rio Lento.

And that's the best thing – it *was* legal, if it worked. Anyone has a right to make a citizen's arrest if they suspect the law is being broken. We suspected the Planetary Director was breaking the law in not responding to the Executive, and all Nuevans are equal before the Lawcore.

It had to be Volunteers who would do it. They were young – even the veteran David Krauss was only eighteen – and they didn't remember the Event. They didn't share the awe and the respect of older generations for my father. They had no memory of his single-handedly saving our world. They had the stories, they had the second-hand accounts, but the young need a good reason to carry on their parents' beliefs and it had never occurred to their parents to give them one.

"Hey, they're nibbling," the pilot reported. She turned up the volume so we could all share the experience.

"*Rio Lento Traffic Control to unscheduled rigi flight. Please identify yourself.*"

It was almost certainly a blackbox speaking. Unscheduled rigi flights were so unusual that surely no human could sound so uncurious.

The pilot looked at me; I nodded.

"This is R474 out of Altiplano City, special flight on behalf of the Citizens' Volunteer Patrol, en route to Rio Lento," she said back. Someone in the cabin sniggered; David impaled the offender with a glare.

"*R474, please state your business in Rio Lento.*"

The pilot stuck firmly to the script, though not without another glance at me.

"Rio Lento, regret unable to comply with request. All queries to be directed to office of Resettlement Co-ordinator Joaquin Mateo in Altiplano City."

There was a pause, and then an undeniably human male voice took over.

"*R474, we need to know your business now.*"

The pilot swallowed.

"Rio Lento, repeat, unable to comply with request. All queries to..."

"*R474, we are taking control of your craft. Do not attempt to override. We will bring you in to Rio Lento main field.*"

The pilot broke into a huge grin; so did I, so did David.

"Rio Lento, we will comply," she said simply. "You have control. Over."

She relaxed her hands on the controls which were now moving of their own accord, taking their guidance from Traffic Control. There was no need for her to fight it because Traffic Control were kindly taking us exactly where we wanted to go.

As coups go, it may seem a little tame. To anyone from an old Earth nation with a more entrenched tradition of revolution and overthrows, the minimal security around my father might have seemed laughable. At the very least, anti-aircraft satellites or orbiting laser platforms should have been tracking our every move, and an unscheduled flight like ours in the proximity of Rio Lento should have put everyone on red alert.

But Nueva simply wasn't used to this kind of thing. We had no military, no counter-insurgency force, no militia more dangerous than the Constabulary. Ours was a ground-breaking venture.

"Stand by," David ordered. The Volunteers were suddenly a bustle of activity, pulling on snowcoats and hats and checking their stunners.

We flew on, no longer talking or laughing. Ten minutes later, something on the ground below caught my eye. It was a pair of giant metal hoops, side by side, raised on stilts out of the snow that coated the floor and sides of the valley. There was another pair, a hundred metres ahead. And another, and so on. We were flying along the ringrail track. Half a kilometre ahead, the hoops vanished into a dark tunnel bored through the mountainside. I knew exactly where we were.

"It's just over that ridge," I said.

The ridge fell away beneath us, the ringrail re-emerged and there was the Rio Lento valley. The glacier oozed down from the Barreras, dirty and jumbled and ragged. The steel grey sheet of sea lay beyond and there was the villa, perched on its summit. It wasn't snowing, though the stuff was thick on the ground, and visibility was good. I could take in the entire range of my childhood with one glance.

"Go, go, go," said David, and he pulled a trip switch. It looked, and was, old fashioned: it mechanically severed the fibres connecting the rigi's blackbox to the comms unit. At the same time the pilot pushed the throttle forward and pulled back on the stick. The engines protested with a rising howl and the rigi surged forward, free of the invisible grip of Traffic Control.

Now it was just a race. People on the ground would spot us, of course, but they had to guess where we were going – fairly obvious, really – and get there quicker than a rigi.

"Take us..." I said, pointing ahead, and the words suddenly dried up. I hadn't been here for six years but I had been confident I could immediately pick our landing spot. Had it changed? Had some sheer perversity made my father randomly decide that the tennis court should be moved somewhere else?

"Landing site acquired," the pilot said, and the rigi banked. She had taken a conceptual on Rio Lento geography and she didn't need my instructions. I breathed out again as my perceptions caught up with reality. Nothing had changed – except that everything was so much smaller than I remembered. The court was exactly where it should have been.

The rigi bumped down thirty seconds later. Cold, dry, rock-smelling air flooded into my nostrils as the hatch cracked open.

"Squad B, go!" David barked. He stood by the hatch, fanning ten of the Volunteers on their way. Squad B's job was to secure the back door of the villa, in case the Director tried to make a run for it. "Squad A, with me. Señor Mateo, sir?" He looked hopefully at me, and glanced significantly at a chair.

Earlier on, he had made it quite clear that in his opinion his tios could handle this. I was the boss, I was the mastermind, but he knew how well I could fight and I should just safely sit in the rigi until they brought my father back.

"Thank you," I said, and jumped down to the ground. I pretended not to see his look of irritation. "Lead on."

"Squad A, with me," he muttered.

We set off at a brisk jog through the ankle-deep snow. Below a powdery surface it was frozen hard and it crunched beneath us. The tennis court was on a flat terrace cut from the hillside. On one side it dropped sharply down towards the town. On the other there was a steep bank a couple of metres high, with steps up to the driveway. The driveway had also been cut out of the hill at this point, and the ground continued to rise sharply above on the other side. The villa lay to our left at the end of the drive. Squad B was to our right; they would cross the driveway and the raised ground behind it, and approach the villa from the other side. We were heading for the main entrance.

There was a strange movement in the corner of my eyes.

"What the...?" David exclaimed. Squad B had all taken it into their heads to have a lie down.

And then the boy next to me gasped and suddenly dropped flat on his face. Two more followed suit. I stopped and stared at them.

"*Run!*" David bellowed. He grabbed my collar and yanked hard. I stumbled forward and our little squad charged towards the embankment. I had a fleeting glimpse of figures on the high ground on the other side of the drive, clasped hands held in front of them and pointing at us, and then there was solid rock between us and them, and the stunner fire couldn't reach us.

I swore and glanced back at the rigi. A trail of five or six slumbering bodies marked our passage. But I had *checked*. And *double-checked*. I wanted to scream. Rio Lento had *no* army or any kind of security force. The Constabulary were based down in the valley and they couldn't have got up here in the time available. So who the hell were these people?

Now I could hear the stunners. Our crunching footsteps had masked the distinctive buzz of the discharges. It was a strange experience. I almost felt that being fired at by projectile weapons would be preferable. At least then you would feel you were being honestly shot at – bullets cracking through the air, ricochets bursting off the rock in front of your nose. This is probably not an opinion shared by anyone who has actually been through that experience but it rankled that we were cowering from nothing more than a distant swarm of insects. Those thirty years in jail suddenly seemed a lot closer.

"*Throw your guns up onto the road*," called a voice. "*Then stand up nice and slow with your hands on your heads.*"

"Oh Christ, I don't believe it," I exclaimed. David looked at me oddly.

"You want us to fight it out, Señor?"

"No. Stay down here. All of you." I filled my lungs, then raised my head as far as it could go without being exposed. "*Ilo!* I want to talk to you!"

There was a silence.

"*Who's that?*" the voice shouted. It's hard to put suspicion into a shout but he managed it.

"Quin."

"*Quin who?*"

I grit my teeth. "Joaquin Mateo."

A longer pause. "*Never. Prove it.*"

David grabbed my hand to stop me getting up. I gently plucked his fingers away. I wasn't going anywhere without guarantees.

"If you like," I called, "you can just call me Spawn."

No reply.

"Can I talk to you? Please? Without being shot?"

"*Okay, Spawn. Stand up where I can see you.*"

David grabbed me again; again I had to pry myself free. Very slowly, very reluctantly, I stood up.

A bulky figure rose slowly into the skyline above me. I clambered up to the drive, he just as cautiously descended, and then we stood face to face. I pushed my hood back to give him a good look at me.

"Well, well," he said. He was the one thing in Rio Lento that didn't look smaller. Still just as big, still just as much of a swagger. All that had changed was the badge he wore. Apparently he was now Captain of Rio Lento. "Homesick already?"

I shook my head.

"We're here to arrest my father," I said.

He nodded slowly. "He thought someone might try that."

I was seeing where the unexpected opposition had come from.

"So he moved the Constabulary up here, didn't he?" I said through my teeth.

"Yup. Didn't think it would be you, though. I'm disappointed."

"Didn't you think I had it in me?"

"I didn't think you'd try an obvious trick like the not-remote controlled rigi. How stupid do you think we are? An unscheduled rigi flight comes to Rio Lento! Well, gee, that's a tough one!"

I carefully kept a poker face.

"So are you going to let us pass?" I asked. His grin got wider.

"Nope. Are you going to surrender?"

It felt strange, talking to him like this. Previously, as the son of his boss, it had always been that he gave, I took. Now I could no longer demand services from him by right. I had to earn his favour.

"Sorry I didn't write to congratulate you on your promotion," I said, with a nod at his badge. I pulled my hood back up. "I suppose it's as much as Rio Lento is going to give you."

"Let me worry about my own future, Spawn," he said. "You've got enough to worry about on your own."

I strolled theatrically to the edge of the driveway. I could see David at my feet, staring up as if I was mad. He held his gun up with an obvious question on his face: *can I shoot him now?* I shook my head and looked out over the town.

"It's spring, Ilo," I said. "The fields should be busy." I looked down at the snowy wasteland. "Where is everyone?"

"We switched from crops two years ago," he said slowly. "It's myco now. Indoor production."

"Ah, myco," I agreed. "Can't remember the last time I had that. Breakfast this morning was ham and eggs, fresh rolls and some good, strong, black market coffee."

Which was an outright lie.

He patted his mouth in a polite yawn. "There a point to all this?"

"Rio Lento's got ten years, max," I said, and that was the honest truth. I just hadn't realised it without seeing the place first. "Half the population have moved to APRA already; most of them are resettled in zones that hardly even see snow." I pointed into the valley. "The glacier used to be at least three metres below the bridge. Now it's almost up to the base. And what about you? You can't last forever, Ilo. You're not young anymore. What are you going to do when your turn at APRA comes up? You won't be Captain there."

"I heard about your own fancy outfit," he said, measuring each word. "It sounds like a good ticket. Maybe I'll look at that."

"Except that it's my force, as you point out..." He opened his mouth; I held up a hand. "And a whole lot of my friends are lying unconscious in the snow here. You won't be a popular man, and believe me, Ilo, in APRA you need friends if you want to maintain your lifestyle. You so badly do *not* want to be just another evac. No possessions. No privileges. And no protection, if the Volunteers decide not to protect you. A lot of scores get settled at APRA. It's a very equal sort of place."

"And you have a solution to this?" he said, sounding very bored.

"Let us pass, Ilo. Then apply for the Resets. There's a whole load of positions for a tio of your experience and talents – I'll give you the pick of them. A section commander gets thirty grand and as many, um, additional benefits as he can manage."

I heard a squawk of protest from the direction of my feet.

"You'll be set up for life on a collective somewhere, if you like," I said, "and, best of all, you'll have the friendship of a rising star in the government of our fair planet."

"And that would be you."

"None other."

We held each other's gaze and I could see the wheels turning. All the time I had been at Rio Lento, he had been investing time and effort in buying my favour – the special treatment, the offered introductions to various adult experiences. Now, I hoped and prayed, he would decide his investment had matured.

Ilo slowly tucked his gun away in its holster, then opened his coat far enough to tug a tablet from an inner pocket. I had no idea what he was doing but I was obviously expected to watch. He turned it on and entered something with grand, showman-like gestures.

"No..." he murmured at what he saw. He was deliberately drawing it out to make me squirm. And: "... no, not that one." Then his eyebrows rose slowly. "Hmm. Maybe. Uh, no. Um..." A pause. "Yes!" He flipped the tablet round so I could see it. "I'll take this one."

It was a job vacancy – section commander of the Resets at the Ochoa chemical processing post. Equatorial, a direct ringrail link to Alti, and its manufacturing capacity would open up black market opportunities that could make a man salivate. Ilo would go through it like a knife.

I sighed. "Okay. You'll get that one."

"Show me."

I produced my own tablet, called up the ad, gave it my personal endorsement. It beeped: *accepted*. I showed it to him.

"Congratulations, Section Commander Bast."

He stepped back and, with a sweeping gesture, indicated that the way into the villa was wide open.

"Last time I saw him, about twenty minutes ago, your father was in the study," he said.

ALREADY, OUR ACTIVITIES had caused no little stir amongst the villa's usual population of government officials. Some of them stood rooted to the spot as we passed through, barely daring to follow us with their eyes. Some sidled away into nooks and crannies. And at least one person called ahead of us, because when we burst into my father's study he didn't look surprised. It was strangely like the time I had confronted him over my mother, though this time a couple of civil servants cowered in one corner. He sat upright in his chair and fixed me with the familiar glare from those dark eyes.

"If you'd said you were coming, we'd have set a place for dinner."

I drew a breath; my grand little speech was spoiled by a suddenly dry throat. Had he always been this *old?* He almost looked frail – face thinner, skin slightly more baggy and just beginning to look outsized in the way it hung on his bones. I hadn't been around for six years in which to absorb gradual change – instead those six years' worth of aging just hit me.

"Take a father's advice, Quin," he continued. "Turn around, walk away."

"You just mind it," David snapped. "And you lot." He waggled his stunner at the people in the corners. "Out."

"Stay," I said quickly. "We need witnesses. This is a legal operation. Planetary Director Mateo, we are here in the name of the Executive to escort you to Altiplano City for ques–"

"In the name of who?" His bark of laughter cut me off. "'In the name of the Executive'? My, we do sound grand. You'll be telling me you're here in the name of the people next."

"I can zap him," David muttered. But the one thing I couldn't do was see my father shot in front of my eyes.

"No," I said. "Just get him out of here."

David clicked his fingers, and two burly young men who had been chosen for the task stepped forward and dragged my father from his chair. He struggled until he was halfway across the room, but then he remembered his dignity.

"Thank you, that will do," he said, and he stopped resisting. They glanced at David and me, then slowly let him go when I nodded. He carefully straightened his clothes with precise, deliberate tugs. "I know the way." He walked out with his escort, leaving the rest of us looking at each other uncertainly.

"Go with him," I said, and David followed quickly after him with the rest of the Volunteers. The civil servants were still in the corner.

"Now you can get out," I said, and they fled.

And that was it. Nueva's first coup, over. I was alone in my father's study.

I felt I should report to the Executive. I sat down at the desk and shifted uncomfortably in the chair. It was moulded to his form.

INTRUDER!

The word blasted into my brain and I clutched at the desk for support. I sensed the fury of a vast presence. It was angered and was a hair's breadth away from swatting me like a fly.

I had forgotten there was a neural pickup in my father's study – one of the few left. My father had been linking with the Discourse and the Lawcore when we barged in and he hadn't had time to terminate the link formally. I was in the same pickup field as he had been, the headspace was still up and they wanted to know who this interloper was.

I identified myself hastily. The Lawcore checked with itself and decided I had a right to be there. Then the Discourse politely asked if it should transfer to me all the privileges of the Planetary Director. And it showed me what it meant.

"Wha–?" I could only manage a small whimper of surprise as the full impact of being Planetary Director swept into my brain. I felt that I was God. I could twitch my finger and move populations. I could channel every atom of food grown on this planet to Rio Lento and let the rest of them starve. I could think a nasty thought about someone, and he could be arrested. I could...

But about a quarter of a second later, the Lawcore just as politely rebuked the Discourse. Such an order, it pointed out, would need the consent of the Executive.

"Oh, thank God," I muttered. I sagged in the chair, slack jawed. My father had had this for twenty-three years? No wonder he had stuck with it so long.

But to me, it had been a glimpse into Hell. And what is the first step on the path to Hell, as Father Adolfo had drummed into me so long ago? Temptation.

I called up my grandfather.

THE CONVERSATION DIDN'T last long. It was hard to tell if he was delighted, furious, or a bit of both or somewhere in between. We agreed I would fly straight back to Alti, with my father, and in the meantime the Executive would be convened.

In theory, when my father left Rio Lento, he would still be Planetary Director; I doubted it would still be so when the rigi touched down at the other end.

I strolled slowly out onto the hall and stopped, surprised. The hall was full of Volunteers and civil servants, no one quite sure what to do. My father was still there, silent and aloof, while his captors milled uncertainly around him.

"David?" I asked.

"Um..." David looked very abashed. "It's snowing out there and we can't, um, find his outdoor clothes. And, um, he's not telling us where."

I slumped against the doorpost while some strange feeling that wasn't quite laughing or crying bubbled inside me. The overthrow of the Planetary Director, stalled by the weather. But David was right – it was bloody cold out there and it wouldn't be right to frogmarch him to the rigi in his indoor clothes.

"Through there." I waved a hand at the walk-in next to the main doors, and someone was immediately dispatched to investigate.

The sound of my mother's voice spun me round.

"Tomás? Tomás! What's happening?"

My mother was at the top of the stairs, and now she was running down, running towards me, pushing aside anyone who tried to stop her. "Tomás, they're saying you've been arrested? What is this? Who are you people! Get out of my house now…"

I drank in the sight as she came towards me, though she was obviously in the middle of a big relapse. Her hair was dishevelled, her face puffy and not made up, but she was my *mother*, and I stepped into her path.

"Mama…" I said soothingly, and she just pushed me aside.

"Get out of my way! Tomás, what is happening?"

My father smiled and came forward. He took her hands in his. "You remember Quin?" he said, with a nod at me.

"Quin? Quinito?" She looked around vaguely. "Quinito is asleep in his cot…"

Can you imagine your own mother standing right in front of you and not recognising you? For a moment I actually thought she might have had another baby and named this one Joaquin too. But the truth was, she just wasn't there.

She began to weep. "Tomás, what is happening? I don't understand…"

"I have to go, my sweet," he said. He pulled her into a hug and rested his chin on the top of her head. His voice was warm and soft but his stare at me over her head was cold and hard. "I have to go to the Altiplano. Official duties, that's all. I'll be back in a couple of days."

"Oh! Oh, but..." She sighed. "Oh, I find it so hard to remember these things. Quinito will miss you, you know how he loves to play with you..."

"*Mama!*" The word was torn out of me. I really should have known better, not least with David and the others looking on, baffled and appalled. "Mama, *I'm* Quin!"

She seemed to notice me for the first time and she blinked with mild surprise. "Feli?" she mumbled. Then: "No, Feli went away too..." She blinked again at my father. "Didn't he? Don't I remember that right?"

"Yes, mi amor, Feli went away. This isn't Feli, this is just some ..." He glared at me again. "Just the kind of bungling incompetent the government is hiring nowadays. You see why I need to go away? I need to make this right." Gently, he disengaged from her and with a very soft motion he pushed her away. Then he turned towards the door. "Come on, let's get this over with..."

"No! No..." She began to shake, her voice sliding up the scale towards panic. "No, you mustn't go, don't leave me..."

My father stopped, exasperated, and didn't quite turn back to her. "I have to go, querida. I'll be back soon ..."

David nodded at the Volunteer standing nearest to her. The boy moved forward, reaching out to escort her away.

She screamed, "*No!*" and grabbed for the stunner in her escort's holster. They grappled together for it – it would have been amusing if not so tragic – until she managed to fire it into his thigh. He crumpled with the mother of all dead legs, and she stood over him, waving the stunner wildly about.

She was surrounded by people trying to make calming, soothing noises. God knows what she actually saw as her madness spiralled chaotically away from any kind of reality. Someone would step forward. She would scream again, "*no!*" and wave the gun at them, and they would quickly step back.

The one man present who might have been able to help moved forward slowly.

"Mi amor," my father said. Step. "Maria. Don't be frightened." Step. "You know me, don't you? It's Tomás..."

There was no recognition and no hope in her face, just desolation.

"You're going to leave me..." she wept.

"No, you know I won't..." He was almost at her.

"*You're going to leave me!*" And she jammed the gun into his stomach and unleashed a full charge straight into his central nervous system. Then she dropped the gun, sobbing. "You mustn't leave, you mustn't leave me..."

My father was lying on the ground like a boneless corpse. Every now and then a tremor would run through him. His mouth and eyes were wide open, not moving.

For a second, no one did anything. Then it was uproar as Volunteers piled onto her. Out of the hubbub came:

"Get her out of here!" That was David. And:

"Get off her!" That was me. And:

"Get a medic! Someone get a medic!" That was David again. Only, we didn't have a medic. We were a bunch of amateur abductors. Why should we have a medic with us?

And while they ran around and panicked, I ran outside.

"*Ilo!*"

Ilo and his Constabulary came running. They at least had medical training, but by the time they got in it was too late. My father wasn't a young man and the stunner had been on full charge. His brain had already shut down and he died like a stranded fish, lying on the tiles in the hall of his family home.

Someone, probably David, escorted me back to the rigi. But I remember very little of the flight back.

EVER BEEN BRAIN scooped? You can't be involved in the killing of the Planetary Director and avoid it.

They scooped everyone who had been in the hall when it happened, minus my mother who was excused after psychiatric evaluation. A total of forty-seven tios left with a splitting headache, retching and trembling for the next twenty-four hours. The good news was: no, we hadn't committed treason, just monumentally screwed up.

Scooping only gets the facts, not the feelings. The facts I could live with – it was the feelings I badly needed to explore. I wanted to scream to anyone who would listen that I hadn't wanted him to die, that hadn't been part of the plan, I wanted him alive and stripped of power but I didn't want him *gone*. I think anyone who knew me already knew that, but I wanted to scream it anyway.

The scooped facts spoke for themselves – a testament gleaned from forty-seven separate eyewitnesses. No one of sound mind was to blame for the death. No one went to jail. The official version rose out of the ashes. The Director's death was due to a sudden heart attack. It was made generally clear that my mother's part was not to be made public. And the one up-side to all of this was that my mother was now safe in Alti, finally receiving the best care available.

But after that comes the moral responsibility. There had been grumblings about the amount of power concentrated in my youthful hands, and this was what I did with it! Even my grandfather's influence couldn't protect me, the architect of that day's grand disaster. I formally resigned from every one of my posts, the empire was dismembered and Executors fell over themselves to seize control of their own private army, totally missing the point that the private army wasn't interested in being part of the hijo power structure. The Volunteers simply stopped Volunteering and the force evaporated overnight. My successors were left clutching an empty shell and the gleeful Resets moved back into the vacuum that was left behind.

But there were some who still thought I hadn't been punished enough – it's bad taste to overthrow the head of government but it's social death to involve segundas in it. My grandfather had to act, or face their wrath himself.

"There's one way I can keep you in the Ministry," he told me. "You'll hate it but it will keep your foot in the door."

He was right, I hated it, but the alternative was to be thrown to the wolves altogether. And so I accepted my banishment, to La Nueva Temporada's one inescapable prison, while the world stepped comfortably into its handbasket and slid off for Hell.

PART 3
EARTH

CHAPTER 12

DEPARTURE

ALEX NEVER SAW *Phoenicia* blast out of orbit. He and the rest of the crew had been put into longsleep on Puerto Alto before being loaded on board.

The ship as it blasted away from La Nueva Temporada made a double star in the Nuevan sky – the flame of the strap-on fusion boosters and the sparkle of the ice shield, pristine and white. Compared with what was to come its progress was sedate and stately, humming across space until it was scooting along the edge of the gravity well of the next planet out, the gas giant Pelayo. The planet's gravity felt like a tickle against the ship's skin, growing over time into an insistent tug and then an irresistible pull which the ship welcomed. Now it was falling towards Pelayo, faster and faster, and at the precise moment when it was travelling as fast as it ever would simply from gravity, the boosters fell away and the main drive came on. *Phoenicia* hurtled out into space past Pelayo at twice its previous velocity and kept accelerating, riding the surge of annihilated matter from its miniature black hole with a cybernetic whoop of triumph. It also started to transmit ahead, letting the Terrans know it was on its way.

For the next ten years...

After a decade the ship was travelling as fast as it safely could, a quarter of the speed of light. With a sense of obedient regret it cut the drive and coasted through cold space on momentum only. Every so often it trembled slightly as the ice shield took the impact of interstellar dust, striking it with enough force to destroy a city.

Twenty more years and it felt the first faint trickle of the solar stream coming from Earth's sun. It was time to deploy the solar brake. Slender masts extended from the ship in all directions and a powerful current ran through the superconducting cable that stretched from tip to tip. A powerful magnetic field wrapped around the ship and bit into the stream of charged particles from ahead. The ship started to slow.

After a few more years it was slow enough that it could safely spin around by 180 degrees. It emerged from behind the ice shield, exposing the rest of its structure to the direction of travel, and fired the main drive again.

By the time *Phoenicia* entered Earth's system it was no more than cruising. By the time it reached high Terran orbit, obediently following the commands of Orbital Traffic Control, it was moving at a sedate trot, as if the whole mad rush from La Nueva Temporada had never happened.

The Terrans had had twenty years to prepare and were ready for it. The ship had expected them. Indeed, all their actions from the time they intercepted it were entirely in accordance with what its Nuevan masters had predicted.

CHAPTER 13

WAKE-UP CALL

HISTORY HOVE INTO sight in the narrow frame of Jo Odembo's faceplate, and she bit back a triumphant smile. Earth and Luna hung in space on either side like the weights of a massive dumbbell, and their combined light reflected off the spars and frames and modules of the starship *Phoenicia*.

From a distance the starship still looked cold and empty, with no sign of the crew who had boarded it when it was only just inside Mars orbit. It still dwarfed her little scooter, which was just a framework holding a basic life-support system, fuel tanks and thrusters. Up at the ship's prow the ice shield was dirty and scarred, winnowed down to a fraction of its starting size by forty years of sub-lightspeed impacts. The ship had extended the ring of Command & Habitation and it was spinning again for the benefit of the waking humans on board. The kilometre-long spines on either side of the ring were almost bare. An obvious exception was the small module halfway down the aft one. Jo already knew what the module contained and didn't need the headspace overlay: it was the wormhole terminus, the whole point of this mission.

Jo's attention had been riveted to the broadcasts as the boarding party had made their way through the ship's passages to the longsleep chambers. She had been itching to be there with them – but the Hired Sword clan had claimed the ship for their own, all signed off by the Lawcore. They had been responsible for bringing the ship into Earth orbit, though as far as Jo could tell the ship was perfectly capable of bringing itself.

But the great and the good had decided that now *Phoenicia* was here it would come under the jurisdiction of High-Kili station, and that made it hers. When Hired Sword's Team Leader Szabo had made his unexpected discovery, Jo had been out of the door almost before he finished speaking.

As the scooter carried her forward, a neutral voice spoke in her head.

Unauthorised access–

She blanked out the messages that started to chatter back and forth in headspace. Hired Sword was telling her the ship was out of bounds, her scooter was bouncing back the authorisation she needed. She let the blackboxes slug it out between them and continued to approach the airlock.

"Sergeant Odembo, what are you doing? There's no police business here."

Jo smiled. The Team Leader himself had butted into the conversation. She wondered how he had got this job. Had he just been the one on watch when it came up? Headspace said his team had been handling the security for a mining city on Mars, until it was abruptly pulled out to go and board *Phoenicia*. That was what Hired Sword did: security and related functions. So, a professional head-butter was put in charge of a marvel like a starship. Not a match she would have chosen herself.

"I beg to differ, Team Leader," she replied, calm and professional in response to his abruptness. "You reported deaths on board."

"Deaths? What has that–" He broke off for a moment, then came back. *"I suppose, yes, but that's still no business–"*

"A report must be filed, Team Leader," she said. "Procedure."

Always quote procedure, she mused. The Szabos of this world like procedure.

There was a long pause; she could picture him counting his options.

"*Very well.*" He conceded with very bad grace. "*I'll be waiting for you.*"

THE SHIP KINDLY put up a map in headspace to guide her after she docked, but before long Jo was being guided by her unassisted ears towards the concourse. She followed the sound of voices and the knocks and clatters of the engineering crew at work. The open space when she got there was dotted with engineers, heads buried in cable conduits or waving instruments at bulkheads.

"Sergeant." Szabo was just as curt in the flesh. He had a wide, flat smile that never reached his pale eyes and conveyed no humour or warmth at all. "Ara Szabo. Shall we get–" He moved aside with an irritated scowl to let a drone pass by on some mission for the ship. "Shall we get this over with? I've got a lot going on."

"Ship keeping you busy, then, Team Leader?" she asked as he turned his back. He snorted without turning round.

"This ship is giving us minimum co-operation, it questions and double-checks everything..." She smiled to herself at the litany of complaint, and then slowed to a halt as something caught her eye. A huddle of equipment had been piled up by the Hired Swords and one of the open crates was full of guns. Sidearms. Plasma pulse projectors.

"You'd think it'd be grateful for an overhaul after forty years, but..." Szabo glanced over his shoulder to check she was following and realised she had slowed down.

"You came on board with all this?" she asked. He followed her gaze and then she got the flat smile again.

"Just precautions, Sergeant. This way."

Precautions? Jo thought. There were precautions, and there were boarding parties armed to the teeth, and it looked like the Hired Swords had erred more towards the latter kind. But then they were essentially a bunch of mercenaries; maybe this was just how they travelled normally.

What exactly were they expecting? *Phoenicia* was here because the Nuevans wanted help. She had seen the recording that the ship sent ahead of itself, of course: the speech by the Nuevan Planetary Director himself. "*Our world has suffered a catastrophe...*" Obviously the Terrans knew all about it as well – the wormhole explosion hadn't been confined to La Nueva Temporada – but it sounded like the Nuevans had had it far worse than Earth.

Glowing lines in headspace showed the way along the upwards-curving corridors to the longsleep chambers that held the two thousand, two hundred and seven crew on board. The Nuevans had reduced their population slightly by sending home every Terran stranded on their world.

"First on the left," Szabo said.

Reflected shimmers defined the curves of the longsleep coffins lining the floor of longsleep chamber A. Each one held an adult-sized human shape, a faceless grey smear in the faintly glowing depths. Hired Sword medics hovered over the coffins, taking readings and prepping them for the move to High-Kili.

"There's two in here," said Szabo, "one in chambers B and D, none in C. Just average wastage for a journey like this."

She had already seen the empty spaces. The gaps in the rows of regular, smooth shapes stood out like missing teeth in a friendly grin. She made her way over to the nearest. There were coffins on either side but here was nothing. The connections were there, the tubes and the power feeds that would have been plugged into it – just no coffin to plug them in to.

"Was–" she asked. Szabo obviously braced himself for a question, and she stopped before she made herself look a complete fool. She had been about to ask the standard question at the scene of every non-natural death: "Was the scene like this when you arrived?" But she knew from the broadcasts that Szabo had been the first into this chamber, and she doubted he had personally picked up and hidden the coffin that was missing.

Every coffin had a nameplate fixed to the bulkhead beside it and this space had one too. *Alejandro Mateo*, she read.

"Request whereabouts of Alejandro Mateo?" she asked the ship.

"Died mission year 27.6.2 due to coffin malfunction," Szabo said casually, just as the ship gave her exactly the same information.

Corpse ejected into space, the ship added.

She gave the supplementary data a quick check. Mateo had been nineteen. That was young for a voyage like this but hey, there had been kids on *Phoenicia's* first voyage. But this was an emergency trip, not a colonisation endeavour. Maybe he had been a cadet or something. *Fuck,* she thought.

"Poor guy."

"One less Nuevan to worry about," Szabo remarked and Jo had to force herself not to snap something she would regret. "Ship's master. The other three were ex-pat Terrans taking a free lift home." He shrugged. "As I said, average wastage."

"Right..." She gritted her teeth. She hadn't expected it to get her like this. Colleagues, people known to her, had died in freak accidents or the line of duty. Space was not a safe place to work. She had only used the reported deaths as an excuse to get on board *Phoenicia*, but suddenly it was almost like she had met the guy.

This Mateo was a complete stranger who had made a brave journey for the sake of his world. Nineteen years old, adult life just beginning; he had travelled between stars, trusting his life to the machines, and the machines had let him down. On general principle: *damn.*

Jo turned away, angry with... whom? The universe? Maybe. But angry. Average wastage, the man said.

"More like a bloody massacre," she muttered. She said it quietly, but Szabo overheard her.

"Considerably more died on the outward voyage," he pointed out. "On long voyages, longsleep coffins occasionally fail. Fact. Start from there."

"Yeah, yeah." Jo didn't pursue the matter. "Have you checked all the coffins? There may be more–"

He rolled his eyes. "Yes, Sergeant, we have checked all the coffins on board and they're all fully functioning. Now, I'll leave you to your job. I expect you'll want to get back to High-Kili once you're done, so you can see yourself out when you're ready to go. If you'll excuse me, we have the ship to secure."

Those last words were full of carefully enunciated satisfaction. He very briefly met her eyes as he said that, just long enough for a flicker of a triumphant smile that was genuine. Jo wondered if he always showed it when he was pleased with himself.

But: 'I expect you'll want to get back to High-Kili'? She wanted to shake him. *Are you crazy? I want to explore every centimetre of this ship from stem to stern.*

Only...

There was no 'only'. She was out of excuses for being here. The ship could give her the details of the deaths and she could do the rest through headspace.

"I expect I will," she said formally. "Thank you for your co-operation, Team Leader."

They turned away from each other and Jo knew she was already forgotten.

She took one last look at the space where Mateo had been. Four deaths, out of two thousand. A fifth of one per cent. For antiquated longsleep equipment, hurriedly pressed into emergency service, maybe it wasn't bad. But for the unlucky ones...

On general principle, and for one last time, she thought, *fuck*.

CHAPTER 14

THE MAN WHO FELL TO EARTH

ALEX WOKE UP at the heart of a fireball.

His awareness kicked up out of the depths of a murky well. There was light and sound and consciousness ahead of him, and suddenly he was back in his body drawing a huge, deep breath. He was strapped to one of the padded couches that ran around the wall of a small, domed cabin that shook violently. His couch was the only one occupied. Invisible restraints held him down and a heavy weight sat on his chest. Bright orange light flared the other side of the viewports as if someone was playing a very large blowtorch against the glass.

There was a heavy weight on his mind too. Somewhere at the back of his brain was the knowledge that quite some time had passed since his last conscious thought.

Where the hell am I? It was an instinctive question and it was immediately followed by the obvious answer. He could see with his own eyes that he was in a lifepod, and the fire outside, the shaking, the weight, the restraints – it all said that the lifepod was falling through a planet's atmosphere.

Report? he sent. There was no response, not even an empty click in his headspace.

Emergency! What's going on? Emergency!

Calm down, take a breath, stop panicking, he told himself. Maybe you had an accident or... something.

The flame had died away while he was thinking. He hadn't noticed it go or counted the minutes since. Outside the windows it was just dark, the slightest hint of light growing. The rocking had died away and the whistle of rushing air lurked just at the edges of his hearing. He was still falling.

Then an angry roar bellowed through the walls of the pod and the weight that sat on him suddenly doubled. The pod's rockets were firing, which meant they were close to landing–

Smash, and the noise and shuddering were so intense that he might have blacked out for a moment. The cabin pitched violently up and down, over and over again. It hadn't landed, it had splashed down. Water sluiced past the viewports as the rocking died away. Lights set around the ceiling came on and the restraints that had held him retracted into the couch.

He tried to lift his head up, then groaned and let it fall back onto the padded headrest. After that, he had to make do with squinting about through narrowed eyes. He didn't see anything to tell him more than he already knew.

With an effort Alex pushed himself up on his elbows. Then he took a deep breath and heaved himself so that his upper body was upright. Last of all he planted his feet on the floor and slowly, achingly stood up. He had to hang his head to get over the blood rush but finally he was vertical.

There was an instrument panel next to the hatch and he took in the key readings at a glance. The air outside was breathable; acceptable temperature and pressure; background radiation easily tolerable. Something nagged at him for attention and he double-checked the readings. No, everything was in the green.

There was also a small box attached to the wall next to the panel, with the words 'Open me' stencilled on it. He ignored it for the time being and instead tapped out the 'open' code for the hatch.

A sharp hiss filled the cabin as pressure equalised with air that was surprisingly warm and humid. The hatch swung open and Alex braced himself for a chill blast, but there was none. For the first time he noticed what he was wearing: not a shipsuit, not even normal day clothes, but something like a surgical tunic, which shouldn't offer any protection against the cold at all. Cautiously he poked his head and shoulders through the opening.

He was a couple of feet above the waves that lapped gently around the pod. He reached down and dabbled his fingers in the water, which felt silky and soft and noticeably didn't chill his fingers to the bone.

But... it really was warm, the kind of warmth you only got indoors if the thermostat was turned up too high. You never got it outside at all. At least, not if you were on La Nueva Temporada...

He looked down at the water. It had a strange inner glow which, he realised, was a reflection. With infinite reluctance, he looked up.

It was hard to say what he noticed first – the absence of El Grande; the full spread of velvet black night sky from horizon to horizon, ablaze with a million stars; or the bright silver, coin-sized planetoid above the horizon. It was a full circle marked with patterns of craters that looked vaguely like a face turned on one side.

"That's Luna," he murmured. He looked down, around him at the endless sea. "So this is Earth."

He was twenty light years from home and had no idea why he had even left.

There were more discoveries, now he knew what to expect. The air moved over his head in a strange way; in fact, he could feel it on every centimetre of skin. He quickly ran his hand over his scalp and found he was completely bald.

He held his arms in front of his face and studied them closely. The smooth skin had a strange tint to it, a very faint shade of yellow that wasn't just a trick of the light.

Another quick check showed that it wasn't just his head. There wasn't any hair anywhere on his body.

As a final test, though he really didn't need it, he rolled up the tunic and checked his thigh. There was the dark puncture, healed up with skin sealant, where the tubes had been.

"Longsleep?" he murmured. It could be nothing else. He had been in longsleep. You lost your body hair, the preservative fluid stained you yellow, and it wiped out your memories for anything from the last few hours up to months, depending on how long it lasted.

But it was not a comforting thing to learn. *Why* had he been in longsleep? There were only two possible reasons he could think of: sometimes it was the only way to save the life of an accident victim, and it was the only way to get through a very long space journey without ageing. Like, for example, the forty-plus years it would take to get from La Nueva Temporada to Earth without the shortcut of the wormhole...

That was when the sinking feeling hit him. He ducked back into the cabin and made himself look at the readings again. The environment readouts still gave no cause for concern. The chronometer was something else.

"Oh... God..." he whispered. He sank back onto one of the couches and curled up, hugging his knees. He felt his breathing start to speed up, like in his basic spacesuit training many years ago. He forced it down again.

"Oh, God."

His voice rose and tears pricked at the back of his eyes. He blinked furiously but couldn't tear his gaze from the display.

"Oh, God..."

He really was twenty light years from home and he had been asleep for more than twice as long as he had already been alive.

ALEX KNELT ON the floor of the pod and scrabbled at the little box marked 'Open me'. It held a pair of conceptual crystals and the small plastic crescent of a linkset.

He held up one of the tablet-shaped crystals between a shaking thumb and forefinger. A figure '1' was stamped on the surface. Level one – full and lasting memory restoration. Glints of light sparked in its crystal depths like the hidden memories it contained. Swallow it down and within minutes RNA viruses would have restored his memories, or implanted whole new ones. Alone on the ocean of the wrong world, still no idea at all what he was doing there – there were memories that badly needed restoring.

Was he still nineteen? Had he graduated? Were his family alive? Did he have a girlfriend? These were all questions worth asking, every bit as important as what he was doing on Earth.

But common sense and prudence said the linkset might be the better idea. The implants that made it possible to access headspace without even thinking about it would have been removed before he went into longsleep. The linkset was the next best thing until he could get new implants grown. Alex fitted it into place unobtrusively behind his ear and sat back in a couch. He twiddled his thumbs nervously and waited for something to happen.

There were a couple of clicks and buzzes inside his head.

Good. You are awake. How are you? The voice was strangely androgynous; it could be man, woman or other.

"I'm fine," he said. "Who are you?"

I am Phoenicia.

"... ah." The starship? So, that was presumably how he had got to Earth. "And, uh, what am I doing here?"

So you have not yet taken either of the conceptuals. It was a bald statement.

"No, not yet."

I recommend you do so. Have you deduced you are on Earth?

"Um, yes, but I..."

Good. I have now managed to pinpoint your location. You are–

"Couldn't you just track the pod's beacon? It must have one."

A distress beacon could be tracked by anyone and so I disabled it. As it is, I am communicating through a highly distributed system that is almost untraceable. You are–

"Almost?" Alex asked nervously.

Another starship could do it, or a blackbox of equal complexity to myself. Did the ship sound a little complacent?

None exist in local space. For the third time, you are in the Indian Ocean, midway between two sea clan communities known as the Maldives and the Seychelles. This is a most satisfactory outcome. Assistance will be with you within four hours. Taking–

"Assistance?" Alex felt a gush of relief. "You've contacted the emergency authorities?"

The assistance is not of that nature. Taking–

Then it struck Alex. "But, hang on, you appear to be working okay?"

I am in perfect working order.

"So why are you jettisoning lifepods? In fact, why did you disable the beacon? Why–"

Taking the conceptuals will answer your remaining questions, as well as all the ones you have yet to ask. For the time being, take it as read that the Terran authorities believe you to be dead and it is desirable that you should remain that way.

"Desirable to who?" Alex yelped.

To you, for a start.

"And they think I'm dead because...?"

That is what is indicated by the evidence they found when they boarded me. As ship's master, you were the first one they looked for.

Alex had been steeling himself to take the first conceptual. His hand was almost at his mouth but at the ship's last statement it dropped down again.

"I'm the master? That's not right!"

It is.

"Excuse me, I remember that much! Felipe and I were going to get you out of mothballs but he was going to be the one in charge. He was the one going on the expedition. I just–"

Alex stopped. Felipe?

He had been about to say: "I just provided the money." Yes, he and Felipe had been going to mortgage their inheritances to fund this venture... but they certainly hadn't been planning on returning to Earth. And now, for the first time it struck him that if he was here, so should Felipe be.

"Ship," Alex asked, "where is Felipe?" Though he could already guess what its answer would be, and sure enough:

Take the conceptuals. It was blunt and to-the-point. There was no easy way out of this. Alex glared resentfully at the crystal held between thumb and forefinger. It could give him all the answers but suddenly he wasn't sure he wanted to know them.

He popped it into his mouth.

CHAPTER 15

NASTY, SUSPICIOUS MINDS

JO GOT BACK to the office on High-Kili just as her Constable was heading for the door. From his stricken look, she guessed Bob had been about to take advantage of her absence and bunk off early from his shift. He recovered quickly and she pretended not to notice.

"How was it?" he asked.

She dropped down into her chair and looked speculatively at him. The entire wall behind her showed a real-time view down the cable towards Earth. It was night across Africa and it looked as if the silver line disappeared into the dark, hit something and broke up into speckles of light – the lights of the Ken-Tan-Moz megalopolis that sprawled along the east coast. The view kept Jo focused on where she had come from, and where she hoped to return one day on her own terms – though when she had busted one bad guy too many and the clan gave her twenty-four hours to leave, the hint had been strong that she shouldn't even dream of coming back until a lot of people had either died of natural causes or otherwise moved on.

How was it? she thought. The question was meaningless, just his usual conversational seed. Where to start? She held his gaze just long enough to make him shift a little, wondering what he had done wrong.

"Coffin failure," she said.

"... Yes...?"

"The longsleep coffins were stripped down and rebuilt, they're self-sustaining, built-in redundancy as far as the eye can see. If there's to be a failure rate you'd expect it to be low, wouldn't you?"

"Yes..." he said again, carefully, like a man with a toe dipped into the conversation, not quite sure how deep or heated it might suddenly become.

"And it was low. Four out of two thousand..." A fifth of one per cent, she reminded herself again.

Bob pulled a figure from headspace.

"Twenty-three never woke up on the original *Phoenicia* mission," he pointed out.

"Twenty-three out of ten thousand," she agreed. It was a similar figure: a fifth of one percent, give or take. But... And yet... But.

"Go home, Bob," she said. She suddenly felt very tired. "I'll close up."

"Right!"

She dropped down into her chair and he darted for the exit. "And you're on night call," she added over her shoulder.

"Right," he muttered, a little less pleased, and the door closed. Well, there was no point in not being a bit of a bastard if you had the rank for it. Night call meant that if any emergencies arose while the office was closed for the day, he would be the one contacted. Whereupon, of course, he would contact her, but her sleep would be undisturbed for a little longer.

Jo leaned forward and rested her head against the desktop.

"Crappity crappity crappity crappity crappity crap."

It wasn't just the deaths. It wasn't just that one of them was a kid. (Note to self: the three Terrans who also died might have families who would need notifying.) It was the realisation that making a pointless trip out to the starship (which could just as well have been done through headspace) to record four deaths (which could just as well have been handled by a blackbox from the coroner's office) was the highlight of her... month? No, more than that. Year, at least. In fact, today's contrived distraction was quite possibly the highlight of her career.

God, how boring was her career likely to be?

Extremely, if current signs were anything to go by.

It was a sad fact of life that there was only one Chief Constable of the Orbital Police Force. The way to get to Chief was to be Commander of one of the four big stations – High-Kili, Atahualpa, Garuda, Basilé. The way to be Commander of a station was first to be one of its Sergeants. But Commanders tended to hang around for a long time, not creating any further vacancies; and Chief was such a plush job that whoever got it tended to stay forever, pulling up the ladder for their contemporaries and only creating a vacancy for the next generation down.

She sighed and called the first of the dead Terran names out of headspace. She could squeeze a bit more official activity into the end of the day.

"List known relatives of Katharine Trinq, last known whereabouts La Nueva Temporada."

Headspace told her there were no known relatives on Earth. Well, that made the job slightly easier.

"List known relatives of Samuel Ahudi, last known whereabouts La Nueva Temporada."

No known relatives located.

Jo sat up, frowned, sent off the request for the third name.

No known–

"For goodness sake," she murmured. She thought for a moment, then picked three names at random from the list of *surviving* Terran passengers. Then three more and another three after that. All had family – a spouse, a child, a parent, at least. Usually more.

Maybe a fifth of one percent dying was the statistical norm, but what were the odds of the three dead Terrans being the only ones not to have any surviving family at all?

It was too late, she was too tired. She would come back to this.

* * *

SHE CAME BACK to it in the middle of the night.

Jo had gone to bed, turned off the lights and had the kind of sleep where she was convinced she hadn't slept for hours, until she remembered getting out of bed in the middle of longsleep chamber A, and her mother being on *Phoenicia* saying all the things that Szabo had said to her earlier, and strolling down the ship's spine in the sunlight...

So she probably had slept. A little.

The last straw was Ara Szabo, apparently standing next to her in her room, with his broad, flat smile of smug satisfaction.

"*We have the ship...*"

Jo's eyes opened into the darkness.

"Yes, Team Leader, you certainly do," she murmured.

Phoenicia was built to fly between solar systems and establish colony worlds, and it was programmed to do it in one way only. It would give unswerving loyalty to its designated master, until its mission was accomplished or its master died, in which case it changed its loyalty to the nearest civil administration.

She remembered Szabo's complaints about the ship's lack of cooperation. If the Terrans now owned *Phoenicia*, it seemed to be news to the ship itself.

She dug a little deeper into headspace, looking back through publicly available records. She soon found that it wasn't just Szabo. It questioned Traffic Control, it had been very reluctant even to let the Hired Sword people on in the first place... in fact, *Phoenicia* was showing no signs of loyalty at all to any government or public body of Earth.

Yet, it also claimed to have personally ejected the body of its master, Alejandro Mateo, into space. In mission year 27. It really should be aware that its master was dead.

It could just be a case of blackbox psychosis, simultaneously holding two contradictory beliefs in its mind. It happened.

Or...

Jo snorted. It was a nasty, suspicious thought based on the flimsiest of evidence, and she was probably still delirious from dreamland and not thinking clearly. And while there were times in her line of work when a nasty, suspicious mind was a positive asset, this probably wasn't one of them. So instead she asked a question she really should have asked earlier. Szabo had said Mateo was... ship's master?

"Query: how did a nineteen year old become ship's master?"

Headspace quickly told the story, retrieved and synchronised from the ship's own archives: how Alejandro Mateo was the reluctant junior partner in an enterprise founded by his older brother and, what with one thing and another, he was the one to come to Earth.

She also glanced at the sketchy data on the kid's father, Tomás Mateo, the man who made the speech. Planetary Director, eh? That certainly sounded grand. By definition he must be a successful politician. She would bet he also had a nasty, suspicious mind.

Jo had the strangest feeling there were threads here. But as yet she had no reason to tie them together.

CHAPTER 16

SAUCY SUE

ALEX CRIED OUT and his fingers scoured into the cushions of his seat. Though his face was screwed up and his teeth clenched together, still a faint whine squeezed its way out.

But there was no stopping the restored memory reclaiming its place in his head. The conceptual had been recorded before he went into the coffin back on La Nueva Temporada. Along with everything else that had happened the night of the Event, he relived the news of Felipe's death.

He had taken conceptuals before, of course, but never had a full restore like this. You latched onto something, some vaguely remembered concept; you gave it a little mental prod and your past life just unrolled in front of you. Once started, you couldn't stop.

The news was worse the second time round. The first time, he remembered the shock, the numbness, the cushioning that his mind gave to the blow by only gradually letting him take it in. With a restored memory, apparently, there was no such trick. You got it all at once. Alex sagged down into his chair and his body shook with silent sobs.

The memories continued. The rush programme to recommission *Phoenicia*, the ship's refusal to be commanded by anyone else... They had left Nueva less than six months after the Event, which he had to admit was pretty damned good work.

There was no memory of saying goodbye to his parents. Maybe he had done that after recording the conceptual. Maybe he just hadn't wanted the extra pain.

And at least he now knew why he was on Earth. What he didn't however know was why he was on this bit of Earth, pretending to be dead rather than enjoying a proper red carpet reception, but that was presumably in the second conceptual, and right now he would rather be alone and grieve for Felipe all over again.

He wasn't sure how long he sat there, hunched up in misery, but the sound of engines made him lift his head up. At the same time a new voice came into headspace via the linkset.

"*Mateo?*"

"Who's asking?" he muttered.

"*Well, there's gratitude for you! Boy's just like his father…*"

Alex pushed himself to his feet with a sigh and a grunt and went back to the hatch.

Dawn was fast approaching, a band of light against the eastern sky, and a vessel was silhouetted against it. It looked like a cross between a boat and an aircraft the size of a rigi. At the stern a pair of tall slanting tail fins supported two large, powerful propellers, though neither was moving at the moment so presumably it had some other kind of propulsion for slow speeds. Stubby triangular wings sprouted from the hull on either side and waves slapped against the bow that pushed its way through the water towards him.

Saucy Sue, ekranoplan registered in the Non-Territorial Gerontocracy of the Glorious Crown, said headspace. *Ekranoplan: amphibious ground effect vehicle commonly used for long-distance intercontinental transport on Earth–*

Alex knew what an ekranoplan was, though he had never seen one. He was more interested in who was on board. Someone from the Non-Territorial Gerry-thing of whatever, presumably. Headspace primly told him he didn't have the permissions to know the crew manifest.

A streamlined transparent dome was set into the top of the fuselage and one of the people he didn't have the permissions to know about was looking down at him. The outline looked like a woman. She waved as the craft came closer, looming over the pod, and Alex cautiously lifted a hand in return.

Saucy Sue slowed and stopped with a final surge of noise, and a wave washed towards the pod. Alex was gripped with a sudden fear that it would burst through the hatch and sink him, though the pod rode the wave with ease.

"*I'm bringing the dinghy over now. You should have a red metal case in there somewhere. Bring it with you and do not drop it, or I swear we'll send you down to retrieve it and the sea's three kilometres deep here.*"

"Who–" Alex began, but headspace said the channel had closed again.

The red case was easy to find, clamped to the wall below the hatch. It had a carrying handle but no way of opening it. In fact it didn't look as if it was meant to be opened. There were grooves down the edges and ports down one side which suggested it was meant to be slotted into something. By the time Alex had unclipped it and put the second conceptual in a pocket, the dinghy had cast off and a single man was rowing it across the few metres between them.

His unidentified friends were still staying silent so Alex tried the ship.

"Won't people get suspicious when they find an empty pod floating in the sea?"

They will not because I installed a small explosive charge–

"What?" Alex yelped, and he peered around. He didn't want to be near an explosive charge, even a small one.

– that will sink it once you are away.

The oarsman was an old man: the coming dawn reflected off a bald scalp ringed with a line of silver hair. Alex saw his teeth bare as the man grinned and held out a hand, but it wasn't for him.

"Particles?"

"Parti– Oh, right." Alex looked at the red metal case with renewed respect. Particles were used to open the wormhole.

161

This little box was what the entire forty year flight had been about. Even a new terminus could be built from scratch here on Earth, but without the particles, still quantum entangled with their cousins back on La Nueva Temporada, the mission was a non-starter.

A sudden fear hit him: that once they had the particles, he would no longer be necessary and the ekranoplan would depart without him.

"Uh… why do I have these, exactly? Why not just keep the particles with the terminus? On the ship?"

"I believe the terminus is indeed fully loaded."

"So… what …"

"Wasn't my plan, boy. Let's say, just in case. A little bit held in reserve never hurt anyone."

The man carefully placed the box under the dinghy's bulwark before holding out a hand to help Alex climb in.

The explosive charge went off with a muffled *pop* as they were rowing back. Air gusted out of the open hatch with the sigh of a tired geriatric and the pod began to settle. It sank with a quiet dignity that was only a little let down by the sound of submerged gurgles and belches. Alex watched the patch of ocean where it had been until the last bubbles had gone, and even then it took an effort to look away.

"It's just a machine," said the oarsman kindly as they came up to the ekranoplan.

"I know that," Alex muttered. Yes, it was just a machine, but it was just the machine that had kept him alive and brought him safely down to this place.

"You're sentimental," said a voice above him. The speaker was an old woman, silhouetted in the doorway in *Saucy Sue's* hull above him. "Just like your father. Are you strong enough to climb up?"

It was the second reference in a very short space of time to Alex's father.

"Yes," he said through his teeth. He didn't feel particularly strong and would have welcomed a hand up from someone capable, but from the sound of her voice he would have ended up dragging her down into the three-kilometre-deep Indian Ocean. "And you never met my father if you think that." He stood on wobbly legs, braced himself against the foot of the doorway and heaved. His arms gave out and he sprawled on *Saucy Sue's* deck at her feet. She stepped back to give him space and he felt the old man behind him, shoving him up into the ekranoplan. It was not a dignified entry.

He slowly picked himself up to stand in front of her. They were in a narrow passageway and it was the first time since arriving on Earth that he had been able to stand straight without his head hitting something. His spine enjoyed the feeling of unfolding properly. The old man scrambled up behind him, the dinghy absorbed into the hull and the doorway healed shut behind them.

"You know, there are rungs if you care to look out for them..."

Now Alex was finally standing upright, he found himself looking down at the couple. Neither of them came up beyond his shoulders. The man's grin was wide and the sparkle of the eyes said it was genuine friendliness. The woman had been pulled down by age from the graceful, upright poise she might have had when she was younger. She wore a simple pale blue smock and a bun of pure white hair was pulled tight behind her head. Her face was lined and grim, not a square centimetre of smooth skin, but the set of the mouth suggested she might have been smiling. Or perhaps she just enjoyed taunting amnesiacs.

"Typical Mateo respect for his elders," she declared. "And you were such a sweet baby too."

"So we met when I was a baby?" Alex felt the impatience growing inside him.

"And a couple of times since, plus birthday and Christmas greetings each year."

"We *last* met on your sixteenth birthday," said the old woman.

"Came all the way from Earth to see you into adulthood."

"We never did get a thank-you letter for the whisky."

The penny dropped.

"Aunt Marietta? Uncle Nathan?"

Alex found himself staring at his godparents. Nathan and Marietta Sulong, Nuevan legends in their own right for being the pair who opened the wormhole. They were so *old!* But they had to be. They had travelled on board *Phoenicia* before his parents were born, and so they had to be well into their century, but even so...

"And you're no portrait yourself, yellow bald boy," Nathan told him, reading his mind. "*Sue*, give Alex all crew member permissions."

The ekranoplan's full headspace abruptly opened up for Alex: identity tags for Nathan and Marietta, and access to any other shipboard data and connections he might have wanted to call upon. There were still blanks that were only open to a full-fledged member of the Gerontocracy of the Glorious Crown but it was still enough to make him feel human again. A control panel appeared outlined in the air in front of Nathan, who moved his hand over a couple of virtual switches. Power displays surged and Alex felt, then heard *Saucy Sue's* engines fire up: first a whine that rapidly rose into inaudibility, chased by an increasing bass roar that turned into a steady thrumming vibration as the blades bit into the air. He felt the deck shift beneath him and the gentle surge of acceleration pushed him a couple of steps back down the passage before he caught himself on a handrail.

Marietta had already turned away down the passage.

"I'll show you your cabin. There's some things for you there. How many conceptuals have you taken?"

"Just the one..."

"Then you'd better take the next. And when you're all done, you'd probably like something to eat after forty years."

Alex forced a smile.

"Yes, I think I would, thanks."

"Though I warn you," Nathan put in, "your first solid bowel movement after four decades of longsleep is *excruciating.*"

*   *   *

WEARING HIS NEW identity, Alex stepped out of the cabin. He held up his arms and studied the sleeves, and then looked closely at the datacloud that followed him. Everything seemed to fit.

The clothes were colourful and light – trousers, shirt, slippers, all his size. What was really impressive was that the data identity seemed tailor-made as well. Headspace assured him that he was Henry Sulong, great grandson of Marietta and Nathan, resident of Samoa Sea Clan, aged eighteen. There were datastreams going all the way back to his non-existent childhood and try as he might he couldn't pick any holes in them.

He was in a circular lobby. Three or four other doors led off it, and a flight of steps set into the wall opposite him led up towards daylight. The walls were lined with wood panelling and the carpet beneath his slippers was soft and caressing. He didn't know much about life on Earth but the general level of luxury hanging around *Saucy Sue* was impressive. It would be: headspace said the Gerontocracy of the Glorious Crown was a clan of retired, well-off people who pooled their life savings together and sold their expertise to other clans on a consultancy basis. (There were over 100 million of them, which put Nueva's total populationof sixty million into interesting perspective.) His godparents had got rich by sleeping for forty years on the *Phoenicia* mission from Earth to La Nueva Temporada, with all their assets in the bank back on Earth in the care of some financially astute blackboxes while they were gone. As well as the handsome fee paid by the Nuevan government they had returned to Earth through their own wormhole to live off four decades of compound interest; plus, they had got a percentage of the transit fee whenever a ship went through the wormhole in either direction. Nice work if you could get it.

He made his way cautiously up the stairs, still clinging onto the stair rail to help his unsteady legs, and emerged into a lounge. It was a circular recess in the hull covered by the glass dome, sides lined with comfortable couches done out in white leather. Marietta and Nathan looked up from the game of chess they had been playing. As far as Alex could tell, his godparents were the only crew on board – the blackbox did the rest.

He glanced back through the dome towards the stern. *Saucy Sue* skimmed so close to the sea that it sent up graceful fans of white water in its wake. He knew how ekranoplans worked. A cross between an aircraft and a boat, they thrust themselves forwards with old fashioned turboprops or jets until a cushion of air lifted them out of the water and they could skim a few metres above the surface. It was stylish, efficient and graceful – everything a machine should be.

"He's in love," Marietta commented. "You can tell he's an engineer."

Nathan chuckled. "Just like his–"

"Please don't say 'just like his father'." Alex turned back towards them and suddenly the entire room contracted into a single object at the centre of his vision – a tray of sandwiches set out on a table. His body had been quiet on the subject so far but now it reminded him he hadn't eaten for forty years.

"I was going to say mother." Nathan indicated the tray as an invitation and Alex dropped down into the white leather chair next to it. "Go on, tuck in. Just like your father? Good Lord no. Tomás is a middleman through and through – someone to have ideas and make others do them for him. Linda's the creator in your family."

Alex was already finishing the first sandwich off and he didn't even know what was in it. Every bite sent a wash of energy into his system: he could feel his head clearing, strength returning to his muscles. Headspace identified the sandwich contents as meat paste laced with the required vitamins and nanites to purge his system of the last of the longsleep preservatives and get him back to full strength. Yummy.

He felt a corner of his mouth quirk at what Nathan said.

"True." He picked up another and gave it another mighty munch. "Is there really a Henry Sulong?" he asked, a bit indistinctly.

"Oh, he's real," Marietta chuckled. "He's lying low for a few days, on a fishing trip, out of headspace."

"But I'm not just masquerading. I mean… the past I'm seeing is *me*. It describes me so well, I could actually believe I'd been born on Earth."

"We started planning this a long time ago," Marietta agreed, "just after he was born."

"A purchase here, a registration there…"

"… and we built up a parallel identity, just for you. And speaking of family…" Marietta had her concentration back on the chess board, and she moved a piece to take something of Nathan's. "We were very sorry to hear about Felipe. Very sorry indeed."

"Thank you," Alex said after a pause.

"But of course," Nathan added, "we heard it years ago when signals from the ship started reaching Earth, so we've had a little longer to live with it. How are you?"

His tone was friendly but he gave Alex a direct look that was dark and solemn, and although Alex still flinched from the fact of Felipe's death he appreciated the candour – though not enough to answer the question.

"What was it like at this end? Did many die?"

"There was a ship in transit through the terminus at the time. Two hundred and fifty-seven crew and passengers. Otherwise, the terminus was angled away from Earth, so no collateral damage at all from the blast."

"We got hosed," Alex muttered.

"So I gather."

"Have you taken the second conceptual now?" Marietta asked.

"Yes."

"So you know–"

"Everything. Mostly everything." Alex pushed himself up into a more comfortable position and reached for another sandwich. "I can't believe… this was all planned?"

"'Planned' is a strong word," Nathan objected. "Say rather, 'the possibility was anticipated.'"

"Four words," murmured Marietta.

"So you were recruited by Nuevan Intelligence *just in case* the wormhole ever closed? And there's such a *thing* as Nuevan Intelligence?"

"As government departments go, I don't think it was ever more than your father plus a blackbox inclined towards paranoia – but yes, Tomás did draw up contingency plans with us for what to do should the wormhole ever close so firmly that *Phoenicia* had to return to Earth. It was not beyond the bounds of possibility."

"It still seems... I mean, are you sure? Everything on that conceptual was just theory when I left..."

"Oh, believe me, we have every reason to believe your father's theory was entirely correct." Nathan had given up on the chess. He swung himself round to face Alex and leaned forward with his hands clasped together at his knees. "I don't think anyone at our end has the slightest intention of ever reopening the wormhole to Nueva."

CHAPTER 17

GHOST HUNTING

"*MY NAME IS Emiliana Devesa.*" She was a young woman, about Alex's age. Long dark hair framed an oval face. Set against her pale features, her eyes darted from left to right like a pair of trapped insects. She spoke whenever her gaze settled on the camera.

"*I loved him. I loved him so much. He broke my heart. They don't care. No one cares. I'm going to show them what it's like. I will split Nueva and Earth apart like he has split our hearts.*"

There was a pause, more eyes darting left to right as if she was trying hard to think of something to add. Then she stated simply:

"*That's all.*"

The image froze, then faded away into the walls of *Saucy Sue's* lounge. When Alex closed his eyes the outline was still there. One heartbroken Nuevan girl, responsible for... for...

He opened his eyes again and the outline vanished. She was gone. If only he could unmake what she had done so easily.

"She was a Nuevan student, over here to study drama and contemporary dance," said Marietta. "The last anyone heard of her, she was returning home for the holidays – on the ship that was going through at the precise moment of the explosion. Turns out she accessed some pretty high level conceptuals which would have driven her even more batty."

"How did she do it?" Alex asked quietly. He looked up at the two sceptical old faces. "Allegedly?"

They glanced at each other: Nathan took up the story.

"When you travel through a wormhole you don't just travel through space," he said. "You also arrive slightly in the future because you have travelled instantly while the rest of the universe is taking the slow route. This doesn't matter because when you travel back again, you go back the same distance into the past. And if you go back the slow route, through space – well, no problem, you're still in the same timeframe. So, it's impossible to create a paradox, like go back and kill your grandfather or whatever. But, open another wormhole too close to the first and potentially you *could* have a paradox. You go down one, back up the other and suddenly you're in the past, even if it's only half a second. Which the universe hates, and it gets round it by closing both wormholes. Happened all the time with the Nuevan wormhole, and it still happens today with the wormholes to Mars and Jupiter. The universe naturally creates the things all the time, and they only last a split second before closing up of their own volition, but if one wanders too close to your own wormhole – poof! There's no way to stop it. But it was never a problem because you lot – and the Martians, and the Joves – both had plenty of spare particles to open another with."

He smiled and opened his hands as if to say, 'got it so far?' Alex anticipated what was expected of him.

"But?" he asked, and Nathan looked pleased.

"But. Say the second wormhole was created *in transit* through the first, at the actual moment of going through. There's a paradox within a paradox. The universe can only deal with this by effectively cutting out a bit of itself and destroying it. Utterly. All the energy contained within that portion of it must be expelled violently."

"Result," Marietta contributed, "something very like a powerful nuclear explosion, a burst of really quite exotic radiation, and to really make its point the universe wipes the links with all entangled particles associated with that particular region of space."

"Which is what happened."

"Textbook."

"To be precise, the textbook we wrote." Nathan pulled a face. "And guess what it turned out Emiliana had been reading?"

Alex stared at the two of them, sitting side by side, both gazing at him like a pair of lecturers with a dim student. Nathan pursed his lips, raised his eyebrows and half turned to his wife.

"I think he's about to make a response to our hypothesis, my love."

"That is bloody ridiculous!" Alex shouted. He leapt to his feet and paced about the lounge. "A *dance student?*"

"Drama and contemporary dance," Nathan corrected him. "Very important distinction."

"And her boyfriend was a physicist," Marietta added, "for that extra touch of verisimilitude."

"A *drama and contemporary dance student* can just pick up your textbook –"

"– and a few conceptuals. The enquiry noted that too."

"– and get hold of all the right equipment and override all the security protocols and... and..."

"Alex, Alex." Marietta stood up and took both his hands, forcing him to slow down. She gazed patiently into his eyes from a distance of thirty centimetres, and Nathan came to stand beside her. "Of course it's ridiculous. It's a complete and utter lie."

"Her involvement, anyway."

"Oh, yes. There's no doubt at all *how* the wormhole was destroyed. Maybe that wasn't what *she* did but someone did it, and set her up."

"Of course, she also died in the explosion."

"Making it hard to call her as a witness."

Alex stared from one face to the other, and the sheer scale of his incomprehension seemed to choke off any coherent words.

"But... you... couldn't..." He forced himself to calm down, took a breath or two and tried again, "Couldn't you say something?"

"We were called as witnesses to the enquiry and we endorsed the account one hundred per cent," said Nathan. "We couldn't do otherwise."

"But the whole Emiliana story…?"

Nathan suddenly couldn't quite meet his eyes. Marietta was made of sterner stuff. She looked right into them.

"May I repeat – someone set her up. Someone with the resources and organisation to do this, and to make it look convincing enough for the Discourse and the enquiry to swallow, and someone who obviously didn't care who lived and died to protect the story: not Emiliana, not the other two hundred and fifty-six people on the ship with her and not everyone who was going to die on Nueva, from Felipe downwards."

"They were *murdered!*"

Suddenly, it was hitting him. While he had thought the wormhole explosion might have been a natural phenomenon, it hadn't been so bad. But now … He felt the anger rising within him. He had to speak slowly, to let it out bit by bit, because otherwise he knew the sheer rage might make him explode.

"Fe… Fel… *Felipe* was *murdered!*"

"Indeed. So, no, Alex, we didn't say a thing about Emiliana, because it wouldn't have made the slightest difference, except to draw the attention of whoever was behind this to the fact that two people in a position to cast doubt on their story were rocking the boat. We kept quiet because we knew the chance would come to make good."

"In forty years, when *Phoenicia* arrived back here."

"Of course, we didn't know it would be you on board."

"But if someone did this," Alex objected, "they must have known *Phoenicia* would return?"

"Dear boy," Nathan said patiently, "I think they were counting on it. And now," he added in a decisive bark, "we need to be getting on. This is the plan; we've already told it to the ship. You, by which I mean Henry, and I have tickets booked on a Mars liner, departing High-Kili in a week's time. We take the elevator to High-Kili, obviously, but from there…"

The plan will not work.

Alex had forgotten the ship could listen in at any time.

He frowned and held up a hand. Nathan didn't notice and continued to chat.

"We get hold of an engineering pod and use that to travel…"

Marietta had to nudge him, and nudge him again, to make him shut up. Eventually he trailed off, seeing from Alex's slightly glazed look that Alex's attention was elsewhere.

"Right…" Alex felt a grin tugging his mouth apart as he turned his attention back to the two old people. "Sorry. The ship says it's analysed the plan you sent, and it's fine in principle, but it's been probing the High-Kili security systems and some of the details need to change."

And how! Just the thought of what the ship wanted sent a thrill through his body. Some of it must have shown on his face because both Nathan's and Marietta's faces suddenly clouded with identical looks of suspicion.

"Change how?" Nathan asked.

Jo STEPPED INTO the dry shower and closed her eyes while the warm jets of scented, astringent powder pummelled her, dissolving grime and invigorating her muscles for a new day. Headspace had assembled a number of stories based on her current topic of interest and she pulled up the first.

Doubts expressed as to integrity of Phoenicia *particles.*

"Play," she sent.

Scientists commissioned to examine the viability of opening a new wormhole to the stranded colony world of La Nueva Temporada have expressed doubt that they will be able to do so with the equipment to hand. A preliminary study of the entangled particles carried on board the ship, which are vital to such an operation, suggests…

"Conclusion," she ordered, and headspace jumped to the end of the piece.

It could be a year or more before we can ascertain whether or not a wormhole could in fact be opened. Link: new proposals for starship Phoenicia *received by Hired Sword.*

Jo let herself linger on the conclusion of the first story for a moment. A year or more, eh? A nice, imprecise length of time to stall and think up fresh excuses?

"Credibility?"

Headspace displayed arguments for and against the first article that gave it approximately 50% credibility, meaning most people either didn't know or didn't care. It was interesting that the arguments for it, which were backed up by reams of scientific data, citations and reports, outweighed the very simple arguments against, which were essentially that quantum entanglement was a very simple business and unless the particles had been prepared by a Nuevan schoolchild whose supervising adult was temporarily distracted, there really shouldn't be any problems.

It did look a lot like the faction saying the wormhole couldn't be opened any time soon were having to shout twice as loud to be convincing.

Did no one else see that? A quick glance at the Discourse suggested that perhaps they did: the problem was, they didn't care.

Even before the wormhole explosion, apparently, before Jo was born, there had been a lot of resentment towards the Nuevans. Their world was seen by much of Earth as a drain on its own resources, and that memory still lingered. Ethnically, too, most Nuevans were of European or Eurasian descent, which also weighed against them. The madnesses of the Committee had just about healed but Europe was still a dustbowl, the worldwide economy had been brought perilously close to the edge and just building *Phoenicia* had been the dictatorship's final, fatal vanity project.

Earth was a comfortable world to live on. It could feed and support itself almost one hundred per cent. Not many people wanted to risk that again.

A small but vocal faction had been in favour of shooting *Phoenicia* down before it entered orbit, and not all of them had been in favour of unloading the sleeping passengers first.

There was no single, killer argument against re-opening the wormhole – but there was a lot of subconscious resentment, background rumour and legacy interest backing it up.

Interesting, Jo thought.

"Play link."

Hired Sword is understood to have received proposals from interested parties for further missions to be undertaken by Phoenicia. *The starship was designed to travel at slower than light speeds to other solar systems to help crews found colonies on other Earth-type planets. The most likely and favoured prospect has been observed in orbit around the star Epsilon Eridani, 10.5 lightyears away –*

"Conclusion."

… the spokesman added: 'Such a venture would be a fitting tribute entirely in keeping with the pioneering spirit of the brave people of La Nueva Temporada.' Next: Hired Sword petitioned to expedite revival of Phoenicia *crew.*

Jo nodded to herself and ordered the shower to end.

"Play," she sent as she climbed out of the cubicle.

The Nuevan Expatriate Association together with representatives of Terran families with members stranded on La Nueva Temporada have petitioned Hired Sword to expedite the unloading and reviving of the crew of Phoenicia. *Facilities at several hospitals in Ken-Tan-Moz are standing by to receive the crew but it is understood none have yet been unloaded from the ship. Association chairman Teódulo Bahamonde.*

The voice changed. After four decades-plus of enforced exile on Earth the new speaker still had a Nuevan accent – rhythmic and with a slight emphasis on its closing syllables.

"Those of us who were stranded on Earth by the wormhole collapse have waited forty-three years for this moment. We do not understand why Hired Sword seems to be dragging its feet over this very simple matter. I address this to all those members of Hired Sword who have families of their own. You can understand how we long to be reunited with our loved ones. Please, Señors, revive the crew so that we can reopen the

wormhole. Nueva's need must be urgent by now. We cannot do this ourselves: that power rests with whoever controls the ship. So, I ask you–

"End," Jo ordered, and the feed fell silent. Yes! She thought. Yes, that's why they'd do it...

Power rests with whoever controls the ship.

"Who lost, financially, as a result of the wormhole closing?"

Headspace showed her the list. At the top were several banks, corporations and others who had had substantial sums invested in La Nueva Temporada, or were owed money by the Nuevan government. The sums of money involved got smaller as the list went on. The individuals who lost out the most were a husband and wife couple called Sulong, who had opened the wormhole in the first place and who got a cut of every transit fee. After them the sums got smaller still until she was just looking at people stranded on Earth with bank accounts back in Altiplano City.

"How many of these debts are still current?"

None. The individuals had received charitable assistance or got jobs and one way or another picked themselves up again. Some corporations had had to retrench, cut back, lay off some divisions. They had all long ago disappeared into the usual whirl of mergers and acquisitions. Remaining debts had simply been wiped by the banks as unreclaimable. La Nueva Temporada had vanished from the financial market.

"Who would gain financially, under known existing arrangements, if the wormhole reopened tomorrow?"

Absolutely no one.

Jo slowly, thoughtfully stepped into her clothes and let them climb up around her. As they pulled themselves together she went back to the Discourse.

"Query: assuming crew of *Phoenicia* are revived, will they be allowed to reopen the wormhole?"

The Discourse reckoned that if the matter were decided by a simple majority vote, here and now, the answer would probably be yes, based on sheer sentiment and because it was possible. It also suggested that a powerful vocal minority could sway the voters' feelings to say no.

One more question for headspace:

"Why didn't the Nuevans just come out of longsleep in deep space and open the other end of the wormhole while they were still a safe distance away from Earth? Or even, why not just open it back home and then tow the terminus out here?"

The problem (with a link to a textbook written by the Sulong couple) was one of basic supradimensional engineering. If the two ends of a wormhole moved apart too quickly, the connection was lost. To keep the wormhole open, *Phoenicia* would have had to travel so slowly that the voyage would have taken ten times as long. And opening it in deep space would require more complicated and expensive travel to and fro to close the gap, losing the financial advantages of having it in orbit.

As Jo pulled her shoes on she thought back to Planetary Director Tomás Mateo, father of Alejandro, who had made that impassioned speech that the ship had broadcast ahead, appealing to the better natures of the peoples of Earth. He would know exactly how badly La Nueva Temporada need the wormhole open, and he would surely have worked out everything Jo had just got from headspace. It wouldn't have failed to occur to him that whoever controlled the ship, and the wormhole terminus with it, held the fate of La Nueva Temporada in the palm of their hand.

So he would do everything in his power to see that that control rested with someone he knew and trusted, and that did *not* mean the Terrans.

She was fully dressed now. Her door opened as she strode out into the corridor, thinking ahead in headspace.

"I want access to the ghost files."

CHAPTER 18

A VISION FOR NUEVA

KEN-TAN-MOZ rose like a solid wall out of the sea as *Saucy Sue* cruised in from the east. Sunrise washed rosy light across ranks of gleaming skyscrapers that stretched quite literally from horizon to horizon, and in headspace the megalopolis glowed and thrummed with the public streams of data from its millions of inhabitants. Standing at the front of the lounge bubble, Alex stood and quite frankly gaped. Ken-Tan-Moz made Altiplano City look like a small village.

He heard the now familiar shuffling sound of two pairs of feet on the deck behind him, and muttered bickering.

"Go on, then, tell him."

"I'll tell him when I'm ready, woman! Stop nagging me."

"Oh, just stop playing around or I'll say it for you..."

Alex maintained the discreet fiction that he couldn't hear them until Marietta called his name and he turned with a look of polite, neutral interest. Marietta's smile was nervous, darting between him and her husband. Nathan's glare was like thunder.

"I'll do it," he said tightly, "because I don't have a choice and neither does Nueva and it's the only way the ship thinks will work, but by God you're straining our friendship!"

It wasn't just anger, Alex realised, it was hurt – the feeling that trust had been betrayed.

"I'm an old man, hadn't you noticed? Or, to lay the blame where I suspect it's due, hadn't your father noticed? You have no right… you have *no right* to be asking that when you know I'll say yes!"

Marietta took his hand, stroking it; he yanked it away angrily.

Possible answers flashed through Alex's head. "*If there was any other way…*", "*I'm in this too, you know…*"

"Thanks," he said simply. "Thank you."

"Go to hell," the old man muttered, and turned abruptly back to the stairs. Marietta watched him go, then turned back to Alex.

"He certainly isn't as young as he was," she pointed out mildly.

"The ship's seen his medical records." Alex did feel guilty at what he was asking of an old man, but he had trusted his own body to the ship's tender care and it had looked after him. It had a reasonable idea of what the human frame could take. "It says he can do it."

She came forward, turned him back to the view.

"So what do you think of our little city?"

He shook his head, eyes back on the skyscrapers.

"It's… it's…"

"I know," she agreed. "Ghastly, isn't it? Nothing but people everywhere."

"It's…" Alex wasn't sure what the word was but it certainly wasn't 'ghastly'. Maybe terrifying, but only at first; only because the mind first rejects unfamiliarity wholesale, then gradually lets it back in again bit by bit.

Headspace told him that this was Mombasa District, the city's main port. It gave him an elevated view, as if he was flying in at a height of a few hundred metres rather than sea level. After the harbour, which looked big enough to take all of Alti, the grids of buildings continued inland for tens of kilometres, further than the unaided human eye could see. They reminded Alex of an old-style electronics chip. He couldn't see a single tower of less than a hundred stories, which was eighty higher than Alti's tallest building. In fact each tower probably held more people than the total population of his world's capital. The whole city held many more people than all the Nuevans put together. Earth could afford to lose a chunk of people the size of La Nueva Temporada and not even notice. It might even breathe a sigh of relief.

It was something Altiplano City could only dream of aspiring to and for precisely that reason Alex was seized by the determination to make it happen. There was plenty of land around the Altiplano plateau. Plenty of room to grow...

Saucy Sue was heading for a break in the wall, and as it drew closer Alex could start to see that the wall wasn't that solid. There were gaps between the buildings: large ones, too. Boulevards, parks, wide avenues. Once you realised that then you really started to appreciate the scale.

They were no longer alone on the ocean. Without moving his head or consulting headspace, Alex could see three other ekranoplans; seven or eight smaller ships that bounced on the blue waves, propelled by kites or sails or wind foils that spun sedately on deck; a couple of tankers; and any number of sailing dinghies. He had now spent several days on a world of many billions of people, and the number of them that he had seen in the flesh was precisely two. Occasionally there had been the odd ship on the horizon, a passing ekranoplan, an aircraft passing far overhead – but no *people*. It was a strange feeling to think that he was now going to be thrust into the middle of millions of them – and, if all went to plan, he would barely have time to take it in. He resolved to pay attention while it lasted.

Saucy Sue had already exchanged protocols with the harbour's defence systems. The Gerontocracy of the Glorious Crown was in good standing with Ken-Tan-Moz and so the ekranoplan was allowed to approach and pass through its territory. It barely slowed down as it headed down a wide channel. Headspace showed it keeping to a precisely defined virtual highway that extended across the harbour and then onto dry land. Alex watched the approaching shoreline with only a little trepidation. A blackbox had piloted *Phoenicia* and kept him alive all the way to Earth: it wasn't too hard to trust that the blackbox in charge of *Saucy Sue* could do its job too. Still, it wasn't an entirely pleasant feeling to watch the shore approaching at such a speed. But then they were over it and there was only a slight lurch as *Saucy Sue*'s air cushion boosted them up a few metres, adjusting to the new level of ground beneath it. Now the ekranoplan was barrelling down the kranway, a smooth concrete apron 500 metres wide that led through the city and out to the plains beyond. It was lined on either side by those serried ranks of skyscrapers.

Alex continued to gaze in awe. They merged with a whole stream of ekranoplans and fast travelling groundcars heading out of the city, passing another stream heading in. Pleasure craft, freight vehicles, small family units, business travellers. The side streets were a-crawl with lines of groundcars, some hovering, some wheeled; and above all there were people, *people* everywhere, all with their own lives and purposes, not one of them aware that they lived in what Alex considered to be a marvel of the universe.

"If our wormhole had been angled more towards Earth like yours was... if the pulse had hit here..." Marietta sucked in her cheeks thoughtfully. "All this would just be big lumps of foamcast. Civilisation is a transient thing, Alex."

It took about ten minutes to pass through Ken-Tan-Moz, and the great buildings whipped by too quickly for Alex to take anything really in. Headspace revealed much more information than the eye could see but even those glimpses were fleeting – not so much because they passed quickly but because they were so quickly superseded by the next fascinating datastream, and then the next, and then the one after. Alex felt like a five-year-old again, constantly grasping for the next shiny distraction. But all good things come to an end and it wasn't long before *Saucy Sue* was zipping through the suburbs.

Alex looked mournfully back through the lounge canopy at the receding megalopolis. The towers were sinking as *Saucy Sue* carried him away: the ground was reclaiming the vision it had offered him.

Marietta seemed to have read his mind.

"You don't want Altiplano to end up like that place. Too big, no soul. If you really want inspiration for Nueva, look around you."

So Alex looked. Beyond the city the kranway was a concrete channel through an endless vista of crops, rocky crags that glowed under the baking sun, and soil so red the ground seemed to bleed. At first it didn't seem much, not after the vision that was Ken-Tan-Moz. But it did look familiar… and now he came to think of it, it was very like the plains around the Altiplano – or how they could be, once his native planet had thawed a bit.

For hundreds of kilometres in all directions, this was the breadbasket of Ken-Tan-Moz. The city had to eat. Endless fields of wheat, sunflower and maize stretched into the shimmering distance beneath a sky of purest blue and clouds of pristine white, but it was dotted with much smaller pockets whose boundaries only showed up in headspace – mini- and micro-clans of farmers, twenty or thirty of them already in the space between horizons, making Alex wonder how many must be dotted throughout the whole continent. The datastreams over them all flowed in one direction, back to the city on the coast.

As a vision for Nueva it was inspiring. A world of warmth and plentiful food where a good day's work guaranteed a reward, whether you wanted to be small and independent or part of a larger whole. He was dimly aware that Earth had taken a long time to get to this point but it was a point worth getting to.

But none of this would come to pass if his mission failed, and for that they first needed to get to their destination. He wandered to the front of the lounge and peered into the distance.

Headspace showed it at once, of course – the elevator cable slicing down from the sky, lost to the naked eye in the blue haze. Its endpoint was still below the horizon but as the journey went on it began to appear. Shades of grey and white, hard rock thrusting up out of the soil, each successive view as it grew closer making it seem further away because you realised how big it was, how much detail you were taking in. It was the triple cone of Kilimanjaro, 6000 metres high and the terminus of the elevator that would take him up to High-Kili and his ship.

Alex studied the great mountain with interest as they drew near. The station at the Earth end of the cable, Uhuru, was at the top of the highest of the extinct volcano's three peaks. Puerto Bajo back home was buried within the Altiplano plateau, but Uhuru here clung to the peak of the mountain. It seemed strange to see the massive buttressing and the workings exposed, like Puerto Bajo turned inside out. Above it, the elevator cable shone like a pencil-thin laser beaming up into space.

A flicker of movement in the sky caught Alex's eye further up. An elevator car was sliding down the cable at landing speed. In a moment it had disappeared into the terminal. He wondered if that was the car he would be taking back up again.

Saucy Sue was slowing down and a town was growing up around them again. Blackbox traffic control guided the ekranoplan to a parking area, a designated spot on a wide concrete field dotted with other vessels like it, some barely visible because the superheated air shimmered so. It slowed and extended wheels, touching down on the concrete with barely a jar and coasting to a stop precisely in its allocated position. The wings folded into the hull, the engines whirred into silence and Alex finally felt that he had arrived somewhere.

The three passengers assembled by the hatch. It was the first time Alex had seen Nathan since being told to go to hell, and the old man so pointedly didn't refer to the conversation that Alex knew he still wasn't forgiven.

"Ready?" Nathan asked, one hand poised over the headspace control.

No, Alex wanted to say, *I feel about as unready as you can get*. It wasn't just an attack of nerves, or fear of discovery. He shouldn't stand out in a crowd – they had cruised in circles around the Indian Ocean until the yellow had flushed from his system and his hair was growing back. His head already itched with the dark shadow of a new thatch.

"I feel naked," he protested. Perhaps it was an exaggeration but he did feel distinctly under-dressed for the outside. He *felt* that he ought to be freezing.

"You'll get used to it. Hat?"

Marietta had given him a hat to wear, which seemed unnecessarily floppy and bohemian – something only an artist would wear, or maybe it was just normal everyday Terran headgear for any gender. The other two were both wearing something similar and Alex was struck by an even worse fear than public nakedness: that he was wearing an *old person's* hat.

They each slipped a pair of dark glasses on and then light and heat flooded into the ekranoplan as Nathan told the hatch to open. Alex actually cried out as a furnace blast of air hit him in the face.

"It's only heat, boy."

"You're human. You evolved in weather like this."

"And if you could look a little more like our great grandson who's only ever lived in the tropics and a little less like a Nuevan ingénue who's never experienced anything above five degrees, that would be good."

"But try not to say anything because you'll sound Nuevan the moment your mouth starts flapping."

Saucy Sue extruded some steps and with his godparents' encouraging badinage at his back, Alex finally made his official landfall on Earth beneath a blazing sun. Heat actually bounced back up at him from the ground. He stood on the concrete with slightly shaky legs and breathed deep. He could feel the warmth of the air as it was sucked into his lungs, heating him up from inside. His skin felt like it was glowing in the sunlight.

He had known it would be hot, of course. It was just a heat that was so outside his experience it was something he could never have expected. This was the first time he had been outdoors in daylight since arriving on Earth. The polarised canopy of *Saucy Sue's* lounge had reduced the sun of the equator to something that, yes, was obviously *warm*, but not... not... *this*.

He looked back up at the old couple. Mindful of their remarks about his accent, he used headspace to send instead.

"*This is what Earth's like?*"

"*Just the middle bits,*" was Nathan's answer.

"*Do you see why we didn't visit Nueva that often?*" Marietta added.

"*I finally understand my parents' generation. They want to make us like this.*" Grinning, Alex held out his hands to indicate the sheer perfection of the weather.

Nathan patted him on the shoulder as they came down the steps. With his other hand he was carrying the red particle case that Alex had taken from the lifepod. Through the shimmer Alex could see a taxi approaching.

"This way," was all Nathan said.

THE TAXI CARRIED them to the station of the funicular railway that led up to Uhuru – a brief but welcome relapse into air conditioned comfort – and they took their leave of Marietta in the shadow of Kilimanjaro's mighty peak. Nathan suddenly made himself busy checking the readout on the red particles box, so Marietta moved over to Alex, and took his hands in both of hers and gave him a peck on each cheek.

"You can do this," she said.

Then she moved back to Nathan, who had run out of readings to make. There was no hand-holding. The two stood a close distance apart and looked at each other. Their looks were cool, resigned, appraising.

"We're mad," Marietta said.

"At least one of us is stark staring raving," he agreed. "Come, boy."

He walked away without a backward glance.

It was a short walk into the station. Alex forced himself to think like an engineer, keeping his eyes fixed on the approaching terminal, ignoring the people around him and not making contact with anyone as they passed without effort through security and onto the train. He would have loved to press his face to the window and watch the unfurling view as the carriage climbed the mountain, but Henry Sulong would probably not have done that and so Alex Mateo did not either.

Their tickets were confirmed to Mars; their headspace tags said it was to attend a funeral. Therefore, Alex and Nathan hoped, no one would try too hard to get them into conversation, and the ruse seemed to work as no one did. Their tickets were handled by the blackboxes without human intervention; Marietta and Nathan's forgeries stood up perfectly, and everything went as smoothly as it possibly could. Alex found he took great comfort from Nathan's slow but steady company. The old man simply plodded on as if he had every right to be here – which of course he did – and Alex followed in his wake, automatically assuming the pose of a slightly embarrassed grandchild. The only time he truly felt nervous was crossing the departures hall of Uhuru. The polished stone of the floor seemed to stretch into the distance for kilometres and Alex felt as exposed as a nudist on top of the Altiplano plateau, but he was completely ignored, and after that it was much easier to breeze innocently through the security checks, where the red particles box was scanned and classified as electronic equipment, non-interactive and non-explosive, so no danger to anyone, which was all technically true. Then they could take their places in the departures lounge and while away the couple of hours it would still take before boarding by watching vids, eating and drinking a little, and saying not much at all.

When they finally got on board the elevator car was almost a clone of the ones Alex knew from home – streamlined like a teardrop, three passenger decks with circles of seats facing inwards and outwards, and a panoramic view out of the windows. In fact, barring a few modifications and updates, it was almost exactly the same, built by the same company as the ones Alex remembered arriving at Puerto Alto when he was a boy. His mother had been very pleased with the purchase from Earth – faster, smoother, greater passenger and cargo capacity than before. Back then she had been expecting them to last their natural lifetime and, by the time they needed upgrading, they would be replaced by cars built on Nueva. He doubted that had happened.

At long last, the car rose above the level of the terminal like a very slow take off. Alex often wondered what it would be like to be blasted into orbit, like everyone had been for the first decades of space travel. Exhilarating, probably; noisy, certainly; and bloody expensive. This was smooth and they barely seemed to move until Alex looked out of the window. The view over Kilimanjaro and beyond was spectacular.

He closed his eyes and breathed out. This was commitment, the point of no return. He had a sudden image of himself walking down an ever-narrowing corridor. He had come here on a starship that could have taken him anywhere in space. After splashing down, he had had the entirety of Earth to play in. Then he had chosen to come to Kilimanjaro, and his horizons had been encompassed by the terminal and now the elevator. Always, at each stage, less and less freedom of movement, fewer and fewer options. Ultimately he would have no options at all except to follow the plan.

Well, it was what he had chosen.

Nathan stood up slowly.

"See you in a few hours."

"Where are you going?"

"To the bar, boy, to get as drunk as I possibly can in the time remaining."

Alex shot to his feet. "What! But..." he blurted, then looked around and drew Nathan closer to him. "You can't do this when you're drunk!" he hissed.

"Oh, believe me," Nathan said, still glaring dislike at him, "I'll be well sober by the time I have to do anything."

"But..." Alex moaned, but he didn't dare make a scene.

"Come and join me? Sorry I can't lay on any dancing girls with it..."

"I'm fine," Alex snapped, "thanks." He retired to his seat to see what the in-flight entertainment had to offer for the next eight hours.

A woman walked up and plonked herself down beside him.

"Mr Mateo? Sergeant Jo Odembo, Orbital Police Force, High-Kili." Identification glowed briefly in the palm of her hand. "I think we should talk." She glanced across the cabin. "And perhaps you'd like to join us, Dr Sulong?"

CHAPTER 19

LIFT UP

Jo HAD SPENT a long time thinking how to handle this. Eventually she had decided on the completely calm, matter of fact approach. She wasn't arresting anyone. She wasn't even sure what crime had been committed. Yes, Mateo was travelling under a false identity and has passed through the territory of several clans that way, but that was probably a matter for the Ken-Tan-Moz authorities. On board the elevator, they were in her jurisdiction. So, she would keep it quiet. There wasn't exactly anywhere the two putative miscreants could run to.

They sat at a circular table on the lounge deck, deck two. It had subdued lighting and a few other passengers sat around. She had bought soft drinks for herself and Mateo: he was over-age by Nuevan laws but under by local Terran ones. Dr Sulong had something much stronger.

Now the old man raised his glass in salute.

"Very clever," he said.

"Why, thank you. It was ghosts that did it," Jo answered. "Well, that clinched it. There were all these little bits and pieces that didn't *quite* work…"

She felt a sudden need to explain this to someone. Handled right, it should be an enormous career coup and not do her promotion prospects any harm at all – but still, the scale of the accomplishment would be lost in the flat anonymity of her report.

"Make a note of that, Alex." Sulong gave the boy a nudge. "Tell your father, didn't *quite* work."

Mateo still didn't say anything. He was just toying with his drink in his hands, and when from time to time he glanced at her she only saw a dark wound behind his eyes. The Alejandro Mateo in the datafile from *Phoenicia* was younger, more innocent than this one, and the dark, wavy hair had made him look younger still. This one had dark stubble on his head like a convict and he had seen the wormhole explosion and the deaths of loved ones.

But, finally, he did speak. He lifted those dark eyes up and asked:

"Ghosts?"

"That's what we call them. You know – suspected space objects that turn out to be electronic illusions or forgotten satellites." On one occasion a particularly big ghost had been the entire contents of one of High-Kili's septic tanks, accidentally ejected and freeze-dried into a solid mass in space. One job of the orbital authorities was to protect Earth from space debris and the ghosts could almost have been invented by God to make their job harder.

She smiled, to reassure him, and he simply looked away again. She kept talking.

"I did a search on any ghosts that had apparently come in on the same vector as *Phoenicia*. And guess what? There was one. Non-massive, non-metallic, barely enough to register on radar or mass detector... so they ignored it. They didn't think it was going to do any harm. And here you are."

He slowly turned his glass around 180 degrees, studying it as if it was a complex engineering problem.

"And do you think I'm going to do any harm?"

She half laughed, half snorted and waved a hand around to indicate the almost empty bar. "As you can see, I'm surrounded by armed back-up. No, I don't think you're dangerous. But you are what we would call an illegal immigrant."

His face stayed expressionless.

"I do understand your plan," she said. "I think I do. You had to be sure the mission wasn't compromised, right? Just in case we did something to take it over, you – the master – had to be safe and able to give your ship overriding orders?"

He made a strange gesture that was something between a shrug and a nod.

"They thought there was a good chance *Phoenicia* would be boarded by you lot before we were within range to open the wormhole," he said. "So they sent me on ahead."

"Just in case."

"Just in case." He looked moodily at his hands.

"But if the ship just sent you, alone, that would look *so* suspicious. So it claimed you had died, along with three others, to make it look more statistically likely. I'm guessing they never even got on board in the first place."

The faintest ghost of a smile flickered around his mouth. "Weren't going to kill them, were we? No, they're safely back on Nueva, growing old."

"But you chose the three who had no relatives here to miss them. If you'd mixed it up a bit I might not have got suspicious."

That shrugging gesture again. "Wasn't my plan."

"Well..." Impulsively she reached over and squeezed his hand. He looked down at it with an abstract curiosity and she took her hand away again. "I'm on your side here, Alejandro –"

"Alex."

"I'm sorry, Alex. I don't want your world to freeze or starve. I understand there's... um..."

"Resistance?" Sulong offered.

"... *resistance* to a new wormhole, but that doesn't bother me. But I hope you realise why I couldn't just leave you running around Earth on your own. We have to do this properly."

Another shrug/nod.

"I am curious," she added. "What were you going to do when you got to High-Kili?"

Now he looked up at her again.

"Get in touch with my ship," he said innocently.

"It might not have been that easy."

He smiled, faintly. "It got me this far."

There was the slightest hint of mockery there as well. Jo told headspace to shunt the conversation up to High-Kili for voice stress analysis. If he was hiding anything... well, she might not be able to tell what, but she would know there was something.

A second later, she cancelled the instruction. Of course the kid was hiding something. He must have about ten thousand secrets. She didn't need voice stress to tell her that. It was up to her to work out if any of them were relevant.

But, would he have been able to lie low on High-Kili, aided only by the ship's remarkably easy way with the Terran systems? Maybe he would.

"Yes, it did," she agreed. "Your ship's an amazing piece of work. It was a real honour to go on board. When I thought how far it had come... forty years of cold and dark–"

He looked at her sharply, for the first time a flash of emotion in those wounded eyes.

"You've been on board?"

"I have. She's..." Jo shrugged. "Beautiful. It was a real privilege." She gave a twisted smile. "And for the record, you've probably guessed I'm not one of the Terrans who wants to shoot her down."

"Uh-huh," he said again. Another slight smile, warmer than before. So this is how you get to him, she thought; talk about his ship. But then, he is a boy.

"And you – you Nuevans – you did a... a *fantastic* job in getting her out of storage and ready for the trip here, so quickly," she added. The praise was genuine.

He really did smile. With one corner of his mouth. "She was already out of mothballs. We were prepping her for a new voyage anyway."

"I read about how you ended up on this mission." Another flash from those dark eyes – resentment at her prying? Well, it was all publicly accessible thanks to his ship. "What were you going to do before that?"

A pause. She was digging into personal information that wasn't in headspace: if she was going to find out, he had to want to tell her.

"I was about to take my engineering diploma. There's a project I wanted to join – diverting the equatorial sea currents so they flow around our continent and warm it up. That's what I wanted to do – keep working on the Thaw. Make Nueva somewhere worth being." He snorted. "Until the explosion changed my plans."

She nodded. She had seen those recordings too. "It must have been terrible for you. It didn't affect us much at all–"

"Well, it affected every single one of us." His voice was suddenly sharp and bitter. "My brother was killed."

The last word hung between them like an accusation, as if it were her fault.

"So I gathered." She said it simply. What more could she say about the death of a brother she had never heard of, of someone she had only just met? "I really am sorry."

"Well..." He seemed suddenly nonplussed, maybe a little embarrassed at taking his bitterness out on a complete stranger. "Wasn't anything to do with you."

"Even so." She bit her lip and spent the next minute taking a little too much care about sipping her drink. Eventually she spoke again. "Do you have anyone else back home? Any other family?" She could ask headspace but she wanted to take every opportunity to encourage him to open up.

"Just my mother and father and br–"

He stopped, with a look of complete astonishment stamped on his face. "My brother," he finished. "My *other* brother."

Sulong looked almost as surprised as Alex.

"You have another brother?"

"Well, he's my..." Alex shook his head as if to clear it. "Never mind what he is. Uh, yeah. Maria had him on the night of the explosion. Quinito. It's..." He tapped his head. "Not long ago enough for long-term memory. It was in the conceptual but I never had a reason to go down that route so... Yeah. Apparently

I have another brother, who will now be in – wow – his early forties. He's also my godson."

"Ah, another godfather!" Sulong raised his glass in salute. "To a worthy breed. I hope you read the baptismal vows carefully, boy. They're very big on renouncing the devil and all his works but apparently there's a whole lot of small print I failed to notice about helping your godson to open wormholes."

"To brothers!" Jo said, spontaneously. Alex gave a sheepish, one-sided grin and all three of them clinked their glasses together.

"Of course, that'll make all the difference," Sulong put in. "I mean, once they hear Alex has a brother they're bound to let us open the wormhole." He looked at Jo with an old man's eyes that had not a shred of good humour in them. "Wouldn't you agree, Sergeant?"

And Jo felt the pall settle right back down on the three of them again.

"We will get to High-Kili," she said distinctly, "and what will happen will happen."

PART 4
SAGA OF THE EXILE

CHAPTER 20

THE LAIR OF A MAD SPIDER

Quin is 23

AH, PUERTO ALTO! What superlatives shall I best employ to extol my home for the next eight years after my fall from grace?

It was... warm.

And...

Do you know, I believe I've plumbed the benefits of Puerto Alto, that barren, miserable, godforsaken, vacuum-parched, *boring* rock in the sky. I wasn't even kept busy, to take my mind off my misery. At the time, the small Ministry of Supply office was there to oversee the trickle of goods into and out of the port, and its demands were not great. The facility was only kept in operation to service our satellites, do a bit of weather observation, and a handful of other things that are easier to do from a height of 35,000 kilometres. And so, it supported a small clutch of scientists and engineers and technicians who scuttled about in the shadows of the empty docking cradles and cargo bays, the lounges for departure and immigration – all the legacies of the days when the place bustled with thousands of passengers, tens of thousands of tons of goods coming through in a month, and Puerto Alto was Nueva's gateway to space.

Before the Event there had been elevators in either direction every twelve hours. Now the frequency was one a week. You went up to Puerto Alto, and there you stayed for at least the next seven days with as much to occupy your mind as a musgovore during one of Father Adolfo's sermons.

Eight years! Eight years of not even being able to have a decent shower in hot water – though it was a good way of hoarding energy credits to splurge when you hit Alti on leave. But meanwhile, everyone up there stays clean by blasting their bodies with dry grit and inevitably they become a bit dry and powdery themselves. Some of them would blow away if you turned the aircon up a fraction.

The carousel gives the appearance of gravity and stops the calcium leaching from your bones, but because you're basically standing on the inside of a giant spinning wheel, your feet are moving slightly faster than your head and after a while you need one of a variety of pills to stop the feeling that you're about to fall over. That's along with side-effects that can include wind, water retention, appetite loss, constipation or rashes, depending on which of the main ingredients you're most allergic to. All it needs is loss of sex drive to round off the bill of fare. That actually wasn't a side-effect, though I found myself wishing it was as month piled on celibate month. The port facility operated on a skeleton staff and most of them were already married or just shacked up for sheer companionship. The opportunities offered by Alti for casual liaison were a fond memory and my new rank had nowhere near the pulling power of the old.

The pastel colours of the décor, the comfortable feeling of space in the safely enclosed cabins in the living quarters, the smooth organic curves of the layout – it's all designed to make humans feel at home. But the hum of the air conditioning forever hangs in the background like a subtle tinnitus, and just as you're convincing yourself this is normal, something happens – a glimpse of an upwardly curved corridor, a gust of stale air from a vent, a pixelated flicker across a breathtaking ocean view that you've been admiring out of a fake window – and you remember that it's all illusion, you're stuck on an asteroid, and there's nothing you can do about it.

Eventually a visitor came to my office and saved my sanity.

"I've been wanting to meet you," she said.

No knock-knock, no how do you do, Señor Mateo. I was trying to find some statistics interesting. My brain was jellifying under the relentless scrolling of columns of figures; my reactions were slow and my social graces non-existent. I managed to glance up for a second and take in the fact that she was obviously a local – her hair was cut short to go inside a helmet, and the typically slim spacer physique was made positively gaunt by the dried-up scrawniness that seems to afflict some women of a certain age. Then the deadweight gravitational attraction of the numbers drew my concentration away again.

"Can I help you?" I grunted, or something equally dismissive.

"I've been wanting to meet you," she said again. "I believe you knew my ex-husband."

"Really." I couldn't think of any close contacts who might have been married to a woman of her, ahem, seniority. "And who was he?" If I could get a name then I could deny knowing anyone and hopefully she would go away.

"Tomás Mateo."

Well, *duh!* It got my attention and years of good breeding finally made themselves felt. I stood up to greet her.

Of course, I had known Linda Hahn was on Puerto Alto. The woman was a legend. For crying out loud, she had been in charge up here during the Event, twenty-three years ago. The port had taken the brunt of the wormhole's outburst and she had driven her crew for days on end without sleep to get it back up and running again. She had been one tough lady.

But I had had exactly no desire to meet her. She was Alejandro and Felipe's mother, not mine. I had been complicit in the death of her husband. Ex-husband. It would still be awkward. So, though I had already had several invitations from the Port Administrator to meet up, I had never replied to any of them.

"How do you do," I said. Maybe I still didn't want to talk to her but there was a sudden, strange masochistic interest in comparing and contrasting her with my own mother. The known set of women who had married Tomás Mateo had suddenly expanded by one hundred per cent. It meant a lot more data to work with.

"Since you're not responding to invites," she said. "I thought I'd come down and do it personally. Anyone else I wouldn't bother, but I thought meeting you would be interesting."

"Why?" I said through gritted teeth. "Because of our mutual acquaintance?" If she was going to get heavy on me for what had happened, she was getting a smack in the face and I didn't care how old she was.

"No," she said thoughtfully. She put her head on one side and regarded me analytically. "It's because they usually give your job to someone who's waiting for his pension or who's fouled up somehow, but I don't think I've ever met someone whose career has made it so effortlessly far up shit creek as yours." She straightened up. "Look, Mateo, we're going to have to work with each other and there's something I really need to ask you. About work. But first, let me just show you around. You're going to have to get used to living here and I know the short cuts. Let me show you the ropes and get you dinner. Unless you have other plans?"

I looked down at the figures. I looked up at her. Never mind who she was – she was the first human being to reach out to me since I managed to get my father killed and I suddenly realised how badly I just wanted simple, one-to-one company.

"No," I said. The full weight of the truth came slowly crashing down on me as I said it. It was true now and it was true for the rest of my foreseeable life. "No, I have no plans."

AND YES, OKAY, it was quite interesting. She knew the ins and outs, the nooks and crannies of her little domain, and she was so obviously proud of the place that she could make it attractive to other people too. I learned things I had never previously suspected.

Like, the fact that Puerto Alto was armed.

Of course, I knew it had small scale, high precision lasers to protect the elevator cable and cars from space debris. A full-blown military installation was something else.

"Just in case," she said. The control blister was a transparent module clinging to the surface of the asteroid. Outside I could see the prisms and cables and barrels of the giant laser. We were outside the carousel so we were in freefall – I was getting used to the strange feeling of an exo guiding my movements and keeping me steady.

"There was no way of knowing who was coming through a wormhole until they got here," she said. "In principle, especially in the early days, anyone could have come through at any time, done an emergency landing down below, set up their own little colony."

"You've been here a very long while," I commented, as we made our way back through the hatch into the rock.

"I do go down to the surface from time to time," she said.

"Yes, but... I mean, you were in charge here twenty-three years ago – why are you still here now?"

And – oh, God – she gave me the look my father would give when someone had said something silly. I wondered which of them had learned it off the other.

Yes, I could probably have worked it out for myself. She had one surviving child, and if he ever came back to her, it would be through a new wormhole. Up here, she would be the first to know about it.

AND SHE SHOWED me how, up in Port Control – another of those empty caverns where the ghosts of the glory days clung obstinately on. She led me over to one particular console.

It was nothing special – just a simple display – but the single seat was worn as if someone spent a lot of time sitting here. Data was scrolling across the display and, when she touched a control, a small, repetitive beep sounded.

"Telemetry from *Phoenicia*," she said. She pointed at one part of the display. "Twelve light years out." The finger moved to another area – a list of names, each followed by a row of statistics. "So, twelve years ago, Alex was alive and well."

It took me a moment to work out: Alex – Alejandro. But of course. Alex is a perfectly good contraction of my brother's name, for hijo or segunda; but I had only ever heard hijos talk about him until now and they invariably used the full version just to eliminate any doubt.

Alive and well – that could be one way to describe longsleep, I thought, but it wouldn't be my choice. Nanogen-laced preservative coursing through his veins in lieu of blood and lymph fluid; his brain patterns constantly rewritten from the backup taken before he left. My brother was the output of a machine. He was alive because the ship said he was: otherwise, he was just so much lightly-warmed meat.

"Are you hungry?" she asked.

"MY PARENTS WERE one of the first to come through the wormhole," she said over lunch. The Puerto Alto lunch shift was one of the few times you could feel part of a crowd, as humanity in all its shapes and sizes and odours descended on the canteen. One thing I can say for Puerto Alto – see, something else nice! – is that it's a meritocracy, pure and simple, and the divisions between hijos and segundas just aren't there. "The Sons of Castille wanted an orbital port and an elevator for their new world and they weren't afraid to hire in expertise if they didn't have it themselves – like, experienced orbital engineers, which is the Hahns for generations back, or like the Sulongs to open the wormhole for them in the first place. But they didn't *approve* of us, oh dear me, no. You should have seen the raised eyebrows Tomás got when he took me home."

"What got you together?" I asked, curious despite myself.

"For me? He could be funny, he could make me laugh..."

I took a moment to recall that we were talking about the same Tomás Mateo.

"... and for him... well, he was quite the rebel when he was young. He got such a thrill from shocking his parents. He hit the roof when he learned about Feli and Alex buying up the ship, but I wanted to ask him what he expected. Had he never heard of DNA?"

I really didn't know what to say.

"So you got married to upset his parents?" I asked.

"No." She made a dismissive gesture. "We got married because we were both too full of our grand schemes and we actually thought it would work. He had great plans for turning Rio Lento into the richest estate on Nueva. I had taken over Puerto Alto from my parents and it was opening up into a real port. Put those two together and it was like a union of earth and sky. The unstoppable Mateos, rulers of all we surveyed!"

She was smiling, and it was genuine. Broken dreams can so easily become full of bitterness but she really seemed to find it funny.

I felt safe enough to ask: "what happened?"

"What happened? Our good friends R. Lento and P. Alto got in the way. We both realised we would far rather spend time with them than with each other. And with me up here, him down there, we never really got a chance to talk through our differences and we were both too stuck up and proud to be the one who went to the other. I could never see why he couldn't just unwind a bit and admit he was wrong." She gave me a roguish smile. "And I'm sure he thought the same of me. It was all very clean and civilised – we just didn't renew the marriage."

We ate quietly for a while.

"What was it you wanted to ask me?" I said a few minutes later, to break the silence, remembering our first conversation.

"Good question." She mopped up her soup decisively and pushed her chair back. "Ever been Outside?"

I HAD NEVER been Outside. I had no desire to go Outside. The vacuum of space was just one more example to me of what a good idea planets are.

We actually weren't *that* much Outside. She took me out of the carousel again and down to an airlock in the depths of the asteroid

– a small chamber hacked out of the bare stone. All I could see the other side of the membrane was blackness. For the first time ever I put a pressure suit on, still nervous as the exo guided my movements, but I felt comforted and enclosed as the suit sealed itself around me. Depending on your preference, you could set the helmet for anything from 360 degree panoramic view – for those who really like open spaces, I suppose – to a tunnel, dead-ahead view with all peripheral vision ruthlessly cut out. I chose the latter.

Hahn touched a control on my sleeve and the view reverted to the former.

"I need you to see it all," she said.

We pushed through the membrane into a wider chamber. Much wider. Lights mounted on our shoulders and helmets threw circles over a rock surface a hundred metres away. It was faceted in large, smooth planes, which told me this wasn't a natural hollow – it had been cut out, probably for raw material, but never filled in again with habitat. To our left, an oval opening led directly out into space. One quarter of it was filled with the curve of Nueva below us, but the planetlight only made it partway into the cave before the sill blocked it out. The rest of our surroundings was in pitch black shadow, until Hahn operated a control and the cavern slowly lit up.

"What," she said, "is this lot?"

We were in the lair of a mad spider. The walls of the cavern were thick with crates and containers, all securely lashed down with restraint webbing.

I whistled. I had no idea what it all was, but it was a stockpile of something, and that alone made it unusual. Nothing was just left lying around on Nueva. Everything was meant to be serving a purpose.

I was obviously expected to take a closer look, so I obliged. I read the label of the nearest box – an anonymous, blank container the height of a man.

"0570-Y reaction nozzles," I said.

"Try another," she suggested. I moved along to something much larger, the size of a couple of habs.

"8519-G ablation plating?"

"You getting it yet? No? Spare yourself the trouble," she said, and handed me a tablet. I took it from her and scrolled the list. Items like ablation plating and reaction nozzles, I recognised. Others were more abstruse. I had no idea what a primary drift compensator was, or a tubular dampening buffer latch, but the overall idea was quite clear.

"Spare parts..." I said.

"A lot of spare parts," she agreed. "Enough to build several spaceships. But check the origin."

I checked. I checked again. It made no sense at all.

"Office of the Planetary Director?" I had also noticed the date. This lot had been up here for about as long as I had been alive.

"They started arriving... oh, a few weeks after we sent *Phoenicia* off. They came up the elevator for a couple of months, bit by bit, then they stopped. I asked Tomás what the hell was happening, but of course he couldn't see why I needed to know. Some of my people tried to use the supplies themselves, for some routine maintenance, and all kinds of hell blew up – official reprimands straight from the desk of your dear father. He made it quite clear we were to tuck it all away and forget about it."

I recognised the usual Tomás Mateo approach: the genuine inability to see why anyone would want something explained to them when all they had to do was obey.

"Any query," she added, "ever since then, just got bounced back by the Office of the Planetary Director. But since that no longer exists – guess what? I did a check and this has all defaulted to the Ministry of Supply. I don't know what it is, but it's yours now."

Oh, great, I thought. God bless blackboxes and the virtual neurons that make up their tiny little minds. The value of this lot had to be several million nuevos, and guess who would have to account for that sudden addition to the Ministry of Supply inventory?

"Do you have much need for..." I checked the nearest container. "Anti-stressor torque braces?"

"Of course – spare parts for the service capsules, that sort of thing. The government likes to think we're kept pretty well supplied but you have to pull teeth with red tape every step of the way."

"Well, as far as I'm concerned," I said quite frankly, "dip in whenever you want."

Only, it's never quite like that, is it?

I got back to my office and sent off a purely routine memo announcing the find. And next thing I got a direct person-to-person call from my grandfather, no less, on the secure Ministry line.

"Under no circumstances are those boxes to be touched, Quin," he said bluntly. "See to it. Have that cavern sealed off."

"Why?" I said. I believe in following the easiest solution, and everyone's lives would be so much easier if the Puerto Alto staff could just take what they needed from this treasure trove.

His face hardened. "Those are your instructions. That is all."

I was face to face, but also 35,000 kilometres away, which made me a little foolhardy.

"Si, Señor Director," I said. He glared at me, then managed a reluctant and stiff smile.

"I suppose I deserved that, but only from my grandson," he said. "Your father left certain records that have now come into my possession. Based on that information, which I don't intend to discuss on a link, it's best that they be left alone. In fact, that's probably the most important part of your job. That's all."

And he broke the call, leaving it up to me to explain to Linda Hahn that actually she *couldn't* just use the stuff. Which of course I couldn't do without reverting to the "just trust me" approach, which of course drew comparisons with my father, and led to a certain coolness between us.

CHAPTER 21

THE CASCADES

Quin is 27

THE DOWNFALL OF Ilo Bast made for entertaining viewing, until it got nasty.

There are classic lessons from history about transplanting species. Ilo was a predator but he grew up in an environment with plenty of natural controls – the perks of working for my father, his reputation, the fact that everyone knew him and carefully gave him just the right amount of slack. His predations never grew beyond a certain limit.

In his new home at Ochoa, as Reset section commander – job application endorsed by yours truly about eleven minutes before I became incapable of endorsing anything – he had all his old instincts and absolutely no checks. Ochoa processed chemicals and rare earths. Some of its output was exported to manufacturing plants. Some went straight into components on the premises. Goods flowed, money flowed, and all Ilo had to do was insert himself into the stream somewhere.

When he first turned up for work, while my own downfall was still echoing around different levels of government, there were doubts expressed by the management. They checked the public record and it assured them that their new Reset chief was an experienced lawman, elected Captain in his old home town, with an excellent record at keeping petty crime down. All true, and they withdrew, grumbling.

Meanwhile, up on Puerto Alto, I began to pull myself together. I reached an uneasy truce with Linda Hahn. I think she realised I wasn't keeping her from the treasure trove in the basement out of spite. In the meantime I quizzed her about the process of getting her spare parts and supplies up from the ground, and I was able to cut a little red tape for her. I lived on Puerto Alto too, you know – I wanted it running as smoothly and comfortably as possible. And so we met each other halfway, meaning that we had lunch together a couple of times a month, nothing more. I had a structure to life again, something to look forward to, and she seemed to enjoy having someone in my office that she could actually work with.

To pass the time between meals, I started a small black market racket. I also thought it might be handy as something to discover and brutally shut down if I needed to enhance my record in any way. Puerto Alto became a teeny bit more fun, its crews more receptive to the idea that being a natural born spacer didn't automatically condemn you to a lifetime of puritanical drabness.

For the next eight years...

Oh yes, the riots. APRA erupted as several thousand displaced segundas finally decided they had had it with complacent patronising hijo incompetence and corruption. A month of angry demonstrations spread to the collective farms and even a few established towns. There was frantic negotiation with the segunda leaders, some judicious sackings on the hijo side, and some letting go of the trappings of power that the Executive didn't really need anyway. The riots died down; a new, tense normality was restored.

And Ilo got arrested.

I said Ilo just had to insert himself into the cashflow stream. In fact he tried to insert himself into several streams, some more than once. He overstepped and got caught. It was the kind of anti-corruption thing my beloved Volunteers of fond memory would once have taken care of. They no longer existed and the arrest could be put down to Ilo giving himself so much rope that everyone noticed.

Then Mr Bast got in touch.

"Ilo!" I said, genuinely surprised when his face appeared on my wall. "How are you?

He didn't look pleased to see me.

"We have a problem, Spawn," he said. I raised an eyebrow. As far as I was concerned, *we* had stopped the moment he had stood aside to let me into the villa. After that point, our obligations to one another were fully discharged.

"Yes, I heard about that. How's that going?"

"My trial comes up in a couple of weeks," he said. "I'm on bail in Alti. I can't leave the city limits. I'm considering my defence and I thought of you."

I had to laugh. "You want me as a witness? To your character, maybe?"

He leaned close and growled. "Shut up and listen. There's a defence I can't give to my lawyer and this is it. I know things about what happened at the villa..."

I still couldn't see where this was going, but I wasn't sure I liked where it might be.

"Ilo, I got scooped too. We all did. There's no secrets."

"That's right." He jerked his head in a sharp nod. "We all got scooped, but a lot of what came out of us never ended up on the public record. Small details about exactly who did what, unless..."

I wasn't even aware of getting to my feet. "*You leave my mother out of this!*" I screamed.

He very slowly smiled the old Ilo smirk at me. "Wow, that was easy. I was afraid I was going to have to spell it out."

I started to settle back into my seat and became aware I was trying to sit on air. I had knocked the chair over when I got up. I stayed standing.

"I don't have any power to help you, Ilo," I said, "but I swear that if you–"

"'Course you don't have any power," he snapped. "You're even more screwed than I am. What you do have is connections. Use them. Tell them what will happen. They don't want your mama brought into this any more than I do, but that's how it will go."

Connections, of course. I was just the messenger boy. This little item was expected to end up in the lap of my mother's father.

He reached out to cut the display at his end, while I just glared hatred at him. "Preliminary hearing is in a week," he said. "If the charges haven't been drastically revised by then, I start remembering things. Get it done, Spawn."

I KNOW WHEN I'm out of my league. I took the problem straight to my grandfather, but not like a little boy running to a grown-up. You see, once I'd calmed down, it dawned on me that he had just as much to lose as I did. Sure, I didn't want them to drag out my mother's name and her involvement in my father's death. But she was of unsound mind, and I had told everything to the investigation. My grandfather, on the other hand, had been of completely sound mind when he pulled strings to get the official version sanitised.

But any feeling of comfortable superiority I may have entertained evaporated under my grandfather's displeased glare. The distance between us suddenly didn't mean that much as I nervously explained the situation. After I had finished he looked at me for so long, not saying anything, that I quietly went through what I had told him and tried to pinpoint the bit he didn't understand.

"How the hell was a situation like this allowed to arise?" he said just as I was about to start repeating myself. "What were you thinking?"

Which was just a *little* unjust. I opened my mouth to defend myself and was pre-emptively interrupted again.

"Still, he seems to trust you. When's the next car down to Alti?"

"Three days," I said.

"Be on it. You got us into this, you can get us out, and here's how."

AND SO, FOUR days later, I was in Alti, at Capital Main, awaiting the arrival of a ringrail from the west. It drew in on schedule and David Krauss stepped out of a carriage, looking around him at the sights of the big city with wide eyes.

I had been a sobbing wreck the last time he saw me. I rectified the memory by offering my hand with a firm gesture. He returned it with a wary caution.

"Good to see you, tio," I said.

"And you, Señor, though I'd really like to know what this is about."

All I had told him from Puerto Alto was that I had a job requiring his talents. That, and a Ministry travel warrant, had apparently done the trick. I waited until we were in the ground car that took us to the hotel.

"It's just a bit of bodyguarding," I told him.

"Your body?"

"Correct." I didn't expect Ilo to turn nasty, but then, I hadn't expected to be almost killed, that time four years ago at Cabrera. That kind of thing makes you wary and I never again wanted to go into a situation that I didn't know I controlled. "So what are you doing now?" I asked.

"Oh, this and that," he said with a shrug.

"Volunteer stuff?"

"Yeah. No. Sort of. Not really. Sort of... yeah, it's the kind of thing Volunteers would do but it's not... not really Volunteer stuff."

Which told me absolutely nothing, but I didn't push it.

We had lunch at the hotel, then set out for our rendezvous with Ilo.

It was usefully remote, a kilometre from the city centre along the plateau. The light covering of dust on the road said it wasn't used much. Sol 2 was below the level of the plateau on one side, Sol 1 below it on the other and as our car drew nearer to the scarp there was a strange effect ahead – red sunset rays and long, dark shadows of bumps in the plateau's edge, a kind of anti-light that lanced up from the ground itself.

Finally the road sloped down into a sharp, dry gully carved naturally out of the rock, signposted 'The Cascades'. The car pulled into what had once been a car park but was now just a fenced-off area of land. We wrapped up well, stepped out, and descended some stone steps carved into the side of the gully.

We had arrived, and David looked about with frank curiosity. "What is this place?"

"It's a restaurant," I said.

"Well, yeah, but..."

It seemed to defy all sense, but yes, we stood in a deserted alfresco restaurant. It was built on a dry riverbed, right above a dead waterfall, on a series of natural terraces that stretched back up the gully. I told him about it.

"There used to be a lake on the top of the plateau, thousands of years ago. This was its overflow channel. Water ran down here and over the edge."

More recently – but still not in my lifetime – smartly dressed men and women and children had sat at stone tables that were built out of the ground. Of course, no one went to smart restaurants anymore. The Cascades had served their last customers around the time I was born.

"The idea was that Nueva would warm up again and the lake would refill," I finished.

"But..." David glanced up the gully. "They dammed the lake up, then, right?"

"Nope." I had to smile, because I had always found the idea absurd, and I could see it was bothering him too: an intelligent but unimaginative man trying to make sense of something that was naturally stupid. "This place was designed by some art movement." Something else Nueva didn't have nowadays. "The lake would fill up again and there would be torrents of water running through here. Down the terraces, over the tables.

People would gather to watch and think what it must have been like. We would have our own ready-made ancient ruins, like on Earth."

He snorted. "Bet it was a hijo who thought that one up."

The far end of the restaurant was the edge of the plateau, and I couldn't resist peering down over the safety rail. The drop was sheer and the ground far, far below. The waterfall that had been where I stood must have been very spectacular.

"It's a long way down, Spawn. I hope you weren't thinking of me being down there."

I jumped; David deliberately turned more slowly. Ilo stepped out of a doorway. We stood twenty, thirty feet apart, just the three of us and the cold wind that wound its way between the stone tables.

"Never crossed my mind," I said, not with complete truthfulness.

I'd wondered if he would look older. Nope, Ilo was ageless. Same iron-grey stubble, same massive chest, same suspicious stare in those narrow eyes.

He nodded at David.

"Who's this?"

"You have met..."

"I'm just some tio," David said.

And that was where my carefully laid plans went awry.

What should have happened was this. I should have explained to Ilo that we couldn't change the way the Lawcore conducted a case. Ilo would have known that because the Ilos of this world know how the world runs. They don't waste time complaining about what can't be changed – they just concentrate on bending what could be to their will. So I would have paid him half a million nuevos. He would be able to buy off a couple of key witnesses and the prosecution would have to depend entirely on some more circumstantial evidence. If he still went to jail after that, it wouldn't be for more than a couple of years, less with good behaviour. On his release he would get another half million.

That million total was a lot more than I had on me. My grandfather had contributed a large amount from personal savings. The rest came out of the estate I had inherited when my father died, and a large garnish on my salary that would last for many years to come. But he didn't need to know that.

That was what should have happened. What really happened was that David pulled a gun out of his coat and shot him.

It seemed like a joke. My mind detached itself from the scene and withdrew to a safe distance, so I could watch with a strange sense of detachment. There was very little noise. The gun chirped a couple of times, and Ilo simply crumpled to the ground while massive gouts of scarlet blood flowered from his chest. It was an assassin's gun; it unleashed a small stream of barely subsonic razor-sharp plastic chips that slipped through the victim's clothes and skin like a knife through butter and tore him up inside. There was a strange gushing noise, which I realised later was the air in Ilo's lungs leaving him through the holes in his torso. He stared up at me from the ground, a look of puzzled surprise, which faded as the life left his eyes.

That was when my mind decided it was okay to return to my body, and I found myself standing in the middle of the Cascades with a murder victim at my feet and the murderer standing next to me.

I screamed.

"What the fuck did you do that for?"

"Sorry, Señor, he had to be silenced." David casually walked to the edge of the restaurant and chucked the gun over the edge; which, a small part of me noted, meant he wasn't going to shoot me too.

"Who... what... why..." *Get a grip, Quin!* I took a couple of breaths. "Did my grandfather send you?"

"Your grandfather? No." He reached into his pack and pulled out a cylinder like a fire extinguisher. "We have to..."

"Then who? *Why did you kill him?*"

He gave me the barely patient look you give a small child.

"He was telling people he was going to get off the charges because of stuff he knew. Now, I know he meant stuff he knew about you, but the people I work for know what else he knew and they thought he meant something else. They weren't taking chances."

That was the most frightening thing he had said so far.

"The people you work for? Who are they?" It was complete news to me that there was anyone on Nueva who felt empowered to order hits on other Nuevans.

"You'll... probably find out. Look, Señor, I'm sorry this had to happen. Did anyone know you were meeting him?"

"Um... no. Yes. My grandfather. He didn't know where or when, though."

"Cool. You tell your granddad that you waited, but Bast never showed. Now, stand over there. No reason for you to be any more involved."

So I obediently stood over to one side and watched the thing I had created get to work.

David released the contents of the gas cylinder over Ilo's body. Ilo's clothes dissolved into a powdery dust and left a dead, naked, torn up corpse lying on the stone floor in his own blood. My throat rose and I had to look away.

I remembered the little boy, Davy Krauss, glaring at me for daring to eat his family's food. That little boy should have gone on to be a farmer, and marry, and have lots of little farmers, and one day die of old age.

When I dared look back with one eye, David was taking another cylinder out and undoing the seals on the cap. And now I remembered the tall, burly teenager with his Volunteer badge, so pleased to be officially fighting corruption, with his face proudly covered in bruises from a fight he had got into through working for me.

Then I remembered the eighteen year old, my accomplice in Nueva's very first coup, and now he was a twenty-two year old assassin. I had no idea how David had got to this stage of his life, or what lay ahead, but he was somewhere along a path that I had set him on.

He sprayed the second cylinder over Ilo's body, leaving him covered with what looked like cobwebs. Then he replaced both cylinders in his pack and turned towards me as he swung the pack onto his back.

"We should go," he said. He took my elbow and led me to the exit.

"What was..."

"Nano stuff. It will break him down and in a few hours there'll be nothing but dust here." He looked approvingly around the Cascades. "Good choice. Wind blows right through... it'll all be clear in no time."

We didn't talk much on the drive back.

I was sure that if he thought I was a threat, he would kill me in a moment. Yet he had immediately disposed of the weapon after using it on Ilo. He just seemed to assume I was safe, and I wasn't sure if I was flattered or insulted. What was to stop me turning him in straightaway his back was turned? I would gladly submit to a scooping to prove my case.

Yet I didn't.

I didn't mourn Ilo. He had been a large part of my childhood but never a friend, never someone to like. The world wouldn't miss him. But there was still one thing I thought I should check. Back in my hotel I got details of all the unsolved murders, anywhere on Nueva, committed in the last three years. There were eleven, all in resettlement camps, and if they were unsolved it was only because the authorities were having difficulty narrowing the culprits down. They had all been obvious cases of one lowlife falling foul of another and meeting his end in a brawl or a stabbing in a dark alley. There was nothing to match the sophistication of what I had witnessed, not in the unsolved murders and not (I checked) in the solved ones either.

So whatever David was, he didn't seem to be a contract killer working his way around the planet. Innocent people didn't seem to be at risk.

But then I thought – what about disappearances? No one would ever know Ilo had been murdered but before long they would certainly know he had disappeared.

Well, yes, there were disappearances. There always were. Just say that there was nothing outside the statistical norm. If there was a pattern it would take more detecting skills than I had.

And so I didn't turn David in.

His last words to me before he boarded the ringrail were almost as frightening as everything else that had happened.

"Take my word, Señor. The best thing you can do is go back to Puerto Alto and stay there. When it's all over – then you'll know you can come down. We'll be in touch."

I turned his last words to me into a prayer: "Dear God, please may he *not* be in touch again. I want exactly nothing to happen for the rest of my life."

But as Father Adolfo was so fond of saying, if you want to make God laugh, tell him your plans.

CHAPTER 22

INDEPENDENCE DAY

Quin is 31

I SUPPOSE NUEVA'S slide into perdition had a kind of graceful inevitability to it. Maybe that was the problem. You watch the leading edge of a glacier approaching down the mountainside and do you ever think of diverting it *before* you're crushed by the dead weight?

After the riots, things looked briefly rosy for both sides. The segundas got a little more recognition and dignity than before and the whole affair neatly paved the way for my grandfather to take the reins of government.

Say what you will about my father's rule as Director, but things got done. After his death the Executive had tried to run the planet by power-shared committee again and, guess what, nothing got done at all except that a lot of hijo incompetence came to light. And so the Executive decided it needed a single man in power at its head again, only this time, accountable to them. They called him First Executor, and it was Luis Alcantara who got the job. He looked good for his years, standing at the podium, nodding gravely at the cameras, stately and distinguished. His moustache still bristled. He was not much younger than my father would have been, but he wasn't weighed down by years of single handed Directing. Just looking at him, you felt confident that this was the man for the job.

And me? Did I bathe in my grandfather's reflected glory?

I did not, because a door had slammed in my face. I was still a regicide. While my grandfather was just a minister, I was a useful but embarrassing relative tucked away in orbit. Now he was First Executor he really did not want to know me. Up on Puerto Alto I was contained and useful. Down there... no.

So, I blew a week's leave in Alti with as much drink and women as I could manage. Then I returned morosely to Puerto Alto to do my job.

There was a strange moment as the car glided into motion up the cable and the Altiplano slid away below us. I looked out at the city and actually thought, *thank God that's over*. Since when had plenty of booze and sex started to seem like an obligation rather than fun? At the grand age of twenty-eight, was I getting too old for this?

THE NEXT THREE years kept me busy enough not to worry about it. We had a decade, give or take, until the wormhole reopened and Puerto Alto really would be a Puerto again. We had to ramp the place up and get it ready for space commerce once more. It would be a gradual process but we couldn't let it slip. I drew up the plan.

Maintenance teams started to come up the elevator. For the first time, you could pass strangers in the corridors of the port. The expectation began to grow that, you know, Alex and *Phoenicia* might actually make it. We would be in touch with Earth again. The older people began to look thoughtful. My younger generation didn't really know what to make of it.

Rio Lento finally gave in to the approaching winter and was officially evacuated. Snow and ice now blew unhindered through the rooms and passages where I had lived for my first seventeen years. And as if there was some psychic link between the two, my mother died. She hadn't lived there for eight years and she rarely showed any sign she knew she was living anywhere, but around the time Rio Lento shut down, so did she.

I had done all my crying in advance. The funeral in Santo Cristóbal and the cremation left me strangely dry-eyed. I suppose there has to be some internal pressure to force tears out, and I had none, just a massive vacuum in place of my soul. While the priest waffled on, my mind was replaying every conversation I had ever had with her that had gone wrong. That terrible birthday party, and a thousand incidents like it. But this time, in my fantasies, I would find exactly the right words of love and assurance that would slice through her madness and bring sense back into her life. And then I would wonder why I hadn't said those words at the time.

Later, for the second time, I had a strange feeling as the elevator car rose out of Puerto Bajo to take me back to work. I felt like I was going *home*. There was more for me up there than down here. La Nueva Temporada now had nothing to deserve my love or my loyalty. It was an ugly and charmless lump of rock that existed to keep me alive, and no more.

BUT IT WAS a bubbling, dangerous Nueva that I left behind. Promises had been made following the riots. The vague assurances that followed them up were being tried and found wanting.

And so more riots erupted and this time there was bloodshed. A couple of Resets here, some angry segundas there. A regular Constable tried to step into a fight and got knifed.

"The Executive of this planet follows the will of the people," my grandfather announced. "It does not follow the demands of an unrepresentative minority of anarchists." And he went on to belabour how we all must pull together, or freeze, or starve. That was still a powerful argument.

Again, segunda leaders met with the Executive in Alti, and this time they emerged with a genuine surprise.

I heard the sounds of cheering down the halls of Puerto Alto.

It wasn't the kind of thing you usually heard and it carried a long way in the asteroid's echoey chambers. I followed it to one of the old maintenance bays. Among the gantries and docking cradles, the mostly segunda workforce had downed tools and were having a party. Across the hall I could see Hahn and her friends already having a good time. Our eyes met and she raised a styro cup to me in cynical salute.

"It's elections!" a girl exclaimed as she pulled me into the crowd and pushed a cup into my own hand. As you generally do when there's a lot of black market around, I took a careful sniff before an equally careful sip. Interesting – I was pretty sure I hadn't supplied this stuff. "We're getting elections!"

Yes, elections, no less – an ancient concept, long since made redundant by the notion of Discourse. We were creating a brand new assembly: a place where elected representatives of the people could stand up, and state grievances, and be heard by the government.

It's always nice to reach adulthood and be taken seriously; now, in one small stroke, it was like the greater part of the Nuevan population had been allowed to grow up. Not a lot of work was done that day.

Somehow I ended up back with the girl, who liked to dance with her arms round my neck and her body pressed very tight to mine.

"I'm Amy."

"I'm Quin."

"I know, but what's your name?" We had both had enough alcohol to find this incredibly funny. We retired back to my cabin, and either what followed was a vigorous symbolic celebration of the new spirit of Nuevan democracy that brought hijo and segunda together, or it exemplified exactly what hijos had been doing to segundas all these years and were going to keep on doing for as long as they could. Either way it made a pleasant change from the usual self-service.

I mention that only because I want to show that at least I got something out of the elections promise.

The new assembly would be called the Council of Representatives.

"Might as well call it the Council of Segundas," Hahn remarked, when she heard. Most of the population of Nueva were segunda, so what would an elected chamber representing them consist of?

The next day this must have finally occurred to my grandfather, because the brakes came on with a screech you could hear in orbit. Representing the people was one thing; letting go of the hijo stranglehold on power was quite another. Everything I was saying about reaching adulthood – well, imagine someone then admits it was all pretend and you're actually still a child. Disappointed? Angry?

Thought so.

Then some fool started another riot, which was all the excuse the Executive needed to tear the agreement up.

"We have tried to negotiate with those elements that would bring down our society," my grandfather declared. "We need no further proof of their bad faith and their inability to act in a considered, mature manner. The Executive has considered the way forward and finds that it has no choice."

He stared directly at his audience, which was most of La Nueva Temporada.

"We are invoking the emergency protocols once again, and I have agreed to the Executive's request that I should become Planetary Director for as long as the emergency lasts."

I shouted angrily at the display and blanked it. A moment later, Hahn appeared in its place.

"You have to wonder how an intelligent man can be so stupid, don't you?" she said.

"I hereby renounce my entire hijo heritage," I told her bitterly.

And then the Nariz Doblado peninsula, population three million, declared independence.

* * *

IT SEEMED A joke at first. I like to believe I'm lateral minded, able to think sideways on to the general viewpoint; even I never thought of breaking off bits of Nueva and saying "this is ours now". It just couldn't happen. Nueva had one hostile, inhabited continent and sixty million people on it. We had to get through the isolation years together, or not at all. We didn't have the luxury of dissension.

It's quite scary how I can default so quickly to thinking like my father.

The peninsula has the geographical advantages. It's slap bang on the equator. It has a narrow neck on the far side of the Cuchillos, so it could quite easily be held by one army against another, if either side had armies. It sticks out from the west coast of the continent, and with our north and south surrendered to the glaciers it's the most far-flung habitable part of land. But it's only just habitable and that's the problem. I knew the facts from my job. It had three collective farms, the Cabrera manufacturing plant – scene of my run-in with the ex-Resets and my first introduction to the Volunteers – and that's it. Those farms could just about feed its population but it wouldn't be easy.

Of course, we all downed tools to watch the official announcement from the new peninsular government. We got a nervous looking bunch of men and women with a larger crowd behind them. Some faces I knew, or knew of vaguely. Others were complete strangers.

The new President of the Republic addressed the planet.

"This is not a move we have taken lightly," he said, "but the Altiplano government has shown that it cannot be trusted to negotiate. We have considered the situation carefully. We of the Peninsular Republic can run our own affairs until this planet re-establishes contact with Earth. Earth is a world of more than one nation–"

"*Clan*, you moron," I muttered, "*clan*, not *nation*, completely different…"

"… and there is no reason we cannot be too. In the meantime, we will naturally contribute all that we can to the survival of La Nueva Temporada throughout this trying time. No Nuevan will starve or freeze, inside or outside the Republic, because of us. But we will no longer accept the rule of the self-satisfied autocrats of the Altiplano."

He opened up to questions, and I could guess what the first would be. My lips moved quietly in unison with the speaker off camera:

"What about Cabrera?"

My grandfather could conceivably let the peninsula go – though I doubted he would, because losing even a pebble of La Nueva Temporada under his government would be an unbearable blow to his pride. But losing Cabrera, the main manufacturing facility on the planet, was unthinkable. Cabrera had to be wholly owned by the government. There was no other way. Any element of competition here was just too risky.

With the President's first words, I knew the Republic was doomed.

"The Cabrera facility is vital to the Republic's well-being," he said. "We recognise the importance of the plant to the planet as a whole and we have sent representatives to Altiplano City to negotiate how all parties can best benefit from it."

I could bet that those representatives were sitting somewhere in an anteroom in the Executive Building in Alti, and that was where they would stay.

The President's voice grew harder as he dredged up a little more nerve.

"In the meantime," he said, "it is conceivable that the Altiplano government will try to retake the plant by force. We strongly advise them not to do so. Our Minister of Security has already taken steps to ensure its protection."

The camera panned briefly to some other stranger sitting near the President, a round, grumpy bald man who nodded curtly before the camera moved back again. But suddenly I was sitting bolt upright. It wasn't the Minister of Security that I recognised, but the tio standing behind him. My own pet self-made monster, David Krauss, looking bored and fidgeting like he had more important things to be doing.

That was when I began to take the Republic a little more seriously. I just knew that David wouldn't put himself in harm's way without making damn sure he was going to win.

I set a feed to let me know of any developments, and thoughtfully went back to work.

An hour later a development splashed up on my wall. This time it was the Minister of Security.

"We have heard that an attempt is being made to seize the Cabrera plant from the Republic," he said. "We are broadcasting this to bear witness to the intransigence of the Altiplano government."

The scene changed to a slightly pixelated snowy plain. There were mountains in the distance and the sky was blue-grey. Three silver dots loomed shakily just above the mountains. The view zoomed in and the dots focused, over-focused, blurred and eventually settled down as three rigis, flying in echelon formation.

Captioning said that the rigis were heading for Cabrera, on the coast. They had the entire peninsula to cross first.

Other voices streamed in, broadcast live. An anonymous traffic controller was telling the rigis, over and over again, that their flight was an illegal invasion of the Republic's airspace, and they were to turn round immediately. They kept flying.

They were told that armed force would be used. They kept flying.

There was a *whoosh* and then two small burning balls of light were streaking towards the rigis. A moment later they blossomed into two fireballs and the *boom* of their explosions reached us a few moments after that.

They had exploded well ahead of the rigis, but the point had been made. The Republic could defend itself.

Two of the rigis took the hint and immediately backed off. The third stuck to its orders. It swerved slightly in its course, but then kept on coming.

Stats in the bottom of the display showed that most of the population was watching.

The Republic controller became more insistent that it should turn back. It kept coming. Nueva held its breath.

A third missile flew off. At the last moment the rigi lost its nerve and started to turn, but too late. The missile exploded close by. The rigi shuddered and twisted, then began to plummet, with black smoke pouring from its rear. It tried to pull up but long before it hit the ground the stresses proved too much for a machine basically designed to transport equipment from A to B without being shot at en route. Its spine snapped and it disintegrated at two thousand metres in a shower of flame and debris.

The image froze, pixelated, and faded back to the Minister. Even he looked shaken, but he hid it with a scowl at the camera.

"Th–" he started. He tried again, more firmly. "That action was forced upon us by the stubbornness of the Altiplano government. You all heard the pilot being told to turn back. You all heard us saying that we could defend ourselves. The blood of the men and women onboard that rigi is on the hands of the Planetary Director and his cronies. We apologise to the husbands and wives and children of those who died today, but you must refer the matter to your own government. We will negotiate with any government in Altiplano City that is prepared to act in good faith–"

I cut the display and fell back in my chair.

This kind of thing might happen on Earth, but not Nueva. We had our differences but despite everything, we generally pulled together. We could argue. We could overthrow governments, even, but we always stuck to the big picture. Nueva stayed as one.

Sometimes Nuevans killed each other. I had seen this happen. We called it murder and we usually punished it.

Seeing one group of Nuevans cold bloodedly shoot down another in the name of a government... no. No. Just, no. It was wrong. It was inconceivable.

Something was nagging at the back of my mind. Missiles. Surely you didn't just run missiles off a nanolathe when you needed them. I asked about the missiles used in the attack and it came back quickly. They were of a vintage design, centuries old, developed during Earth's Third Himalayan War but perfectly good for their present purpose. Just because Nueva had never needed surface-to-air missiles didn't mean the knowledge wasn't there. Someone had dug it out of the banks and no doubt got them made at Cabrera.

But the fuel? And the explosives? What about that? There was no precise knowledge but it was the kind of thing that the Ochoa plant could have handled. And Ochoa was very close to the Nariz Doblado.

In fact – I checked – the new Republic's claimed land border made a deliberate wiggle eastwards at that point. Ochoa was something else that they wanted.

It's very anticlimactic to solve a murder single-handed and realise no one will care. But four years ago, Ilo Bast had been gunned down by the tio who now stood behind the Peninsular Republic's Minister of Security. I had been on the scene because Ilo had been trying to blackmail me with what he knew. I strongly suspected he had been in on their activities also – and maybe threatened them with exposure too. So he had been silenced.

If this had been at least four years in the planning, it was not a spur-of-the-moment uprising and we were all in a lot more trouble than my grandfather's government seemed to realise.

CHAPTER 23

LASER SURGERY

Quin is 31

I PASSED ON a message to my grandfather, summarising my deductions: that I suspected certain parties behind the new Republic had been stockpiling weapons for years, waiting for the right moment, and that they were a lot more determined and more dangerous than the bunch of desperate insurrectionists he took them for.

I got a terse message in response to say that the matter was in hand. And then communications went out. None of the blackboxes would put any kind of message through, and Hahn's people picked up an unscheduled elevator departure from the Altiplano.

It takes the better part of a day for a car to get all the way from one end of the cable to another. A day is a long time when you have no idea what is going on and your imagination fills in as many details as you like. We didn't know for sure that the unscheduled car and the blackout were linked but it would have been an awful coincidence if they weren't.

Hahn led the reception committee to the docking area. I tagged along and was interested to see that her people armed themselves from the port's small supply of stunners. If whoever was on the car was dangerous then surely someone at Alti would have found a way to warn us by now... but I could see her point. These were uncertain times.

Nine men and seven women spilled out of the car, moving with an awkward lack of grace that even their exos couldn't overcome. As they came down the transparent tube towards the pressurised area, we could all see a strange deadness in their eyes that went well with the robotic stiffness to their movements.

"They're conceptualed to the eyeballs," Hahn murmured. "I remember that look from college."

I had seen concept-junkies too but never anyone quite so far gone. They came into Arrivals, and newcomers and reception committee gazed warily at one another.

"Administrator Hahn?" demanded a particularly scowly individual. He thrust a tablet at her. "You are required by the Office of the Planetary Director to render all assistance required to myself and my team. Please confirm that you have received and understood these orders."

Hahn waited just long enough to get an impatient grimace before reaching out and taking the tablet. She then read it through very slowly, as if there was a lot more than its terse couple of lines that essentially repeated what he had already said.

"I confirm," she said eventually. "Welcome to Puerto Alto." She handed the tablet back. "Can I ask the purpose of th–"

"Just do not interfere with our operation," he said. "That is all."

And they dispersed into the depths of the asteroid.

NOW OUR NEW guests had arrived, communication with the ground was partially restored and Port Control became a tense, snappish place. Hahn was seething and wasn't able to take it out on anyone who could actually do anything about it, so her staff tiptoed around and I took myself back to my office.

Then Hahn turned up in my doorway.

"Your pet goons–" (I rather resented that 'Your'.) "– are moving the laser."

It took me a moment to realise what she was talking about. It was eight years since I had arrived on Puerto Alto and got given the grand tour, which had included the laser turret – our planet's one-time defence against unauthorised incomers through the wormhole. It was a separate module planted on the asteroid's surface, and because it was a module, it could be moved.

External cameras tracked what was happening. Suited figures glided about the turret, burrowing industriously away like cavadors at its roots in the rock and affixing thruster packs to the supports. The laser came away from the transparent control blister and hung in space a few feet above the surface. Then a satellite chassis, just an open framework of supports and thrusters guided by more of the strangers, hove into view around the edge of the asteroid. The laser and its various workings were fastened to the chassis and an array of maxitoks was plugged in. The crew withdrew and, with a final burst of white thruster gas, the new satellite fell away from Puerto Alto and towards Nueva.

It took twenty-four hours to reach low Nuevan orbit. Twenty-four hours and thirty minutes later, my grandfather had his response to the insurgents.

This time, the view broadcast to all Nueva was the other way round – a shaky picture from the nose of a rigi en route across a white plain towards the distant jagged line of the Cuchillos and the Nariz Doblado beyond.

We got the same exchange of pleasantries between ground and air as before, culminating in a final warning from the Republic that if the rigis persisted on their course, they would be fired upon. All the rigi pilot said was that if the Republic fired first, retaliation would be taken.

The Republic fired first. We saw the tiny spot of light against the mountains that meant a missile had just been set off. The view changed to a magnified view of some foamcast bunkers, high on a craggy mountainside. Small figures, well wrapped against the cold, were looking straight at us through binoculars. On the slope above them was the missile rack, one of its chambers empty but still primed with plenty more.

"Power spike from the laser!" someone shouted.

"Oh God, no," Hahn murmured, and the scene whited out. A second later it was back, but changed: flaming wreckage tumbling into a blackened crater a hundred metres across carved into the mountainside. No buildings, no missiles, no people.

Suddenly we were back in the nose of the rigi again. In the distance, the mountains looked unchanged but other specks of light suddenly appeared – more missiles from other installations, all conveniently giving away their locations. White balls of flame blossomed against the mountains like a row of nuclear pinpricks.

An anonymous voice was droning.

"This is an official statement by the Office of the Planetary Director. The action we have taken today was forced upon us by the obstinacy of the illegal insurgents of the Nariz Doblado. We offer our deepest sympathies to the families of the men and women who have died. We bear the people of the peninsula no ill will. We urge them to rise up against those who have led them to this point and to renew their loyalty to La Nueva Temporada..."

It was strangely easy to stop listening. The rigis flew on across the peninsula unopposed, towards Cabrera. Either the insurgents had gambled everything on one line of defence or they weren't going to give away any further positions and call down more fire upon them.

Hahn looked slightly dazed.

"Not even your father..." she said. "Not even at the height of his rule. Holding his own population at gunpoint? He's mad! He is utterly and completely mad. He won't get peace that way. It's never worked before and it won't work now."

I had to agree, and I wondered how this was scheduled to end in my grandfather's mind. Did he see the insurgents peacefully rolling onto their backs with their legs in the air? I thought otherwise. There would be more accusations and counter-accusations, more riots, more promises, more lies. Anything...

Anything to keep the hijos in power. It wasn't a particularly blinding revelation, but suddenly I saw the key difference between my father and my grandfather. My father had ruled the planet single-handed and treated everyone like shit, but at least it really had been *everyone*, hijo and segunda alike. He had had a vision for the whole planet and everyone was expected to weigh in equally.

My grandfather simply couldn't think outside the rigid framework of hijo supremacy. He looked the part of a wise and distinguished elder statesman, but when you scratched below the surface you just got a small-minded aristocrat.

My father's rule had grated, but it had been twenty years of peace that kept us all alive.

"What will you do?" I asked.

"Me?" She laughed bitterly. "What can I do? I'm buggered if I'm going to help him indulge his little dictatorship fantasies."

"If you don't, he'll replace you." I wondered briefly if Puerto Alto would go the same way as the Nariz Doblado, declare its independence from Nueva. But even if Hahn's group of spacers did discover a sudden militant streak and shut the elevator down, the rebellion would last exactly as long as their food supplies. And there was still the laser crew to contend with.

Interesting thoughts began to hover at the edge of my mind. I took it as a given that Nueva had to stay as one, regardless of who ran it, and that everyone had to work together...

She shot me a cold look. "Let me worry about that, Mateo." She turned and stalked away, and I slowly began to walk in the other direction, back to my quarters. Those hovering thoughts would suddenly skitter away if you looked at them too closely, but if you left them alone then they coalesced into something positive. By the time I was at my quarters, and with a slightly detached sense of disbelief, I knew what I was going to do – and why I was going to do it. It was two words that, for me, had never really hung together before as a phrase: for Nueva.

MY HEAD WAS still buzzing with conceptuals freshly taken as I moved down the tunnel. My movements were stiff and slow, not just because I was using an exo in freefall but because my clothes were necessarily bulky to hide what was under them.

Lights were dim in this little-used part of the asteroid. The tunnel was narrow, not even lined, very little sign of the hand of man apart from the light panels, and there was always a patch of dark in the distance that never came closer. It had only been drilled to give access to the laser control bubble. The laser was now in low orbit around La Nueva Temporada but it was still controlled from up here.

And suddenly there was the metal door, guarded by one of the goons.

"This area is off-limits to all–" he began.

I held out my credentials. "Mateo, Ministry of Supply. The Director has made me your official liaison."

He looked suspiciously at the tablet, and at me, and called up something on a tablet of his own. But there was no getting round the fact that I was who I said I was.

"What's your business here?"

"Ministry business."

"Which is...?"

"Ministry... business," I repeated, trying very hard to imply it should only be told to his superior. The conceptuals these people had taken obviously included some kind of over-cautious security set-up. I hoped I was fitting the right way into his artificially induced view of the world.

He stood aside and let me pass. I entered the airlock and climbed up into the control blister.

Nueva hung in the sky above our heads, the cloud patterns hovering over the continent pierced by the thin diamond needle of the elevator cable. There were just six others present – most of the sixteen who had come up had just been to get the laser moved. The others were in their quarters now, which was the best place for them.

You couldn't see the laser with the naked eye from up here but a red spot on the transparent blister wall marked its position in orbit. The six crew were practising, reading off coordinates of places on the surface and aiming the laser at them. They would name places on the west coast and the east, to the north and to the south, and time how long it took the laser to traverse the distance.

The chief goon, the one with the deadest eyes and the worst attitude, scowled over at me when I identified myself.

"Wait there," he said, indicating one corner of the blister next to a computer bank. I moved dutifully into my corner and waited for them all to start ignoring me again. Then I reached into my pack and pulled out the charge.

Puerto Alto carried a small amount of explosives – for seismic testing of the asteroid, for emergency excavation, maybe just because they were fun to have. I used a small tube of puncture sealant to fix the charge to the wall of the blister. A light on it started to blink.

Then I moved a few feet away, squirted a line of sealant down my forearm and slapped it against the wall. I gave it an experimental tug. My coat was bonded to the wall like rock.

"May I have your attention, please?" I said loudly. A couple of them scowled at me afresh.

"You may speak when we have completed the exercise," the boss said, apparently not noticing my unusual stance.

"No, I'll speak now," I said. "I've just fixed a blasting charge with a two minute fuse to the side of this blister. That's it, over there. I've also fixed myself, here. I know how to stop it, you probably don't. You can detach the charge, and you can detach me, but not in the time available. So you need to evacuate the blister within... um... ninety seconds. And counting."

Now *that* got their attention. All except Scowly. He glared at me, hard, then turned back to his console.

"Carry on," he said. "Recalibrate laser to co-ordinates..."

"He wasn't kidding!" One of the others had checked the charge on the wall. "We have to leave now!"

"Yes, now," I said helpfully. "Right now. Really good idea–"

"He would die too," Scowly said logically. "He is bluffing."

"Um, no." I bent my arm behind me to reach down my neck and pull out the hood of the pressure suit I was wearing under my clothes. I yanked it forward and down across my face so that it could seal with the collar. My lungs filled with slightly stuffy, recycled air. "I'll be fine," I said, a little indistinctly.

"You... you're... you're mad!" one of them exclaimed. "You're insane, you're–"

"– going to be the only one alive in sixty seconds," I said.

"Sod that," he said and made a dive for the airlock. Others followed.

"Return to the exercise. Remove this person. Return to the exercise..." Scowly intoned.

"Fuck you," said the last of them, and they were gone. Except for their leader.

I looked nervously at the charge.

"You really should be going," I said. "I'm not kidding. Look, I'm fixed to the wall and I can't..."

"The exercise will continue." There was a slight, a very slight tremble in his voice. Behind his eyes and the barrier of conceptuals that had forced his brain into an unyielding clockwork machine, there was a frightened man trying to get out.

"You're going to die!" I shouted. "Get out now! The exercise is over!"

"You do not... have the authority... to end the exercise..." The words were grinding out as free will started to exert itself.

"Thirty seconds!" I begged him. "You can still make it..."

And when he still showed no sign of moving, I swore and plunged my hand into my pocket for the laser cutter. I turned it on, pointed it to where my arm was still stuck to the window... and stopped. And swore again. To free myself to cancel the charge to save his life I had to cut away the pane, which would let the air out and kill him.

"The exercise must continue, you are not authorised, the exercise must continue..."

I screamed angrily and started trying to wriggle out of my clothes. Not easy when one arm is fixed to the wall.

The charge blew.

There was no bang, just the suggestion of a sharp crack which was instantly carried away by the blast of venting air. My entire body was lifted up and pulled towards the hole, jamming up short when my arm refused to move. Loose objects – tablets, food capsules, instruments – flew towards the leak. And Scowly, who was clinging onto a support, hung on all he could until his eyes bulged and his last breath gusted out of his mouth and his fingers went limp. The blister wasn't large and by now the very brief hurricane had died down to a mere trickle of wind. His body drifted slowly across the enclosed space, bumped into the wall and drifted slowly back again.

"You fucking *lunatic!*" I yelled. "I didn't want you to die! Why couldn't you just do what you were told? Eh? Why?"

The problem was, of course, he *had* done as he was told. My grandfather had told him to take conceptuals on... I don't know, engineering, high energy physics, basic laser operation. And some covert ops spin-offs: security awareness and advanced paranoia. And look where it got him. He had needed the knowledge of how to work the laser. He hadn't needed to know how to act like a government goon. If my grandfather had just been able to trust a simple man to do a simple job, this wouldn't have happened.

"*You there, Mateo?*" said Hahn's voice in my helmet.

"Yeah."

"*We all heard you talking to the fool. It wasn't your fault.*"

"Thanks."

"*Look, you did the right thing. Now, get yourself out of there and we'll–*"

"I'm not getting out."

A pause.

"*What?*"

"If we just gave the laser back, it would start all over again. I'm going to end this."

"*How?*"

"Just... wait and see." I glanced up at Nueva and swallowed. It had all seemed such a good idea ten minutes ago. "I'm going to fix all this."

Another pause, and angry voices in the background from Port Control.

"*The rest of your friends have just turned up. They're insisting that we mount a raid on you,*" she said.

"I wouldn't," I told her. "I've mined the blister and the tunnel with more charges. Try and take me, and they go off."

It was a lie, but it was what I would have done if time permitted. So it was almost true.

A third pause.

"*Look,*" she said, "*Mateo boys tend not to be stupid so I'm trusting...*"

"Trust away," I interrupted. "Just let me be for the time being."

"*Your choice. Let us know if you need anything.*"

"Whatever," I muttered. "Stand by."

First, I freed myself from the wall, and shucked off the extra clothing so that I could move more comfortably in just the pressure suit. Then I took spare panes from a locker, and sealed them over the one that had blown out and the one I had cut. Then I repressurised the blister and opened my hood up again.

I sat myself in the main operations couch and let my newly conceptualed knowledge of how this thing worked come flooding into the front of my brain. Then I called up Hahn.

"Can you put me through to the general channels?" I said.

"*You're on.*"

I spoke again, and this time I knew I was addressing the whole of Nueva. Suddenly the grand plan seemed a lot less grand.

"My name is Joaquin Mateo," I said. "I have taken control of the laser that my grandfather's government put in orbit to destroy the Peninsular Republic's missile installations. I intend to use it for a different purpose."

I paused, both to take another swallow and – to be honest – to savour the moment. What were people thinking? Was I going to go mad and wipe out the entire Nariz Doblado? Take out the Altiplano?

"In one hour's time," I said, "I will destroy the Wheeler collective farm on the Nariz Doblado. In two hours' time, I will destroy the Haregano collective farm. I don't know how accurately I can pinpoint this thing so I advise everyone down there now to move well away. In the meantime, watch me take some practice shots just to get my eye in."

"*You what?*" Hahn was bellowing in my ears. "*I take it back about stupid! We're coming for you now, you psychotic little brute, and we're–*"

"Charges," I reminded her, and cut her off.

Well, that was my bridges well and truly burnt, I thought. Now, those practice shots. For the sake of balance I really thought they should be in hijo territory, and there was one place that immediately came to mind. I glanced up at the red spot marking the laser's position. Yes, it was in line of sight with my intended target.

I called up the co-ordinates. 30 degrees south, 16 degrees east. The instruments told me that the laser was locking on to a small spot on the south east coast called Rio Lento.

There was a display that showed me the view from the laser. From orbit, the ups and downs and hills and valleys of the Barreras all blended into one mottled plain and I still needed artificial enhancement to make out the lines of my former home. But the regular shapes of the buildings and the pale lines of the roads helped me get my bearings, and I was able to guide the crosshairs up the hillside from the valley until they were poised squarely over the Mateo villa.

Rio Lento had been evacuated long ago; everything that could be moved had been shifted to APRA. But the buildings remained and none remained more solidly than the villa. It had been built to last, to survive the transition from Nueva the snowball to Nueva the sultry paradise, when it would dominate a sun-drenched valley of vineyards and olive groves and a chuckling, clear river. Even now, with snow piled up against the walls and filling the yard, its lines were firm and proud.

I put the crosshairs in the courtyard and pressed the FIRE button.

The snow flashed into steam a split second before the yard blazed with white light and the solid lines of the buildings melted away into the glare. It cleared and the villa slowly emerged from its pall of steam and smoke – a slagged, charred mass that cooled before my eyes in the chill sea breeze up from the valley.

Hahn spoke.

"Very symbolic. Your grandfather would like a word."

I HADN'T EXPECTED him to shout and swear, and I wasn't disappointed. He sounded like he had passed through the shouting, swearing, hair tearing stage long ago. Now he was just in sheer, utter disbelief.

"Quin...?" His tone even seemed to suggest he doubted my very name. *"Just what are you doing?"*

"I'm taking control of this situation."

"By... destroying Rio Lento?"

"Just the villa," I said. "And it is mine. Was."

"But... all that about the farms..."

"I'm taking out two of the peninsula's three farms," I said. "The rebellion will be over because the surplus population will have to depend on the rest of Nueva for food, which you will provide."

"Quin..."

"This is how you win people," I snapped. "You earn the right. Down there they're not rebelling out of perversity, they're doing it because you have shown you have nothing to offer them, and people who've planned this for a very long time have managed to take over. So if you discredit those leaders and put them in a situation they can't handle, those people will come back to you. But not if all you can offer is the same old. You're going to have to change too."

"Quin, we have this situation well in hand, and–"

"You do not have it in hand," I said bluntly. "You haven't had it in hand since you first provoked this by going back on your promises, and nothing's going to change now."

"*Now listen here, you–*"

That was more like it – he was starting to revert to type.

"Talk me through your version," I said. "What happens now? Elections?"

"*Elections? Are you joking? These people have shown they can't be trusted to run–*"

"And neither can you!" Suddenly I was shouting, though I had resolved that I wouldn't. "Why can't you just get it into your head that people aren't prepared to do what they're told by you because Papá knows best! Most people down there are every bit as intelligent as you and in the short run most of them have a hell of a lot more to lose. And in the long run we all lose equally anyway because this isn't about you, this isn't about hijos versus segundas or the peninsula versus the rest of us, it's about all us Nuevans working together and not starving in the next ten years! Won't it just be great when Alex gets back here just in time to watch the last Nuevan die of starvation because the planet he left behind tore itself to pieces over a petty little matter like who gets to run which bit of it!"

"*And so, you're removing the danger of starvation by threatening to destroy a couple of farms?*"

"I am going to couple a destroy... I mean..." I took a breath. "I will destroy a couple of farms because that's the only way I can see both you lot being forced to work together. I'll talk to you again after."

I recognised the danger signs in myself: get too agitated, lose control of your words, let someone who is very good at words – like my grandfather – run rings around you. So I broke contact.

Hahn was back on again.

"*Interesting,*" she said. "*Okay. Thought here in Port Control is that you may not be completely stark staring mad after all. But I'm warning you, if it looks like even one person down there gets killed through your actions, we send in the drones to get you out of there and we risk a few of your alleged mines.*"

She didn't wait for a reply and I didn't give one. I spent the rest of the hour thinking.

* * *

AN HOUR LATER, confident I had the undivided attention of Nueva, I destroyed Wheeler.

Satellite view confirmed the fields were empty of people. I started at the south west corner and worked my way by zigzags across to the north east. Land charred and turned black under the beam. Hundreds of acres of cold weather crops flashed into flame and ashes in seconds. The protective domes took one lick of the blazing light from above and crumpled in on themselves, then exploded in violent paroxysms of superheated air.

The foamcast buildings that housed the myco production plants stood up for a few seconds more before exploding in great gouts of black, greasy smoke. And then I came to the livestock.

That was when I hesitated. Cattle and sheep were rare commodities on Nueva, and the most innocent of bystanders in our civil war. Fires a hundred metres high raged all around them and the sky was black with smoke. They had clustered in the corners of their enclosures furthest from the flames and were terrified out of their stupid little minds. But I knew that if I started showing pity to animals, I would be in a very poor position to be merciless to humans. So I whispered, "sorry," and finished them off too.

It all just took a few minutes, to undo years of work and the livelihoods of thousands of people.

"That was Wheeler, Nueva," I said. "The Executive and the government of the Peninsular Republic have an hour to agree to my terms before Haregano goes the same way. Now, these are the terms that I expect both parties to agree to…"

And just in case there was any doubt about it, I had Hahn post them on every node she could get access to. I was probably less succinct when I said them out loud – I'd neglected to bring anything to write on – but in short they were:

1. Both sides to lay down their arms immediately.
2. Elections to be held across La Nueva Temporada

within a month for a new assembly that would replace
the Council of Representatives and rule the planet.

3. A full, total and complete amnesty for all actions
taken on either side concerning this rebellion.

I phrased that last one to make the rebels feel safe in laying
down their arms. The discerning reader will also note that it
covered the case of yours truly.

I hadn't expected a reply within an hour so, as promised,
I destroyed Haregano. To tell the truth, I think I would have
found an excuse to do it anyway. The Republic could still have
survived with two farms and I couldn't have that.

This was where events entered that grey area in my plans that
I hadn't really looked at very closely.

Within the following hour, the Republic announced that it
accepted my terms, and I thought, *damn!* because I had wanted
my grandfather to blink first: to commit, once and for all, and
in public, to the reforms that he needed to make. But if the
Republic blinked first...

As a sign of good faith, the holders-out at Cabrera laid down
their weapons. My grandfather promptly announced that the
government of Nueva had won a great victory for everyone,
welcomed the non-combatants of the former Republic back
into the fold, and announced treason charges against the former
leaders. Elections would be held, he announced vaguely, once
the present state of emergency was over – but recent events had
done nothing to hasten that end. As for those ridiculous terms
posted by that lunatic in charge of the laser, *he* hadn't agreed
to anything.

And I thought, *bugger*.

That was when the anaesthetic gas they had been quietly
pumping into the blister for the last twenty minutes finally
overwhelmed me.

CHAPTER 24

THE END OF THE BEGINNING

Quin is 31

THEY HADN'T CUT through the hatch, which I would have noticed. They had used nanites to drill a very small hole through the rock next to it. The gas came from the supplies stored in some backroom of Puerto Alto, a leftover from the long-ago when a million people a year passed through the station and it might have been needed in the event of civil disturbance. I don't know if they told Hahn what they were doing; I don't know if she would have told me if they had.

I woke up, under guard, in an elevator car that had been given clearance for an unscheduled descent. So, I didn't even get to say goodbye to Puerto Alto. I did think about asking what would happen to my personal possessions... but I realised I probably wouldn't be needing them for a long time.

At this stage, I was reasonably well treated. They let me eat and drink but I wasn't allowed near anything technological. They weren't thugs, they were just well meaning functionaries who had volunteered for the laser job. They had come down from the conceptuals and, after all, I had kindly spared their lives.

On the ground it was different. I was handed over to the Altiplano Constabulary, hijos all, for whom the career of Judas Iscariot had been but a low-budget dress rehearsal for the life of Quin Mateo. I was whisked off to a cell somewhere in the precinct house and I managed to fall against a few unyielding objects, to add to the ones I had already fallen against whilst sitting quietly in the back seat of the groundcar. The only time anyone mentioned a lawyer was when the booking officer told me, with a malicious smile, that under the emergency protocols I could be held for up to a month without one.

And then I was in a brightly lit cell with a table, a toilet, and a bunk with no bedclothes, all smelling of cleaning chemicals and body odour. They left me my clothes and I wasn't put on suicide watch; they were probably hoping I would spare them all the trouble. Then the door slid shut and locked itself with a decisive *clunk*, leaving me on one side and my entire life, career, hopes and aspirations squarely on the other.

I probably sat for a couple of hours, stewing in my own misery. Then I paced about a bit, then I sat a bit longer. Eventually the door unlocked and slid open for one of the guards.

"Can I get you anything, Señor Mateo?"

"Something to drink and eat?"

"Sure. Anything else?"

He was looking expectantly at me, like I was supposed to get a hint. I took him in more carefully.

"What's your name?" I asked.

"Robertson, Señor."

Segunda, then. Possibly more sympathetic towards me than his hijo brethren. I thought I would press my luck.

"Could you get me a tablet, tio?"

"Sure."

He gave a friendly nod and the door closed. A short while later he was back with coffee, and some sandwiches, and a tablet, albeit one with any kind of access disabled.

The tablet had only really been a test to see what I could get away with, but now I had it, I thought I should use it. It would pass the time.

And so I've been writing this, all the key stages in my life that have got me into this particular pickle. I had no real purpose or target audience in mind, at first. For posterity? Maybe. But gradually I've come to realise who I'm really writing it for.

Hola, Alejandro, big brother of mine. You're still twelve years away from Earth but you've got that far and you'll probably make it all the way. You may even get the wormhole re-opened. And what will you find when you get back here? Probably a handful of Nuevans clinging on to their existence in caves, because the rest of them – us – were too stupid to work together and hang on. Maybe one of your Terran friends will pry this account from the frozen fingers of your dead brother, trapped in his cell when the power went off after the fall of civilisation.

Believe it or not, that's a more cheerful thought than some of the ones I'm having.

I'm sorry we let you down, Alex. I would so love to have met you. You did more than enough on your part but we couldn't manage the simple act of staying alive for forty years. Still, the infrastructure is in place. Maybe you and yours can get the Thaw going again. Make Nueva somewhere worth living, with no bloody hijos to screw things up. If any of us survive, put us all on Puerto Alto and cut the cable.

I just wanted you to know that your brother did what he could.

PART 5
THE COMING OF THE NUEVANS

CHAPTER 25

JUMP

Wake up.

Alex came awake with a shudder. He hadn't exactly been sleeping but he hadn't really been awake either. The ship had alerted him because they had left Kilimanjaro eight hours earlier. It was time.

Half of Earth was spread out underneath the car and it occurred to Alex this was the first time he had seen it with his own eyes from space. Sparkling blues and whites were a dazzling contrast to the world of his birth. The atmosphere below was a haze layered over the crystal fineness of the planet; they were so high up now that high grade vacuum was wrapped around the car on all sides. He couldn't tell just by looking that he was moving at all. Weight had almost vanished. The car was still accelerating but only very slightly, creating a very small sense of gravity. A loose object would tumble very slowly to the floor.

Lights in the lounge were low. Jo Odembo wasn't in sight; he assumed she was taking a bathroom break. There were other passengers scattered around, taking up couches and chatting quietly over their drinks.

Alex grunted and stretched. Then he reached his headspace out to *Phoenicia*, and despite his nerves the ship's delight at the renewed contact made him smile. In contrast to its usual aloofness he could picture the ship in orbit, jumping up and down with eagerness, wagging its tail, loving what it knew was coming.

Like any passenger unaccustomed to microgravity and held down only by the overshoes issued by the elevator staff, he made his way slowly over to Nathan. The old man was slumped in a chair with the particles box hugged tight to his chest. Alex had to shake him awake and he looked up out of blurred eyes.

"It's time."

"Oh, crap. All right." Nathan woozily unstrapped himself and got up.

Ready, Alex sent, and he had to smile again at the cybernetic equivalent of *whee!* that flooded into his mind.

Alex and Nathan headed together for the central spiral staircase that connected all the decks. The only deck above them now was deck one, crew territory, authorised personnel only. Alex kept slightly behind Nathan so that he could surreptitiously guide the old man.

"Uh, excuse me..." the barman called. Then more loudly: "excuse me! Hey! That's only for crew members–"

"Oh piss off." Nathan muttered. "It's not like we're hijacking you, we just want to get off..."

Two of the elevator's stewards had registered the misbehaving passengers. Their expressions settled into a fixed mask of grim politeness and they began to come forward. At the same time the barman's polite smile vanished and he also started to move towards them.

Nathan suddenly threw the box through the hatch above, straight up through the middle of the spiral stairs, hard enough to overcome the vestigial gravity, and jumped after it. He soared through the hatch above like an experienced spacer and looked back down at Alex.

"Well? Coming?"

Alex kicked his way up after Nathan in one bound while the barman was still making his way across the lounge. The man made the classic mistake of trying to hurry. His overshoes came unstuck and he swore as he tumbled slowly in mid-air. The stewards were making much better progress and their eyes were fixed on Alex. He took one last look down into the lounge, where other passengers were slowly waking up to the unusual events, and grinned at the sight of the barman gently bouncing off the floor. Then he pulled the emergency close switch. An alarm began to sound as the hatch hissed shut into its airtight seal and he threw the lock.

The top deck was much smaller and more spartan than the one below. White plastic walls were studded with lockers and equipment, and hatches led to the innards of the car's mechanisms and the control cabin. Nathan and Alex only had seconds with that alarm going off, but they were already right next to where they wanted to be: the upper airlock. Alex poised his fingers over the keypad next to it.

"Code?"

5136A.

Ever since it had arrived, the ship had slowly been worming its way into the confidences of most of the blackboxes in orbit. It was an intrusion that only a very clever security system could detect because it was all in idle chat and it wasn't after any deep secrets. The point of a code like this wasn't to keep anything confidential or hidden – it was just to make sure only authorised personnel could get through, and to slow down any unauthorised ones who tried it long enough for them to be apprehended. It was very top level data and the ship had been able to skim it up along with a thousand other possibly useful facts.

Alex tapped out the code and they slipped inside as the hatch slid open. He pulled the lever that shut the hatch again and locked it tight. It was purely mechanical and couldn't be overridden by any blackbox. The only way in was to cut, which the crew probably wouldn't bother doing until they reached High-Kili. And even if they did try now, they would take too long.

"God, I'm mad," Nathan grumbled, but he had already opened the locker containing the suit belts. "How's our friend?"

Alex checked.

Phoenicia was falling down out of orbit, swooping gracefully towards Earth and the hair-thin line that was the elevator cable sticking up from it. It reported that it was free of all waking personnel. The ship had warmed up from its interstellar voyage and no one on board had now expected to need a spacesuit, so when it began to close bulkheads and pump air out of compartments, the crew had been easy to shepherd. Once they were all corralled in the auxiliary equipment module they had been unceremoniously ejected from the ship's spine for pickup. Meanwhile Traffic Control was on high alert but the ship was blithely ignoring its increasingly anxious signals.

"Doing fine," he reported. Nathan just grunted. Together they slung the lifepacks over their shoulders and pulled the collar rings over their heads, and as always Alex tried not to squirm as he felt his spacesuit grow out over him. It always tickled as the smartcloth slid and tightened around him, adjusting to his body shape. The background hum of the airlock died away as the helmet extended up from his shoulders to cover his head.

Finally they helped each other on with the thruster packs that hung on one wall. Alex carefully chose the command pack – the one that could slave all the other packs to its will. Nathan fastened the particle box to his wrist.

"Do these things handle being sick?" Nathan's voice asked in Alex's ears.

"Yes," he answered shortly, as he turned to the airlock controls.

"That may be as well..."

The ship gave Alex the code for the outer door. It slid open and all that stood between them and harsh vacuum was the airlock membrane. A sourceless metallic blue light filled the airlock. Straight ahead was a field of pitch black – no stars, no planet, just a well of infinite depth that the eye could barely focus on. It was only when they moved to the edge of the door, their toes on the very edge of space, that they could look down and see Earth below, the source of the light.

"Oh my God," said Nathan, looking down towards the world beneath his feet. "Told you. Sober." He checked the life display on his wrist. "I hardly need this thing." The display showed that the suit had detected his physical condition to be sub-optimal for spacework – a polite shorthand for too old and too drunk – and was taking care of it for him. The suit was running his body, supplementing him back to full health and the prime of life.

Alex looked down into the abyss.

"Ready?"

Nathan's head turned very slowly towards him.

"No," he said with heavy sarcasm, "I'm completely unprep–"

Alex gave his friend a powerful shove, pushing him through the membrane and toppling him out into space.

"EVENING, LADS. ALL behaving?"

Jo stepped through the hatch into the control cabin and the flight crew smiled back at her, always happy for the distraction. She always thought 'flight' was a rather grand term for operating an elevator that was limited to going up or down, though she was ready to admit it probably required more training than she had.

The flight captain passed round the drinks.

"So, who's the prisoner?"

Jo smiled at him over the rim of her cup. She hadn't made a scene when she moved in on Mateo but it must have been obvious to the cabin crew that she had reeled one of the passengers in. She had left him in a doze on the deck below. "He's not a prisoner, and I'm not at liberty to say."

"Oh, come on!"

"Just a hint!"

It was all good humoured joshing and she decided to tease them with some facts that were technically accurate.

"He's a nice kid who took some bad advice."

"He's pretty young to be getting this kind of attention," the flight captain said perceptively. He looked directly at Jo as he said it and she sensed a challenge.

Frighteningly young, she agreed, but she kept it to herself. She had been younger than Alex Mateo when she first officially trod the streets of Ken-Tan-Moz but it had been a long time before she was entrusted even with driving a squad car, let alone taking command of a starship and the full weight of a mission to save a planet.

For the flight captain's benefit, she just smiled and shrugged.

"Hidden depths..." she began to say, and then the alarms went off. The crew leapt for their stations.

"Code four," the flight captain reported. Jo took half a second to run through the list of code alerts in her head. *Unauthorised orbital manoeuvring in proximity to elevator cable.*

That could be anything from a capsule to –

"It's *Phoenicia!*" the flight captain exclaimed to the room in general. "Coming right at us!"

Images filled Jo's headspace – Earth, High-Kili, cable, car, full orbital deployment... and *Phoenicia*, on a projected arc that intersected with their present position nicely.

And then the internal alarm went off, at the same time as a seething barman cut into headspace.

"*Sergeant Odembo, this is the chief steward. Your friend just jumped up to deck one.*"

"Mateo!" she exclaimed.

"Who?" The flight captain glanced at her, and she saw the realisation. "Your little friend downstairs? What's *Phoenicia* got to do with –"

"Revised velocity projections," said the co-pilot, and the flight captain's attention was diverted. If *Phoenicia* was heading right at them then they either had to slow down or speed up – either way, just not be there when it hit.

Jo was already out in the corridor, just in time to see the hatch of the upper airlock close and the 'locked' light appear.

"*What?*"

It wasn't hard to link the two strands of thought. Mateo was here, *Phoenicia* was approaching...

He was going to get back to his ship.

Rage, spiked with a grudging admiration, surged up within her. The conniving, sneaky little bastard! He must have intended this all along. Acting all like the kid out of his depth who just wants to get back home... And now this.

But how was he going to do it? He couldn't possibly have hidden a capsule outside the car. Was there one somehow poised in orbit, ready to pick him up? A quick check in headspace said there wasn't – and besides, with the elevator moving at 1,500 kilometres an hour straight up, any rendezvous would take split second timing. The only possible way to do that was–

"Oh my God," she murmured. "He's mad."

NATHAN VANISHED INSTANTLY from view with an angry yell as the elevator's continued acceleration yanked him from sight. Alex flexed his knees and jumped after him.

Vapour flashed as Nathan's suit fired its thrusters to control his tumble. Alex drifted gently down towards him and fired his own thrusters to match speed. The elevator car had disappeared and just the cable remained, a flat grey face stretching up and down into infinity with the two of them hanging next to it. It was too smooth and featureless to give an idea that they were falling, though Alex knew they were.

They glared at each other through their faceplates.

"You're as bad as your father," Nathan grumbled. He flashed readout figures to Alex's headspace. "And I've just checked. You know these things are only for small range use? We don't have the fuel for the kind of manoeuvring you're talking about."

"Bit late now, isn't it?" Alex said absently as he sent commands to his suit. "How's life support?"

"Huh? Well, fine, thank you for asking, as long as I'm wearing this thing I feel like I'm your age but, you know, the fuel? I can't help noticing you're not worried, so I assume there's some kind of plan– *woah!* What's that?"

His suit thrusters had fired again, in unison with Alex. Like freefall dancers, the two of them were turning in unison.

"That was me overriding your suit. You're slaved to me. And there's enough fuel–"

"There isn't, there really isn't..."

"... including reserves, for one long thirty second burn to get us away from the cable," Alex finished. "Three..."

"What?" It was a panicked yelp. "That wasn't what you said! You're mad!"

"... two, one, go."

Their suit thrusters fired and they plummeted down, away from the cable and towards Earth.

Phoenicia came to meet them.

The ship had already reached the right orbit and Earth's cloud systems whipped by beneath it. It had tilted itself up so that the stern pointed down towards the planet and the bow up towards space and High-Kili. The jagged, dirty mass of the ice shield was between the ship and the station.

Alex and the ship had known what would happen because it was precisely what Puerto Alto would do back home. The safety of the elevator cable took precedence over everything else and there were laser emplacements ready to defend it. Now they opened fire and the ice shield took the brunt. Terawatt energy pulses dashed against it and gusts of superheated steam flashed into space, whittling down the shield bit by bit but leaving the ship behind it unscathed. Nathan and Alex watched the show from a distance as the ship approached over the curve of the planet.

"Very pretty," Nathan grudgingly admitted.

Alex smiled grimly as the ship rushed towards them with no signs of stopping. Some complex low orbit manoeuvres, the chance to show off a little... he could tell *Phoenicia* was just loving this.

Something wrapped hard around his foot, which startled him and made him look abruptly down, though he should have been expecting it. Two drones, fired ahead by the ship, had come up towards them from a lower orbit. The drones grasped their feet with their manipulators and thrust themselves on a course and a speed that gradually converged with the approaching ship.

Phoenicia turned on its external lights as it approached, and its long hull became a mass of brightly lit spars and struts and impenetrable pools of black shadow.

The aft spine passed slowly beneath them as the drones carried them down to Command & Habitation, where the airlock was already open. They passed through the membrane and their feet touched down inside. Alex was puzzled by a strange sound in his ears until he realised it was Nathan, laughing. It started as a very mild chuckle, and grew louder and louder until his body was visibly shaking.

"We did it! We did it!" Through his faceplate, Alex could see Nathan's face-splitting grin. Nathan clouted him on the shoulder. "You're a mean little bully with no respect for an old man but we did it!"

Alex laughed. "What do the godfather's vows say about jumping off elevators?"

"Hmm. That is definitely a theological grey area, best left to the conscience of the individual..." Nathan glanced over Alex's shoulder and his eyes widened. "Who the hell are you?"

It happened fast and later Alex had to reconstruct the scene from his fragmented memories. A blurred motion: three more spacesuited figures jetted through the membrane even as the outer door was sliding closed. Two flashes, two loud retorts that were almost simultaneous, and the drones shuddered, then drifted away with blank status displays to bump into the walls. A charred hole in the casing of the nearest one showed where it had been shot. The three spacesuited strangers stood with weapons in their hands raised and aimed at Nathan and Alex.

Then the strangers shot them.

CHAPTER 26

ON BOARD

THE FEELING WAS like falling down a long flight of concrete stairs, all compressed into a single second. Alex's mind seemed to retreat a long way to the back of his skull, pulling away from his body, not wanting to go back to that physical world of blood and tissue and sensation because it would hurt.

One of the men grabbed him to hold him steady, as he spun in mid-air with twitching limbs. The man jabbed at his waist controls so that his suit retracted back into its shell.

"Just in case." The man who had shot him sounded complacent. "Nothing personal." He had a broad face with a high forehead, and pale eyes that regarded Alex as a scientist might view a captured specimen.

"Wh... wh..."

In his mind, Alex was very clearly saying "Who the *fuck* are you?" but the words weren't able to squeeze past his swollen tongue. Headspace was telling him nothing, not even their names. These three weren't tagged in any way. They were walking vacuums of information, and that would have made Alex very nervous even without being shot. All the triumph, all the elation of the jump had been zapped away by the stun charge. It was all too sudden for anger or fear; his jolted brain couldn't quite get a hold on itself to feel emotions like that. To the ship, he sent:

"*I thought you got rid of everyone who was on board?*"

I did. These people seem to have waited outside me. Take hold of one of the hand rails. I will open the outer hatch and expel them –

"No. *They've taken my suit off.*" They thought ahead, these people, whoever they were.

"The old guy's in a bad way, Ara," a man said. Nathan's form hung unmoving in mid-air. Alex made a croaking noise and twitched a hand towards his godfather. It was the only outward sign he could make of an inward shout of rage and a desire to get to Nathan and look after him.

"*Ship, are you getting anything from Nathan's suit?*"

I am getting nothing. The suit's intelligence has been completely disabled.

Alex cried out. He had done this! He had got Nathan Sulong into a position where the old man depended on his suit to keep him alive. With the suit knocked out by the shot, suddenly he was just a very old, very ill man who had been through physical stresses no centenarian should be made to endure.

The leader looked down at Alex as if he had just revealed a very interesting weakness.

"Stabilise him," he ordered. He fumbled behind Alex's ear.

"*Zero interface!*" Alex ordered. "*You communicate only with me…*"

And then headspace went dead as Szabo's hand came away, holding the linkset that Alex had worn ever since leaving the lifepod. Alex's streaming eyes tracked the little sliver of plastic. The man grinned down at him without humour and winked. "Now bring 'em both."

ONE STEP AHEAD, Alex thought bitterly as they dragged him, powerless, through the corridors of his own ship. They had been one step ahead all the way.

Jo Odembo had been almost there. She had guessed he was still alive and that he intended to rejoin the ship; she just hadn't guessed how. But these... Had they followed her to him, and then worked it out for themselves? Or had they worked it all out right from the start?

Well, here they were, and it justified every paranoid precaution his father's mind had come up with to protect the mission. For what it was worth. It was now a sad fact that the ship was not his.

They put him and Nathan in the flight crew's quarters behind the bridge. It was basic but liveable in. They dropped Nathan onto one of the bunks that were set into the bulkhead and dropped Alex into one of the chairs that were fixed to the floor. Alex had time for a last look at his friend, and then the three men crowded around him like wolves cornering their prey and blocked his view. Alex felt the cool touch of a spray nozzle on his neck. He heard a hiss and immediately his head cleared.

"You are Alejandro Mateo, the not remotely deceased master of this ship. I'm Team Leader Ara Szabo of Hired Sword. First, you order—"

Alex could still barely move a limb but his mind at least was almost back to normal.

"My friend..." he gasped, expelling so much breath he needed to draw another, "needs help."

"We have a medico on him. It's doing what it can."

Alex glanced over at Nathan. There was indeed a small box lying on his chest, humming away to itself, but the old man's face was drawn and sheet white, and his eyelids were barely flickering.

"As I was saying, first, order the ship to return to its old orbit."

"Or..." Strength was returning to talk, but it was was still an effort. His tongue still felt thick. "Perhaps I could fire the... main drive and head... back home."

"Yeah, perhaps you could." Szabo leered down at him. "Let's assume you don't. Look, kid, this ship's too big for an orbit this low. It'll be a navigation hazard to itself and to others. Now, you can fire the engine, or we get tugs down here from High-Kili to tow us back up and you've cost us – oh, all of an hour."

He tucked the linkset back behind Alex's ear and headspace returned.

"So make life easier for everyone, and tell your ship to interface with Traffic Control for a return path."

Alex let his head fall back and passed the order on. Szabo took a pause to confirm it was happening in his own headspace. His smirk was smug and satisfied.

"And now get my friend into a healer," Alex said.

Vibrations ran through the ship as *Phoenicia* made the manoeuvres needed to resume its old orbit, and the men instinctively put hands and arms out to brace as the room shifted around them. The ship could have done the journey in minutes but out of consideration for the organic lifeforms on board, Alex knew it would take a few hours of gentle boost.

"Dr Sulong is an expert on wormholes, I believe?" Szabo asked. Alex nodded and Szabo's eyes went cold. "Then his services won't be required in the near future."

A headspace window opened. The view was from an external camera mounted on the hull, looking back across the spars of the kilometre-long aft spine towards the ship's drive. The view was interrupted by the single module that contained the wormhole terminus.

Szabo gestured again and the terminus soundlessly erupted. Glittering fragments burst out into space. Two more explosions followed the first and a dim echo of the vibration rumbled down the hull. It was muffled so that it sounded like a faint storm on the horizon, safe and gentle, a good distance away. But there was nothing safe and gentle about what had happened to the terminus. Alex could see at a glance that it was utterly wrecked. It would never be opening any wormholes.

He let them read what they would into his increasingly heavy rate of breathing.

Szabo picked up the precious red case that Alex and Nathan had brought so far and held it at arm's length as if it were a pair of soiled underwear. Then he dropped it on the deck and with one swift movement pulled out his gun, thumbed it to max, aimed and fired. The box leapt and crackled. The casing split and a trickle of smoke crept from the cracked seams.

Szabo stopped before it could set off the fire alarms and reholstered his gun. Then he reached behind Alex's ear again and removed the linkset.

"So shall we agree," he said, "that talk of wormholes is now redundant? Good. Now, since we have time to kill, I've been instructed to make you an offer…"

Alex looked him in the eyes.

"Get my friend into a healer."

Szabo rolled his eyes, then nodded at one of the other men. Alex still didn't know their names. One of the two had blond hair streaked with red, the other was a dark brown. Blond moved over to Nathan's bunk and Alex felt relief that at least Nathan was going to get help.

Blond whipped the pillow from beneath Nathan's head and pressed it down over his face.

"No!" Alex lunged forward but suddenly Brown's strong hands were holding him down from behind.

At another nod from Szabo, Blond pulled the pillow away again.

"Did no one ever tell you not to interrupt a grown-up? No? Well, maybe I've cured you of that habit." Szabo crouched down in front of Alex. "Now listen, Mateo. Believe it or not, we're making you an offer, and it's a good one. One you could even enjoy. We want you to leave Earth, in this ship."

"And return to Nueva," said Alex, dully, not bothering to meet his eye.

"Nope." Alex looked up in surprise. "We want you to go onwards, to Epsilon Eridani. We give you a fresh set of particles from Earth and you open a new wormhole."

"Epsilon …"

"It's ten light years from Earth and there's a ninety-one percent chance of an Earth type planet, and I mean a proper planet actually orbiting a proper sun, not like the frozen little moon you were born on. It's all set up. The finance, the plans, the recruitment drive. A twenty year journey, a new wormhole and then, in twenty years and one month's time we're shipping out colonists by the millions. Look, I don't know how much you saw of Earth when you were down there but it's either way too crowded, in the cities, or it's barely habitable in the outback where they grow the food for the cities to eat. Oh, no one starves, people stay clean and healthy, but for every rich guy like your friend with his own private kranny there's fifty families living in a room not much bigger than this. How many were on the voyage to La Nueva Temporada? Ten thousand? So, we promise everyone a farm with plenty of space around them and we can get that many volunteers tomorrow, just like that." He snapped his fingers. "But there's no point if we don't have a ship. Oh look. We do!"

Alex frowned up at him. He could see the flaw in the argument, and so presumably could Szabo, so what point was he missing?

"The ship's plans must be on record. Build your own."

"A ship like this is beyond any clan or even a group of clans. There's too many for that kind of direction. Sure, we could cobble the main structure together eventually but the annihilation drive is something else. You need good, solid, reliable industry for that. *Phoenicia* only got built in the first place because all the European clans banded together, and look what happened! The effort broke them. No, kid, Earth won't be building any new starships any time soon. The Martians might, but they won't; ditto the Jovians, because neither of them are going to take away resources from developing their own worlds. Nope. This is the ship we need and this is the ship we have. Now, there's ways and means of convincing it to go along with this plan but the best and easiest way, and so the way we'll try first, is for you to tell it to. So, Mateo, what do you say?"

Alex took a moment to marshal his thoughts.

"First," he said, "you left out the bit about all the backers getting incredibly rich, because believe me, I know that's what they'll be planning because that's what we were going to do ourselves. Second, your vision doesn't seem to include Nueva."

"Because it doesn't *need* Nueva!" Szabo urged. His eyes shone with a strange zeal and he seemed to have forgotten it would be completely wasted on a Nuevan audience. He obviously believed and held it in his heart. "The place is – was – a *drain!* We need it even less now than we did back when..."

That was when he did seem to remember who he was talking to.

"Back when the wormhole so conveniently exploded in the first place," Alex finished for him. He slowly bunched himself up in his chair, hands pressed loosely against the chair's arms, feet flat on the floor.

"That was certainly... convenient," Szabo agreed with his flat smile.

"Do you have a third point?" asked Blond.

"The third is, go to hell."

Alex kicked hard and flew at Szabo. He planned to ricochet off the Team Leader, grab the linkset en route, head out of the hatch and close it on them, gambling they wouldn't hurt Nathan if he wasn't around to be coerced by it. As a bonus, he had had enough practice with Felipe to know that he could inflict pain if he made contact and he was hoping that he would. Once they were on separate sides of the hatch he would make contact with the ship again and send in drones to take Nathan to sickbay.

He was betrayed by his own legs. He hadn't realised they were still so weak and he stumbled as Szabo moved abruptly out of the way. Brown tripped him up and held him down with a foot on the back of his neck. And then one of them shot him again.

This time it was just a low power jolt, still enough to make him scream as fire blazed in every nerve.

"Now, you could have seen that coming." Szabo said. For just a moment his calm vanished and it was the cold, harsh voice of a man prepared to condemn sixty million Nuevans without a qualm. "Look, we're not going to ask you to forget your world, or get over it in a hurry. We're not that stupid. But I will give you these alternatives. Suck it up, work for us, and take your ship to Epsilon Eridani willingly. Or, we pump you full of pentalthine and make you so susceptible that you'd fly into the sun and be glad to do us the favour. Your ship won't know the difference."

Alex took several deep breaths until the raw agony shooting around his nervous system had settled into a mere ache. Brown's foot in his ribs helped him turn over to look up at them. His voice shuddered with suppressed pain and rage and humiliation.

"All I want to do…" he gasped, "wanted… is… was open a new wormhole so that we could get the resources we need. There's sixty million of us. What right do you have to condemn us all to death?"

Szabo rolled his eyes. "Okay, we tried." He nodded at Blond. "Pentalthine."

Blond grinned and pulled a capsule of yellow fluid from his pocket. Szabo and Brown heaved him back into his chair and held him there, arms pinned behind him. He writhed in their grip but the double charges to his system had made him too weak to fight.

A new voice spoke from the hatch. "Szabo! What the hell are you doing?"

CHAPTER 27

SUPPLEMENTARY SUPPORT

"HE'S JUMPED!" THE flight captain was pale as Jo ran back to the control cabin. "He just jumped!"

"Of course he jumped, and I'm jumping too. But I'm not a spacer so you'll have to help me."

They looked at her, blank and baffled.

"He – and his ship – they've planned this," she urged. She tried to keep the momentum going, keep one step ahead of the common sense that would stop her doing this. "They know exactly what they're doing. If they can do it then it's safe. So help me do it too."

She was too aware that *safe* might be a very relative term here. She didn't have the welfare of a planet hanging on this.

"We can't just let our passengers go jumping," the captain pointed out. "It's bad for business." Jo drew a breath to object but the captain, very slowly, grinned. A hint of buried mischief sparkled at the back of his eyes.

"On the other hand, Sergeant Odembo, if the Orbital Police Force requests the co-operation of the elevator company in capturing a fugitive–"

"I do!" Jo said immediately. A fugitive was what Alex now was. He had to have broken some law.

"Right." He turned to his crew. "Put the seatbelt sign on and reduce speed by fifty per cent. I'll get the permissions. You two, get the sergeant suited up..."

Five minutes later, Jo stood in the entrance to the upper airlock. Her toes were on the rim of the void and she stared with wide eyed horror down at Earth. She barely heard the instructions of the crew as they strapped extra fuel packs onto her. She would be slaved to Traffic Control, it was all out of her hands – and she was much more interested in second thoughts.

So the boy was going back to his ship. What was the worst he could do? Open the wormhole? But that was what everyone wanted anyway...

Well, not everyone...

But it would be so much easier if they just all caught up with him naturally *and she didn't have to jump out of an orbital elevator thousands of kilometres above the planet's surface and plunge towards the atmosphere and–*

– and be known for ever more as the one who let Alex Mateo get away.

"*Sergeant.*" The captain's voice was in her ears. "*Turns out you won't need to do this anyway. Hired Sword have a crew on board–*"

"Hired Sword?" Jo exclaimed, and she jumped.

Hired Sword! she fumed as she plummeted towards Earth. The one thing that could make losing Mateo even worse would be Hired Sword claiming a victory by recapturing him. That was just not going to happen. She would get on board the ship, casually reclaim the situation, maybe give a breezy "thanks for your help, boys, I'll take it from here..."

A million points of light sparkled from the Indian Ocean below. It looked close enough to touch and she reached out to brush her hands against the clouds. Abruptly perspective returned and she knew she was at the same height as some satellites above the waves with *absolutely nothing* between them and her. She swore and closed her eyes. In headspace everything looked much safer – a graphic representation of the planet, of herself, of *Phoenicia* below and ahead. The starship was a dwindling point approaching the horizon at a speed she could never match. In headspace she could continue to watch its course around the curve of the planet but somehow that just made it even more unattainable.

Her suit announced that it was turning her round. She spun in space so that she faced back the way she had come, away from the way *Phoenicia* had gone – and in the direction *Phoenicia* would be coming when it had orbited around Earth in thirty-seven minutes' time. And then the booster fired, a full-burn roar that vibrated throughout her body, and she started to fall.

Phoenicia was in a lower orbit, and to get there she had to drop down, which would also mean picking up speed because the lower she got, the less time it would take to go around the planet. She knew the basics but was happy to leave the execution up to cleverer people than her. And she was very glad for the absence of air, which meant no wind, which meant no feeling of movement – nothing at all to tell her she was in fact travelling fast enough to rendezvous with an orbiting ship.

Booster exhausted. Burn will recommence with first reserve pack in thirty seconds.

To use the extra packs she had brought with her, she had to plug the fuel line in herself. Her gloved fingers scrabbled at the valve.

The fuel line was in, the booster fired again and she resumed her downward plunge. She risked opening her eyes. She was diving head first towards the planet and it reared in front of her like a wall she was about to hit. She closed her eyes again quickly.

Fuel pack exhausted. Burn will recommence with second reserve pack in thirty seconds.

Another fumble. The carefully planned flight path assumed each pack would be discarded, and if it was still attached then the flight plan would be wrong because she would be the wrong weight and... Her fingers trembled and seemed to bounce off the buckle. *Hold steady!* she screamed to herself. *Just hold it... and turn... turn... TURN, you little...*

The empty pack fell free, the line was in the new pack. The booster continued its oblivious countdown and fired.

The second pack went the way of the first and the third pack took over. But she had reached the orbit she needed, so, no more precipitous dives. Now she had to cancel speed and stay there. The suit turned her around and boosted gently – a soft, ten minute burn that put her exactly into the orbit she needed with just drops of fuel to spare.

Phoenicia approached and headspace showed their relative orbits and speeds. The ship was travelling slightly faster than her, and a few hundred metres lower. It would pass between her and the planet, easily close enough to snag with her suit's grapple.

She felt safe enough to open her eyes. The starship was a point of light that slowly grew and unblurred into the familiar tangle of struts and spars. It was still distant enough to look delicate and light – an illusion that slowly wore off as it drew ever closer and she was able to make out more and more detail – the stubble of vacant docking ports and access hatches that ran along the spines. Somehow this seemed different to the first time she boarded it. Then, she had been the one approaching while it waited for her. Now she couldn't shake the feeling that the ship was bearing down on her.

Headspace told her to raise her right arm and aim at the ship. A target point appeared in her vision. She gave the *fire* command and the wrist-mounted grapple shot towards the ship, a thin monofilament line trailing behind it. It would attach to the hull and reel her in–

The line went suddenly rigid as it reached its maximum length, and slack again as it recoiled from its own elasticity. It hadn't fastened on. It hadn't even reached the ship. Jo screamed in frustration.

"Distance to *Phoenicia*," she demanded, and at the same time ordered the grapple to coil back in.

Approximately five hundred metres, said her suit.

"Insufficient! I need to know exactly!"

She would have to get closer. She fired the booster to close the gap, and it burned for all of five seconds before finally running dry. Jo screamed again.

Five hundred and thirteen metres and closing.

And it was a five hundred metre line. The ship drifted by beneath her feet, but she was moving in on it by momentum and if she could just get the line recoiled in time for another effort–

The ship's main drive unit was passing beneath her. That was the end of the aft spine. She didn't need to use headspace to see she wasn't going to make it.

"*Phoenicia!*" She hadn't been going to talk to the ship just in case it took Alex's side. Now she couldn't be so choosy. "Help!"

To all parties who try to make contact with starship Phoenicia. The words were cool and undramatic. *The ship's master has forbidden contact with any external parties and therefore no further interaction with you can be undertaken. Thank you for your attention.*

"No! *Phoenicia!* Screw you! I need help! I need... um... mayday! *Phoenicia*, mayday! I am out of thruster fuel and–"

Mayday acknowledged, zero interface order overridden. Please identify yourself.

The voice was just as cool and unremarkable as before, but Jo almost burst into tears.

"Odembo. Sergeant Jo Odembo, Orbital Police Force."

Thank you, Sergeant Odembo. Your position is noted. I am sending a drone to retrieve you.

FIVE MINUTES LATER she touched down in the same airlock where she had arrived days earlier. When her helmet retracted she took a deep breath of ship's air with considerably more gratitude than before.

"Thank you, *Phoenicia*! Now, where is everyone?"

No answer.

"*Phoenicia*, I... oh, yeah, right."

Now there was no longer an emergency, no lives in danger, the ship could return to its former zero interface. Jo stepped through the inner hatch into the body of the ship.

"Mateo? Hired Sword people?"

Okay, she thought, where would they put him? Somewhere with doors if they wanted to hold him securely.

Headspace was closed to her and she couldn't consult stored memories of the ship's layout. She just had to use her own recollections and follow her nose down to Command & Habitation. At one point she thought she heard a couple of distant explosions. What the hell?

And then a scream echoed in the ship's empty passages as she approached the bridge. Again, what the *hell?* She broke into a wary run.

She poked her head into the bridge, caution and speed mingled together. It was empty but there was another hatch beyond the pilot's couch. Now she could hear voices and she was pretty certain she recognised the one doing the talking.

"... take your ship to Epsilon Eridani willingly. Or, we pump you full of pentalthine and make you so susceptible that you'd fly into the sun and be glad to do us the favour. Your ship won't know the difference."

She could hear heavy breathing – long, shuddering breaths – and then Alex Mateo:

"All I want to do... wanted..."

Jo moved closer.

"Okay, we tried. Pentalthine."

Jo got to the hatch. She saw Alex pinned down in a chair, and around him were a blond man and a brown haired man and...

"Szabo!" Jo exclaimed. "What the hell are you doing?"

She hadn't meant it as a distraction but it was all Alex needed. The three men all looked up in blank surprise. The one with brown hair slackened his grip slightly and Alex pitched forward, smashing his head into Szabo's midriff so that the Team Leader doubled over, too winded to utter more than a gasp of pain. But even as he was on his way down, Alex actively fell into Szabo's grasp, wrapping both arms and legs around him and pulling him down to the floor. Szabo writhed to get free but Alex clung onto him like a parasite. Szabo thumped him in the ribs with fists and elbows but he held on, scrabbling for something in Szabo's pocket. It only took a couple of seconds before the other two could pull him off their leader but that was all it took. They threw him back into his chair and he grinned as his hand went to his ear. Jo just caught a glimpse of the linkset being put back into place.

"Gracias, tios…"

Restraining straps flashed around him, pinning him into his chair, and around the still form of Nathan Sulong in his bunk.

She started forward, drew a breath to shout "*Get the linkset, you fools!*"; and then a bass rumble filled the room. A force took hold of her body that plucked her feet from the floor and tried to throw her across to the far bulkhead. She just had time to grab the door frame. For a second it was as if the room had turned ninety degrees so that the far wall was suddenly the floor. Mateo was strapped into his chair and it was fixed to the floor but the three Hired Sword men, with nothing to restrain or support them, fell three or four metres to the far bulkhead.

It was simple acceleration, Jo realised: for just a second, *Phoenicia* had suddenly throttled up its main drive.

The men slammed into the wall and slid to the floor in a groaning, grunting mass as the drive cut back to normal.

"Freeze the blackboxes on all guns," Alex ordered out loud, for everyone's benefit. "Drones to flight quarters – medical emergency. And you lot, just lie there. Spreadeagle. I want your hands and your feet well apart from each other. One twitch and I turn the drive back on again."

The three men very slowed moved to obey him. Jo could see the calculations in their minds. They could leap up, cross the gap between them in no more than a second… How much time did Alex need to fire the engine again? And how high could it go?

It wasn't worth finding out. One by one they spread themselves out on the floor as he had instructed, though their eyes burned with hate and never left him.

"And, Sergeant Odembo. You get over with them. Go round the side of the room. Now."

Jo sidled around the room. Alex in his chair turned to keep an eye on her. Four drones appeared in answer to his summons when she was halfway round, at her closest point to Alex, and they darted over to where Nathan lay.

"Sergeant! Get the little fucker!" Szabo shouted. Jo held up her empty hands.

"What with, Team Leader? Force of personality?"

One of the drones waved a sensor over Nathan, and then together they lifted the mattress out of the bunk and carried the old man out on the makeshift stretcher. Jo got a clear look at his lolling, pale face as they moved past her. He looked already dead.

The Hired Sword men lay still, glaring at Alex with a hatred that could have powered the ship. Jo didn't know whether to applaud or commiserate.

Jo reached the end of the room. The straps that held Alex released him and he climbed up on wobbling legs. He grinned over at her, though malicious glee burned behind the smile.

"I'm sorry, you seem nicer than these tios, but you need to stay with them."

"You know," she said, "I'm almost sure I am nicer?"

Alex staggered to the door, never taking his eyes off them.

"I'm locking you in and... um..." His smile was a brief flash of embarrassed apology through the pain. "Sorry."

BY THE TIME Alex got to the sickbay Nathan was almost hidden by a healer. He lay like a corpse inside the casing that covered his entire body. A mask covered half his face. The displays barely flickered and the fact that the healer was still operating was the only sign that Nathan wasn't already dead.

"Oh shit oh shit oh shit…" Alex leaned over him, peering into the half open eyes, trying to see something in there. "I'm so sorry, I'm so, so sorry, I didn't… I shouldn't…"

Nathan's head moved; the eyes opened a bit further and then crinkled. The old man had grinned as if in response to something coherent that Alex had managed to say. Then the head lolled again.

"I shouldn't have made you do it!" Alex blurted. "I'm so sorry. I didn't…"

"Oh, shut up." Nathan's voice was barely more than a whisper through the mask. Even his lips barely moved. He tried to say something else; Alex had to listen more closely. "Tell ship… enable… patient compensation."

"Ship, enable patient compensation," Alex said cautiously.

Enabling.

After a couple of minutes there was a noticeable change. Nathan's face was a little less white and his head could move more. He could actually lift it up off the pillow by a fraction.

"Thank you." His voice was still very weak. "These things won't let the patients give orders themselves."

Alex cast an anxious eye at the datacloud. To his non-medical eye there were still readings that looked too high and readings that looked too low, but nothing nice and comfortably in the middle of its range, where he felt they should be. The healer was pumping health and well-being into Nathan and even then all it could produce was this incredibly weak old man. Just how damaged was his friend?

"I shouldn't have made you do it," he said again.

"Of course you should. It had to work. Always get the best in."

"But… but…"

"Alex… could you hold my hand? It's very lonely in here."

Alex had to slide his hand into the healer casing, but he felt his fingers close around Nathan's. Nathan's grip had almost no strength.

"Is there a display with the word 'supplementary' in it?"

Alex studied the datacloud.

"Uh… supplementary support?"

"That's it. What figure does it give?"

"Seventy-six per cent."

Nathan closed his eyes. "Oh, bollocks."

"What does it mean?"

"That shows how much of the input needed to keep my body going is coming from the machine. On a healthy lad like you right now it would read zero. If it's up to seventy-six per cent… draw your own conclusions. I'm a walking corpse, boy. Except I'm not walking."

"But… but you can get better! It heals! It's a healer!"

"Get better from seventy-six per cent? Maybe if you got me into longsleep and even then it would be touch and go…" His hand clutched Alex's, hard, in response to the sudden surge of hope that Alex had felt. It must have shown on his face. "And you are *not* putting me to sleep for the next five years on the off-chance I'll wake up again. Look at me! Seventy-six per cent of a healer and I barely have strength to talk. No, Alex. They killed me."

"They didn't!" Alex's eyes filled with tears. "They didn't, you won't die, you–"

"If you don't shut up I'll give the euthanise command right now." Alex shut up. "They killed me," Nathan whispered again. "My heart's just too weak. Fact."

"Are… are you sure? How do you even know how a healer works?"

"Believe me, by my time in life, you know."

"But… Marietta…"

Alex remembered their parting back at the base of Kilimanjaro. They had said goodbye and that had been it. That couldn't be the end! Not the last they would ever see of each other!

"I happen to believe I'll be seeing her again and she believes the same. I'll see you too." He pulled his lips back to bare his teeth; it was probably meant to be a grin. "We both thought there was…" Nathan's voice dissolved into a racking, wheezing cough before coming back. "… was a good chance of me not… not returning."

"Then why the hell did you do this?" Alex cried out in disbelief. "Why did you even think of going through this if–"

"Sixty million lives. And I'm your godfather."

Alex grasped desperately around for any kind of suitable response that would match Nathan's logic. He could only find:

"*And?* I'm Quinito's godfather! I wouldn't do this for him!"

Another corpse grin. "Wouldn't you? Now there's a command I want you to give in a moment. 'Resume patient levels'. Got that?"

"Resume–"

"Don't say it out loud!" Nathan found the strength to snap at him, just, at the same time as Alex worked out in horror what it would mean. It would mean the machine withdrawing its supplementary assistance. It would mean turning Nathan off. "Not yet. There's still one thing to do…"

"You blew it, Sergeant!" Szabo's temper exploded the moment the hatch closed. The men clambered to their feet. "You so blew it! God, you are so finished–"

"I blew it?" Jo asked with wide-eyed innocence. "Little old unarmed me, when there were three of you, with guns, who took him by surprise? Yeah, I really slipped up."

Szabo glowered down at her.

"That's not the point," he said tightly and turned away to thump his fists against the hatch.

"Look," Jo said, "he's said all along that he just wants to save his planet. And we don't just want to leave them? Surely?"

Szabo flung his hands in the air with an exclamation of disgust. To him, Jo reflected, this was high-level debate. She excluded him from the process and looked at the other two.

"Do we?"

"All academic," said the brown haired man, "given that we blew up the terminus."

Jo stared at him in horror.

"You did what?"

"The point is," said the blond man, "we needed the ship. We didn't need a wormhole back to Nueva."

"You needed the *ship*? Why…" But then she remembered that snippet she had picked up from headspace. "The Epsilon Eridani expedition? Fine! Let the ship complete its mission and then it's all yours…"

"The expedition's ready to roll *now*," Brown insisted. "We need the ship *now*."

"Now? But an expedition like that would take ages to set up." Jo half laughed to dismiss what she was about to say in advance. "Unless it was all being planned while the ship was still en route and…" Three glares suddenly turned away from her as three men could no longer quite look her in the eye. "Oh. My. God. The plans really are that old?"

Szabo turned his head back and frankly met her gaze, waiting for her thought processes to get there.

"And if the Nuevans got back in touch it would just take resources away from this other expedition…"

Szabo raised an eyebrow to encourage her along.

"… and so," Jo realised, coming to a conclusion she really didn't want to reach, "there was never the slightest chance of a new wormhole?"

Szabo swore, vehemently, as if it was a personal affront.

Brown sighed. "There were policy considerations," he said.

Jo actually felt her own jaw drop.

"There's sixty million Nuevans on a planet that's slowly losing the ability to support them all! How can any policy be against that?"

"Living on a frozen rock was a choice the Nuevans made," said Szabo.

"Playing nursemaid will just drag us down with them," Brown added.

"You…" Jo had to start again. "You've had a really long time to square this with your conscience, haven't you?"

"Natural wastage will get the Nuevans down to a population that their world can support," Blond chipped in. "It's not like we're exterminating an entire race."

"No, you're just..." Jo's word trailed off under a heavy sense of *why bother?* They *had* had a long time to square this with their conscience, and they wouldn't be the only ones. Everything she had heard so far had the ring of a stock response to it. It was like communicating with a particularly dumb blackbox. If it can't parse the question, it just selects the nearest appropriate pre-recorded reply and plays that instead.

"Leave it out," Szabo said harshly. "She's chosen her side."

Never argue with an idiot, Jo had long ago been counselled; *people might not be able to tell the difference.* So, even though she longed to say something like *yes, I've chosen sides and that's why I'm stuck in here with you morons*, and generally skewer and humiliate him on the rapier of her wit, she instead just turned away and let a bitter, recriminatory silence fall over the room. What thoughts were going through their heads, she didn't know. What was going through her head was that she was in the same room as three men who had just written off a population of sixty million, and were okay with it.

Eventually the silence was broken by the hatch opening again.

First a pair of drones flew in and took up position on either side of the door. Only then did a red-eyed, sulky-looking Alex Mateo appear. He looked better than the last time they had seen him. He must have had some healer time of his own. A gun from Hired Sword's own cache was bulky and incongruous on his hip. His eyes were no longer dark and sullen – Jo could tell he had been crying recently. She could also see he wasn't going to cry again any time soon.

"He's dead," he said. He looked directly at Szabo. "You'll be charged with murder."

Szabo just laughed.

"By who?"

"By the Nuevan Lawcore."

281

"Update on current events, kid. The particles are fried and the terminus is–"

"Ship," said Alex out loud, "forward view, please."

The headspace window showed the forward spine of the ship, foreshortened in its kilometre length down to the dirty, ragged bulk of the ice shield at the end. Szabo squinted suspiciously at it, obviously wondering what the point was. Jo looked at the picture too, but then she looked at Alex and saw unmistakable triumph behind the mask of bereavement.

"Jettison shield," Alex ordered.

The shield didn't come away all at once. Blocks of ice began to peel away from the ship, one at a time, first drifting off into space and then suddenly changing course as drones that were too small to see clearly took control and guided them down into the atmosphere. It took several minutes for the shield to whittle itself away, and the growing triumph on Alex's face exactly matched the growing disbelief from the three Hired Sword men.

Slowly, surely and inevitably, the outlines of a second terminus emerged; a terminus that had spent the last four decades buried at the base of the ice shield.

"Just in case," Jo murmured. Alex shot her a pleased glance.

"Just in case," he agreed. He bared his teeth at Szabo in the most amused-yet-humourfree grin that Jo had ever seen. "And it's preloaded with particles. The red case was just extra insurance." He coughed. "And now, this is kind of awkward... I need a volunteer."

His only reply was silence from four different people.

"To help me open the wormhole," he added helpfully.

There was another long silence until Szabo gave a short, barking laugh of derision. Another of his reasoned arguments, Jo thought.

"You what?" Brown asked.

"Nathan made me record a conceptual off him before he went. I've taken it. I know everything he knew about wormholes, and a second person is strongly advised."

"Or what?" asked Szabo.

"Or I die too, maybe."

The casual tone was almost convincing, except that his jaw was set and there was the tiniest tremble in his voice. Jo didn't know enough about wormholes to know what might be lethal about them, but whatever it was seemed to frighten him more than he was going to let on.

Szabo just snorted. Blond's smile was wintry. "If you die, the ship becomes ours automatically."

"It transfers to the nearest civil authority," Alex corrected. "If the wormhole's open, that will be Nueva." A pause. "Look. There's still two thousand sleepers on board. I could wake one of them up to help me, but it would take longer. But one way or the other, I'm doing this."

"Then it'll have to take longer," Brown said, "won't it?"

Every brittle word of the conversation, Jo thought, was coated with a thin layer of testosterone.

"I'll do it," she said. She met three outraged stares with bland defiance. "What? It's going to happen, people. Let's get this over with."

CHAPTER 28

ALTERNATIVES

"THAT'S ME FINISHED on Earth," Jo said as the hatch closed behind them. She fought to keep her voice light as if it was a small matter. "Any vacancies where you come from?"

He just looked at her and then turned away, so that she had to follow to hear his answer. She didn't miss the drone that was trailing them, though she had no intention of jumping him when his back was turned.

"So, why?" he asked. "I wasn't really expecting any help at all but I thought I'd try."

"It got me out of a room with three really unpleasant people," she said. To her surprise he stopped and looked back at her.

"Well, you're out, and even if you changed your mind now I wouldn't put you back in. But I meant what I said. I could wake someone else up. I know this is going to cost you."

"How long would it take, starting from scratch, to get a sleeper to the state where they could help you?"

"About a day."

"Well, Alex, I'd be very surprised if you're allowed to sit up here for a whole day."

He looked a little uncertain, and spoke with more bluster than usual to hide it.

"We're above the orbit of the stations. It will take them time to scramble this high."

"Believe me, they'll be working on it. You might not realise just how badly some people don't want you to succeed. It's a lot more than those three. You want a wormhole, I suggest you offer Earth a nice big fait accompli. I'll help."

Somewhere in a parallel universe, Jo was sure, the future Chief Constable Josephine Odembo of the Orbital Police Force was screaming at her, telling her there was still time to redeem her career, still a chance of overpowering the boy and taking control of the ship. And in another, the ex-Sergeant Odembo, now reduced to beggary in one of the less salubrious streets of Ken-Tan-Moz – because even beggars have a pecking order and she was disqualified from the nicer areas – was congratulating her on sabotaging her career in such a truly epic way, because even though she was starving and would be dead within five years through hunger or disease or murder, the sheer style with which she had done it still kept her feeling warm at night.

But in this universe, Jo kept going because she knew sixty million Nuevans would stare accusingly at her in her dreams every night for the rest of her life if she didn't.

THE WORMHOLE TERMINUS was at the far end of the forward spine, as far as human crew could go before the solid buttressing of the ice shield began. Moving handholds carried them along to the unassuming round hatch. Alex was not talkative. He spent the journey gazing into the distance with a meditative expression. Sometimes he chewed a little on his lip. Jo still had no idea what role she was expected to play.

The terminus control cabin was small, spherical and crowded. Banks of old fashioned instruments – physical, not virtual – surrounded a large circular porthole that occupied most of one hemisphere, covered by a protective shield. A pair of side-by-side seats with neural interface hoods attached to the backs took up most of the central space of the cabin, awaiting human operators. A hum and a vibration through the walls said the terminus's maxitok reactors were powering up to full output.

Alex pulled himself into the lefthand couch and the banks of instruments wrapped themselves around him, arrays of lights and displays lighting up. He ran a conceptualed eye over them.

"Make yourself comfortable," he added to Jo. She pulled herself slowly into the righthand couch. He pulled the hood down over his head and nodded in gruff satisfaction as he interfaced directly with the terminus systems.

"State of entanglement, excellent," he reported. "We're ready to go."

"And you're going to... what?" Jo asked. "Just, turn the wormhole on?"

"Well, I'm *hoping* the people back home have done their bit. They knew the timetable; they were to get their terminus up and running at the same time as we reached Earth. Then we just send the signal through." It was almost a speech compared to his recent reticence.

"'Just'," Jo said disbelievingly.

"Well, maybe a bit more. Ship, jettison shield and disengage."

A series of *clunks* vibrated through the cabin and suddenly the view through the porthole cleared as the protective shield tumbled away. *Phoenicia* had taken them up into a geostationary orbit far above the equator, a safe 180 degrees away from High-Kili, which put them over the Pacific. Being a hemisphere from High-Kili still put them halfway between Garuda and Atahualpa but they were well out of range of those stations' laser emplacements. There were still excursion vehicles on either station that could reach them at this distance, but it would take time. Jo guessed that the presence of three Hired Sword personnel on board would stop their friends from doing anything too hasty.

More *clunks*, more pronounced than the first, and the entire cabin shifted. The terminus had cut loose and a cluster of drones were carrying it away from the ship.

More tremors: the terminus was expanding. The cabin they were in was on the edge of a metal hoop that had been bound tight to the hull, and now it was growing. Segments of metal moved smoothly across each other and clicked into place, making larger segments which continued to grow outwards. Jo had seen pictures of the old terminus so she knew what it would look like fully grown – a thin, graceful circle of metal, a kilometre across, with the control cabin clinging to the rim like the small stone of a much larger diamond ring.

It took half an hour for the terminus to reach its fullest size and Alex took the opportunity to brief Jo, haltingly, on what was expected of her. She looked at him in disbelief.

"Really?"

He bit his lip. "Really."

"You mean, you could..."

"Yes," he said abruptly. "I could." He looked away a bit too quickly. Sitting there in the control couch, surrounded by the instruments that could manipulate dimensions, he suddenly looked like a little boy playing with his daddy's toys, in the wrong place and completely out of his depth. Jo had to fight the urge to hug him.

He checked the instruments one last time and said simply: "Let's go. This won't take long." He paused for a final, grim smile. "And if they haven't prepped the terminus back at Nueva, it will take even less." Then the hood enveloped his head completely. Jo's own hood dropped down and she saw what he was seeing.

It didn't have the neural bandwidth to let her share the experience fully. She wasn't living and breathing it, feeling it and tasting and touching like Alex was with every one of his senses. But it was stunning.

She saw the universe as it was. She saw the illusion that was the world she had always known, a tiny bubble marked out by the laughably small set of dimensions of space and time that defined her life, while all around them were – the others.

If an amoeba saw a human being, how would it describe the experience? Its whole life was lived in essentially two dimensions with only the slightest extension into the third. It could never see beyond that. Humans were in a similar position, with only the tiniest extension into the realms beyond – just enough to mark out their position, nowhere near enough to interact.

It was as if God had said, "this is where you will live and you will never leave it". There was no way out – no way past these building blocks of existence.

Except that now there was. A tiny, tiny trail, the thinnest of thin lines, led away from them, back towards La Nueva Temporada. Somewhere in the mechanism of the terminus was a set of particles that had been entangled at the quantum level with their twins back home. What happened to one would affect the other, even at a distance of light years. As the ship had carried the particles from one world to another they had left a track back through the dimensions: breadcrumbs of pure information, which Alex could follow.

Now Alex plunged into that trail through the high dimensions and Jo had no choice but to–

> *She saw a world she had never seen before, but she knew it was La Nueva Temporada, cold and dark, its single continent pinpricked by the bright sparks of nuclear explosions. Puerto Alto tumbled down past her, trailing fragments, starting to glow as it hit the atmosphere.*

–follow.

Alex twisted and turned; he swooped and soared through echoing gulfs and dived down into tiny, curled up passages that surely led–

> *Fire blazed and pulsed across the sky as the wormhole collapsed.*

–nowhere. The track of information was growing thinner and branching off in different–

> *Ice sheets from the north and south lapped at the base of the Altiplano; the city above lay cold and silent.*

–directions, just as Alex had briefed her. There were different realities in here, different possibilities, shadow La Nueva Temporadas where they could never–

A statue with Alex's face was raised before cheering crowds in the plaza of Altiplano City. The plaque at its base simply read: "Mateo".

–live, and the trail had to lead to them to the concrete reality of La Nueva Temporada in the here and–

He sat at the controls of a laser in orbit around Nueva. The sights zeroed in on a cluster of buildings below and he fired.

–now.

But Alex knew enough to keep to the true road. That wasn't why Jo had been made to–

His sobbing mother lay in bed. His father sat with his arms around her, clueless as to how to let out all the comfort and love he could offer past his own internal barriers. Together they tried to explain to four-year-old Feli that he wasn't going to have a baby brother after all.

–follow him.

The light ahead that was Alex was growing dimmer–

Rigis approached a mountain range, to be met by a barrage of ground-to-air missiles.

–as well, thinning out, suffusing into the dimensions around it.

And suddenly they were–

His father lay dead on the floor of the villa, and he stood over the body.

–there. The trail came to an end, disappearing into a glowing ball that was the entangled particles in the Nuevan wormhole–

He stood at the foot of the ramp extending from the belly of the shuttle. He breathed deep and scanned his eyes across the vast plain of blue grass that waved gently in the breeze. He linked hands with his wife and they stepped onto the virgin ground. Coming out from the shadow of the shuttle's cooling wing, they lifted their eyes to the horizon where the rings of a mighty gas giant rose above the clouds.

–terminus. They had found–

Haltingly, his parents explained to little Alex and only slightly bigger Felipe that they had decided to separate. Alex guiltily tried to hide the surge of relief.

–their way.

But there was no time for self congratulation. Alex's consciousness had come to an abrupt halt, spreading out as if it had splatted suddenly against a wall. It was disappearing; bits of it trailed off, fading into the highs–

"Help me! Now!"

And this was why Jo was here. She leapt forward and seized his mind before it could fade completely, though it was like trying to hold onto a handful of sand in running water. She wrapped her own mind around it, sealing Alex off, guarding his being with her own existence. Firmly surrounded by Jo's consciousness, there was nowhere else for Alex's to go. The light of his mind began to rekindle, to glow again, gaining strength as they backtracked the way they had come.

*　　*　　*

THE REALITY OF the control cabin materialised suddenly around them and Alex blinked, astonished. It was all so small, so puny. He could reach out with his mind and crush it. He could *think* it into another existence. He could–

Jo released his hood and it sprang back up into its old position at the back of his couch.

"No!" Alex shouted. He gathered his mind together again to plunge back into the dimensions. That was where he belonged. That was where he could do anything. "Leave me alone!"

But the link was broken. He was fully back in this place and his memories of what had been were fading like a dream; once so crystal clear and immediate and real, now dissolving wherever he looked at it and tried to remember. He glared pure hatred at her, until his mind picked up that it was back in the warm, living body where it belonged. His glare turned into a slightly sheepish scowl and he couldn't quite meet her eye.

"Thanks," he muttered. "What did you see?"

Jo's face was almost as sweaty and grey as his own felt. She took a moment to collect his thoughts.

"Weird things," she said. "All about you."

"Me, or almost me. Things that have happened, or might have happened, or will happen, or might yet happen. Unfortunately there's no way to tell which is which. Until it happens." He pulled a face. "We'll find out, won't we?"

His hands moved over the instruments. "Watch out for the feeling that you're about to turn inside out. This close, it's going to be strong..."

Power surged through the tiny tunnel that their trip had carved through the high dimensions. Existence shimmered for a moment and a ripple ran through the universe. For a moment Alex felt that several strong hands had seized every part of his innards and relocated them somewhere else. He was dimly aware of a shout that made his throat raw.

Something blossomed outside the porthole. The wormhole started as a twinkle a billion kilometres away but in a moment it flourished into a sphere that filled the terminus. It was a ball of nothing, not even black or grey with the absence of light. It was just *there*. Its outer edge was just a few metres from where the two of them sat.

It seemed such an anticlimax. Forty years of longsleep, and now Alex felt that he could reach out and touch Nuevan space. He wanted to stretch his arm out through the porthole and plunge his hand into it. The feeling was made stronger by the distinct sensation that he was *leaning* – that the cabin, floating free in orbit about Earth, was on a slope and poised to plunge into the hole.

Somehow, conventional radio just seemed a little dull after all that, but he reached for the microphone and pulled it towards him. He left it up to the blackbox to find the right frequency.

"Hello, Puerto Alto, hello, Puerto Alto, this is *Phoenicia* calling from Earth orbit. Do you copy?"

There was a pause. Then they both jumped as a voice boomed and the cabin filled with a background of shouts and cheers.

"*Yes, Earth, we copy! You're coming through loud and clear. Who is speaking?*"

"This is Alex Mateo..."

"*Jesus Christ!*"

"No..." Alex felt good enough to make the weakest joke of his life. "Alex Mateo, in orbit about Earth."

"*Uh – yeah – this is the duty operative on Puerto Alto. Confirming voice print ... Oh my God, I can't believe this. The wormhole's really open! The terminus is working!*"

"I'd noticed," Alex said, rolling his eyes at Jo. She smiled warmly back and mouthed: "well done."

A bit louder she added: "maybe you should ask if he has a superior with a brain you can talk to?"

She had said it loud enough to be heard at the other end.

"*Oh, uh...*" The voice suddenly grew abashed. "*I'm sorry, Señor. There is a procedure for this eventuality which I have to follow but I'm kinda out of practice...*"

"I suppose you would be..."

A new voice took over: also a man, but harsher. "*Colonel Krauss here. Voice print confirms your identity, Señor Mateo. Is anyone else from* Phoenicia *with you?*"

"Um." Alex and Jo exchanged glances. "From *Phoenicia*, no–"

"*Alex!*" Alex sat forward suddenly at the woman's voice. It was distant and echoey, as if its owner had been in the background. There was the sound of a small tussle at the other end and suddenly the voice was louder. "*Alex! Are you there?*"

Alex suddenly felt tears pricking his eyes. He had only been gone a few days by his own time; he had barely missed her. But suddenly it hit him just how much she might have missed him. He had to move his mouth a couple of times before words came out. "Yes, Mama," he said. "I'm here."

"*Oh, Alex, you–*"

Another tussle, and Colonel Krauss was back.

"*We'll send someone to collect you and then you can talk all you like. We've established contact with* Phoenicia. *Stay where you are; we'll be with you shortly.*"

Earth's first radio link with La Nueva Temporada in forty years went dead. Alex looked absently out at the wormhole until a slight noise made him realise he had completely forgotten Jo's presence. He twisted round to look at her.

"Once I've got a little more backup, I'll release your people."

"Hardly my people," she muttered. Her face clouded, the smile dimming as reality settled in. She gazed out at the wormhole. "God. I'm finished on Earth. They'll never forgive me."

Alex didn't quite know what to say.

"Well, the wormhole's open and the world hasn't ended," he pointed out, annoyed by the sudden air of gloom in the cabin and determined not to let it get any thicker. "That's what matters."

"Hmm."

Suddenly instruments were calling for his attention.

"Hey, there's something coming through already…"

Something blurred its way past the porthole. It was too close to get a proper view and they had to rely on the feed from a cam mounted on the rim of the terminus.

It was a lot of somethings – a steady stream of what looked like excursion capsules, coming through one after the other. The ship reported that they all seemed to be under blackbox control, no human crews. With little puffs of thruster gas they began to move apart, an expanding cluster of dark shapes against the backdrop of Earth.

"Alex." Jo's voice was strange. "Headspace."

He had tuned headspace out while he opened the wormhole. Now he went back in. A frantic background gabble, keywords of fear and alarm, seeped back up the links. He looked hard at the cloud of unmanned space vessels swooping down on the Terrans. None of them was tagged in any way and they were giving nothing in headspace. What were they doing?

Then there was a sudden energy spike as one of the Nuevan capsules, already down in an orbit miles below *Phoenicia*, opened fire on an Earth satellite.

Alex took a moment to try that again. One of the Nuevan capsules *opened fire* on an *Earth satellite*…

Larger ships were coming through now – one, two, three, four, big enough to have to come through one after the other. These weren't capsules, they were full-sized interplanetary people carriers of the kind that used to go through the wormhole in either direction, several times a day. They were basic and cut-down – a simple framework of modules and engines, built for speed and distance. They kept on their way, heading down towards low Terran orbit with a speed and purpose that gave away their intentions.

"Oh my God…" Jo murmured. Alex stared in complete bafflement at the receding ships.

"Huh?"

Jo's voice was barely a whisper.

"It's an invasion…"

"No!" But the denial was more instinctive than based on fact. His mind couldn't quite make sense of it. Two concepts that didn't belong together – *Nuevans* and *invading*.

But like it or not, the very real invasion fleet fell upon Earth.

CHAPTER 29

THE COMING OF THE NUEVANS

ALEX COULDN'T LOOK away from the display, if only because it meant he didn't have to meet the condemnation in Jo's eyes. Did he just say the world hadn't ended? The hollow echo of those words hung in the air.

It was a deceptively peaceful invasion. The fleet of Nuevan ships settled down on Earth like a sheet flung over a bed, soft and enveloping. Alex and Jo weren't tuned in to Terran frequencies. They had no idea what panicked gabble might be going on in orbit and they were out of range of Earth's orbital defences. To the naked eye, it looked like it was all happening so quietly that the Terrans hadn't even noticed.

"What the hell are they doing?" Alex whispered.

The decision was made before we left La Nueva Temporada, said the ship. *The wormhole explosion showed how badly La Nueva Temporada depends on Earth's goodwill. It has been resolved that from now on La Nueva Temporada must control both ends of the wormhole. I was told to omit this from your revival conceptual.*

"Told? Who by?"

By you.

Earth's laser defences were there to protect the planet and other satellites from space debris. They were designed to take out something that had been tracked for weeks beforehand at a leisurely pace, not repulse a sudden, lightning-swift invasion on their doorstep. The automated weapons simply fell silent as Nuevan ships approached. *Phoenicia* said their blackboxes were being swamped, forced into obedience.

The larger, manned Nuevan ships closed in on the orbital elevator stations, the largest human presence in orbit. A pair were approaching Basilé, above the west coast of Africa. It was a little smaller than High-Kili; headspace gave it a population of 4,713. Under human control one of the station's lasers suddenly came to life, swung up to bear on one of the Nuevans, and fired. The nearest ship flared red, then white, then disappeared in a soundless explosion of gas and vapour.

The other Nuevan didn't bother with niceties. It returned fire with kinetic weapons that shredded the laser module into flying chunks. The module split open like a cracked egg and its crew spilled out into the vacuum.

"Shut it down." Jo's words were controlled and precise, clamped down on top of her rising fury. "Just close the wormhole now–"

"Can't…" Alex's mouth was dry; he had to work his mouth a few times just to say the one word. He didn't, couldn't take his eyes off the display where he had just been watching people die. "It stays open until it closes of natural causes."

"So make it happen!"

"The link's been made," he reminded her. "Even if we shut down the terminus, make the wormhole vanish down to the size of a pinprick, they'll be able to restart it remotely from the other end…"

She lunged forward, and suddenly there was a gun in her hand. It had been at his hip and he had forgotten all about it until now. His attention suddenly focused in on the dark opening of the barrel.

"Put… put that away," Alex said. "It's not going to–" He shut up and bit his tongue as she tightened her grip.

Jo was pressed to one side of the cabin, far enough away to cover him, but still the barrel looked very big. Alex knew from experience what a stun shot felt like and it wasn't a feeling he intended to repeat. And if she turned up the power to max, it could easily kill.

Ship, could do with your help, he sent, at the same time as talking out loud: "The link has been established." The effort of doing both at the same time made his voice wobble, which he thought was understandable. He tried to put persuasion and reason into his tone, and fight his voice's urge to tremble. "Even if we close it down …"

I am responding to your situation.

Jo flicked a switch on the gun, and it hummed as it powered up to a higher discharge level.

"Just closing it now will be a start," she said. "Then, I slag the gear here." Her voice shook. "Oh God, I can't believe I just let you do this… I can't let you just walk over us…"

"There's sixty million Nuevans…"

"Shut up!" Jo's voice was rising. "Shut up about sixty million Nuevans, you can't just…"

"They'll freeze to death eventually…"

"*Shut up…*"

In position, the ship reported silently, and Alex responded: *do it*. The drone that the ship had quietly positioned in space, just outside the cabin hatch, twisted the emergency release.

The roar of a storm filled the cabin as the air twisted into a violent hurricane through the small dark circle of the blown hatch. The noise was cut off in a split moment as his helmet snapped up.

Alex was strapped into his couch. Jo had been right next to the hatch and she was plucked out into space in a second, her helmet also safely up. Alex let the initial surge of the storm die away, then released his straps and let the last vestiges of air carry him out into space after her.

Jo had lost the gun – which had been the point of the exercise – and was falling away from the capsule, arms and legs flailing. Alex tumbled after her. These suits didn't have thrusters attached and it was impossible to orient himself. Woman in spacesuit, two-kilometre-long starship, wormhole and planet swam at random around him, and the feeling of falling towards the wormhole just added to the problem until finally the drone took him and held him steady.

He tuned in to Jo's suit's frequency. As he had expected, she was cursing loudly and fluently, and a lot of it involved him. It didn't stop as the drone towed him over to her, caught her and stopped her tumble.

A Nuevan ship, a mid-range excursioner, was approaching *Phoenicia*. It looked less rugged and ready for combat than the first wave of invaders, built for a more leisurely turn of speed.

Señor Mateo is half a kilometre away with a companion. The ship suddenly spoke as if answering a random question. *I have three further waking people on board.*

"Ship, who are you talking to?"

I have been contacted by–

The ship's voice suddenly dissolved into static.

"*Unidentified space suited personnel, cease contact with* Phoenicia *immediately,*" said a new voice with a Nuevan accent.

"I'm Alex Mateo," Alex snapped, "and I'll talk to my ship if I want. Who are you?"

The voice's tone became a little more respectful, but only a little.

"*Señor Mateo, please identify your companion and the personnel now on board* Phoenicia."

Alex paused. Jo glared at him through her faceplate, waiting for his answer. It was very tempting to make Szabo's team someone else's problem. Ten minutes earlier he would have happily handed them over to the Nuevan authorities; now, he had no idea how these new Nuevans would treat Terran prisoners.

"Not important," he said. "They're on my ship and they're my concern."

"*As you will, Señor. We'll find out when we dock in five minutes time.*"

Alex did a quick check. The drones couldn't get him and Jo back to the ship within five minutes.

"Negative! You do not have permission to dock with *Phoenicia*."

"*We were stating, not asking, Señor. Over and out.*"

"What will they do to them?" Jo asked on private frequency. Her voice was taut with accusation, already aimed at him in advance, just in case the Nuevans did something to the prisoners that he could be blamed for.

"I don't know." *Phoenicia* was approaching but it was still too far off. He wouldn't have *thought* the Nuevans would just, say, shoot any Terran prisoners they got their hands on... but then, he wouldn't have *thought* they would invade Earth either. Only, apparently they had.

"It doesn't matter," he said out loud. "I'm telling the ship not to let them on–"

But the ship was showing alarming signs of co-operation. There was another command feed inside his headspace, alongside his own, and it was swamping him. It was as if he was shouting, *I'm here!* and someone else was copying his voice exactly, but shouting louder, *no, over here!*

The status lights on the drone went out and suddenly it was just a lump of plastic and metal, no longer receiving orders from the ship's blackbox. The ship had cut them off, and he and Jo were drifting towards the ship on momentum alone.

The Nuevan ship was closing in on *Phoenicia*. Its airlock extension snaked out and then the small vessel was nestled against the starship like a parasitic tick that *Phoenicia* hadn't even noticed.

CHAPTER 30

SCOOPING

IT WASN'T A happy reunion.

The captain of the Nuevan ship was a coldly respectful segunda in his mid-thirties, who greeted them as they emerged from the airlock: "Welcome on board the *Santiago*." His voice seemed unfocused, his thoughts on something else. He looked at Alex as he spoke but seemed to address a point slightly to one side of his eyes.

"And you are?" Alex demanded.

"Welcome on board the *Santiago*." It might as well have been a recording of the first time he said it, with exactly the same distracted tone. "Please come to the ship's lounge." The captain turned away, a contemptuous dismissal that sent a stab of irritation into Alex.

"I said, and you are?" he repeated.

"Please come to the ship's lounge..." The captain didn't turn round and an escort of four large crewmen moved in around them. They all had the same look in their eyes as the captain and the way they walked was... disturbing. They crowded in just a bit too much, pushed a bit too far into personal space by a fraction of a centimetre. Other people were less important than their programming.

It was something Alex had heard about but never seen.

"They've had one too many conceptuals," he murmured to Jo.

"Well, yes," she agreed with irony. "How else were you going to train up an invasion fleet?"

They were shown into the lounge and left there. Soon after that, Szabo, Blond and Brown were retrieved from *Phoenicia* to join them. The three Terran men lurked on one side of the room and Alex on the other, with Jo somewhere in between, and then everyone watched the fall of Earth from the comfort of the *Santiago's* lounge.

Nuevan ships fell onto High-Kili and the other elevator stations, fastening onto the station's locks or fixing their own onto the superstructure and blasting through the bulkheads. Other Nuevan troops buzzed around the exteriors to secure the external facilities. Clouds of landing craft equipped for atmospheric flight spiralled around the cables to drop down on the base stations. It would take them hours yet, but even with all that warning, Alex wondered what the Terrans on the ground could offer by way of resistance. From what he remembered of Uhuru, perched on top of Kilimanjaro, it hadn't exactly been bristling with weaponry.

Bit by bit, surrender was acknowledged, resistance crushed. One by one the other installations in orbit fell, at first taken over by suited Nuevan shock troops, then simply surrendering when it became obvious what was happening. Some remained occupied, some were left untouched, some were taken out by laser fire, all according to some great unseen plan in the mind of the Nuevan high command.

"Happy now?" Brown asked Jo with soft condemnation. Jo turned away in the direction of Alex.

"So what do they do now?" she asked. Alex gazed blankly back at her. How the hell was he meant to know?

"He's out of the loop, Sergeant." Szabo didn't look at either of them as he spoke. "He's forty years out of date and his worldview begins and ends with opening up the wormhole. This could have been foreseen by anyone who gave the matter just a little thought." He swung his head round to give them the full blast of his pale eyes. "We gave it much more than just a little thought. What will they do? They won't occupy the entire world, because they can't and they don't need to. They just need to control Earth's capacity for getting into space and its capacity for defending itself. Now they have that, I expect life for everyone else will go on pretty well as normal... for those of us who didn't used to work up here–"

"Identify yourself."

The *Santiago's* captain was in the doorway, again flanked and backed up by armed crewmen. Szabo looked at him for a moment before answering, as if assessing a trick question.

"Team Leader Ara Szabo, Hired Sword Clan," he said.

The captain's unfocused gaze moved on to the other Terrans in the room, one by one. Alex finally learnt the names of Blond and Brown.

"Senior Spacer Titus Akken, Hired Sword Clan."

"Senior Spacer Robert Piwnica, Hired Sword Clan."

"Sergeant Jo Odembo, Orbital Police Force."

For just a moment the captain's eyes unfocused even more as he consulted some unseen table in headspace.

"Compliant with invasion plan, appendix seven, section twelve," he said, "all personnel occupying *Phoenicia* of level five and above to be held for scooping. Take them."

The crewmen moved forward, guns raised.

"Scooping?" Alex shouted it above the outraged shouts and exclamations of the others. "What for?"

The captain looked at him vaguely.

"Invasion plan, appendix seven, section twelve," he repeated. "All personnel occupying–"

"I said, what for?" Alex demanded. He glared into the man's dead eyes. "Don't just quote regulations. Explain! Why the hell do you want to scoop these people?" He was no legal expert but he knew scooping was a matter of last resort. There had to be good cause to get at the information inside someone's head quickly.

"Invasion plan, appendix seven–"

Alex moved to stand in front of Jo. Then he thought about it and shifted slightly to put himself between the *Santiago* men and all the Terrans.

"No one gets scooped," he said tightly, "without a damned good explanation. These people were on my ship and–"

The captain's eyes finally settled on him.

"Invasion plan, appendix eight," he said. "Aid and comfort given to enemy personnel; possible subversion of individual. Hold him for scooping too."

THE ANONYMOUS VOICE sounded through the ship.

"*Five minutes to transit.*"

Alex barely heard it.

He was under lock and key again, this time in a solitary cabin on *Santiago*. His linkset gone, no contact with anyone in the outside world and a strange, bubbling feeling inside. Anger, and fear, and a leavening of grim humour so that he could have laughed or cried at the same time. They were going to scoop him.

They were going to... scoop?

Him?

For what? Fury and fear surged inside him. For being decent. For standing up for the others – for what should have been the basic rights even of idiots like Szabo. That wasn't the La Nueva Temporada he had left behind. What had it become?

But first there was the wormhole.

Your first warning was the feeling that you were moving. You *were* moving, you were on a spaceship – but you shouldn't be able to feel it. Yet suddenly you knew. You felt as if the ship were pointing downhill. You were tumbling into the guts of the universe. You felt your whole being inclining towards that hideous point ahead where some fool had tunnelled a way through all those tiny dimensions, which God or the universe or someone far better qualified than you had thought were better left tightly packed up together. And as the ship plunged down that dimensional gradient you felt it rushing, picking up speed, falling and falling and falling and the sides of the ship closing in and every particle of your body being hideously stretched and warped and distorted and you squeezed your eyes shut and ground your teeth and tried *so hard* not to scream and the entire ship collapsed into a single massive point and suddenly you were through.

And he was back home, in Nuevan space. Puerto Alto was a short distance away and he had absolutely no way of contacting it.

Then they took him for scooping.

It was like a drill, a diamond bit of pure pain. It worked its way relentlessly into his head, boring down through every layer of memory and identity. Everything he had ever learned, everything he had ever known was cut out, a shining jewel dug out from the comforting mud of life experience and conscious memory that could have obscured it. Every single datum in the mind of Alex Mateo, from his knowledge of engineering down to how to walk, laid out bare for all to see, handle, study, poke, prod. And on top of it all, the screaming – his own shrieks mingled with the whine of the drill in his mind.

When it was finished he lay curled in a ball on a bunk in his anonymous cabin. His stomach heaved, his head was splitting, his gorge heaved with self-loathing and disgust from the violation.

Someone sat on the side of the bunk; he felt the mattress go down. It was a blurred figure through his tears, but he knew the scent and the feel of the gentle arms that went around him. He had missed his homecoming, not seen any of his arrival at the station, but now he knew where he was.

"Alex?"

"Mama! Oh, Mama..." And he sobbed into her shoulder like a little boy, while she held him and comforted him as any mother would.

CHAPTER 31

QUIN

THEY SAT IN the Puerto Alto canteen and caught up. No cheering crowds, no well-wishers or supporters. She had banned them, to his eternal relief. And no conceptuals either – his head had been played with enough in the last few days. They were going to use *words* to catch up.

He concentrated on gulping down coffee and spooning down the high-energy, vitamin laced soup that was meant to help the recently scooped to recover, and listened while she told him a sad tale of the breakdown of La Nueva Temporada, and coups, and the death of his father.

He had expected that last bit, but that didn't make it easier.

She looked good for a woman of ninety-seven. He had been braced for her being ancient, but it wasn't that bad. Her hair was well on its way to being white and her face was a little more lined. It was only when she walked that he really saw the change. She held herself with a little more care; when she moved it was with a little more effort and often a very tiny grunt.

Her voice grew quieter, dropping down to a flat level of pure fury.

"And they had you scooped? I can't believe it. I'll have someone's balls, I swear. I mean, you hear of these things, down on the ground, and we're up here and relatively untouched so we can still get along but when it happens to *you*..."

Alex looked up from his soup. "You hear of what things?" he asked, and was surprised, because for the first time ever she looked... uncertain. Possibly even ashamed. And she didn't quite answer the question. Instead she looked around the canteen before answering.

"Alex, darling, we came damn close to self-destructing. Nowadays... as long as you accept that the entire point of Nueva's government, Nueva's people, Nueva's industry is to reunite us with Earth then it's fine. We live and breathe and serve to re-open the wormhole. That's it. And nothing gets in the way."

Frankly, Alex would have thought Nueva was like that when he left. Clearly it had become much more so, and in the process, it had become the kind of world that invaded others. What other changes had there been for the people living there? He sensed that if he pushed further, if he looked deeper into this new Nueva – well, he might not like what he found, and he might end up judging how his own mother had acted in a situation where he couldn't speak for himself.

"Due process of law?" he asked. "Right to a fair trial?"

"No problem, as long as you're not accused of anything to do with the wormhole."

"Voting?"

"Vote for who you like, as long as they want to open the wormhole."

"Freedom of speech?"

Her mouth twitched. It was turning into an ironic game and her tone was bantering.

"As long as you don't question opening the wormhole." Then she looked up at someone approaching behind them. "As this gentleman will tell you."

"Freedom of speech is over-rated," said a cheerful voice. A broadly smiling stranger came around the table and pulled back a chair to sit opposite him, slouching down with his hands in his pockets. He wore a sleek black suit with slim lines. He was twice Alex's age and had thick dark hair, wavy, like Felipe's. In fact he could have been Felipe's twin, which was enough to tell Alex immediately who he was, and the similarity was like a stab in Alex's heart.

"Hahn," Quin added by neutral way of acknowledgement, though not looking away from Alex.

"Mateo," Alex's mother acknowledged in kind. Quin's smile turned into a delighted grin when he saw Alex had worked out his identity.

"I prefer freedom of data." Quin carried on talking. "Just let your government do its job, let it be seen to be doing it well, and if it isn't, sack it and get another."

And that was when Alex noticed that the canteen had been cleared, and they were all alone, apart from the guards posted around the room, and Quin, and the man standing behind him. This other man had short hair, and a square chin, and appraising eyes which suggested they were only friendly if they chose to be. When he registered Alex looking at him, he touched one finger to his head in an ironic salute.

"So you're my brother who jumps off elevators," Quin said. He held out his hand across the table. Alex reached out slowly and took it.

So you're the one who got my father killed?

He had heard his mother's account. Quin had been there – but he hadn't been the one to pull the trigger. He had initiated it, but he hadn't wanted it and it had destroyed him when it happened. So Alex didn't punch the broad smile off the other man's face.

"It was just orbital mechanics," he answered. "We were perfectly safe."

"Well, that's one of the many things you need to tell me all about," Quin said. He pushed his chair back. "Let's go somewhere more private..."

"So, do you work for the government?" Alex asked. The man behind him snorted and Quin's smile grew wider.

"Ignore David. I am the government. First Executor Mateo. Papá would be proud."

"And surprised," Alex's mother murmured.

"So I blame you for having me scooped?"

Quin looked him in the eye. "Trust me, chico, you get over it." He stood up. "Let's go."

It sounded more like a summons. Alex glanced at his mother, but she just nodded slightly, and so he went.

Alex was aware of the bodyguard as they walked to the living quarters. Quin moved in the middle of a bubble of constantly cleared space around him. They all withdrew to a discreet distance as they came to the door of what ought to be a senior manager's suite, and the man called David positioned himself next to it. He gave Alex a nod and a twisted smile. Lines in his face showed that he could laugh; a twist to his lips implied that when he did, it might not be at something that amused you. The door closed between them and Alex had a feeling of being sealed into the inner sanctum.

"They keep this place for me," Quin said, moving towards a locker. There was a pair of pictures on the counter. Alex recognised one as his stepmother, Quin's mother Maria. The other was of himself. When had that been taken? For some reason he was wearing a suit: had it been Maria's wedding? "I come up here a lot when I need some thinking time. Come in. Sit down. Christ, you're young. I mean, of course you're young but I've always thought of you as my *big* brother..."

Alex sat while Quin took out a bottle and some glasses.

"I have waited so long to meet you." Quin was still smiling as if he couldn't quite believe Alex was sitting there, and no one had said anything about scooping. "God, where do we both start... Here. It's the best stuff." Quin passed him a glass. "So, are they taking good care of your ship?"

"Apparently there's a crew on board now."

"Good." Quin gave a satisfied nod, lips pursed. "Anything you need, anything at all, just ask. Don't go through channels, come straight to me."

"I will."

"We need it and you deserve it," Quin added earnestly. "Just ask. Anything. Seriously."

And Alex had no doubt that his brother could make it happen.

His whole manner breathed the easy confidence of a man who had the infrastructure of a planet geared to doing his will.

He looked down at his glass. He would have preferred tea but he took a sip and pulled a face. It was bitter and would take a lot of getting used to, much like Quin's La Nueva Temporada.

"What happens to Earth now?" he asked. Quin waved the question away.

"Don't worry about Earth. What you need–"

"I'd like to know."

Alex only put a little asperity into his tone but the temperature plummeted. Quin looked at him with an expression stripped of all warmth, humour or brotherly goodwill. It was the kind of expression Alex might give a crawling bug before he squashed it.

Then the bonhomie was back, as if a switch had been thrown.

"As long as Earth doesn't threaten our interests then Earth can do what it likes. And in the meantime, I expect we'll be able to do business with friendly Terrans." Alex raised his eyebrows and Quin shrugged. "There'll be some. There always are after an invasion. After a while they stop being traitors and become forward thinking visionaries. So, Alex–"

"And the ones who were captured with me?"

"Exhibit A for a prosecution in which we both have a vested interest." Quin grinned without the slightest hint of mirth. "I looked at the scooping results on the way up. Three of them were working for a very large interest group of clans which was actively conspiring to stop the wormhole opening and I have no doubt at all were responsible for it closing in the first place. They have the blood of everyone who died in the Event on their hands, including our brother, and if they think that after forty years it's time to let bygones be bygones then they are going to be sorely disappointed. My advice to them would be to right now disconnect from headspace and go and live in a small hut at one of Earth's poles, or even better a small space station orbiting within the magnetosphere of a gas giant, because otherwise I will find them and bring them to justice. I *will*."

Somewhere during that little speech Quin stopped smiling, and his eyes began to burn, and by the end he was breathing heavily and his drink trembled in his hand.

"The Sergeant had nothing to do with it." Alex kept one eye on Quin's glass, wondering if it would shatter. The pattern of vibrations in the surface of the drink was quite fascinating.

"No." Quin shrugged, abruptly back to normal. "She was just doing her job. She's in the clear. But they're all small fry. They're too young to be the really guilty ones. They'll be returned to Earth once we have what we need and we'll pursue the matter with the people giving them the orders." He took a gulp that drained half his glass. "When we planned the invasion we had to consider everything. Everything! We've got contingencies for the clans rolling over and welcoming us, and for them fighting back with everything from pocket knives to nukes, and for everything else in between."

Alex remembered the captain of the *Santiago*, and his reciting of appendices and section numbers.

"And to help them remember it, you filled their brains up with conceptuals," he said. He got another of Quin's artless grins.

"I don't generally go for mindless obedience but there's times when it's useful. We had to get this right." His voice dropped, became more thoughtful and more desperate. "We *so* had to get this right."

"All for Nueva," Alex murmured. He recoiled when Quin suddenly leapt to his feet.

"*Nueva?* I hate fucking Nueva! I *hate* it!"

Quin gulped down the second half of his glass and paced around the cabin.

"Do it for Nueva? Are you joking? Do it so that frigid lump of rock can become..." His voice changed to mocking. "*Warm* and *lovely*. Or maybe you meant do it for the *Nuevans*?" Now his voice crackled with disgust. "Sixty million inbred ingrates who can't just shut the fuck up and get on with the simple matter of living together? Christ Almighty, Alex, sixty million people who are so fucking useless they need *me* to get anything done? Was that who you were thinking of?"

He dropped back into his chair; his voice dropped to something near a whisper.

"I did it because I want to be warm and alive. That's all. Warm and alive. Is it so much to ask?"

An embarrassed silence filled the room. Alex felt the ghost of his father standing at his shoulder, offering a bit of paternal advice: "*Let them be the ones to lose their dignity but never let them be the ones to end the conversation...*"

He kept his tone steady and level.

"So, if you want warm and alive, you'll be retiring to a Terran island somewhere in the Pacific?"

"Retire?" Quin raised his glass and glared at Alex over the rim. Then he realised it was empty and put it down again. All the energy drained from his voice until it was almost a slur. "Retire? You can't retire, Alex. This job won't let you retire. No one who's run the planet since the Event has retired. There's too much that goes with it. Too much responsibility. Too much to oversee. You know no one else can do it. They'll just balls it up and we'll freeze and... no. I can't retire, Alex. I'm stuck in this job for the foreseeable or until someone bumps me off. Which they won't." He grinned again, but it was a weary grin. "You want to know my secret?" He leaned forward conspiratorially and jerked a thumb at the closed door. "David. He's my secret. None of the others had David. He loves me. Thinks I'm the greatest. Poor deluded sod, but anyway. David won't let them get to me. Keeps me alive."

He pulled himself together with a visible effort: braced himself, flexed his shoulders, took a breath, as if forcing whatever was confusing his brain down his body and into his feet. Suddenly he was businesslike and back to normal.

"So, Alex, your ship. You are going to show me round her. Personally. Promise me."

"I promise," Alex said. Quin nodded, pleased.

"We'll be seeing plenty more of each other but let me tell you one more thing about my plans, because there's something I need to ask you..."

"I WONDERED IF he'd ask that," his mother said later. They were back in her quarters and the tea she had served was much more pleasant and easier on the stomach than Quin's best rotgut. "How was he?"

"I'd have said he was drunk," said Alex. He remembered his brother's diatribe against Nueva and the people who lived there. He remembered the swings of mood, the ever changing tone of voice. "If he'd had more than one glass."

She snorted. "Quin spends his entire existence half cut. You're privileged if you get to see it, though. One of the select few. He's a great actor in public. No, that would not have been his first glass of the day."

He heard the pity in her voice. "Why?" he asked.

She looked at him. "It helps him live with himself. So, what did you tell him?"

Alex looked at his tea. It was easier than looking at the hope in his mother's eyes.

"I don't know," he mumbled.

He was master of *Phoenicia* for one voyage, and that voyage had been made. The ship would let him relinquish control if he wanted; it would return itself to the care of the Nuevan government.

And the Nuevan government badly wanted it. La Nueva Temporada and Earth were reunited, in an unhappy union. The crisis was over; La Nueva Temporada would not freeze. But those two worlds were never going to coexist, side by side, for long. They badly needed something to take their minds off each other. Something big, something requiring their mutual cooperation, something that would show: look, everyone, we really are friends.

That something had been handed to them on a plate in the form of the Epsilon Eridani expedition, exactly as Ara Szabo had already described to Alex. Everything was all set up, all they needed was the ship... And Quin agreed almost one hundred per cent, except for the small detail that it would be a cold day in hell before he let the Terrans take charge of *Phoenicia*.

The ship was still in Earth orbit; it was too big to transit the wormhole safely and wouldn't be coming back to Nueva. But it would be Nuevans who worked on it, Nuevans who prepared it and, crucially, Nuevans who commanded it. Which meant a Nuevan had to be in charge, and if it wasn't Alex then it would be one of Quin's stooges. He wasn't sure he would wish that on the ship, or on the expedition.

His mother took his hand between both of hers. "You were always planning to stay while Feli went on the ship," she pointed out. "You always said you wanted to help Nueva transform."

"Maybe that was when I thought it was worth transforming," he said. Her eyes flashed.

"We are a long way from perfect, sonny boy, and the way to change that is to stay and work from within. You've done more than could ever be expected, Alex, sweetheart. Let someone else do the hard work from now on."

"I'll... think about it," he said quietly. He disengaged his hand with an apologetic smile. They held each other's gaze, and Alex knew his mind was made up, and he was staying on Nueva whatever Quin wanted, and his eyelids grew suddenly so heavy that he had to jerk his head awake again.

"Look, can you show me where my cabin is? I just want to... I just want to lie down. And sleep. Forever, or until Nueva warms up, whichever comes first."

"Of course, sweetheart." He was a little boy with a temperature again, and his mother was fussing over him, helping him to his feet. He was too tired, too drained of energy to mind; in fact it was the nicest thing to happen to him for a long time. "I'll show you... What's that?"

When he stood up, a tablet had fallen out of his pocket and stayed on the chair. He picked it up to show her.

"Quin gave it to me. He just said I might want to read it. Apparently he kept a diary."

CHAPTER 32

QUIN'S LAST ENTRY

Quin is 31

WELL, HERE'S A thing! Talk of my demise was premature.

I'd been existing in my cell for a couple of days, with the monotony only broken by the occasional visit from my friend Robertson. A pleasant lad, though I soon discovered he only knew how to make coffee and sandwiches, and only one kind of sandwich at that. Since I can only guess what his hijo colleagues would do to any food they served me, it's probably better that way.

I passed the time lying on my back and staring at the ceiling. The plaster makes a pockmarked relief map of a non-existent little world, but with practice you can shape the contours and splotches into anything you like. And while I did that with half my mind, I used the other half to give La Nueva Temporada a complete and thorough overhaul and work out how I would run it, given half the chance. Probably not the first political manifesto dreamed up in prison, probably not the last.

But it was all pretty academic. Even then, I thought that the half of my mind doing the ceiling-mapping had the more productive task.

But on the third or fourth day, my concentration was broken by the unmistakable sound of rigis flying overhead. Then I sat up and started to take notice. Even one rigi was unusual because Alti is officially a no-fly zone, so close to the cable, and these were rigis, plural, flying low. From the increased whistle of the jets it sounded like some were landing.

I stood on tiptoes to peer out of the window but could only see the blank walls of nearby buildings. Then, just as I was sitting down again, the building shook to what sounded like a nearby explosion. Then sounds from outside – angry shouting and the alarms of emergency response vehicles and shooting. The buzzing of stunners and the more abrupt, angry pops and cracks of projectile weapons.

It wasn't too hard to work out that Alti was under attack, incredible as it may seem. Who would? Who could? The only likely contenders were the Peninsular Republic and they were three thousand kilometres away. Defence was never a design consideration when Alti was built, but still, it's on top of a massive plateau that is surrounded by flat tundra for hundreds of kilometres in all directions. It should be hard to creep up on.

The fighting didn't take long. There's no one in Alti equipped to withstand a sudden assault. It didn't stop various heroes from trying. Every now and then the shooting would flare up again, always ending abruptly as presumably the other side capitulated and someone died.

Then it all went quiet for a while, and suddenly things became abruptly personal when the sounds of conflict erupted again within the precinct house. First I heard raised voices as a dim, barely heard background murmur. They quickly escalated to angry shouts, and then a couple of shots, inside the building.

That was when I decided it might be a good idea to hide under the bunk.

Then there were boot steps in the corridor outside. There was a purposeful rhythm to them – slow down, speed up, slow down again – and I could picture their owner moving along the rows of doors, pausing as he read the cell numbers, then hurrying on. Outside my door, they slowed and stopped. I heard the clunk of the mechanism unlocking and the door sliding open. The boots walked into the cell and paused. Their owner was in combat overalls with the legs tucked into his boot tops. I cowered back against the wall as he crouched down to peer under the bunk.

"Morning, Señor."

David Krauss pushed up the visor of his helmet and grinned out at me. I really wasn't pleased to see him. Was he the execution squad, here to remove my grandfather's embarrassing mistakes? But no – surely he worked for the wrong government? David pushed the bunk up so that I could climb slowly to my feet and spoke into his wrist.

"Subject located. Lock it down."

He sat back on the edge of the table and swung his legs, looking very pleased with himself. Then he glanced pointedly at me, at the bunk, and back at me. I sat down, warily.

"Okay," I said. "Surprise me. The peninsula has taken over Nueva?"

"Yeah, we like to think big," he said affably. "But no..."

Dear grandfather, as he explained to me, had shown fatal signs of weakness in the peninsula debacle: the fact that he hadn't expected the crisis in the first place; the fact that he let it get so far; the fact that he allowed such damaging transmissions to be shown – in fact, had positively gloried in them. It had been enough for some of the braver Executors to make their own overtures to the leaders of the former Republic. If the muscle could be provided, they would connive in the overthrow of Luis Alcantara. The muscle had duly turned up, headed by David, and now we had a new Government of Planetary Unity.

You can have too many of these Portentous Phrases in Capitals.

"And," he said, "you know those demands you made up in the laser?"

"Um..." It took me a moment to remember my little list. "Yes?"

"The new government's agreed to them. Including the amnesty. Means you're free."

"I heard shots..." I said.

"Oh, yeah, that. One of my men got his safety catch stuck. Sorry."

"So why are you here?" I asked. "Right now, in this cell? Are you freeing everyone?"

"You must be joking! This place is full of crims. No, we're just releasing those covered by the amnesty, which basically means you. You're in demand."

"Who's demanding?"

For answer, he produced a tablet from inside his overalls and handed it over. It was an invitation from the new First Executor, one Alfonso Illescas – a complete non-entity, if ever there was one, as I recalled – to join his government as pro-tem Minister of Supply, pending the election of a proper government in a month's time.

"He's kidding!" I said. David shrugged.

"You're a popular man out there, Señor. Even on the peninsula. Not everyone there was really backing the government. They didn't want it to come to war."

"You were," I pointed out. "You did." He shrugged again.

"Yeah. They had what I wanted."

"You mean, an excuse for a good fight?"

His grin widened and he swung his legs a little faster. He looked like an innocent little boy being asked if he had enjoyed his birthday party.

"Yeah," he said again.

That was my David. Never mind the cause, just measure the opportunities afforded for a good rumble.

There was more on the tablet. Illescas had declared the date for the promised election and there were invitations from no fewer than seven of the new electoral districts, all predominantly segunda, asking me to consider standing for them. David nodded approvingly when I read that out to him.

"Damn right. You should stand. I'll vote for you."

"You might not be in my district," I pointed out.

"So?"

I looked into his eyes and saw no guile there. David's basic sense of fair play really was unclouded by notions of democracy.

I sighed. "Thanks."

* * *

I MANAGED TO grab a shower and a meal that wasn't sandwiches. Someone found me a clean set of clothes, and then it was off to the Executive Building with an honour guard of David's men, to the smiles of the segunda Constabulary and the sheer hatred of the hijos. We got there just in time for Illescas's press conference. He had assembled all his ministers before the cams to broadcast to a world newly at peace. His words, not mine.

I smiled until my face ached, I listened to the bold declarations and I wondered how long it would last.

For the time being, I decided, everyone would get along, because they had seen the alternatives. And the new government had a good mix of ethnic types – that would help send a signal, at least. But was it a good mix of competencies too? Would these men and women be enough to save Nueva? Or would we just slip into more inept dictatorship and another civil war?

I could already see how we might. My grandfather's administration had stuck rigidly to one course of action, regardless of whom it upset. The new lot could do the opposite – go so far down the meandering trail of good intentions for everyone that they would get bogged down and achieve nothing. Nueva had to be kept ruthlessly on its middle way, giving and taking where necessary but always keeping its eye on the goal. The government could lead but it also had to nudge.

I glanced across the room to the back, where a bored looking David was chatting to one of his cronies. Was I looking at the nudger-in-chief?

I realised, with a slight measure of surprise, that I was already thinking in terms of actually *being* the government. Maybe I would rise up in the new one... Or maybe I would have to wait for it to implode and then take over. That assumed a power base, resources, a following... all built up from what I currently had, which was nothing. Almost nothing. I had David, and apparently a lot of goodwill from the people.

I had built an empire for the greater good before, at the age of twenty-one. Now I was thirty-one. Still young. I could do it again, and this time I could build it to last.

CHAPTER 33

FRESH STARTS

Jo FINALLY SNAPPED on the elevator back up to High-Kili.

Three months since she had made this trip with Alex Mateo, she mused as she headed back to her seat from the bar. Three months since the last time she had made this trip as a respectable member of society doing her job...

A man was walking the other way. She stepped aside, and he quite deliberately sidestepped a couple of centimetres to bump into her.

Jo looked at his receding back, blinked slowly, started to count to ten.

No, sod that, she thought and left out three to nine.

"That's all right," she called after him. He stopped, turned.

"What?" His tone was cold and hostile.

"I said, that's all right." Jo carefully stripped the expression out of her own voice. That was how best to rile a suspect under interrogation. Stick to the facts, make it quite clear you're the better person. "It's what you usually say when someone bumps accidentally into you. I just said it before you said 'sorry'."

He did something with his lips that might have been a smile. Or a snarl.

"And why would I say sorry?"

"Well," she said innocently, "it was an accident, wasn't it?"

"Go fuck yourself." He turned away. "Like you fucked every–"

Jo kicked his legs out from under him, brought his arm around behind his back and dropped down on top of him, all in one smooth movement. He shrieked as she pushed his wrist up to touch the back of his neck.

"You've got an attitude problem," she murmured into his ear.

"Get off me, bitch!" he howled.

"Hey!" The on-board security officer was hurrying towards them, baton drawn and fully charged. "What are you... Oh." Jo looked up at him and his expression slowly turned wooden. "Sergeant."

"Constable," Jo said pointedly. "Can I help you?"

She guessed he was hurriedly checking her status. Yes, she was still a sergeant. She wasn't on duty but she still outranked him.

"Just..." He scowled. "Just take your seat and don't cause any trouble." He prodded the man on the floor with his foot. "Either of you."

The man looked up, aghast with betrayal. "But–"

The constable crouched down, pointed his baton in the man's face. "I said, either of you."

Jo did as she was told. At least, she mused as she watched Earth recede, she didn't have little glowing 'TRAITOR's floating in headspace around her any more. She still didn't know who had performed that hack. Eventually the Lawcore had ruled in favour of her right to privacy and overridden it. Her life was her own again, as long as no one recognised her face.

The constable loomed in the corner of her eye and looked warily down at her.

"Taking your old job back, Sergeant?" High-Kili still belonged to the Nuevans, but they were slowly letting the Terran personnel back and they had reopened the Orbital Police Force office.

"No." She made her smile bright and open. "Purely holiday."

"Uh-huh..." He wandered away, with a final, suspicious, backwards glance.

Jo looked up out of the windows, away from Earth, at the darkening sky and the floating headspace tags that identified the points of light as stations and ships and satellites. The cause of all her problems, and their solution, was just passing in front of Luna.

ALEX STEPPED OUT of the flight crew quarters into the bridge, and stopped dead.

"How did you get here?"

He was instantly aware of how unfriendly that sounded. He had been cherishing his solitude more than usual of late.

Three months had passed in a blur. Life had become a non-stop succession of meetings and interviews and shuttling between High-Kili and Puerto Alto and *Phoenicia*. Really it was his own fault because he knew he could let go at any time. There were already engineers on board who were way more experienced than he was. But even though he wasn't going to Epsilon Eridani, he felt he owed it to the ship to stay as long as he could and oversee its overhaul.

Meanwhile *Phoenicia* had all but disappeared inside a cloud of humans and drones, weaving their engineering spells within it and without. And now Quin had announced the date that he would come to tour the ship, so David Krauss's Security Division had been added to the mix.

She raised an eyebrow.

"It's a pleasure to see you, too."

"Yeah. Sorry." He added in headspace: *Ship?*

"The ship let me in," she said. "I got in touch from High-Kili. I'm surprised it didn't tell you."

"Yes..." Alex cocked an eye up at the ceiling. "Me too?"

I thought it would make a nice surprise, the ship said blandly. *You need her.*

"I–?" Alex stared blankly at the nearest sensor. He needed her, did he? Put another way – was his starship *fixing him up with someone?* He knew the ship was meant to look after him but he wasn't aware that particular task fell within its parameters.

He looked back at Jo. "Um... yeah." An awkward silence. "Um... how are you?"

"Not as busy as you. You're looking well. More hair."

He smiled and ran his hand over his scalp and its fully restored thick, dark thatch. She looked around the bridge and her eyes settled on the hatch behind him that led to the flight crew quarters. Alex flushed when he remembered that she had been locked up there.

"Happy memories," she said wryly.

"Uh-huh..." The quarters had become his own personal escape pod. The rest of the ship could be heaving, and it frequently was, but not in his personal little realm. Any work that needed doing there, he could do himself – or if he felt like it, he could just settle down with a book. It was relaxing and therapeutic. He had become good at banishing outsiders.

"Still ship's master, I see?"

"Yeah..." He was a little surprised to find the desire to talk growing inside him. "For the time being. I mean, the mission's over so I could hand over to anyone now. But it's, um, easier."

"Yes...?"

Enthusiasm was growing. "I'm helping to prep the ship and the university is adding my experience on board to my diploma. By the time the ship sets off, I'll have finally graduated." He grinned. "The Event kind of set my education back."

She laughed. "I suppose it would. And what do you do with your diploma when you get it?"

"What I was always going to do. Stay at home, join the Equatorial Current Project, help the Thaw."

"I suppose you had to start all over again."

"I guess." She probably meant the Thaw programme, now starting up again after its forty year hiatus, but it struck him she could have meant other things too. Nueva itself could begin again, perhaps, this time without the division between hijo and segunda that had almost brought it down. "So... uh... anyway, can I help you?"

"Yes..." She shifted slightly. "Look, I've tried doing this through channels and I've had five routine rejections. I want to join your crew. I want to go to Epsilon Eridani."

She seemed to take his silence as an invitation to keep talking.

"I'm not a trained spacer," she said, "though I've picked up experience at High-Kili. But I'm basically a cop, and I've been following the news. You were ranting to a reporter about petty theft, items going missing..."

"Yes," Alex said with feeling. The ship was a reliable source of high precision parts and a honeypot for thieves. Never anything major, never anything mission critical – but enough went missing to be a constant source of irritation.

"And your security people can't stop it?" she asked innocently. Alex just raised an eyebrow at her. Security Division were a joke when it came to police work. They could break the heads of dissenters, they could make sure you smiled during Quin's speeches and they could squeeze a confession out of people they arrested. What they couldn't do was pre-emptively keep tabs on petty crooks. Their minds just weren't wired for it.

"Right. So here I am. Give me a badge, give me power and I promise your theft problem goes away."

"But why–" he began.

"Why?" She had been restrained, polite, like anyone turning up for a job interview. It seemed to be wearing thin. "Because I'm finished here! I'm the one who helped you open the wormhole, aren't I? Do you think any Terran will trust me now? Ever again?"

"Ah." Alex tried to imagine what it must be like to have a whole world hating your guts. Actually, he already had a whole world hating his guts – and it was the same world as hers – but it wasn't the world where he had grown up and that he called home. That had to hurt.

"But I can't believe you want to work for Nuevans..." he said.

"I don't," she said, with extremely forced patience. "I want to get to Epsilon Eridani and start again."

"Ah."

For a moment they just stood and looked at each other. A security drone buzzed in through the hatch and circled the two of them, its main sensor focusing suspiciously on their faces. He irritably brushed it aside. To have a security presence on board that wasn't run by David Krauss was an attractive notion.

"You're in," he said. For a moment she seemed as surprised as he had been to see her, but then she rallied.

"Thank you."

"Look," he blurted suddenly, "there's one thing..."

She jabbed a warning finger at him.

"If you apologise for the invasion, or tell me how it's not what you wanted, I walk," she said.

He bit his tongue. "I wouldn't dream of it."

"This is hard enough as it is..."

He held his hands up in peace.

"I said, I wouldn't dream of it."

Their eyes met, and they both broke out into slightly disbelieving, nervous laughs.

"As long as that's understood," she said.

"Right. No problem."

"So, um..." She held her hands out to indicate the whole wide range of options available. "What happens now?"

He thought. "I need to talk to – uh – someone to confirm the job..."

"Your brother," she said flatly.

"Yeah, him. But he said I can have anything I want and I'll hold him to it. And then I'll get Krauss to brief you and you can take over. Quin's coming to visit..."

Jo suspected, rightly, that Quin's visit would be her first headache in her new job.

Alex had just pictured a simple little tour: he and Quin would explore the ship and maybe do some of the brotherly bonding that Quin so obviously yearned for. Alex was wrong. When news crews started setting up discreet cams around the concourse, and Jo was peremptorily told by Colonel Krauss that Security

Division would be handling this (him: "all the guests have been cleared, Sergeant, trust me"; her: "guests?"), it became clear it wouldn't be quite so simple.

Two ships docked with *Phoenicia* in quick succession. The first bought the crowd: journalists, officials from both worlds, space workers from High-Kili who had somehow physically got in on the jolly rather than attend by avatar. Then their ship stood off while Quin and his entourage arrived on board *Santiago*, a ship that Jo had no reason to remember with joy.

And now Jo moved slowly through the throng in the concourse, a pair of human eyes that barely made a difference to the multi-angle surveillance feeds she was getting in headspace. The crowd had got substantial: all the strangers bussed in from High-Kili supplemented by the maintenance crews on board *Phoenicia* itself and of course Krauss's goons, who were stationed at points around the perimeter and also keeping a clear area in front of the elevator from the airlock.

The elevator doors opened and La Nueva Temporada's First Executor stepped out, side by side with his still teenage, technically big brother. A small crowd followed after them.

The sight of Alex made her smile slightly. He was plainly ill at ease, shifting from one foot to the other, hands clenching and unclenching, wearing slightly smarter clothes than his usual worn but perfectly serviceable shipsuit which Krauss had advised him to put on just in case Quin wanted to give him a big hug for the cameras. Quin was just Quin; snappy suit and effortless smile. Headspace tagged the rest of the faces Jo didn't know by sight: most of the mega-clan leaders; the Chief Constable of the Orbital Police Force; the President of Hired Sword; the CEO of the Epsilon Eridani Corporation, all with smiles ranging from modest to huge and acknowledging the applause with nods and waves. Also, Jo was interested to see, high-ranking representatives from Mars and Jupiter's Galilean Federation. Headspace said the same crowd had been following Quin around for days now. It was a simple enough little ploy and Jo didn't need headspace to spell it out for her. Quin's new best friends were people who controlled a lot of public interest in the Discourse: be nice to them and it would trickle down to their followers and, in theory, Earth would become better disposed towards their Nuevan cousins.

Quin shook hands with Alex – and sure enough gave him the hug – and then held his hands up for silence. The clapping died away and just before he spoke, in the wall of faces behind them, Jo suddenly made out one face in particular.

"Ladies and gentlemen," Quin announced, "Terrans and Nuevans, our two worlds stand today ready for a new beginning."

It was Szabo. Wasn't it? He had moved slightly; three-quarters of the face were hidden behind the head of a Nuevan security woman. Jo angled round to get a better look and called up three different angles on him from headspace.

"The unfortunate events that brought us to this point are known to us all..." Quin sounded a little bored, even a bit irritated, already dismissing this old hat. Life and light returned to his voice again. "... but it's time to put them behind us."

Jo craned her neck and nudged past the man next to her without apology. Yes, it was definitely Szabo.

What's he doing here? Why isn't he in jail? she sent and headspace came straight back. Szabo might have been working for people who did something wrong – destroyed the wormhole, etcetera – but none of his actions on board *Phoenicia* had been illegal in themselves. Heavy handed, but not illegal. Both Nuevan and Terran Lawcores even gave him the benefit of the doubt in the death of Nathan Sulong: Nathan had been downed with a legitimate stun shot and it wasn't Szabo's fault that he had been an old, frail man whose body couldn't take it.

So Szabo was in the clear – but still, *not* someone she would have expected to attend this happy event. She started to edge towards him.

Headspace was still wittering.

Ara Szabo is an official representative of the Committee for Reparation of Nuevan Crimes, a Lawcore-recognised legal action group. CRNC exists to advocate an official prosecution against the government of La Nueva Temporada for acts of aggression...

Jo cut it short. CRNC was genuine, she didn't entirely disagree with it, and an accredited representative had every right to be here. But the thought of someone like Szabo being in the same room or even thought process as the finer points of law was not one that came easily to her. She kept on working her way through the crowd.

Quin's speech went on:

"We are all citizens of *Phoenicia's* worlds. We are all humans, we all have the same DNA, and *Phoenicia* is a physical symbol of our mutual ties and our common heritage. So it is appropriate that on this ship we can begin to rebuild our friendship. I regret we came here as conquerors. From this day on, we can be friends."

He waved a hand to indicate his followers, physically present and virtual.

"Let me tell you what we have agreed so far…"

And he launched into a list of agreements and treaties and partnerships that were designed to bring the worlds together in friendship: not just Earth and Nueva but Mars and Jupiter's satellites too. Quin had woven a web that included them all.

"… thanks to our wormholes, you can get to or from Earth and any of the other worlds in an equally short space of time. So why do we continue to think of worlds beyond a wormhole as being on the periphery or a long way away…?"

Headspace was analysing the speech as it went on and Quin's reasoning was transparent. He was making Nueva important to the interests of multiple worlds and he wasn't trying to hide it. But as everyone would benefit in some way, she suspected it would all go down well in the relevant Discourses. Who knew, maybe history was being made here after all.

The concourse was applauding and even Szabo was clapping too, but only in that he brought his hands together, slowly, at about a third of the pace of everyone else. His smile was flat and humourless. She thought he might have looked briefly in her direction, but if he did then their gazes didn't connect.

Alex, who had been standing a short distance away looking ill at ease and out of place, found himself pulled over to stand by Quin.

"And as a first step, my brother Alex has promised us all a tour of this marvellous ship."

The crowd began to shift and shuffle. The ceremonies were over; a lot of them would be leaving. Of much greater interest to her was where Szabo had got to now.

"He's got a gun!"

Jo saw it all so clearly that it was like looking at a picture stamped on her vision: something that had happened long ago to other people and she couldn't change a thing. It was all two or three metres away from her but there were other people in front. She couldn't push through; she could only be a witness.

Szabo thrust himself forward through the crowd towards Quin. He was raising his hand and there was something grey and cylindrical and ugly in it. There were sounds in this picture too – screams and shouts. Bodies milled about; people who had seen the gun trying to move away from it; people who hadn't seen it trying to work out where they should move away to; Krauss, shouting for everyone to get down, fumbling at his waist for his own weapon.

Four drones flashed forward from their recesses in the walls. They grabbed one each of Szabo's limbs with unyielding graspers and straddled him against the nearest bulkhead with an impact that could be heard metres away. One of them extended another grasper and delicately plucked the gun away from him.

The screams continued; it would take some seconds more for the good news to permeate through the crowd. A bunch of security men had pushed Quin and the others down to the deck for protection. Krauss was poised, gun aimed at where Szabo had been, caught out by the faster reaction of the drones. Then he readjusted and aimed the gun squarely at Szabo, face cold with fury, finger tightening on the trigger. Szabo looked dispassionately back at him, then closed his eyes, resigned to his fate; and Jo was running forward even before the conscious thought process had sent signals to her legs.

But another drone flashed forward and snatched the gun from Krauss's hand. She wasn't sorry to see it obviously wrenched his fingers because he yelped and clenched one fist inside another.

The people who had been in the way were gone. Jo could stride up to the pinioned captive who was slowly opening his eyes, not quite believing he was still alive but obviously glad to see it.

"Szabo!" she screamed, but it was a scream of fury, not fear. "You... you... *moron!* My *God*, you've done stupid stuff before but this—"

Somewhere beneath her pounding heart and her churning stomach, queasy from adrenaline, she felt a laugh begin. It was incongruous. It was ridiculous. A failed assassination, and she was scolding the would-be killer like a big sister.

But Szabo's face just twisted in disgust. "Stupid? *I* was *stupid?* So it's not like I opened the wormhole up and let *that* in—"

"David?" It was Quin, climbing slowly to his feet. He slowly came forward, peering nervously at the captive.

Krauss wheeled round. "We have him, Señor." He looked around at the people picking themselves up off the deck. "Stay down! Everyone!" To Quin: "But I want you—"

"All the guests had been cleared," Jo said. "Wasn't that what you told me?"

He looked stone-faced at her. "There will be an enquiry."

Quin was getting over the shock. "This changes nothing," he said. More loudly, for the benefit of the cams and the audience, he repeated himself. "This changes nothing! We will not let our alliance be sabotaged by the actions of a deluded fanatic."

"The First Executor is quite correct." The Chief Constable, Jo's former ultimate boss, stood firmly beside Quin. "We – in fact, all right-minded Terrans – disown this man's actions completely." Jo couldn't help noticing that his gaze slid over her like she didn't exist.

"Respectfully, Señor, I want you back on the *Santiago* now," Krauss stated. His gaze darted over the crowd. "He might have an accomplice and it's more secure than this place."

Alex had caught up with them and Jo saw the stunned look on his own face. "And who's been crawling all over *this place* for the last week?" he demanded.

"Children, children," Quin murmured.

"You get back on *Santiago*, now, or I carry you myself," Krauss threatened. It sounded like an overblown threat but the two men locked eyes for a moment and then Quin had to give in, with a sad nod. Jo wondered what he had seen in Krauss's past to take him seriously.

"I'm sorry, Alex, everyone. Another time, after David's people have done their work."

"And we'll start the enquiry," said Jo, drawing another glare from Krauss. "Right?"

"As you will," he muttered.

Krauss was obviously itching to start the interrogation of Ara Szabo but he didn't want to leave Quin's side until Quin was back on *Santiago*. The cams got one last look at the First Executor waving before going into the airlock and Alex got one last smile from him.

"Keep up the good work!"

David Krauss went into action even as the hatch was closing, striding back to where Szabo was still held down in one corner of the concourse.

"Get those cams off!"

The news people didn't hurry to obey and he gestured at his own security people to do it for them, then turned away, ignoring the protests of the free press. "Lock the ship down – we're going to speak to every one of these people before they go anywhere." To Alex: "Senor Mateo, find us somewhere we can all go..." He grinned like death at Szabo. "... privately."

IT WAS AN empty, bare storeroom. Krauss looked around it and nodded in satisfaction.

"It'll do. Odembo, you stay. Señor, you're excused if you want. Bring him in."

Two security men dragged Szabo in and held him between them. Krauss marched up to Szabo and stood with hands on hips.

"Name?"

Szabo's only answer was for his lips to curl. Krauss punched him, hard, twice, once in the gut and immediately with the other fist in the face. Held up by his guards, Szabo could only writhe and take it.

"Enough!"

Alex stepped forward and Krauss's powerful hand in his chest shoved him back.

"Security matter, Señor. Stay out of it." He drew back his fist for another blow.

"Want me to set the drones on you?" Alex gasped. The fist hovered and Alex met Krauss's harsh stare without blinking.

"Any drone comes near me, I shoot it down." But Krauss lowered his fist and looked at Jo. "I heard you say his name. You know him?"

Jo looked from Krauss to Szabo and back. Szabo's eye was swelling black but he still scowled contempt out of it.

"Team Leader Ara Szabo, Hired Sword," she said. Krauss had grown up without headspace – she marvelled that it didn't even occur to him to try that obvious route first.

"Team Leader Ara Szabo, Hired Sword," Krauss snapped at one of his men. "Tell High-Kili to round up all known associates." Back to Szabo. "What was the plan?"

Szabo sneered. "Scoop me."

"Waste of time. I can do it far quicker my way and it's much more fun." Krauss held a warning finger in Alex's face. "And you mention drones again, I invoke security overrides and I do it to you too. Last chance, Szabo. What was the plan?"

"The plan?" Szabo's face split into a corpse's grin. "The plan?"

Krauss stepped forward, fist raised.

"The plan," said Szabo with careful glee, "was to get Mateo back onto the *Santiago*."

It took a moment for the penny to drop. Krauss, for the first time, was struck speechless. He shook his head, very slowly. His lips pursed. His eyes narrowed. And then he pulled the gun out of his belt and raised it to Szabo's face.

"No!" Jo smashed her baton against his wrist. The gun discharged downwards and blew out a small hole in the deck. The gun fell to the deck and Krauss clutched his numbed wrist while the men holding Szabo were torn – keep hold of the prisoner, or go to their chief's aid? Szabo himself obviously found it hilarious.

Jo held the baton poised like a sword between Krauss and herself. It buzzed as she pressed the charge stud.

"No murders on my ship," she said. "*No.*"

Krauss breathed heavily, crouched down slowly to retrieve his gun. But when he straightened up, he slipped it back into its holster.

"We are going to scoop this guy until he starts to grow roots and leaves," he stated. He looked around blankly. "Where did the Señor go?"

She knew where Alex would be and she started to run there herself.

"Bridge," she shouted over her shoulder.

ALEX HAD OPENED windows to the *Santiago's* captain and to Quin, and called up an orbital schematic: *Phoenicia*, *Santiago*, Luna, Earth, High-Kili, wormhole. He was surrounded by images of people and graphics indicating orbits and spacecraft and gravitational forces.

And he had hit a snag in *Santiago's* captain. The man only looked slightly alarmed.

"A bomb? Who says?"

"The one who just tried to kill my brother! I mean, he didn't say it, but–"

The captain seemed to lose what little alarm he had showed. His smile was condescending.

"Well, my ship's blackbox has a thorough knowledge of all the hardware on board, so–"

Krauss pushed Alex aside. "This is a Security Division matter, Captain. I'm ordering you to–"

"With respect, Colonel, you're not in command–"

Quin appeared in his own window. "Alex? What is it?"

"You've got a bomb on board," said Alex again. Quin's eyes widened.

"Oh, God. Captain, what do we–"

"I shouldn't worry, Señor, I'm not convinced–"

"Look, if my brother says–"

"We swept the ship thoroughly!" That was Krauss's entirely unwelcome contribution. "Where the hell did it come from?"

Alex clenched his fists in frustration.

I have it. Santiago's *blackbox is a lower level intelligence than me and it doesn't know what a bomb is, so…*

Alex passed on *Phoenicia*'s words to *Santiago* as they came to him.

"… my ship says the bomb is actually on your manifest… That's how they hid it from your people because the ship said it was okay… All it knows is that an extra item of equipment has been fitted… secondary cooling system, right next to the tanks."

The captain began to look as if he might be convinced.

"We'll get some people down there to look for it. Out."

Quin's eyes briefly met Alex's. "Thanks." He looked past Alex to Krauss. "David?"

"Señor?" Krauss's voice almost broke, his tone begging for forgiveness.

Quin bit his lip, then just shook his head and cleared.

He was back after ten minutes. It was ten minutes in which no one in the bridge talked; ten minutes in which Alex watched the blip that was the *Santiago* edge along its orbital projection.

"They've found it," Quin said. "The chief engineer is working on it but he can't say when it's timed to go off. We're past the point of no return here, so we're going to transit and then boost for Puerto Alto."

"Just abandon ship," Alex said, baffled. "Get into the lifepods and go!"

"Well, that would be an excellent idea, if our saboteur had confined his efforts to planting bombs. Seems he had some time to kill so he passed it by doing in the lifepods too. Don't worry, Alex. We've contacted Puerto Alto and they're on their way to meet us."

Alex knew how far Puerto Alto was from the wormhole on the other side. This still wasn't the quickest way to get *Santiago's* crew to safety.

"Just get back here!" Krauss exclaimed. Alex knew the answer without even looking at the orbital schematics. Of course they couldn't just 'get back here'. Spaceships couldn't just turn round. For the same reason they couldn't just cut across to another orbit that would put them within range of rescue ships from High-Kili.

"Can't do, David. The wormhole's closer–"

"You can," Alex said suddenly. "Ship, confirm, please. From their present position they can boost around Earth and come back to us."

"No," Quin said bluntly. "If we're about to explode there's no way we're going to risk *Phoenicia* as well."

I confirm. The projected orbit is viable.

"You won't need to come close!" Alex urged. "You get into suits and–" Despite himself, he grinned. "You jump. Then we come and pick you up in our own time."

Quin looked partway convinced. "Okay... I've no idea how many suits we have on board–"

Four suits designed for extravehicular maintenance only, said *Phoenicia* immediately, *for a total crew and passenger complement of forty-seven. I can send out drones with the remaining forty-three suits required.*

Alex passed it on again.

"As soon as everyone's in a suit, abandon ship. The drones will pick you up. It will all be quicker than getting to Puerto Alto or High-Kili."

"Done," Quin said. He looked Alex in the eye. "And if it doesn't work... well, I was never going to retire, was I?" He bit his lip again. "There's no point in chatting, Alex. I've said everything I ever wanted to say to you and I'm glad we finally got to meet. So I'll be seeing you."

And he was gone.

Santiago passed by the wormhole, thrusters firing to bring it onto the planned interception orbit. A cluster of drones fired away from *Phoenicia*, each one bearing a suit.

Alex glanced sideways at Jo. Her breathing was slow and steady, her eyes fixed on the display. He wondered exactly what was going through her mind. How hard exactly would she mourn if something did happen now? She had no cause to love Quin.

She hadn't read Quin's diary; she hadn't had that conversation on Puerto Alto. None of that excused what Quin was, but it did give reasons...

Santiago disappeared. All feed from the ship vanished, the big dot dissolved into a haze of smaller dots and then even they were gone.

Jo drew in a sharp breath. Krauss was sheet white. Alex stared at the empty gap in the display where *Santiago* had been.

He wasn't anything to do with me, he told himself, *not really. He wasn't the little baby I once held. He was a grown man twice my age. He wasn't a friend and I didn't particularly like him.*

But there had been a hole of a particular shape in his life and, very briefly and not very well, Quin had filled it.

Krauss whispered, "Someone..."

For a moment Alex could have sworn he saw tears in the man's eyes. It sounded like the words hit an obstacle in his throat and died away. Then Krauss blinked and suddenly, where there might have been tears, there was only cold, hard anger.

"Someone's going to pay for this," he announced. "I'm going to get to the bottom of it and someone will pay."

"Of course they will," Alex said quietly. "And now just get off this ship."

Krauss sneered down at him. "Respectfully, Señor, there are still a number of people on board who must be questioned..."

"No one entered the *Santiago* while it was docked who didn't return on it," Jo said. "The bomb must have been planted on Puerto Alto. Look to your own people first."

"My... God." Krauss stared at the display as if the thought was occurring to him for the first time. Perhaps it was. A Nuevan had killed Quin? "The ungrateful bastards..." He pulled himself together. "Right. Odembo, take as many of my people at this end as you need to get everyone questioned. And I am going to turn Puerto Alto upside down. Commiserations on your loss, Señor." He saluted and left the bridge.

For a moment Alex thought he heard a voice brush against his mind, saying his name.

And Quin was gone, for good.

CHAPTER 34

DEPART IN PEACE

THE CHOIR FILLED the high vault of Santo Cristóbal with mournful, liquid melody. Alex shifted in his seat and, next to him, his mother gazed stonily up at the cross on the altar. Quin would have been glad to know she made the effort, Alex thought. He knew from the diary that Quin had found an unexpected friend in her.

In the row in front sat La Nueva Temporada's new First Executor. He was called Andrew Petterson, he had formerly been Quin's deputy, and he was a segunda. La Nueva Temporada finally had a non-hijo head of state. Other than that, Alex knew very little about him, apart from what he could see now from the back of his head, which was that he had short hair and large ears.

Szabo's scooping had revealed a conspiracy that blew the current political generation of hijos apart. If they ever came back to power, it would be a long time from now. That alone made Petterson's position more stable than any other leader's since the Event.

In fact his approval ratings were much higher than they had been for Quin in the last days, from non-political hijos and segundas alike. Quin had started on a wave, ending the civil war and bringing enforced peace to the planet. But peace at a cost. He had been the stitches that pulled the wound of La Nueva Temporada together, but stitches have to be removed eventually and natural healing takes over. Was that Petterson's role? Alex wondered. If it was then he deserved support.

Alex switched his gaze to the back of the head of the man sitting next to Petterson, and wished he could read the thoughts going on in there. The head was square and powerfully built, like the rest of its owner.

David Krauss's Security Division had been poised to be unleashed upon La Nueva Temporada in a wave of vengeance; an unprecedented crackdown on political opponents, malcontents and anyone who looked at its members in an odd way. But Petterson had reined it in and now Krauss sat next to his new master. He could barely disguise his fidgeting and was vainly trying to follow the words of the psalm in the order of service.

Petterson was waiting at the cathedral door at the end and they couldn't avoid him. He lunged for Alex's hand, almost pulling it out of his pocket, then changed pace and shook it slowly for all the cams to see.

"We all lost someone very important to us," Petterson said clearly. "My deepest condolences."

"Thank you."

"How are preparations on the ship?"

"Still some work to do."

"Then you had better get back there, hadn't you?" The First Executor said it with a smile and several flunkies laughed obediently.

If there had been the slightest hint of any kind of emergency in the offing, Alex would have been on his ship now. Petterson stuck to his public script.

"It's very good of you to be sticking with the ship to the bitter end. Many in your position would have said they've done their job and come back home."

Alex had his own reasons for sticking with the ship and no intention of saying them out loud. So his only answer, hoping it would be so boring all the networks would omit this conversation altogether, was:

"Yes."

"Travel safely. There's a lot riding on you."

"Yes," Alex said again. He glanced over Petterson's shoulder at Krauss, who looked stony-faced back, not even the usual smirk. He surprised himself with his next words, which were quite sincere. "And on you."

Petterson looked equally surprised at the compliment. His reply was just as sincere and this time it was pitched for Alex's ears alone.

"Thank you. That means a great deal to me."

"Think there'll be another coup?" Alex asked, back in the groundcar. Secure and alone in their warm cocoon, he watched Altiplano City pass by outside.

"Who knows." His mother stretched and sank down into the seat cushions. "Puerto Alto tends to be honoured by all sides in any dispute. I'll stay up there. I'm too old for politics."

Alex looked out of the window again and tried to picture the Alti of Quin's last diary entry. Rigis swarming overhead, bombing important public buildings.

"Nueva's better off without Quin. Isn't it? I mean, it is now."

It sounded a terrible thing to say. She laughed, and pulled him towards her, and kissed the side of his head.

"Alex, my darling, you don't have to convince me."

Her smile when she looked at him was immensely proud. Glum as he was, it ignited a small spark of pride deep within him that gave a comforting glow.

"And even if he was my only grandson – well, I just have to rely on you to give me plenty more."

Alex snorted. "Oh, please!"

They drove in silence for a while until Alex felt he just had to ask.

"Quin… did he ever find… did he know that…"

"That you're his uncle, not his brother?" She shook her head, lips pursed into a thin, twisted smile. "I never saw a need for it to come up in conversation and I doubt Quin ever needed a genetic test… so, no, probably not."

"Did Papá ever find out?"

"I honestly don't know. He didn't miss much but what he did miss, he couldn't have seen if you tattooed it on his retinas. He either knew from day one, or died in ignorance, but I really couldn't say which."

Silence returned while they both contemplated how life might have been different for everyone, if Tomás Mateo hadn't had to be away from Rio Lento one night, and in his absence Feli and Maria hadn't both had a bit too much to drink and both regretted it for the rest of their lives.

"Quin could have been..." Alex couldn't quite finish the sentence, not quite able to find the right order in which to put the words *your only living descendent if something went wrong with* Phoenicia.

If she guessed what he wasn't saying, she didn't show it.

"Oh, my darling. Come here." She pulled him towards her again, and he rested in her embrace with his head on her shoulder until they reached Puerto Bajo.

IF THERE HAD been no real need for Alex to be present while the ship prepared, there was even less for him to be there while the command crew recorded their conceptuals. But he intended to be the very last man off *Phoenicia* before it departed for Epsilon Eridani and this was the only way to do it.

Jo Odembo was the last to be recorded. He smiled down at her as she opened her eyes.

"Ready?" he asked. And even though he knew she still saw him as essentially a boy, he felt warm and happy when she graciously took his hand and let him help her to her feet.

"Ready," she agreed.

The rest of the command crew waited for them by the hatch from the bridge. They would be the last on board to go into longsleep. A full complement of colonists, engineers and mission specialists were already stowed away in the longsleep modules. The ship was green to go. The fusion boosters strapped to the ship's frame were counting down towards burn. Non-essential systems were on standby to close down altogether. A few hours more and the ship would be cold and dark. The ever-present Security Division were finally pulling out. Last minute messages had been exchanged with families, friends and loved ones, and the command crew's memories of the last three months had just been added to the ship's conceptual store, for restoration when they reached Epsilon Eridani.

It occurred to Alex that in that case he could kiss her, and she wouldn't remember. Legend had it there had been a lot of kissing, and more, on *Phoenicia* before it left Earth on its original mission, after the conceptuals were recorded and before longsleep erased the memories; but there again, if no one remembered, how did anyone know?

They left the bridge as the lights powered down and the hatch closed on a black, empty space behind them. There was little chatter as they stepped down into the concourse. They had all worked together for months but this moment overshadowed any casual talk.

A dark figure came to meet them from the shadows cast by the emergency lights and Alex's heart sank. David Krauss's eyes were narrow and fixed on him and his mouth was set in a grim, humourless smile.

"A moment of your time, Señor?"

"I'll catch you up," Alex called to the others. They hesitated, then went on ahead. He was pleased that Jo hung behind. They could square up to Krauss together.

He looked down at them with the same concealed amusement as an adult being threatened by a pair of toddlers.

"I just want you to know that I'm the last Security man off this ship." He looked solemnly at Jo. "From now on you're on your own."

"Thank you," she said.

"Got everything?" Krauss's smile suddenly grew wide and Alex wondered if they should feel nervous. "Been to the toilet? Packed your toothbrush? Clean underwear...?"

"Is there a point to this, Colonel?"

"There is." Remarkably, Krauss suddenly looked ill at ease. He glanced away, glanced back, even took a couple of steps away from them. He held out his hands, palms up. "I just want to show you that I'm unarmed," he said, "and I know you've got control of the drones. So there's not much I could do to hurt you or force you into anything."

"Right. But…?" Alex frowned sideways at him.

"I want… I'd like…"

Alex didn't know quite where to look. Seeing Krauss unsure of himself, almost pleading, was… embarrassing. Krauss pulled himself together and straightened up.

"I'd like to see him," he said. "I'd like to say goodbye."

Neither Alex nor Jo gasped, or denied anything, or reacted at all except to make their faces as straight as they could.

"Oh, come on," Krauss said irritably, and the return to form was a relief. "Just to say goodbye. That's all."

Alex had no idea how he knew. But he knew, and how wasn't important.

"The countdown's too advanced to be stopped," he said. "If you try to make trouble–"

"I know, I know. Look, the lady here can stun me and bring me to Epsilon Eridani with her, if she likes, to make sure I don't tell anyone. Please?"

They regarded each other silently for a moment. Then Alex held out a hand towards the passage that led to the Reserve Power centre, where they had hidden their secret.

"This way."

THE LONGSLEEP COFFIN stood on one end, well hidden in the limited space behind a cabling trunk. Alex, Jo and David Krauss had to squeeze themselves together to see it. The figure of a human was just visible through the translucent cover, embedded in the gel that preserved life. It was impossible to see the body well enough to recognise the features.

Emotions no one would have suspected Krauss of having were flickering over his face. Alex himself gazed stonily at the not-quite-corpse of his brother's son. He couldn't quite look at Quin without wondering how many people he had trampled over to get his hands on one of the four suits on board *Santiago*. There had been no other survivors from the doomed ship.

"How did..." Krauss asked.

"He jumped," Alex said quietly.

"Huh?"

"He jumped. That's what we're guessing. I'd said that was what he should do and..." He shrugged. "He must have done it a few minutes before she blew. His suit's thrusters gave him just the lead he needed."

"Not much of one, surely?"

"Not much at all." Jo was abrupt. "His suit was holed, he suffered a lot of internal damage, major organ failure, shock, and a nasty radiation flash. Couldn't happen to a nicer guy," she added in a murmur that was meant to be heard.

Alex looked at her for a moment, then back to Krauss. "The drones brought him in – I went out to get him myself. Even if he was in a hospital he'd need at least six months in longsleep to repair the damage."

"And he's getting twenty years..." Krauss mused. To Jo: "What's in it for you? You don't owe him anything."

"Like I told you," she said coldly. "No murders on my ship." She nodded at Alex. "He told me because he knew he couldn't keep it from his Head of Security."

"And how did you find out?" Alex asked quietly.

"Oh, one thing and another." Krauss looked very satisfied. "Half overheard conversations... some big secret between you two, obviously, and far as I know you're not screwing so it had to be something else... slight discrepancies in the longsleep supplies..." He grinned. "For what it's worth, thank you. Both of you."

"If you knew, why didn't–" Alex began.

"'Cos I think it's what he would have wanted. If they knew he was still alive, they'd come for him again, and he would have to fight back, and there'd be more trouble..."

"I thought you liked trouble," said Jo. Krauss looked her straight in the eye.

"I love it," he said frankly. "I also like living on a world that isn't tearing itself apart. Everyone should quit while they're ahead."

He turned back to the coffin, reached out, rested his hand against the surface over Quin's dimly seen face. If his voice trembled, it was only a little.

"Adiós, Señor, y gracias."

THE THREE OF them were back at the main airlock. Alex and Jo both glared at Krauss until he took the hint, threw them both a sardonic salute and disappeared through the hatch.

Getting a lift back with Krauss hadn't quite been how he planned it, but Alex's resolution still held. At this end of the journey, he would be the last off the ship. He also sent the ship an order:

"No one else comes on board until Epsilon Eridani. No one!"

Understood.

Jo was scowling.

"You know, the only reason I wanted to come on this voyage was I didn't want to live on a planet run by your brother. And now we're taking him with us."

"Yeah. Funny old world, isn't it?"

I will look after him, the ship assured him.

I know you will, he sent back.

"Hilarious." But the scowl melted into a faint smile. She paused, as if weighing up unseen options in her head. Then she leaned forward and kissed him lightly on the cheek. "Good luck."

"And you."

She winked, and the airlock hatch closed between them. Alex pushed his way through the membrane into the capsule and took his seat beside Krauss. Neither of them spoke as the capsule disengaged and moved away from the ship, or indeed all the way back to Puerto Alto.

Soon after, the vibration of the fusion boosters rumbled the length of *Phoenicia*, but no one was awake to notice.

THE END